The Spaewife's Secret

a novel

by Jessica M. Simpkiss

ALL RIGHTS RESERVED

Publisher's Note:

This is a work of fiction. All names, characters, places, and events are the work of the author's imagination.

Any resemblance to real persons, places, or events is coincidental.

Solstice Publishing - www.solsticepublishing.com

For my mom, because of her undying support and crazy love of Scotland, both of which made this book possible.

Preface

I listened from the top of the stairs, hugging the wall like I always did when they fought. I could tell my father had been drinking, more than usual, which meant my mother would take the brunt of his irritation. If there was any left over, I might catch some punishment as well. I told her she didn't have to defend me to him, that it didn't bother me anymore, what he said about me, but she always smiled and hugged me tightly, telling me that she was my mother and it was her job to love me and loving me meant defending me to anyone, including my drunk of a father.

His words were slurred on a good day not having been brought up proper or been educated like most, and drinking only accentuated that fact. My mother's incessant need to point it out only made it worse for her, but she always did it anyway. Sometimes I think she wanted to show him that she wasn't afraid, even when she was. She liked playing games with him like that.

"He's weak," he yelled, smashing a glass against the wall, no doubt after it flew by my mother's head. "He'll ne'er work th' fields, what good will he be?"

"He's not weak," she cooed in her motherly voice.

But I was. He knew it. She knew it. And I knew it.

My father's words became incoherent mumbles under the clatter and crash of dishes and whiskey bottles breaking into pieces against the walls. I slid slowly, step by step to the bottom. I knew what was coming if my father saw me, but I wanted him to know I wasn't afraid of him either, even though I was. She'd told me not to be fearful of him; fear was what he wanted from us. To the devil, fear was control, and we weren't meant to be controlled.

On the landing, I leaned against the wall trying to listen to the rain falling outside, but the storm inside was louder. I looked around the corner at my mother pushed up against the wall, and my father pushed against her. His words were whispers and the fight she'd had seconds before had vanished.

"Should hae taken care o' it whin ah had th' chance."

I couldn't hear anything else, but that I heard like he'd whispered it in my ear and not my mothers.

My father stumbled, reaching for something before pushing himself against my mother again. The blade of the knife he'd grabbed from the counter glinted in the glare of the kitchen light that swayed back and forth. He moved it slowly, up her thigh and under the hem of her dress until he stopped. He'd nicked her skin with his unsteady hand, and a thin trail of blood was beginning to streak her pale skin.

I moved out from the shadow of the landing and into my mother's line of sight. Even at that moment, she had love to show me, begging with her eyes to leave it be and go to my room, she'd be up when it was over to read me a bedtime story. And she always did.

I snuck back to my room as quietly as I could, trying not to listen to her cries as I went. With the door closed and the rain pelting the side of the house, I could barely hear her. I cowered under the covers with my favorite book, even though I knew I'd outgrown the children's stories of fairies and monsters. She'd read it to me anyway.

"Started without me did yah," she whispered standing in the doorway.

Her face was shiny, painted with tears and she'd done what she could to clean the blood from her leg, but it looked as if it had stained her colorless skin. She crept toward my bed and slinked under the covers next to me.

"What are we reading tonight?" she asked as if the cruelty my father had waged on her minutes before hadn't happened.

"Mither, ye'r bleedin'," I said, pointing to her leg.

"Ach, it's nothing. Dunnae give it another thought."

But I did. It was all I thought about; that, and how I was too weak to protect her from him or anyone.

"This is a good one," she cooed, changing the focus of the evening back to the book. "This is ma favorite."

It was my favorite too, so I let her read without questioning it further, but I wasn't listening. I didn't have to, I knew the story by heart. I knew them all by heart. Instead, I thought about what I wasn't supposed to give another thought to, and the fact that I was too weak to protect my mother from him.

"The horse didn't move as the husband placed the rope around its neck. The creature was still, almost invisible in the night. The husband grasped its long mane and pulled himself up onto the beast, but, as soon as he was seated, a glare of wickedness surfaced in the horse's eyes."

She continued to read the story of the water horse, the beast made of evil that was said to live in deep lochs and rivers. By day the creature could come ashore in the form of man, the devil himself, my mother would say, and tempt women of the nearby villages with the sins of the flesh. At night, the creature would wait by the water's edge, ready to devour them and their children.

In the story, the husband is carried away by the water horse and devoured at the bottom of the loch, leaving the boy to fend for himself and his mother. He defeats the water horse with the words of warning from a wandering old woman he finds in the hillside. The boy puts the creature to work, plowing their fields so that he and his mother have food for winter and can survive without the meager means the husband would have earned.

"'N' that is th' story o' th' water horse. For no man could master th' beast, yet, a wee laddie once did."

My mother closed the book and kissed me lightly on the forehead before slinking back out of the room and down the hall to her own room where she would cry and beg for forgiveness and release from the devil's grip. I looked down at my crooked leg and cursed a God I didn't believe in for sending me into this world a cripple, incapable of protecting my own mother like the boy in the story.

I was old enough to know that the story of the water horse was just that, a story, but I wondered what had made it true all those years ago when someone had written it down and if anyone still believed that it could be real. True evil lurked in the shadows of my own life wearing the skin of my father; why couldn't it take the form of a horse?

Chapter One

Lachlan sat on the edge of the bed in his small one-bedroom flat, watching the unsettled dust drift in the streaks of morning sunlight peeking through the curtains. The band music from the evening before still thumped in his head. He rubbed the side of his face and winced in pain. The half-moon shaped indentation above his right eye always throbbed tenderly when he drank too much. He let it be before the memory of what had given it to him had a chance to creep back into his mind.

His hands grappled with his effects on the nightstand searching for a glass of water. When he pulled it back empty-handed, he noticed the cuts and scrapes along the ridge of his pinky finger down to his wrist, forcing him to wonder what his face must have looked like. He second-guessed a trip to the wardrobe for a glance in the mirror when his legs wobbled unsteadily as he tried to stand. There was nothing to be done about it now.

As his head fell back into the comfort of the pillow, he could hear the running water of the shower and regret filled his already tense body. He hadn't remembered Liri spending the night and wondered what else he'd forgotten from the night before. He hoped it would stay hidden, whatever it was. Nothing good ever came from remembering when he woke up in such a state. The phone buzzed on the nightstand, and when Lachlan saw the distant but familiar number drift across the screen, he slowly rolled over to the other side of the bed, trying to put as much distance between the two of them as he could.

Eventually, the hum of the phone quieted, and Lachlan drifted between bouts of sleep and a semiconscious state of listening to the shower water drip, imagining it was rain. As he drifted, he became aware of the traffic moving outside his flat. He could hear the pump of the brakes from the No. 33 bus, the low rumble of passenger vehicle engines coming to life in the parking spaces outside his window and the voices of pedestrians on their travels. There was too much noise for what he thought was a quiet weekend morning when everyone slept in late and had coffee and Danish at the shop around the corner. He rolled back over and fished his phone from the nightstand to see how late he would be to work. The phone began to buzz again, the same number drifting across the screen.

"Fuck!" Lachlan yelled, louder than he expected in his hungover state.

"What's that, love?" Liri yelled from the shower thinking Lachlan's outcry had been for her.

"Fuck," he mumbled to himself, having forgotten she was standing under the running water. He'd broken his promise to himself and had spent the night with her again. He knew he had to cut her lose, but the sex was good, and it was just easier to sleep with her and then ignore her calls in the morning. Had he not been so hungover he could have dressed and slipped out of his own flat, avoiding the awkward exchange where she expected Lachlan to expel some reference to his deep emotions for her and he would grab her ass and kiss her neck to prevent any actual exchange at all. But he knew he needed a shower if he was going to shake off the previous night and salvage some part of his workday.

He watched as the streaks of sunlight sifted into the room, the dust almost settled. The phone was still in his hand when the young girl poked her head around the corner of his bedroom door, dripping water onto the floor at the threshold.

"You call me?" Liri asked, her bubbly, upbeat voice tearing through the throbbing of Lachlan's head.

"Nah, someone from back home," he whispered, gesturing to the phone.

Lachlan looked up to the naked girl standing in his doorway towel drying her blonde hair, unaware of the gravity that a phone call from back home presented. As he watched her move in front of him, the morning sun catching the beads of water still clinging to her skin, he tried to remember the faces of the people he'd left behind. The memories came quickly, blurred like they were sped up in his mind and disappeared just as fast as they had appeared. When was the last time he'd spoken to someone from Lewis? Perhaps he'd called home last Christmas with a good wish for both his parents. That's what estranged sons probably did. It didn't feel like something he would have done though.

The phone buzzed again, shaking in Lachlan's hand as it begged to be answered. It was too early, and he was too hungover, he told himself, to handle a call from the only person who could be calling from the old number. He held the phone until the screen went black and waited to see if, after three unanswered calls, his father had finally left a message.

"Don't ignore people," Liri's bubbly voice called from the bathroom where she stood, still naked, examining herself in the mirror. Lachlan could see slivers of her flesh from around the corner and felt his weakness for her body wash over him. There was little else in the way of attraction between the two of them, at least in his eyes.

"It's bad karma," she said as the hairdryer she kept under his sink roared to life, deafening his thoughts.

Lachlan stared at his phone, not wanting to listen to the message but knowing that he had to. His father never called, so three calls inside of several minutes meant something had happened. Thoughts of what could be wrong skipped across his mind like the rocks he'd skipped on calm water as a child. Distant memories of his father and his childhood jumped around in his mind but faded as quickly. Reluctantly, he pulled up the voicemail and listened to the stranger's voice on the other end.

"Everything ok?" Liri mouthed after poking her head around the corner and seeing the phone to Lachlan's ear.

"Nah," Lachlan replied calmly. "My mother's died."

The girl tilted her head in confusion. "I thought you said she was dead."

"I said she was dead to me," he answered, drifting to the bathroom like the dust in the morning sun to grab a shower before heading into work.

The rhythmic rocking of the train relaxed Lachlan on his ride from Dundee to Aberdeen. He usually spent the hour-long ride marking papers that he'd failed to get to the evening before, but his bag sat at his feet as he stared out the window, unable to concentrate on anything other than the sound of his father's voice still ringing in his ear.

There was sadness in his voice, but it was not on account of his mother's death. That much Lachlan was sure of. It had always been there, clinging to every word he spoke even though he spoke so few of them. When he didn't talk, there was sorrow in his eyes that took the place of his words. He tried to remember the sound of his mother's voice but could only hear the pain or regret that always accompanied it. When either of them looked at Lachlan, there was hollowness in both their eyes, like they didn't know how to look at him much less love him.

The train pulled into the station at Arbroath, and a pretty brunette took the seat next to Lachlan. He pretended not to notice her and continued staring out the window. She smelled like coffee and pastry, reminding him of how hungry his hangover had made him. He'd not managed to grab anything to soak up the remaining alcohol in his gut before dashing out of his flat and away from the invasive questions Liri would not stop asking about his mother's death and a past he'd done well to keep hidden.

Out of his peripheral, he saw the brunette push something in his direction. He turned and avoided making eye contact with her by looking directly at the bottle of water in her hand.

"You look like you could use this more than me." Her voice was thick, but smooth, like crushed velvet in her mouth. Her long hair fell over the crest of her breasts poking out from under the low-cut collar of her navy-blue dress. The leather of her knee-high boots rubbed together as she crossed and uncrossed her legs. Lachlan's eyes worked their way up from her hand holding the bottle of water, up her arm, over the soft, exposed skin of her neck finally landing on her painted lips, parting ever so slightly as their eyes met.

"Do I look that bad?" Lachlan asked, reaching out and purposely touching the skin of her hand as he took the water from her.

"Rough night?" she asked, smiling as she looked him over, head to toe.

"Something like that," he answered.

The two strangers made small talk as Lachlan imagined taking her into the lavatory, pulling her navy-blue dress up around her waist and pushing her firmly against the closed door with his hips, over and over again. He'd kiss her neck roughly, leaving red marks with the stubble dressing his jawline and she'd bite her lip until it bled. Any other day, he might have done just that, but his mind was a thousand miles away and focused on another woman he'd not actively thought of in years. With the prospect of returning home looming over him, her red hair burned like fire in the forefront of his mind.

The brunette exited the train at the Montrose stop but not before slipping a crumpled piece of paper into

Lachlan's hand, winking seductively as she did. He waited until she'd stepped to the platform and the chime indicating the closing doors rang through the carriage before tossing it on the floor, never even looking at it. He rode the rest of the way to Aberdeen with his head propped against the window, eyes closed, the color of fire burning on the underside of his lids.

***

Rain had started to fall by the time the train pulled into the station. The pitter-patter sound of droplets against the hood of his raincoat mixed with the running and skipping of children's feet as they all made their way to school. A group of older girls a few paces in front of Lachlan giggled and whispered behind their hands as they glanced back at him. He smiled under the hood of his jacket and looked coyly at the ground as he followed slowly behind them. He knew what the whispers and secrets were about. The female teachers at the school did the same thing at times, just an older version of the girls they were meant to instruct. Lachlan knew the extent of his attractiveness and used it to his advantage often, but his good looks did little in the way of filling the void underneath them.

The day dragged more than usual. Lachlan sat behind his desk as his students worked diligently, reading pages from their texts and discussing the passages in small groups as he'd instructed them to do. He was unable to concentrate on anything other than the rain drizzling on the window and a past that was slowly starting to creep into his present.

The thought of returning home to Lewis was agonizing. He remembered the sideways looks and whispered words secreted behind cupped hands when he'd had visitors in the hospital, the majority of whom had been police officers, some from as far as Glasgow. By the time he had been released, almost everyone on Lewis had heard the story and come to their own conclusions about the truth, including the police and his parents, neither of which he cared much about. There was only one opinion that had mattered to him, and she had never come to visit, passing her judgment with her silence.

When Lachlan finally looked up from the window and his drifting thoughts, the children had already dismissed themselves for lunch, and he was alone in the classroom. He pulled his phone from his bag slung across the back of his chair as he stuffed half a lunchroom turkey sandwich into his mouth. He ignored the multitude of text messages from Liri asking if he was alright and if he needed her to make him chicken soup or make their travel arrangements back to Lewis, the answer to all of which was no. He'd let whatever it was between him and Liri drag on too long and become something it was never meant to be, and now he felt her claws digging into his skin. She would, no doubt, see his mother's death as her opportunity to make an emotional move, jumping from casual sex to a real relationship. One she could claim as legitimate. Lachlan closed his eyes tightly and rubbed his forehead with his free hand. He was a coward when it came to women, and he knew it. It was always just easier to sleep with them and leave in the morning.

He played the message from his father again, outlining the details of his mother's death. She went peacefully, his father had noted near the end of the message, in a vain attempt to instill tranquility in Lachlan's mind over the loss of a woman that had been his mother only in the legal sense of the word. He listened to the sadness in his father's voice, laced with something close enough to guilt to call it that. It was hard to tell where the guilt in his voice came from. He didn't recognize the voice or the cantor in the message, only the sadness that persisted. Lachlan wondered if he'd even recognize him should they pass on the street unknowingly. He'd hardly known the man on the other end of the message when they'd lived under the same roof. Anything could have transpired between his parents in nineteen years, manifesting into guilt. Whatever the truth was between them, Lachlan was sure he didn't want to know.

His mind drifted to his last memory of his parents. The tempered glass on the back window of the car sent to take him away had blurred their faces, but the utterly emotionless exchange between them before being placed in the car burned as bright as the sun. There had been no words, only the look of relief. He wasn't glad that she was dead, it was more like indifference. She'd been dead to him since that day. Having to return and face almost two decades of truth because she'd died felt like one last calculated cruelty toward him on her behalf.

"Lach?" a man's voice called, somewhat distant in his ears. "Hello?"

When he turned toward the door, he could see the outline of a man standing on the other side of the glass, hands cupped around his eyes peering into the room from the other side. The voice belonged to a fellow teacher, Mr. McAvoy, from two rooms down. Lachlan must have missed the screech of the lunch bell and had never gotten up to open the door, allowing his students to return to class. When they began to pile up in the hallway outside the room, Mr. McAvoy must have taken notice and began knocking on the door.

"Mr. McGinley," his voice called again over the sounds of children scurrying through the crowded corridor.

Lachlan grabbed his bag, shoveling papers and his half-eaten sandwich into it before he moved toward the door, swinging it open much to the surprise of everyone standing the other side.

"Everything alright, mate?" Mr. McAvoy asked.

"No, not quite," Lachlan answered, still unsure of how a normal person would react to the news of a parent's death. He thought to cry was a little over the top, but still, he had to sell it if he was going to request leave with no notice. "Can you tell Mr. Lennox that I've had a family emergency and that I'm going to have to take leave."

Mr. McAvoy's face creased with concern and confusion. "Sure, sure. Is there anything I can do?" he offered as Lachlan slipped by him in the doorway while his students, oblivious to the situation, filed into the classroom.

"No, I don't think so," Lachlan called from down the hallway, leaving his coworker in charge of his class without so much as two minutes notice.

"How long a leave?" Mr. McAvoy called, his voice trailing off into the empty hallway.

Lachlan pretended not to hear his question and continued walking, crashing into the heavy double door at the end of the corridor and exploding out into the fresh, wet air. He hadn't realized that he'd been holding his breath since earlier that morning until he gulped at the cold breeze around him. The fresh air rushed over his lungs, bringing some relief, but the smell of the wet earth began to remind him of the home he thought he'd left behind.

***

The pub around the corner from his flat seemed like a better choice than sitting at home with his thoughts. Liri found him, despite his apparent attempts to dodge her and the questions he didn't want to answer. She sat next to him as he nursed a warm beer, playing the part of the concerned girlfriend by rubbing his forearm and then his thigh. His involuntary excitement at her touch reminded him of the brunette from the train and all the other women. Most of them were just faces with no names to remember them by. He liked Liri, he just didn't love her. He couldn't love her. He downed the rest of his beer and adjusted himself before standing up to let her lead the charge to his bed a few blocks away.

The bell above the door pealed as they passed underneath it, almost deafening the quiet whisper of a name that had been lost on the winds of long ago. He let go of Liri's hand and stood as still as stone in the doorway of the pub, looking for the girl who burned like fire in his memory.

"Isla!" a woman's voice shouted, her hand waving incessantly in the air above the bobbing heads of the crowd between them.

His eyes darted around the room looking for her, unsure of what she'd even look like nineteen years older than the last time they'd seen each other. He ducked and bumped his way through the crowded room in the direction of the hand he'd seen flapping in the air. He was vaguely aware of someone calling his own name and pulling on his shirt as he moved through the pub, slow, like molasses, cutting in and out of the cohesive groups of friends drinking and conversing with one another.

He heard her name again and spun in the direction it'd come from, his heart pounding and sweat beginning to bead on his brow. He looked for her hair, the color of burning coals at the bottom of a fire on a cold night. Even if he didn't recognize her face, he was certain her hair would give her away. Despite being in a pub on the borders of the Scottish Highlands, not many women shared its color.

He heard sheiks of excitement and found Isla and the woman who'd beckoned her from across the pub dancing in a warm embrace like teenagers. The woman was much too old and much too gray to be the girl he'd known as a child. He watched the golden ale in one of their glasses spill onto the floor between them as they danced together like idiots. The shock of possibly seeing his Isla Gilcrest again wore off and Lachlan was left sweaty and light-headed. He wiped the sweat from his forehead and felt his knees come out from underneath him, catching them just in time to remain upright.

He couldn't make out exactly what Liri was shouting over the band that had begun to play, sending the crowd around them into an uproar. Lachlan pushed through the sea of people, finally finding relief in the cold air outside in the dark alley of High Street. At first, all he heard her yelling was something about a ghost.

"Did you hear me?" she yelled again, trying to find his face as he spun in a circle seemingly unsure of where he was or in which direction his flat might be. He gulped for a fresh breath, but the rain was coming down in buckets, making the air around him hard to find.

"What?" he finally yelled, annoyed that she was still trying to play the role of the girlfriend when all he wanted was to be left alone. *I'll never love you*, he wanted to yell, but her heart-shaped eyes demanded something more from him. He bit his tongue, holding back the only real emotions he felt for the girl whom he knew to be in love with him. He winced inwardly as he remembered the desperate feeling of love unrequited.

The sting of his broken heart had faded on the surface, but the pieces had never fit back together properly, and he realized he was punishing the poor girl standing in front of him for it. He took one last look at Liri Murray and whispered his goodbye into the rain and wind between them. He turned, knowing he could never look back for her again.

"You look like you've seen a ghost," he finally heard her yell as he took off down the dark alley away from her and in the opposite direction of his flat. He ran down the dark street, twisting and turning down the alleys as he went, without knowing or caring where he was going.

As he ran with the brisk wind licking at his skin and the rain clinging to his stubble, he felt a freedom he'd not experienced since he was a child running across the wet moor in spring or over the top of the purple heather in the summer. He could see the faces of the kids he'd grown up with. He could see Isla's dark eyes looking back at him as he chased after her, never quite catching her. As he ran aimlessly through the street, he let himself fall down the rabbit hole of memories he'd done his best to forget because he knew where they led; back to Lewis where everyone knew him as the boy who'd murdered Arden Scott and gotten away with it. He wondered if his twenty-year absence was long enough to warrant forgiveness; both from the people of Lewis and himself.

Chapter Two

The winters were always long and cold, but the one before she arrived on the island was particularly brutal. Snow blanketed the moors and beaches for longer than I could remember in any recent year. Even as kids who were supposed to enjoy the snow, we had all had our fill of the cold and wet that seemed never-ending. I was ready to see the colors of spring painting the bleak countryside and feel the warmth of the sun on my pale skin. I closed my eyes and reopened them minutes later, hoping to have had willed winter away, but the sleet hitting the classroom window said otherwise.

I watched, painfully, as the hands on the clock above the door barely moved, mocking us the way a warden would his inmates. Our teacher, Ms. McNish, droned on in her rough Irish accent about a test that we'd taken earlier in the week. Her nicotine addiction did little to improve the quality of her voice, and when she spoke, it sounded like milk thistle had become caught in her throat. Listening to her for hours a day felt like glass in my ears, the shards so deep there was no hope of ever retrieving them. I tried to tune her out as I watched the hands on the clock, counting down the minutes until we were free of her for another weekend.

When the bell finally rang out above our heads, Ms. McNish tried to yell over top of its shrill scream even though it was evident that none of us were listening. Even the few girls in the front row that had been attentive to her just before the bell were now gathering their things and talking amongst themselves, indirectly ignoring her Irish droll. Her sad eyes said she could already hear the excuses for incomplete or nonexistent homework that she'd be given come Monday morning.

"One more thing," she shouted, her voice was high pitched and urgent. "We have a new student starting on Monday, so everyone, please, be on your best behavior."

She shot daggers at Arden and I from the front of the room as the words left her mouth, then circled around to almost every other male student in the classroom, leading the speculation to conclude that the new student would be a girl. As we scurried past her desk and into the hall, I heard Ms. McNish talking with Sarah Campbell, the goodie-goodie who sat front and center and always knew the answers even when she wasn't called on. I paused long enough to hear a name I'd never heard before. Arden and the others were already steps ahead of me, almost running toward the doors and had missed the conversation. I felt privileged to have been the only one to have heard her name; like somehow, she was already mine.

We all decided that Ms. McNish was an evil Irish spirit sent to torture us with the prospect of a new female student at the very last second of the day, thus making it impossible for us to enjoy our weekend properly as we all bickered and lamented over the possibilities a new girl at school represented. The island hardly ever received new residents. No one ever willingly moved to Lewis, much less to our extreme eastern outcropping of rock and deserted moorland. While Arden and Euan all argued incessantly on our walk home about what she was going to look like and who she was going to fancy best, I wondered what on earth was bringing her to the middle of nowhere, in addition to what she was going to look like and who she was going to fancy best, of course. The possibilities were endless.

When my eyes opened the next morning, the rain was already falling outside my window. It was light enough that the youth of Lewis could still get away with being outside, at least at the moment. I could smell the burnt coffee my father had in the kettle drifting down the hallway to my room, letting me know that my parents were awake and about the house already. It was going to take skill to escape without my mother's notice.

I dressed quickly and stood in the darkness of my room, one ear against the door listening to the noises on the other side. I could hear my father downstairs in the kitchen, fiddling with the kettle and pretending to read the newspaper at the sink while he really stared aimlessly out the window. I did not hear my mother.

After several minutes, I convinced myself that she'd decide to sleep in, which she'd done once or twice in my lifetime. I tried to place the last time I remembered her still being in bed by the time I pulled myself from mine but couldn't find the date. Even still, it was a possibility and a good one in light of her missing movement from the house. Maybe she'd run out to the store, which would have been even better. I knew I couldn't stand at the door forever. I made the decision to risk it.

I spun the handle on my door as quietly as I could, but it felt like the neighbors a quarter mile down the road might hear the metallic crunch of it as it tore into the quietness of the house. I poked my head out and still only heard my father in the kitchen. I tiptoed down the hallway, careful to step over the floorboards I knew would give me away. I stood at the top of the stairs, listing for my mother before I crept like a mouse down to the landing at the bottom. My boots were heavy on my feet and made more noise than I had calculated. I should have carried them on my hands like gloves, I thought regrettably, as I crept around the corner to the kitchen.

I turned and saw my father just as I had pictured him. My mother would knock him for his idleness if she saw him just staring out the window so he held the paper just low enough under his eyes so that he could see past the empty shoreline that spilled out in front of our house. I watched for a moment, wondering what he thought about as he stared out toward the horizon. He was a pensive man and must have thought about many things even if he rarely spoke about any of them. I was just about to make my presence known to him when I heard the door to the carport slam behind my mother as she re-entered the house. I bowed my head, knowing that I was caught.

"Lachlan McGinley, you've tracked mud in the house again. How many times have I told you, no wellies in the house."

I turned to see my mother standing behind me, fully dressed with a basket of laundry resting on her hip. She'd been in the port gathering clean clothes from the dryer, which was why I'd missed any sound of her when listening at my door. I looked down at the floor at the two or three pieces of dried mud that had fallen from my boots, damning me to a morning under the microscope that my mother carried with her always. I turned back to my father as if to ask for help, but he was already walking out the side door to the garden, leaving me to fend for myself. I removed my boots and carried them through the door leading to the port just in time to see the morning sunlight breaking through the gloom that always seemed to be hanging just above our heads. I grabbed the broom from the closet and walked back inside to clean the mess as the sun continued to sneak out from under the monochromatic gray color that was early spring.

"And the mop," my mother yelled from the back room. I slunk back out to the port, knowing that my morning was gone to chores and other menial labors my mother saw fit for me to do. Standing in the drive, I watched three figures on bikes race down the road in the direction of the morning sun, disappearing around the corner and into the freedom of our weekend.

***

We hadn't said a word to each other most of the morning, working independently of the other. My father had not returned and was most likely hiding out at the pier to stay out of my mother's crosshairs. By eleven, I had swept and mopped all the hard surfaces in the house, cleaned my room, put away my laundry and cleaned the hallway bathroom. By now, there was no telling where Arden and the others would be, but I was desperate to find them just as soon as I was freed.

"Ma," I said, making sure not to put the inflection of yelling for her in my voice. Yelling would warrant another hour of cleaning. I stood in the hallway, still as stone, waiting for her to appear from wherever it was she was in the house.

"Ms. McNish tells me that you received the highest mark in the class on your history exam." Her voice came from behind, startling me as I spun around to face her. I stood straight, arms at my side, waiting. There was no elation in her voice like a child would have expected from a parent reciting the same phrase. I waited for her to congratulate me but there would be no praise from her. I stood quiet, looking at the clean floor under our feet, waiting for her to speak.

"She also tells me you're getting a new student on Monday." My eyes sprang from the floor to meet hers which were already burning a hole in my forehead.

"She said something like that as we were leaving yesterday," I admitted, not wanting to seem overly anxious at the prospect of a new student, especially a female one.

"It seems they're Catholic," my mother spat, the tone derision thick on her tongue. I said nothing and returned my stare to the clean floor. "Well," she continued, "That's a shame."

We stood in the hallway, awkward and uncomfortable, for what felt like forever. I knew better than to ask if I could leave to join my friends. I simply stared at the floor, waiting for my mother to be sufficiently pleased with my silence and obedience. I always noticed she had large feet when I was forced into the position to stare at them for longer than anyone would want to look at feet. Larger, by right, than most women.

She always wore shoes, even in the house, even when no one else was allowed to. I tried to remember if I'd actually ever seen her feet but couldn't think of a time that I had. I thought that strange, for a boy never to have seen his mother's feet. I'd spent many nights sleeping over at Arden's or Euan's house to know that not all mothers were like mine. I'd seen both their mother's feet.

"I'm not your maid Lachlan," she said. "I'm not here to serve you."

Her voice was cold and angry, far past any anger she should have been harboring for a few pieces of dried mud on the ground.

"I have a million other things I could be doing instead of being ..." She didn't finish her sentence. She didn't have to. I could feel the pain in the back of my throat, stinging like I'd swallowed a thistle. I wanted to cry but held the tears back since they only ever worsened the situation.

"Homework?"

"Yes, ma'am. Done. Last night." I replied, my words coming out of my mouth so fast they were all jumbled together at points. My eyes finally jumped back to hers, hopeful that I'd suffered enough for her to let me go. I'd be half asleep by the time the sun started falling in the sky but being free for the rest of the day was worth every lost minute of sleep from the night before. She looked me up and down, searching for something to be wrong so she wouldn't have to let me go, but by twelve I knew how to play the game well enough to win on occasion. Our eyes met for a moment, mine begging for freedom and hers begging for something similar.

"Six," she said and turned her back on me, disappearing into her room at the end of the hall. I was already in the side yard throwing a leg over the seat of my bike when she'd pulled the door closed behind her.

***

It didn't take long to find Arden and the others posted up at the pier with their poles, even though we never caught anything other than seaweed and crabs. Arden had managed to lift a few cigarettes from his older brother's room while he slept, and the plan was to ride out of town to a small loch hidden from the road and the prying eyes of adults that knew our names. There, we would smoke the cigarettes like the men we were desperate to become instead of the boys we felt like we were destined to be for the rest of our lives.

The small glimpse of the sun I had seen as my friends rode to freedom ahead of me had disappeared behind a wall of gray in the distance. The rain had stopped for the moment, but we knew the trek to the loch would be soggy. I could hear the slurping noise the mud would make as we made our way over the boggy ground. I would have to remember to clean my boots before going home, or I'd probably never be let out again.

"Lach," Arden whispered, motioned with his chin toward the entrance of the pier. My dad stood at its end, hands crammed in his jacket pockets like always. "Maybe he can get us some bait, to take with us?"

"Sure," I replied, heading in his direction, knowing that he most likely already had it in his pocket.

He looked like a statue, the spoondrift casting off the murky water churning on the rocks below us. He rarely spoke and almost never in my mother's presence. His hair had thinned and turned a soft shade of white in the last couple of years, which, for any man was a sad state of affairs but even more so for my father on account that he wasn't that old. It was my mother that had caused his hair to salt. I was surprised my own hair had not started to turn.

It was hard to imagine my mother as anything other than the cold, emotionless robot she was, but there had to have been something between them at some point. I wondered if he loved her or if he'd ever loved her. People who hate each other don't just get married. I looked at my dad and tried to remember a time I'd seen them kiss or hug or even shake hands, but there was no memory of any of it.

"What's the plan then?" he asked, avoiding eye contact by looking past me to my friends gathering their poles and packs, readying to head out.

"Fishing," I answered, looking back over my shoulder as the three of them awkwardly shuffled about waiting to see if I was able to secure the bait we needed. None of us really wanted to dig in the mud for worms, but we would make Euan do it under protest if we had to.

My father pulled his hand from his pocket, gifting me a small white paper sack, the bottom already visibly wet from the loose earth inside.

"Thanks," I said with a smile, taking the bag before turning and shaking it in the air like I'd won something significant.

"What time?" he asked.

"Six."

"Don't be late," he said, stepping aside so we could pass by, my friends thanking him for the bait as they did.

I looked back at him as I swung my leg over my bike at the end of the pier. Arden, Euan, and Calum already a few pedals down the jetty. He stood there, leaning on the railing, looking out into the gray abyss in front of him. I wondered how long he could stand there before the mist from the water chilled him enough to retreat, but deep down, I already knew the answer. Rarely was he ever home before me.

***

The wind whipped at our backs, pushing us down the winding single-lane road toward Kirkibost. We had all seen the squall hanging in the distance before leaving the pier but said nothing. Each of us knew as well as the next that having the wind at our backs now meant we'd be fighting against it and the rain that was coming on our way home. But there was little else in the way of entertainment on our deserted island for young boys who were not yet old enough to drive. Before being granted that liberty, there was little else we worried about other than the direction of the wind and the rain on any given day.

We stopped at the co-op and gave all our money to Calum for sandwiches and water and any other provisions he saw fit to buy. The rest of us waited outside with the bikes, kicking rocks in the road and listening to the cows talking to each other on the other side of the fence.

"I bet she'll be blonde," Arden interjected into the silence of the moment. "With blue eyes."

"Who?" I asked, scrunching the skin on my forehead to play dumb. I couldn't let on that I had obtained insider information about the girl, that she was even to be a girl, and that I knew her name. I liked having a secret over them. I could introduce myself to her if I saw her before class instead of just staring at her as all the other boys would do. I could call her by name. I'd get my foot in the door and have her eating out of my palm by lunch. All because I knew her name and they didn't.

"I don't know," Euan said as he bent to pick up the rock we'd been kicking back and forth, hurling it into the pasture and landing it square on the smallest cow's backside. "What if she's tall, like too tall?"

Euan was the shortest of the four of us and the thickest. He also wore glasses that he was constantly adjusting and fidgeting with. His parents kept a cottage for a wealthy owner and didn't make much money, so everything he wore was a hand-me-down, some even from us when they grew too small. He'd never seemed to mind before, but this was the year we were certain we would all become men. Turning thirteen meant we'd all be sent to the Nicholson Institute next year for our first year of secondary, where Arden's older brothers already attended. We'd be on the other side of the island from our parents, from Bernera, and may as well be on the other side of the world. There was freedom hanging on the horizon. But that's when your clothes and what you looked like started to matter, and Euan seemed worried.

"What if she's a cow?" Arden laughed. "What if she's as fat and hairy as that cow's arse right there?" Arden threw another rock, landing it on the same cow that Euan had. The beast barely noticed as it bounced off its thick chocolate colored fur.

What if he was right? What if she was hideous or smelled as bad as the pasture? I'd already claimed her because I knew her name before anyone else without ever thinking of her being anything other than the most beautiful thing in the world. I was already in love with a girl I'd never even seen and now the prospect of her being as big and smelly as a cow sent me into a spiral of despair and dejection.

"Ach, what'd you do that for," I yelled after Arden launched another rock, this time at the side of my head.

"You were just standing there like your da, staring into outer space, you half-wit," he said, his eyes asking if I was ok. Arden may have had a rough tongue, but he was a good friend. I was lucky to have the privilege of calling him my best friend, which was something even I knew not everyone could expect to have in this life.

"Got the snacks," Calum yelled as he rejoined us in the parking lot, shoving the lot into his bag before jumping back on his bike.

Calum and Euan rode in small circles, spitting gravel with their tires as they went. I stood motionless, still shell-shocked by the fact that I'd never even considered the possibility of the new girl being as ugly as mud before letting myself fall in love with the idea of her. The chip I'd been wearing on my shoulder since the previous afternoon began to slip down my arm slowly, showing me the depth of my naivety as it did.

"You commin?" Arden asked, punching me in the shoulder, knocking the chip the rest of the way to the ground, leaving me feeling empty inside.

"What if she is a cow?" I whispered to him. He tried to cover his own concern for the matter with indifference but did it poorly. But we all knew why the others cared so much about her. In a place where nothing ever happened, she was the possibility of something happening. Something big.

"Then we'll throw rocks at her," Calum spat from his bike, launching one in our direction but missing pathetically.

"Let's go, the rain's coming," Arden said as he jumped on his bike, joining Euan and Calum as they spun circles around me.

"I gotta piss," I mumbled pathetically and headed into the co-op to use the facilities. I could hear them behind me calling me names like Nancy and Barbara. I'd never been one for pissing outside, which in their eyes, made me a girl. But my jeans never smelled like urine, unlike theirs. I knew better than to piss into a wind that changed direction without notice and rarely let up.

The soap on the sink of the bathroom was a transparent purple color with bits of real heather floating in it. I pumped some onto my chapped hands and frothed them under the warm tap. The smell reminded me of summer, something we were all desperate for by the time it finally appeared every year. I'd almost forgotten what the flower smelled like, even though for two or three months out of the year it would blanket the moor and we'd drift on top of its blooms. I closed my eyes and inhaled the smell of the bubbles gathering in the bottom of the sink thinking of the last time I had felt warmth against my pale blue skin. I opened the door and stepped out into the hallway, my hands pressed against my face in a desperate attempt to hang onto the memories of last summer, the door just missing her as it swung outward.

I was frozen, stuck to the sticky co-op hallway floor that looked like it hadn't been cleaned in months and smelled of wet earth and cow shit. At first, all I could see was her hair, burning like wildfire on top of her head. It was everywhere, wild and crazy strands casting out in every direction. There was too much of it to be held back from her oval face with just one tie, but it was not unkempt. She said nothing but gave a look that made me question if her personality matched its unruliness. The look in her eyes said yes, and I probably should have known better, but I knew right then that I would try to tame her anyway.

Her eyes looked like polished green marbles and fizzed under the florescent lights of the hallway. They reminded me of the color of the sea at Seilebost, when Arden and I had gone with his parents late last summer. The water was cold by then, but we still swam to the sandbar that showed up at low tide and walked almost clear across to the other side of the island. I couldn't look away, no matter how much I begged my body to do so, screaming inside that I needed to say something, anything, before she thought I was some kind of mute dolt who smells his own hands after taking a piss. I couldn't let that be the new girl's first impression of me. I'd never recover.

She looked me up and down, and I instantly wished I'd put on clean clothes that morning or at the very least brushed my hair. I was thankful for the first time in my life that I'd listen to my mother and brushed my teeth before leaving the house. She smiled as her eyes moved over me. Keenly aware of the hold she had over me at that moment, she took a few steps toward me, leaning in with her nose tilted up in the air.

"You smell like summer," she finally said as her eyes met mine, mere inches apart. Her voice was small but powerful, a bullet crashing into my heart, ripping through it only to leave me hopelessly in love with her.

"Heather," I heard my voice answer, unaware that I was still capable of speaking.

"Actually, it's Isla," she said shamelessly. "Isla Gilcrest."

"You're not a cow." My voice was broken and cracked in certain places.

"Would you rather I was?" she asked, perplexed by my inopportune choice of words.

"Sweet Mary mother of Joseph no," I shrieked, realizing the stupidity of my comment. "You're just like I imagined you would be."

I felt the flop sweat take hold of my body. I wasn't sure if anyone had ever died of embarrassment. I would be the first, if not.

"I like summer," she said, slipping past me.

"I like heather," I chocked at her back.

"No," she whispered, turning to look over her shoulder. "You like Isla."

She smiled and winked over her shoulder as she pulled on the door to the women's bathroom. *Bye,* she mouthed before she disappeared behind the door, leaving me to wonder if she had been real or just a figment of my overactive boyish imagination.

"Let's go, Barbara," I heard Arden yell from a few feet behind me. "What's taking so long? Having a hard time finding your pecker?"

I turned and charged at Arden, punching him in the shoulder as he backed away from me when he saw it coming. I hit him harder than I had intended, and he fell ass first into a display of chips, knocking the merchandise on the floor and drawing the attention of the keeper behind the counter. I had minutes, at best, to get him out of the shop and headed down the road before Isla Gilcrest emerged from the bathroom, in all of her blistering glory, for him and everyone else to lay eyes upon. I wanted to keep her a secret, if only until the school bell rang on Monday morning. Until then, I wanted to keep her for myself.

Chapter Three

Lachlan was thankful for the gentle sway of the train below him. The movement comforted him the way he'd always imagined how a mother's embrace would feel. Under different circumstances, he would have found sleep quickly, but his mind raced with memories of a home he'd left behind a hundred years ago. He never imagined that he'd ever have the need to find it again.

The carriage moved slowly as it traveled down the line toward Perth, where he'd hop another train and continue on toward Inverness and then a bus to Ullapool, delivering him to the Calmac ferry terminal. He had no good memories of the Inverness station or the city in general. He tried to focus on the rhythmic movement of the train's wheels as they clicked along on top of the track, but his mind drifted to distant memories of things better left buried in the past.

A voice came over the loudspeaker announcing their impending arrival in Perth, and as Lachlan stood to detrain, the memory all but slipped from his view. On the platform, he looked for the cure-all for dispatching unwanted memories and found it at the bottom of a Highland Special before boarding the train that was to take him back to Inverness.

From Perth to Inverness the carriage jerked and stalled, pulling into station after station, picking up and dropping off fellow passengers as it went. Just as the train felt like it had achieved a comfortable travel speed, the door chimes would ding, and the swaying motion would begin to wane before they shuddered to a stop. Lachlan rested his head against the window and ignored the pretty women that always seemed to find a seat next to him, their smooth skin and silky hair smelling of sex and lies. He wasn't interested in the emptiness they had to offer. He was already too empty inside.

The alcohol in Lachlan's otherwise empty gut swished audibly with the swaying of the train, his Highland Special calling out for company. The closer to Inverness the train crept, the more Lachlan drank, until he eventually had a collection of mini liquor bottles stacked on the tray in front of him. The homely woman running the bar cart took pity on him and handed him a sandwich to help soak up the liquid courage he was trying to find at the bottom of each little bottle. The door chime pinged, and a despondent voice boomed over the loudspeaker; *Last stop. Inverness. All passengers must detrain.* Lachlan waited until the other passengers had exited, leaving him standing alone again at the threshold of the Inverness train station.

The station was bleak at midday, most of its travelers already come and gone until the evening rush. The few people that remained either scurried like seen rats as they jumped from one train to the next or staggered like zombies on the platform waiting for the next leg of their journey to begin. The majority of them appeared to be tourists, dragging wheeled luggage behind them that ticked against the cobblestones in the long walkway leading up toward the mouth of the station. The stones were slick underfoot with rain tracked in from the morning rush.

Lachlan's sneakers squeaked as he walked under the dim yellow lights, climbing the tall staircase at the end of the platform to the upper level. He walked sluggishly, the alcohol affecting the speed with which his legs and brain were communicating. As he mounted the top step of the stairway, the bench on which he'd sat as a teenager, waiting for someone to come for him, crept into his peripheral vision and grabbed ahold of him the way the wet and the cold stuck to Scottish rain.

He stood, paralyzed, staring at the bench in front of him. He'd made every attempt over the last twenty years to avoid Inverness altogether so he'd never have to see it again. He'd never had a need or want to visit the city after he left at seventeen years old with nothing but a change of clothes and two fifty-pound notes the driver had been instructed to give him once he reached the train station. He remembered the feel of the crisp note in his hand as he stood on the sidewalk, watching the only soul he knew in two hundred miles speed away into the darkness of the night. The money felt fake in his shaking hand, and so had his reality.

The yellow lamp hanging above the bench was dull and flickered when a train pulled in or out of the station. Lachlan remembered the comfort of its glow when he'd laid under it, illuminating the darkness that filled the station and keeping the other monsters at bay. The air had been cold that night, even tucked inside the mouth of the station. He sat and waited for the morning to come. He could smell the warm sunlight trying to find him in the tunnel. By then, he knew no one was coming. The nurses had lied to him when they pushed him out the elaborate front doors, assuring him that someone was coming for him at the station. Maybe they had believed someone was coming for him. Perhaps they'd been told it was so. But by morning, Lachlan knew that no one was coming and that he had been left alone in the world.

The brakes of the coaches hissed on the street in front of the station and echoed through the concrete labyrinth of platforms and alcoves. Lachlan blinked away the memory of his night in the Inverness train station and began running for the queue to catch the bus the rest of the way to Ullapool. The bench in the cold, damp station was only the tip of the iceberg of his time in Inverness, and he did not care to stay any longer, fearing the other memories that were likely to find him. He found a seat in the back of the coach, pulled out the last of his liquid courage and drank Inverness away.

The port smelled like a mixture of diesel fuel and the open sea as if the air couldn't decide which one it wanted to favor most. The bay was like glass and reflected the cloudless early summer sky above it. The ferry sat high in the water at the dock, waiting to be loaded with passengers on their way to Stornoway. The smaller skiffs tied up in the bay lay motionless on the polished surface like paintings hanging on an old woman's living room wall. Lachlan looked out over the Minch at the fog sitting just above the surface several hundred feet from shore hindering any view of what laid beyond it.

The queue became punchy when Lachlan did not advance toward the ticket window at his turn. He tried, but his legs refused to move. He stood motionless trying to find a reality that didn't involve the ferry or Lewis or going home at all. He could already see the accusatory faces and hear the hushed whispers, but her memory was crisp in his mind, buried under a crown of fire. Even after two decades, he could still feel the burning of her soul against his own.

Lachlan regained feeling in his legs just in time to step out of the queue as a large man grumbled angrily behind him. He turned his back on the bay and headed into the sea of cottages that dotted the streets of Ullapool. Moments later, the horn from the ferry screamed as it pulled away from the dock, sending teams of startled birds into the air.

Lachlan found refuge in The Seaforth at the end of the narrow, cobbled road. He looked back towards the port as he opened the door to the pub to see the ferry being swallowed by the ash colored fog hanging just above the water's surface. Lachlan found a seat in the corner of the dark pub, determined to drink himself brave enough to catch the 6:30 ferry after the light of day had slipped from the sky and his fear of returning home was well hidden by the black of the night.

The whiskey was successful, and Lachlan watched as the lights of Ullapool disappeared from sight as the 6:30 ferry pushed into open water. He had two and a half hours until they docked on the other side and he doubted that anyone would serve him another drink while on board. The lass at the ticket window had mumbled something to her coworker behind their glass divider when Lachlan fumbled with his wallet and credit cards. The two must have alerted other members of the ferry staff to his condition, meeting their shifty eyes as he tried to find somewhere on board to lie down and sleep away the passage to Stornoway.

The passengers on the ferry looked like Lewis locals returning home from the mainland for the weekend, dressed in dirty work clothes and faces shoved into smartphones or laptops. He felt out of place sitting with them like it was disrespectful to be counted amongst those who actually braved life on the island. Lachlan wondered what people his age did for work if they'd not made it off Lewis. He was sure most of his friends hadn't. That was just how it worked. You lived and died on the island, and so did your kids.

The gallery was quiet, except for two primary age boys playing with toy cars on the floor while they're mother read a small book with a red cover. Everyone looked tired, including the crew who dashed about the ship busying themselves with menial tasks until the ferry was ready to dock in Stornoway. The days' worth of drinking began tugging at Lachlan's eyes. He wanted nothing more than to be lying in his own bed listening to the low rumble of the steady traffic outside his flat. He'd figured on getting to Stornoway, but past that, he'd not given it much thought. Home was another hour drive to the other side of the island.

He needed to clear the whiskey from his head and find a place to sleep before the ferry docked in Stornoway.

The dreams were dark, like always, making them hard to see. The people were always faceless, except for Arden; his face was clear as day. Lachlan could feel the fear in his eyes as they struggled against one another while sideways rain pelted their faces. The half-moon shaped scar above his right eye began to pulse as his sleeping body tensed, readying for the impact he knew was coming, the connection of metal to flesh and bone. Lachlan was thankful for the rousing that pulled him from his dream just moments before the impact. He wiped the sleep from his eyes, shielding them from the torchlight being shined into the backseat of the stranger's car he'd managed to climb into when the whiskey'd finally done him in.

"Sir," a man's muted voice on the other side of the glass called. "Sir, you can't be down here."

When Lachlan didn't move, the man rapped the handle of the torch on the glass almost hard enough to crack it, indicating the seriousness of his request.

"Sir, you need to exit the vehicle immediately."

Lachlan heard the beep and squawk of a walkie-talkie and more muted scrambled words on the other side of the glass. He was moving, but the sum of the alcohol he'd consumed over the course of the day was wreaking havoc on his body. His head spun, and the torchlight shining in his face made him think he was going to vomit. He'd already broken into and slept in a stranger's car, he didn't want to add puking on the floorboards to that repertoire.

He shimmied out of the back seat with the help of the man with the walkie-talkie, just missing his shoes as his stomach heaved fifty dollars' worth of alcohol onto the deck of the CalMac ferry. The attendant stood behind Lachlan, talking into his walkie-talkie, requesting someone to bring a hose to the lower deck to clean up the mess.

"Sir, do you need medical assistance?" The attendant asked kindly, before mumbling *you fuckin drunkard* under his breath.

Lachlan chuckled, still hunched close to the ship's deck. He may have been a drunkard, but that didn't give some shit ferry attendant the right to call him one.

"What did you call me?" Lachlan asked as he stood and spun around, still somewhat off-kilter, staggering to keep his balance before coming face to face with the man with the walkie-talkie.

"Sir," the man started again, taking a step toward Lachlan in an attempt to assert his dominance over the situation. "Do you need ..." His words trailed into the murkiness around them as his eyes fixated on Lachlan's face, his glance darting back and forth between his eyes and the scar above his eyebrow. An expression of confusion straddled the man's face as he took a step back, trying to take in the whole of Lachlan standing in front of him.

"It can't be," the attendant whispered. His walkie-talkie chirped, and the garbled voice of the person on the other end came through, but Lachlan couldn't make out the words. "Aye, I've got it handled, cancel Maddox." He turned the knob on top of the walkie, and the red and yellow lights dimmed and then disappeared, leaving the two assumed strangers straining to see the other in the darkness of the night engulfing them.

"Are you Lachlan McGinley?" the stranger asked outright, a sliver of hope and excitement riding on his words.

Lachlan rubbed his face and spat onto the deck a few times trying to get the tang of twice-tasted whiskey out of his mouth. He didn't recognize the man in front of him even though he'd obviously knew him.

"Do I know you?" Lachlan asked.

"Are you Lachlan, then?"

"Aye."

"It's Calum," he answered proudly, expecting the veil of confusion to be lifted from Lachlan's face at the mere mention of his name. The man's expression soured when his memory continued to elude Lachlan. "Kincaid. Calum Kincaid," he repeated again and waited for any sign of recognition. "Ms. McNich's class. Fourth year."

"Holy shit, man," Lachlan finally said. "Is that really you?"

"Me? Is it really you? I never thought I'd be seeing you again, mate. We all thought you were ..." his voice trailed off as it had before, caught in the blare of the ferry horn. Tiny yellow dots began to appear on the horizon, hanging in the foggy air like lanterns leading them into Stornoway.

"You got anything I can ..." Lachlan motioned with his hands for something to swig on and wash the vomit from his mouth before continuing their re-acquaintance.

"There's some whiskey over there," Calum said, pointing to the puddle of liquid vomit to their right.

The two men began to laugh, first in small, short bursts but eventually progressing into a roar that only two friends with shared childhood memories could manage.

"Good to see you man," Lachlan laughed, throwing both arms around his old friend, and smacking him loudly on the shoulders as men tend to do.

"You too. I still can't believe you're standin' in front of me. It's unreal."

The two men, who'd known each other only as boys, stood facing each other, unsure of what to say next. So much time had passed between them, it was hard to know where to start.

"Your mom died," Calum finally blurted out, immediately regretting his choice of words. "Shit, I'm sorry man, I didn't mean it like that, just that, that's why you're back, right?"

"Something like that," Lachlan answered before they fell back into silence for a moment. The happy reunion had done well to further sober Lachlan, and he felt human again. He could feel the beginnings of summer rush against his face, warm and sweet streaks of air melted in with the mild sea breeze. It smelled like heather and gorse and reminded him of when they'd been kids traversing the hilly terrain of Bernera because there had been absolutely nothing else to fill their days. He looked at his old friend standing in front of him and for a moment, was glad to be home.

"Seriously," he mucked, his mouth still stale with sick. "You got anything I can rinse with?"

"Aye, yeah, yeah," Calum said hurriedly, pulling a half-drunk water bottle from his back pocket.

Lachlan rinsed his mouth and retrieved his bag from the ground. He could feel the ferry begin to slow and knew that Calum would most likely be called away to dock them in Stornoway. He remembered Calum's love of the ferry and his tales of riding back and forth with his father who had been an officer when they were kids. He was happy his friend had found a life in it.

"Are you staying in Stornoway then, at least for the night?' Calum asked, twisting the knob on his walkie so that the red and yellow lights came back to life.

"To be honest," Lachlan started. "I've been too drunk to figure a plan. I'll probably just grab a bed for the night and hop a ride out of town in the morning."

"That's shite," Calum shouted over the muddled voices on the walkie. "You'll stay with me. I'm off after we dock anyway. I've got a few things to take care of, but meet me at The Edge, we'll have a pint and catch up."

Lachlan looked lost. "The edge?" he asked.

"Ha. You've been gone too long my friend," Calum laughed, smacking him on the back as they made their way toward the stairway leading back up to the passenger deck.

They climbed the stairs and pushed toward the bow. Calum pointed off to the right side of the port as they drifted toward the dock. "Just there, those orange lights. The Edge o' the World. I'll buy you a pint." And with that, the only friend Lachlan had in the world disappeared into the night to tend the ferry bringing them home.

***

Stornoway had changed, much more than Lachlan had expected. Evidence of the mainland had crept over the Minch with every ferry load, infecting the island with the syndromes of the outside world. Modern shops lined the streets just off the harbor selling Harris Tweed or Gin, chocolates, and candies, Walkers cookies and cheaply spun plaids; anything a tourist might fit in their suitcase to pull out later and remember the time they visited a near-deserted island. The mom and pop businesses of his childhood whose owners only spoke Gaelic had not survived, driven out by bigger, newer, younger businesses. Pubs filled the empty spaces between the shops, and large, rowdy crowds filled them. That was one thing that had remained the same. The men of Lewis were some of the hardest working men anyone would have known, and so they drank just as hard. As Lachlan walked down the narrow road toward the cluster of orange lights Calum had pointed out from the ferry, he could hear glass breaking, women yelling and men singing in every pub he passed. He knew the Edge o' the World would be no different.

The air was thick with the salt of the sea and smoke, but it didn't touch the perfume of whiskey that clung to most of the men in the pub. The smell made Lachlan's stomach turn, the taste of vomit still stuck in his throat. He made his way through the crowd toward the bar and grabbed a seat at the end, out of the way of all the local men who deserved to be there more than he did.

The barmaid pushed a shot in front of him without so much as a word and returned a moment later with a pint of the pub's homebrewed ale before disappearing farther down the line. Lachlan studied the whiskey in the small glass, holding it up to the yellow glow cast down from the bar lights. He'd always loved the color of good whiskey; golden yellow, sometimes almost orange like the sun coming up over the horizon on a clear summer morning. He remembered seeing that sunrise as a child, creeping up over the horizon and spilling its warm colors into the loch, the silhouette of his father always standing in the middle of it.

"Lachlan fuckin' McGilvery. Is that really you?"

The unfamiliar voice startled Lachlan who had been lost in forgotten memories risen by the whiskey in his hand. He turned and peered into the crowd looking for the person who'd recognized him but staring back was a sea of foreign faces. The catcall had been loud enough to quiet some of the patrons in Lachlan's general vicinity. When no one immediately copped to the shout, Lachlan turned back to his whiskey, trying to place the voice of someone who obviously knew him.

"It is you," the booming voice called again. "You've got a lot of bollocks showing your face 'round here."

The crowd around the bar began to part, creating a pathway leading to Lachlan at its end. He hadn't recognized the voice but instantly knew his face. Ross Scott had been old enough the last time Lachlan saw him that almost twenty years hadn't changed him enough to become unrecognizable. He had the same greasy, dirty blonde hair and pock-marked skin. His dull eyes were too close together and dog-shit brown. A half-smoked cigarette clung to his bottom lip and Lachlan could see the tips of yellow teeth as a smug smile broke out across his face. Lachlan remembered him being bigger than he appeared now, but that may have been due to their age difference. Lachlan had only been twelve the last time they saw each other, Ross probably close to nineteen at the time.

Lachlan turned back to the bar, twirling the whiskey in its glass. "I dunna want any trouble Ross," Lachlan said before throwing the warm liquid down his throat. "I'm here to bury my mother, and that's it. Then I'm gone."

"Aye, that's right, your ma's gone and fuckin' died on you. Couldn't have happened to a nicer lass."

"You'll get no argument from me on that," Lachlan said, motioning to the barmaid for another shot with his empty glass.

"At least you get to bury her," Ross continued, moving a few steps closer to Lachlan who was still perched on the barstool, the ball of one foot resting limply on the ground and the other thumping incessantly on the metal ring tying the legs of the barstool together. "At least you have a body to bury, that is, unlike us, who still have no peace."

The pub was silent enough that Lachlan could hear his own heartbeat as it jumped from his chest to his throat. The barmaid grabbed the bottle of whiskey from the speed wall, shooting daggers at both men as she did. She looked like she'd been around enough to know what was coming next, holding a thin wooden bat in her left hand as she poured the whiskey with her right. She'd hardly finished the pour before Lachlan had the glass to his lips, the whiskey in his belly and his fists balled tight, ready for what he expected would be a fight with a much older and hopefully slower than he remembered Ross Scott.

"I dunna want any trouble," Lachlan said again, setting the glass on the bar top with a thud. "Just leave it be, it's not going to change anything."

Lachlan could see the veins in Ross' neck start to pulse, his face turned red, and he clenched his chapped lips around his soured teeth.

"Yeah, that's what you would say, you fuckin twally-washer. I wonder what my brother'd say if he were here instead of you."

Lachlan was on his feet and nose to nose to Ross before his bar stool tipped and hit the floor with the sound of thunder. Ross smiled, gloating over his ability to rile Lachlan. Voices whispered from the crowd that had gathered around the men, disparaging murmurs thick on all their tongues.

"That's right," Ross whispered, the smoke from his cigarette floating like a ghost in the air between them. "Everyone here kens who you are and what it is you've done."

Lachlan backed up a few paces, having regained some of his composure. He knew that throwing punches with Ross wouldn't change anything. It wouldn't change the opinion of every soul on the island regarding who and what they thought he was. It wouldn't change what he'd done to his brother, regardless if it was the truth. Truth didn't matter to these people. All that mattered was that Arden had disappeared and no one had ever been brought to justice for it.

"You do what you have to do Ross, but I ain't gonna fight with you. It doesn't matter anymore." Lachlan turned his back on Ross and the gathered crowd and retrieved his bar stool from the floor, setting it upright.

"Maybe this will matter to you. I got her," Ross scoffed, guile dripping from his voice. "When you couldn't. All that time you spent lovin' over her, and I got her instead."

The thought of Isla Gilcrest underneath the man that stood in front of him made Lachlan's skin crawl and his blood boil. He clenched his lips tight around his teeth, grinding them together as he did. He knew she would have had a life in his absence, but the image of that life had never involved Ross Scott. The idea was vile, and if Lachlan had had anything in his stomach save one or two shots, it would have been in a pile on the floor. He begged a God he didn't believe in for it not to be true, he begged for him not to have ruined her.

Ross was on the floor before he knew what hit him, Lachlan crouched over top of him. Blood poured from Ross' broken nose, and he spat it back in Lachlan's face, laughing as he did. Lachlan wrapped both hands around the collar of his jacket, pulling Ross' face within inches of his own, a knee in his gut to keep him pinned to the ground.

"You're not worth it," Lachlan whispered.

"Aye, maybe no," Ross replied, his smug smile still dancing on his bloodied face. "But she certainly was."

Lachlan pulled his fist back desperate to cleanse Ross of the lies he was spouting, but a voice called out from behind him that made him stop.

"You lyin' little bastard," she called out, sweet and strong, just how he liked his whiskey. He hadn't heard her voice since they were kids, but it wasn't one he was likely to forget, no matter how much time had passed between them. "Don't' be tellin' folks that you had me when it ain't bloody true."

Lachlan turned in her direction, losing his grip on Ross' jacket. His body went limp at the sight of her. He'd done well to put her likeness out of his mind when he thought he'd never see her again. The mere thought of her was like torture, and when he couldn't take it anymore, he'd banished her from his memory and had tried to move on with his life as best he could. But once in a while when he caught a glimpse of the sun dropping behind the horizon, setting the sky ablaze with streaks of orange and red, he thought of her hair, stopping just short of the image of her sea-colored eyes. She stood before him now, her red hair burning and just as crazy as it had been when they were kids, and all Lachlan could think was that no image he could have conjured of her in his memory would have done her beauty justice.

It may have been his euphoric state and the shock of seeing Isla again or perhaps it was the steady flow of alcohol pulsing through his blood throughout the day, but Lachlan didn't feel Ross' fist connect with his face. Suddenly the Edge o' the World was on its side with the fiery blaze of the sun centered in his sights as all other light left the world.

***

The loud hum of the engine woke Lachlan midway through their drive back to Bernera. He had almost no memory of the evening prior, except one. The image of her hair was burned on the underside of Lachlan's eyelids. With eyes opened or closed, it was all he could see now.

"Welcome back," Calum laughed. "You sure know how to come home with a bang."

Lachlan tried rubbing the daze from his face, finding it was not sleep caking it, but dry blood, stale booze, and only God knew what else.

"What happened?" he asked roughly. His throat dry and stale.

"Well, I only know what I saw, and that was Ross Scott pounding the shite out of you on the floor. By the time I seen you, someone had called the cops. They were right behind me, so I scooped you up and got out of there."

Lachlan suddenly regretted all the mean things he'd done to Calum as kids and was thankful he'd apparently not held a grudge over all their years apart. Calum handed him a bottle of water and a plate of warm biscuits just as Lachlan's stomach started to growl, realizing he'd forgotten to eat the previous day. He devoured three biscuits as he watched the barren landscape pass his window. He'd forgotten how drab and desolate the passage to the other side of the island was. The gray-brown color of the peat fields. Small patches of grass had already turned green, and he could see the yellow buds of the gorse beginning to spread. Trenches from the peat cuts were laced through the hill with empty pallets nearby waiting to be filled. Soon the heather would bloom, and it would be summer.

"Is it true?" Lachlan finally asked, not wanting to know the answer, but needing to know the truth.

"What's that?"

"Ross and Isla. He threw it in my face like he'd done it just to spite me. Is it true?"

Calum said nothing and just stared out the windshield at the road in front of them, but his silence said everything. Lachlan's mouth watered, and he struggled to keep the biscuits down. He tried to imagine what she'd seen in him, but that only put the image of the two of them together in his mind. He wanted to hate Ross, but he knew he was just jealous of him. Lachlan had come so close to having her first, before anyone, and now he couldn't see her without seeing him.

The two boys masquerading as men crossed the small bridge to Bernera. Lachlan could feel the sea breeze rushing over the car, tossing it like a toy they'd once played with as toddlers. He'd forgotten how the wind pulled on the island, constant and relentless. The single-track road twisted and turned through the rolling hills and craggy moorland. The brightly painted sheep dotted the hills, heads down, eating the bits of spring grass popping through the rock. They crested a small hill and passed the school they'd attended as children. The building looked old and run down. Everything on the island was cloaked with age and wear but otherwise looked as if time had stood still in Lachlan's absence.

Up ahead he saw his parent's house, which now belonged only to his father. Calum pulled off the road and idled his car. He said nothing but offered a familiar look. One he'd given as a kid when Ross had the opportunity to torment them, which had been far too often. The door slammed, and his slate-colored Impresa glinted in the sun as he pulled away down the road.

Lachlan stood outside his childhood home, fearful of what he might find inside. Instead, he walked around to the side of the house as daylight began to pull through the clouds. There, standing in the breaking sun, stood the silhouette of his father and the shadows of the ghosts that stood between them.

Chapter Four

The metallic clank of the door slamming woke me with a startle. The two women who'd arrived an hour earlier were sitting in the front seat, looking back at me with half-cocked smiles on their old and saggy faces. They looked like I imagined nuns would look, holier than thou but mad as hell about it. I crouched on my knees and looked out the back window. If I strained, I could still make out my parent's outlines standing on the porch, but they were just blurry figures hidden behind a curtain of rain.

The older of the two women sat in the driver seat, keys in her hand and a sad look in her eyes. She turned without saying anything and started the car. The younger one started talking, but her words stuck to her lips like honey and I couldn't understand them. Everything felt like it was moving in slow motion. I watched as the older woman reached for the shifter to move the car into drive, but I turned to look out the back window again before I saw her hand grasp it. The rain had become a drizzle, and just beyond my house, I could see the sun beginning to break the horizon line, throwing yellow and orange and pink streaks across the infinite gray void of sky.

My parents stood on the porch. My mother had her arms clasped across her chest enfolding her large midsection and a sour look on her face. Her head shook back and forth slightly as I looked at her, our eyes meeting for the first time in a long time and they were filled with something close to relief. She turned to walk inside without so much as a wave goodbye.

My father at least looked upset, like I would imagine a parent should be at the sight of his only child being driven away by two strangers. His eyes were always sad, but now they looked empty, defeated. Before the house disappeared from sight, he stepped off the porch and into the small front yard raising his arm as if to wave goodbye. My father and I had never been close, and his distressing wave goodbye was the closest thing to an I love you I could remember.

I stayed posted up in the back window as the car sped down the familiar roads, splashing in puddles as it went. We passed my school, and I saw Ms. McNich standing at the fence while my classmates gathered in small groups outside, around the community garden we'd started that spring. Calum and Euan ran to the far side of the fence when they realized it was me in the back seat of the strange car, waving and shouting, maybe even crying small tears. Noticeably missing from the fence line goodbye was Arden, making my leaving all the more painful for everyone involved.

The luster of the sun caught my eye, and I turned to see Isla running behind the car, her red hair streaking through the sky after her. I wanted nothing more than to twirl the untamed tendrils around my fingers until my hands were stuck, joining us together forever. But instead, we were being ripped apart. She ran hard. Her face was twisted with pain and tears flowed freely from her swollen eyes. I reached out to her, both hands pressed against the glass, but another second and she was gone, lost behind a bend in the road. We crossed over the small bridge connecting Bernera to the rest of Lewis, and it felt like it was the last time I would see her, my friends, my parents. But I didn't feel anything deeper than the surface for any of them. I couldn't. I was numb, like I'd been the one who'd died instead of Arden.

***

The drugs had worn off as the car came to a stop in front of the large building. The two women jumped out of the car, the younger one opening the door for me, offering her hand for assistance. The building was three stories tall in most places, with rows of windows and peaked roofs, towers and spires, large arched windows and little ones that looked like Irish clovers. The grounds were surrounded by lush gardens, red and yellow and orange flowers sprouting up in thick patches the entire length of the building. Trees swayed in the late spring breeze, singing to each other with the rustle of their leaves. The two women stood in front of the massive doubled doors painted with the thinnest layer of green paint. It looked like giants might live inside based on the enormity of the passageway.

I followed the two women down a long hallway, the slight heels of their shoes clattering against the polished white floor as we walked. We passed room after room, but the building felt empty, as if it had been made for just the three of us. The younger of the two women continually looked back at me, to make sure I hadn't wandered off. The older one never flinched, staring straight ahead as she walked. Finally, at the end of the hallway, we came to a door, and the older women knocked.

A man wearing an expensive gray suit under a white doctor's coat opened the door. The two women stepped aside as if to present me to their master. The man was tall with dark skin and a thick mustache with gray streaks running through it at the sides. He wore small rounded glasses and held a half-smoked cigarette in his left hand.

"Thank you, ladies," he said, motioning to dismiss them. They turned, neither of them looking at me before they walked back down the hall in the direction that we'd come from and out the doors to the courtyard.

"Lachlan," the man continued. "I'm Dr. Rutherford. Welcome to Inverness District Asylum." He spread his arms as he spoke like the ringmaster at the circus announcing his opening act.

"You're not Scottish," I said, inviting myself into his office, stopping to look at the books and novelties strategically positioned on the bookshelves.

"You are correct," the doctor answered, somewhat put off by my initial assessment of him. "My father was a Scot, but I was raised by my English mother, just outside London."

I didn't really care that he wasn't Scottish, but I knew it would put a sour taste in his mouth, as my arrival at the lunatic asylum had put one in mine.

"Right," he continued. "First things first, let's get you settled and comfortable and acquainted with the grounds and the buildings. After that, we'll meet, just you and I, and make an assessment of what treatments you might benefit from."

I couldn't blame them for sending me away like they did. I knew I must have been crazy to think the things I did. But it was the only memory I had of that night. If it was a coping mechanism or a strict matter of denial, as the doctors in Stornoway had told my parents, then surely, I was where I belonged. It was the only reason I'd not been thrown in jail. Without a confession or a body, I'd heard the officer tell my father when they thought I was sleeping, they could not arrest me despite the mounting physical evidence to the contrary. But it didn't matter anyway, the truth had little to do with what people of Lewis believed.

"Now," Dr. Rutherford started, motioning down another long hallway. We walked, passing more empty rooms until we reach another set of double doors at the end of the hall. Dr. Rutherford knocked, and a woman dressed in nothing but white and a bashful smile let us through.

"We don't typically house people of your young age, so for your wellbeing, we've decided to place you in the women's unit. You'll have your own room and private washroom. I think you'll be quite comfortable there."

The room was bare, except a metal bed frame holding up a thin, sullied mattress, a wardrobe and a small writing desk in the corner. There was a window on the far wall, but its promise to let in fresh air was stifled by the buildup of paint and other material in the cracks around it. The bathroom was a blinding white made only worse by the fluorescent light that popped and hissed before springing to life, humming consistently until I cut it off.

"An attendant will be bringing your things up shortly. In the meantime, get settled, maybe take a rest so you'll be fresh-faced for our first session together. The nurses will be round to check on you and gather you back to my office around four o'clock. Do you have any questions?"

I did, but he didn't know the answers. Only I did, somewhere buried deep inside. He looked at me like he could see what I was thinking, like he was already trying to figure out the answer to the question everyone was asking; why had I killed poor little Arden Scott. When the door shut, the sound echoed through the empty room, and I knew I was alone. When the key turned, locking me inside, the sound echoed through my soul, and it felt empty.

"Lachlan, this only works if you tell the truth," Dr. Rutherford started. "You need to dig deep inside and find the truth that you've buried under this story. That's all it is, a story to help you cope." The doctor was growing frustrated after weeks without any epiphany or crazed confession leading to the whereabouts of a missing boy. He removed his round glasses to rub his eyes in defeat.

"Let's start again. What's the last thing you remember?"

The doctor and I held each other's eyes for a moment. His were hopeful that this would be the day I told him what he wanted to hear. Reluctantly, I closed my eyes, and like every night when I tried to sleep, I found the darkness of that night again. The only light came from the sporadic flashes of lightning breaking through the sky. The world was on its side, and the ground shook when the thunder cracked overhead. The mud against my cheek was cold and tasted rank as it seeped into the corner of my mouth. I couldn't move despite being completely free to do so.

"He's screaming," I whispered, listening to Arden's voice in the distance. "But I can't see him."

I strain to keep my eyes open. I want to vomit and cry and scream and run away all at the same time. I'm on the cusp of unconsciousness, and the world fades in and out with each breath I take. A massive burst of lightning illuminates the sky, and for a moment I can see.

"When the lightning strikes, I can see him," I tell the doctor. "But everything's fuzzy."

"Where is he?" the doctor asked.

I don't want to find him, but I strain to keep my eyes fixated where I know he is. I wait, trying to breathe through the pain. There are three short bursts of light, but it's not enough to see through. The world goes silent and dark, and I know it's coming now. I can hear gurgling in the mud, and I taste rust in the corner of my mouth.

The light flashes across the sky, jumping from cloud to cloud for sustained life, and I can see them. "He's in the water, but ..." I trailed off as I took in the complexity of what my mind was remembering. It still made no sense.

"Tell me what's happening," the doctor urged. "Keep going."

"It's like he's walking on water," I muttered. "They both are."

"Who's with him?"

I swallowed roughly, trying to find the courage to answer him even though I already had a hundred times before. The words always stuck in my throat, burning like fire as I tried to get them out.

"A horse." My voice shook as I spoke. It was as black as the night around them and bucked and kicked violently, screaming like a banshee.

"Look closer Lachlan. It's not a horse. It's something else?"

I watched it replay like a movie on the big screen I'd seen a thousand times. The lightning's flash hung in the sky, and I watched as Arden reached out toward the horse. I wanted to scream out to him, but I was already holding my breath. The beast calmed for a moment, and Arden's hand disappeared into his black flesh. Arden's scream filled the air just before the light left the sky. When it returned a second later, they were gone.

I could hear whimpering and was not surprised to find tears and snot leaking from my face. Having to live through that night once had almost killed me. Had I known I'd be forced to relive it over and over, I may not have tried so hard to survive.

"If what you're saying is true, wouldn't the police have found his body in the loch when they dredged?"

"I don't know, I don't know how it works."

"How what works?" the doctor asked.

I thought back to stories and fables we'd read about as young children. Beautiful women who are really seals, brownies and goblins who inhabit your house and do your chores, the water horse who lives in lochs and rivers and preys on young children. I had never paid them much attention, they weren't real, just tales past down over generations. At some point, the tales had served some type of purpose, heralded some kind of warning; beware of beautiful women, don't depend on anyone to do your work for you and stay clear of murky water if you don't know how to swim. The story never included a description of what happened to the bodies after the water horse pulled it into the water. They'd left that part out.

"You don't believe me," I whispered. "So what difference does it make."

"Lachlan, my job is to help you understand what happened to your friend and help you come to grips with what your role in his disappearance may have been. This story about the water horse is just a coping mechanism, a way of not dealing with the truth. When you're ready, you'll let go of it, and the truth will make itself known. Until then, we will continue with our sessions and talk about what you remember from that night."

I watched out the window as he spoke. The tree branches outside his second-story office window were being tossed around by the heavy wind, shifting bits and pieces of sunlight as they moved. The sun was taunting me with her memory, and she was all I could see when my eyes were open. Arden was all I could see with them closed, lost somewhere in the darkness of that night.

"We'll try again tomorrow." He shuffled me out into the hallway where his next patient was waiting, two male orderlies on either side of her like watchdogs. She was thin and pale skinned. It looked like she'd attempted to cut her hair on her own. It was short and sticking up in places, longer in others. I wondered where she'd managed to get her hands on a pair of scissors.

As we passed in the doorway, she whispered something to me, but her words were indiscernible under the thick glaze of crazy surrounding her. The guard dogs ushered her into Dr. Rutherford's office and closed the door. They remained on either side of the doors with arms clasped tightly around their chests, eyes straight ahead. I'd already forgotten her by the time I reached the library at the end of the hall.

The crazies didn't spend much time reading, so the room was always empty. I was sure some of them were too drugged up to manage reading on the most basic level. Most of the books were incredibly outdated. Their rough and tattered pages were covered with dust that flew into the air each time I removed one from the shelf. I was sitting in a small purple armchair covered in just as much dust flipping through a book on the flora of Scotland when I heard yelling coming from the hallway.

She burst through the library door, swinging it shut immediately after she was through it. I jumped from my chair, and we stared at each other from across the room. She smiled, not surprised in the least to see me.

"Well," she yelled. "Are you going to help me with this or not?"

She jumped over a floral printed loveseat to the left of the door and started pushing it, it's feet scraping the hardwood floor loudly as she tried moving it.

"Come on, I won't rat you out for helping me. I'll tell them I threatened you with a shiv."

She pulled a long metal object from her back pocket and in seconds was inches from my face. Her eyes were crazy, with no real life underneath. I could hear the opening and closing of doors down the hall and orderlies shouting as rooms were being tossed in an attempt to find the woman standing in front of me.

"Are you threatening me?" I asked quietly.

She smiled, replacing the shiv into her back pocket. "No. You'd be dead if I were," she whispered, and I believed her.

"There's something in here I need to find before they find me." She ran back toward the sofa and continued her feeble attempt to move it. The sofa had slid less than an inch when I heard the orderlies open the door a room away.

"It's for you," she said, straight-faced and with honest, if not crazy eyes. "It's what you're looking for. Proof of what dragged your friend down into the deep. Proof that he's out there, stealing bodies and killing babies. She said he's far from home, his island where he walks among the living even though they think he's dead - out of his element so far from the shore and the peaks that face west where he takes them and leaves them, but it's still him, and we'll all pay the price for what he's done."

The sound of the book I had been holding landing on the floor may have been what gave us away. I had the small sofa pushed against the door, my back against it and my feet dug into the wooden floor as best I could by the time the orderlies could have heard it. She was scavenging through a stack of books when they came pounding on the door, throwing their weight, which at least doubled mine, into it, pushing the sofa and me slightly. I repositioned and dug my feet in again, waiting for the second blow.

"Don't come in or I'll kill him. I'll do it," she screamed from across the room, books slipping from their stacks, piling up behind her as she moved erratically around the room.

The orderlies threw their weight against the door again and almost sent me airborne. My toes curled under the balls of my feet as they rolled forward with the force of the sofa pushing against my back. I screamed in pain.

"You're killing him," she yelled, now crouched on the floor looking under the bookcase against the far wall. "Keep screaming," she whispered to me. "They'll stop."

I could hear a scuffle outside the door, muted voices. I could pick out Dr. Rutherford's voice over all of them when he finally caught up to all the excitement. The orderlies stopped pushing against the door, but I remained on the floor with the sofa to my back, unsure if I could even walk with the pain that was radiating through both my feet. The voices were quiet, replaced with the gentle knocking of Dr. Rutherford's hand.

"Moira, it's Dr. Rutherford. Who's in there with you, Moira?"

"What fuckin' difference does it make? We're all people, right? Or is that not how it works in here?" She had her arm up to her elbow shoved underneath the bookcase, her face pressed to the ground looking at me and the door as she yelled back at Dr. Rutherford.

"Moira, whoever it is, let's let them go. They didn't do anything to you. Let them go, and we can go back to my office and talk about what's happened."

The look of excitement flashed across her face as she pulled her arm back from under the bookcase, a small book with a blue cover and gold writing scribbled across the front of it. She flipped through the book and stopped halfway through, paralyzed by whatever it was she'd found.

"Moira, if you don't open this door, you know what's going to happen." Dr. Rutherford paused for a moment, whispering to his staff. "We don't want that, now, do we?" More whispers floated in the air.

"No. We wouldn't want that, Benjamin." His name rolled gently from her tongue as she spoke it, making me wonder if that was the only thing of his that had been on her tongue. She flicked it like a snake with a nervous twitch.

Moira shuffled across the floor, grabbed my hand and pulled me to my feet. I winced in pain as my toes went flat against the floor. I was sure at least some of them were broken if not all of them. I rocked back on my heels to relieve some of the sting, trying to balance with the crazed woman inches from my face.

"I'm going to try and break the window," she explained pointing behind her. "They'll come running in when they hear the noise. Hide behind the sofa until they all come in and then you can sneak out like you were never here."

We were nose to nose. Her lips parted, and she leaned toward me, like she might try to kiss me. I pulled back in a panic, not wanting her chapped and cracked lips against mine. She already had her hands around my waist grabbing at the back of my pants. We moved for a few steps together like we might have been dancing. She pressed herself against me and laughed.

"Calm down, laddie," she whispered. "I wouldn't dare take a boy's innocence. That'd be just plain rude."

The embarrassment that my virginity had been so obvious to a complete stranger crept across my face, followed quickly by confusion. I wanted to believe anything she was willing to tell me, but in the back of my mind, I was forced to remember who and where we were. I didn't know how long she'd been at the asylum, but it was long enough to know Dr. Rutherford's first name; long enough to know how to give the orderlies the slip; long enough to know about secret books hidden under cabinets. I wanted to believe her because for some reason she had believed me.

"How do you know what happened to me?" I whispered.

"We talk," she replied. "We knew who you were before you even got here. And you talk loudly. I could hear everything through Benjamin's office door." Her troubled eyes darted away and then back as she admitted to eavesdropping on my sessions with Dr. Rutherford. Her interest in me and my story explained why she'd been present in the hallway at the end of all my sessions. I even recalled once or twice when she was already at Rutherford's door before I arrived. I thought it had been odd, but then I remembered where I was and dismissed it without another thought.

The thought that my story had stretched as far as Inverness was more cause for concern than Moira's indiscretion. It was bad enough when I felt the whole of Lewis thought I was a murderer or at the very least, crazy, but knowing the story had spread almost clear across the country made it feel like there was no escaping it.

"I don't understand."

"That's what the book is for."

"Moira, step back from the door, we're going to have to break it down if you won't open it willingly." Dr. Rutherford's voice was calm but agitated. We could hear them whispering on the other side of the door making their plans.

She had her hands around the backside of my pants, shoving the small blue book into my waistband before she leapt across the room toward the bank of windows on the back wall. She motioned for me to duck behind the overturned sofa and then picked up a small chair and heaved it into the large window. The glass exploded outward and into the courtyard below. At the same time, the door to the library swung open pushing the sofa out of the way as it did. The open door created a small corner between it and the sofa where I remained crouched, out of site of the orderlies and Dr. Rutherford.

Moira stood next to the broken window, looking lost, as if she didn't remember throwing a chair through it not five seconds prior. The orderlies began looking around the room for the poor patient she'd dragged into her manic outburst and perhaps fearing that I'd be found, she sprang from the floor to the empty window frame balancing her feet on the bits and pieces of broken glass left behind. All the attention of the room was back on her in an instant, and I knew it would be the only opportunity for escape. Pushing the door closed, I crawled between it and the sofa, unseen, and into the hallway. Once outside, I stood and tried to run, but something stopped me. Through the crack in the door, I could see Moira standing in the window, laughing at the orderlies as they crept slowly towards her. I could see the blood beginning to drip down the wall as her feet kissed bits of glass left behind by the missing window.

"You'll pay the price; someone always does." Her words were as calm as the wind had become and then she was gone, disappeared below the window well.

I ran as fast as I could with broken toes until I made it to the stairwell at the end of the hall. There, I bounded down the stairs two at a time. I felt faint and weak. I could taste the bile gathering in my throat, but still, I didn't stop. I knew I had to make it back to my room and hide the book tucked in my waistband before anyone suspected I'd been the one in the library with her. Whatever she knew to be in the book had been worth her life. As I ran down the dark stairwell to my room, it felt like it was worth mine too.

**

I didn't dare take the book out of its hiding place for the first two weeks after Moira jumped from the second story window. I didn't even know what the letters written in gold on the cover spelled. I'd hidden it, first inside my dirty mattress and then when I'd been able to lift a few baggies and some tape from the kitchen, I wrapped it tight and hid it on the underside of the lid to the toilet tank, hoping it would take an act of god for someone to look for it there.

Dr. Rutherford knew that someone had been in the library with Moira before she jumped. I had yelped in pain when the orderly's initial push into the door sent my toes curling underfoot in unnatural ways. I avoided the nurse, not wanting to draw any unwanted attention. Everyone's room was tossed, several times, and while the few things I'd been sent to the asylum with were being scattered around my room, all I could think about was the little blue book wrapped in plastic and hidden in the toilet. It was the only thing that mattered anymore.

I continued my daily sessions with Dr. Rutherford. He glossed over the death of another patient and explained that it was a sad fact of life when living and working in an asylum. They wouldn't be able to help everyone, he'd said with a smile on his face as if to taunt me and my own demons. My story didn't change, not much anyway and he grew tired of hearing me retell it day after day.

Finally, almost a month after Moira's death, I felt it was safe to retrieve the book from its hiding place. I waited until lights out, listening to the key turn a full revolution in the lock on my door and the next several doors down the line. When the halls were quiet, I tiptoed into the bathroom, closing the door behind me. The porcelain of the tank was cool against my pulsing skin and weighed a thousand pounds.

Scottish Fairy and Folk Tales were what the gold lettering on the front of the book read. I read it, three times, to make sure I was reading the fanciful script correctly. It was a children's book. I was sure I'd owned the exact same book or one of a similar title as a child. Every child had. The weeks of torturous nights, knowing that the book was only feet away from me as I feigned sleep to keep it hidden had been for a simple and commonplace children's book. None of it had meant anything. There was no proof of anything other than Moira's utter lunacy. I felt just as crazy for having believed in her.

I flipped through the first few pages of the book and found the table of contents and read the titles of all the tales I'd heard as a child, solidifying the fact that Moira had left me with nothing more than a children's book forgotten under the bookshelf. I let the book slip from my hand and fall between my legs as I sat on the cold tile floor. I looked up at the yellow light over the sink as it blinked every few seconds and knocked my head lightly against the wall in a hollow attempt to rid my mind of the image of Moira's blood dripping from the windowsill even after she had jumped.

I wanted to scream, howl at the moon, let the demons out I was harboring inside to roam wild in the night, but I couldn't. I couldn't even cry. I felt every emotion with an intense awareness but had no energy to do anything about them. I'd suspected that Dr. Rutherford had upped my medication after the incident, as he probably had done for most of the patients. He needed to avoid another incident. A dead lunatic was still a dead lunatic and a smear on his somewhat questionable reputation.

The book slid across the floor when I kicked it accidentally trying to get to my feet. The big toe on my left foot was still tender, but the others had healed on their own. As the book skipped across the tile floor, the pages fluttered in the blinking of the yellow light before coming to a rest next to the tub with three-quarters of the stories face down. The ink pen scribbled across the typeface caught my attention as I knelt to pick it up. The mishmash of print and handwritten words made it hard to read. I held the book in my hand and sat on the edge of the tub. There, plain as day, were Moira's last words; *you'll pay the price,* repeated over and over and over again. They were haunting; I'd heard them before.

I flipped through pages of the repeating words, examining them, waiting for them to turn into something else, something that made sense, something that meant anything. After eleven pages of the same scribbled meaningless words, they stopped. Woven into the simple child's fable of the shape-shifting horse lurking at the water's edge was another story entirely.

They were dates, that much was clear, but only labeled with generalities; late summer or winter, the blood moon. The years were the only thing that felt concrete and flowed in sequential order starting with 1990 and carrying on for the next several years. It looked like how I imagined a diary or journal would be set up. The rest of what followed were strings of random words put together without any apparent value or importance. I read for hours, trying to discern meaning from them, without any apparent success. They'd been worth her life. They had to mean something.

Late summer, 1990. Schools in, a brunette now, smaller than the rest with no fight left in her, kids have sucked her dry, peat fields near the inn between while it's tender sleeps, sweat stained-skin and hurried feet. LEWSHAW.

Winer, 1992. Snow blankets and stranded keeps, whiskey to warm when skin is weak. Animals and beasts, the friend's she keeps where Holms and Dores to meet - belly as barren as winter keeps, glens and streams, frozen sleeps. HIGHINS.

The blood moon, 1993. Evening's meet and great with beaches bathed in summer heat with views across the deep of big and little islands peeks – bloodied – blonde and bold, tries to cut and run, beach baby while mother sleeps. LEWKNEE

Fall, 1994. It sees at night things they will always wish to forget. Flashes in the night, spotlights for life. Open windows make for quick escapes. LEWNESS.

Chapter Five

The house was silent, except for the hiss of the kettle from the kitchen. Lachlan looked at the mantle above the fireplace, at the layer of dust that had accumulated over years of emptiness. There were no pictures of any of them set upon it. He tried to remember if there had ever been any pictures placed there, but he couldn't see them in his memory. The sounds from the kitchen fell silent, and Lachlan turned to see his father standing at the window, just like when he was a child. The only thing missing was the rouse of the newspaper under his eyes and his mother's nagging tone somewhere behind them.

They were strangers. They stood awkwardly in the space between the kitchen and the sitting room sipping warm tea with milk, unsure of what to say to one another. Lachlan looked at the old man his father had become. What was left of his hair was white. His face was wrinkled and chapped by the wind, caused by too much time spent on the water. While he'd never really known his father when he was young, what he did know was that he was a tough man, a man's man, in every respect except when it came to his mother. In the shadow of his mother, he became tiny and meek, taking her constant ridicule without ever sending it back. It angered Lachlan to watch his father bend and fold with only an angered look from her. His father was powerless against her, and Lachlan hated her for it.

"So," his father finally mumbled, half into his cup of hot tea. "Good seas on the way over?"

Fishing had been one of the leading industries on the island. Lachlan remembered the blue jumpsuit that stunk to high heaven every evening when he came home. He could hear his mother's voice, yelling at him to strip outside in the dead of winter before he was allowed to come inside.

"Yeah." Then there was silence again as both men looked for the right words, unsure if they existed. Neither of the men was sure how a relationship was supposed to recover after almost two decades apart and barely a handful of words passing between them in just as much time.

"The house looks, about the same." Just older, he'd left out. It was run down and had not been kept up well. Lachlan assumed that it had fallen into disrepair over the last several years when his mother had first fallen ill and taken all of his father's attention. He would have been hard-pressed to find a spec of dirt on the floors or one item out of place when he was a child. Now, a thin layer of dust and grime sat on top of the furniture except for the small rust colored armchair that Lachlan remembered reading in as a child. It must have been the only piece of furniture his father ever sat in.

"Yeah, it's a good house." He father's gaze skipped around the room, no doubt, noticing the lack of cleanliness that had befallen it. Lachlan wondered how his mother had held on for two years with her house in such a state. That alone, he thought, should have killed her.

"How's work?" Lachlan asked, grasping at straws for conversation starters.

"Ach, it is what it is. Slow these days. Some of us have hooked up with a cruising company and charter trips to St. Kila. Sometimes we do some fishing along the way."

Lachlan had forgotten that St. Kilda even existed. The mention of it flooded his mind with faded memories. He had forgotten how, as kids, they had fantasized over their class trip to the island. Only the upper-level students were allowed to take the journey and only those with good marks. They spent the night on the rock in little huts and learned about the settlements of people that had inhabited the island until their final evacuation brought on by illness and starvation. As a child, he hadn't realized the irony in the freedom the island represented to them then when it had been a death sentence to so many before them.

It was a rite of passage, to be allowed the experience of a night away from home on an abandoned island with your classmates. They'd all heard the stories from the older generations; sweet smuggled whiskey, cigarettes and wild behavior. The girls always seemed to be set free of the good-girl shackles that held them while on Lewis, letting them become carefree overnight before returning home to their standard prudish ways. But all boys that age needed was one night anyway, and the trip to Kilda was the way to get it.

A few months after the trip they were all to be heading to the Nicholson Institute, and every boy knew no girl wanted to find themselves at the Institute without having had their first kiss, or sometimes more, to prepare them for the world of older boys. They were using them, and the boys knew it but didn't care. Lachlan had had no strategy, other than to keep the secret he'd been hiding from everyone. He closed his eyes and listened for her voice, the prick and tickle of a thistle against his heart. He was supposed to have found her first, or she'd be forced to make nice with other boys. When he wasn't there to find her, he wondered who she made nice with.

"I've still never been," Lachlan said. "Maybe I could go out with you while I'm here."

Lachlan's father stopped mid-drink with his teacup stuck to his bottom lip. Shock at his son's interest in sailing with him was racing in his eyes. He fumbled to find words in his astonishment.

"Does that mean you're staying then?" he asked.

Lachlan hadn't thought about the implication his suggestion would bring. He had to stay at least through the funeral on Sunday, and it was only Tuesday. They should have time to sail to St. Kilda and back while making up for nineteen years of estrangement along the way. He wasn't quite sure how else he had planned to spend his time on Lewis, but it already felt like he'd been home for weeks in a matter of minutes.

"Until she's in the ground, I suppose. That's why I'm here, isnae it?"

Their eyes finally met and the sadness that Lachlan always saw in his father was transformed into fury in an instant. It was the most expressive he'd ever seen the man.

"That's no way to talk about your mother."

"She was no mother to me," Lachlan responded before thinking about the words coming out of his mouth. They just fell out, and then they were out, and there was no putting them back in. He felt a crack in the dam of his emotions begin to spread and the wall holding back the flood waters began to waver. His mother had been dead to him for twenty years. He had buried his emotions for her, good or bad, in that time. Now that she was dead, he could feel them trying to creep out.

"She did the best she could," his father whispered, his fury reverting to the same sad and dejected demeanor that had always marked him. He walked into the kitchen, setting his teacup in the bottom of the sink and posted up at the window, becoming the statue Lachlan remembered him being throughout his childhood.

"Are you kidding me?" Lachlan laughed, unbelieving that he was hearing his father defend her. He did not turn from his stance at the sink. "How can you defend her? She was awful, to both of us. She's gone now, you don't have to pretend that you love her anymore."

His father bowed his head, rubbing his hands across his face. "Is that what you think; that I was pretending to love her?"

"Are you going to tell me that you actually did?" His stomach churned at the thought. "Nothing I saw in the thirteen years I lived in this house says that you did or that she did. I can't even remember seeing the two of you kiss or give each other a bloody hug. She was the most unloving person, to you and to me. What was there to love?"

"Son," his father whispered. "We did the best we could. It wasn't perfect, but I loved your mother, very much."

"How can you say that? You're just repenting now, so she doesn't come back to haunt you. She's dead, and you're still scared of her, just like you were when I was a kid. You never stood up to her, for yourself or for me. Not fucking once! Especially when I needed you the most, you just let me go, and that was it. I remember her face that day, as the car pulled away. She was happy to see me go. Like she couldnae wait for an excuse to get rid of me. And then it was there, and she fucking jumped at the opportunity."

The quiet tick of the wall clock's hands filled the room. Lachlan stared at his father's back. He began to laugh at the realization that the exchange represented the most fluid conversation they may have ever had. His father turned, desperation in his eyes and his mouth tongue tied with half-truths.

"You may have loved her," Lachlan said, his voice on the verge of cracking in half. "I don't know how on earth it's possible, but I never saw that she loved you back. I never saw that she loved me. Every time she looked at me, all I saw was hatred. I'll not saint her now, just because she's dead."

"She didnae hate you, she just didn't know how to love you."

"You didnae know how to love me! What kind of mindless bullshit is that to tell your kid?" Lachlan was red in the face, his teacup shaking in his unsteady hand. "You probably shouldnae have had me then. What did you think having a kid was?"

The tears in his dad's eyes escaped and trickled down his weather-beaten skin until they reached the cornered of his furrowed lips that quaked with truths unsaid. Lachlan watched as his father tried to find the words, his lips parting and closing with multiple false starts.

"Is this the part of my life where you tell me you didnae want me? That I was an accident? That you would have been better off? It's a little late for the news flash da, that was always very apparent. Do you have any idea how many times I wished ..." Lachlan didn't finish the sentence, not because he didn't want to hurt his father, but because he'd wished for so many things so many different times, his brain was flooded with too many options to pick just one. There were a million times he'd wished for his mother's love, but that was one wish that would never come true.

"No, son." His voice was hoarse, his words struggling to get past the lump stuck in his throat. "We just ..." The words stopped, but the tears kept coming. Lachlan stared at his father weeping. He'd barely seen his father crack a smile before, much less cry. It was almost too much to watch.

"This was a mistake. I don't even know why I came back," Lachlan said, knowing it was a lie. He turned for the front door and was over the threshold and in the front yard without a word from his father, just like the last time. He thought he should turn and see if his father was standing on the front porch, ready to wave goodbye again, but Lachlan didn't think he could bear it twice.

There were footprints in the mud beside the road. Lachlan followed them thinking about how many times he'd done the same as a kid, daydreaming that they would lead him somewhere other than Lewis. He'd escaped the fate the island held for most, but somehow, the footprints had led him right back to the beginning.

Grey clouds danced in the distance as he walked down the one-track road toward the only evidence of civilization in Bernera. The community café, in all its glory, was the mecca of Bernera. A little further down the street would be the school he'd attended. There had been a filling station as well, but it looked like it had fallen from use several years ago. The café was the only shop serving any type of readymade food, and he'd be lucky if it was open at almost eleven in the morning.

The wind died the further Lachlan walked from the water's edge where his father's house sat, and he could feel the warmth of the sun against his face as it periodically broke free of the clouds. He thought of the hundreds if not thousands of time's he made the same walk as a child, to and from school, to and from Arden's house. Everything looked the same, and for a moment Lachlan half expected Arden to traipse around the crook in the road that led to his house like he had done nearly every morning of their childhood.

Lachlan stopped and stared down the road, waiting for someone he knew was never coming. Guilt welled up in his throat as the memory formed. The tang of blood and mud welled in his mouth again, and he could feel the sting in the dent above his eye. He remembered how heavy and warm the rain had felt against his skin as he lay almost face down in the shallow water, struggling to stay conscious as Arden stumbled away from him. Lachlan winced as he remembered the flash of lightning spraying across the sky. With the darkness painted white for a moment, Lachlan had seen Arden walking on water and then he was gone.

The café was opening as Lachlan walked up the gravel drive to the front porch. All he really wanted was a coffee but walked out of the shop to the porch with a bowl of porridge and a handful of sweet pastries. He watched as several other patrons came and went, grabbing coffees or teas before heading on their way, none of them offering so much as a friendly nod. He had been hopeful that twenty years away would have done something to soften people's opinion of him, but their heartless glares said otherwise.

A few other patrons had gathered on the porch to enjoy coffees and cigarettes as Lachlan finished, trying to enjoy the little bit of sun that was left as the clouds began to roll in. A group of three men younger than Lachlan, but still, men, gathered at a nearby table. They all wore identical shirts boosting the local distillery's name and crest. They didn't yet smell like the whiskey or gin that they cooked but come that evening a person could get drunk off their stench. They looked too young to know who Lachlan was, but they knew he was a stranger and that alone had piqued their interest.

Lachlan stood to leave and almost collided with an older man coming up the stairs to the café. They stared at each other for a moment, recognition ringing loud and clear in the older man's eyes.

"Be gaen wi' ye," the man whispered as he pushed past Lachlan, nodding at the three men sitting on the deck before disappearing into the café. Lachlan was at the bottom of the stairs when he heard one of the men call his name from the deck.

"You're McGinley's kid then," he yelled. "The one who murdered the Scott boy?"

The man's words stopped Lachlan in his tracks. He thought he'd come to terms with his involvement is Arden's death, but the return to Lewis was ripping old wounds wide open, leaving them to fester all over again. It was the first time anyone had outright called him a murderer. It had been whispered behind hands and alive in people's eyes, but never so loudly called out on someone's tongue. Lachlan would never accept that he'd outright killed his friend. It just wasn't possible.

The three men were standing at the top of the stairs, looking down at Lachlan when he turned to face them. He didn't recognize any of them, even as younger siblings of kids his own age. They couldn't have been out of diapers when it happened.

"You shouldn't poke your nose in things you don't understand," Lachlan spat before turning and walking into the gravel parking lot. He could hear the men thumping down the wooden stairs and then as their feet crunched in the pavement behind him. His fists balled instinctively, and his pace slowed, letting the instigators catch up to him.

"The way I see it, there's not much to understand about cold-blooded murder."

"I did not murder Arden Scott," Lachlan yelled, trying to convince himself as much as them.

"Oh no? Oh, that's right. It was the water horse that got him, right? Come up from the deep, was it?" All three men laughed, slapping hands with each other as they did.

Lachlan stood motionless, thinking of the boy who'd made up lies about a demon in the depths. His stare shifting from one man to the next trying to decide which one he wanted to strike first. They all deserved what was coming, but the man in the middle deserved the first, most potent strike Lachlan would be able to deliver.

"That's right," the man continued. "We all know who ya' are. You're a legend 'round here. The island lunatic." Their laughs were thick, piercing.

Lachlan's fist connected with the man's face, sending him stumbling backward. Lachlan shook the pain out of his hand and stood ready for the return fire, which came within seconds. The taste of copper filling his mouth as he stumbled in the uneven gravel and into the hands of someone standing behind him.

"That's quite enough for today, boys." The voice was powerful and commanding, breaking up the skirmish instantly. Lachlan spun around and was surprised to see a man shorter than himself, even if his uniform made him seem more substantial than he was.

"I'm on my way to Stornoway already, I have room for four." The constable looked at Lachlan and the three other men, sizing them up, waiting for a response to his rhetorical question.

"Alright then," he started again. "Off to the distillery with you then. And you sir," he said looking Lachlan up and down trying to determine why he didn't know him when it was his job to know everyone in his ward.

Lachlan wiped the blood from his face and spat out that which had pooled in his mouth. He shook his head, trying to dispatch the double vision in his eyes while the constable watched. The temporary blindness made it impossible for Lachlan to see the dumbfounded look on the constable's face as he gawked at him.

"Lachlan?" he asked. "Lachlan McGinley?"

Lachlan turned and walked toward the road without responding to the constable. He'd had enough of what recognition had brought him in the mere hours since returning to Lewis.

"It's Euan," the man called after him.

Lachlan stopped in his tracks. He searched his mind for memories of his boyhood friend, trying to find the resemblance in the man in the uniform. Lachlan turned, unbelieving that his chubby, insecure childhood friend and the constable in front of him were one in the same.

"Euan?" Lachlan asked.

"Causing trouble already, I see," Euan smirked, puffing out his chest and making a show of his uniform.

Lachlan laughed and hung his head, diverting his eyes from the judgmental glare of his old friend. Out of all the kids Lachlan had grown up with, Euan McKenzie would have been his last vote for any type of authoritative position. He had been the smallest and the weakest out of all of them, barely able to speak up loud enough for his friends to take him seriously, much less anyone else he might try and assert himself over. He should have been cutting peat or working a loom like a woman. Anything other than Constable McKenzie would have been believable.

"Did you forget how to count then?" Euan asked.

"Sorry?"

"Did you forget how to count? Three against one doesn't seem like a smart decision."

"Ach, I could have taken them if you hadn't interrupted."

"Right," Euan laughed. "You've obviously not changed a bit."

They both laughed, thinking about all the fights and skirmishes that Lachlan had been involved in and the sidelines Euan had watched from, trying to use his words instead of his fists. Euan had never been in a fight in all the years that Lachlan knew him. He was always the rational one, using reason to talk his way out of some of the worst fights Lachlan and Arden had gotten the lot of them into. Lachlan realized that maybe Euan had been the copper their whole lives. Only now, he'd traded his tattered hand-me-downs for a fitted, dark blue uniform.

"I was sorry to hear about your ma," Euan finally offered.

Lachlan wasn't sure how to respond. He wasn't sorry to have heard of her death. He was surprised to learn that anyone was.

"Yeah, well …" was all Lachlan could muster. Euan would know how he'd felt about her death. It wasn't something that needed explaining. Euan had seen the lack of love when they'd all ended up at Lachlan's house on a rare occasion. He no doubt went home and hugged his own mother extra hard after seeing what the alternative could be.

"So, you're back then, I guess."

"For a bit, anyway."

"Staying with your dad?"

Lachlan's face soured as he thought about having to return home and face his father again.

"How's the old house?"

Lachlan scoffed. "It's exactly the same as I remember it."

The two stood in the parking lot, shuffling rocks around with their feet like they had done as kids. A million memories flowed between them, but they couldn't find the words to reconnect. The awkwardness reached its height before a strong wind blew through and whisked it away like it had never been there.

"So, how about you lay off the fists while you're back? Two fights within a day of being back on the island has to be some kind of record. I'd hate to have to put some hurt on you."

Lachlan started laughing, throwing his head back and wrapping his hands around his mouth before he could look Euan in the eye.

"Put the hurt on me? You forget I knew you as a scrawny kid with glasses."

"I'm a well-trained killing machine now," Euan said, puffing his chest out again, holding his breath while forcing a ridiculously serious smile.

As Euan let out his breath, both men burst into laughter. Euan was no more a well-trained killing machine than Lachlan was a philanthropist or activist or any kind of "–ist", and both men knew it.

"A fucking copper? Really?" Lachlan's sides were hurting from the hilarity of the situation. "How on earth did you land on constable?"

"Ach, it's just a job. And I didn't want to shovel shit all day on someone else's farm, and I can't ride the boats without turnin' green and losing my stomach all over the place."

"God damn man, a fuckin' constable."

"Well, what about you? What grand person did you turn into while the rest of us rotted out here in the middle of nowhere?"

Lachlan laughed, but both men felt the weight of his words. He'd not turned into any grand thing, but the fact that he'd turned into anything despite the odds against him was a great feat.

"Teacher."

Lachlan could see the confusion spinning in his friend's eyes. The cop in him took over, and Lachlan could see the wheels begin to turn; had he lied about his identity to get the job? Did they know who he really was? Who had missed the massive hole of missing time in his record? He knew crazy people accused of possible murder weren't allowed to teach children; could they?

"Teacher, eh," was all that came out.

"Yeah, I saw an advertisement in the paper one day talking about *be the person you needed as a child*. It just kind of clicked, you know."

Lachlan thought about his students. He wondered if he was making a difference in any of their lives like he set out to do. Showing up to work hung over several days of the week, undoubtedly, was hindering that goal.

"I corresponded to finish secondary. The hospital set it up. And since I was a minor when I ..." Lachlan's words trailed into a no man lands of uncertainty. He was thankful for the acknowledging nod from his friend indicating that further explanation was not necessary.

"And so I applied to University and got in, and here I am."

"Ah, you and Sarah should have a lot to talk about then."

"Sarah?"

"Sarah Campbell," Euan said, nodding with accomplishment. "Although most people know her as Sarah McKenzie now."

"Front row, always had the answer, we use to throw paper airplanes at, Sarah Campbell?"

"Yes, sir. She's the head teacher now and my wife."

Lachlan smiled and remember how much the four of them had tormented poor Sarah Campbell as kids. He couldn't fathom what had changed so much that she'd agreed to marry any one of them after that.

"What about you?" Euan asked.

Countless faces of women with no names passed through Lachlan's mind, none of them meaning more than a night or so of carnal entertainment. The only one whose body he'd never known was the one that had meant everything to him.

"Nah," was all Lachlan could reply.

"Ah, well, you'll find someone," Euan responded, even though they both knew he already had. "I'm off to Stornoway to head into the station. I could use some company on the drive."

Lachlan looked around, unsure of what else he would do if he didn't join Euan. He had little appetite to return home and face his father. A dark sheet of rain was already draining into the sea. Stornoway sounded like a good option; the only option.

"Unless your schedule is full up with more fights to pick."

"I didn't pick that fight," Lachlan said, as they walked toward Euan's car.

"I know, I know," Euan answered. "You never picked them."

Both men hung their heads, thinking about who had picked most, if not all of their childhood battles.

"Just had a knack for finding them," Euan whispered into the wind, the secret keeper of boyhood truths.

The barren landscape that blanketed the middle of Lewis trailed out before them as they drove. Outcroppings of gray stone poked through the hillsides. Patches of dead heather dominated the land as far as Lachlan could see. Soon they would bloom, and the hills would be painted purple. Until then, everything remained the color of winter.

The trip was quiet and relaxing, save a few small bouts of shared memories recalled between them. Lachlan explained that he'd made the same drive just hours ago with Calum after arriving in Stornoway, drunk. He recounted his encounter with Ross Scott, which Euan already knew about. He'd wanted to ask about Isla but was fearful of the answers he'd find. He left his feelings for her spinning inside him; twenty years of love and lust bubbling in his blood, tainted with the image of Ross Scott's pock-marked skin. He thought perhaps it would be best if he never saw her again and let the memory of her live on rather than learning the truth of what she'd become. The burning color of her hair and his love of her had guided Lachlan through the darkest time in his life. Perhaps it was the memory of her he needed to hang on to while letting the real thing go.

"I'll drop you here," Euan said, as he turned down Church Street. "I've got to run into the station and take care of some paperwork. I'd bring you in with me and show you around, but I've got to tell everyone's what's what. You know, serious cop stuff."

Lachlan rolled his eyes at his friend and stepped out of his car. He looked around at a Stornoway he didn't remember. The streets were crowded with cars. People lined the sidewalks, traveling to and from the pubs and shops. The city had come alive while Lachlan had been away.

"Walk down Kenneth," Euan said, pointing in the opposite direction that they had come. "Around the corner, to the left, there's a pub, the Twisted Thistle. I'll meet you there in about an hour. We can grab some food and then we'll head back."

Lachlan saluted his friend, the great and mighty constable McKenzie, and turned to head down Kenneth Street like he'd been instructed. He came around the corner at Francis Street and could see the port where the ferry docked. The car park was loaded with vehicles ready to make their way back to the mainland. Lachlan wondered if he should be among them. He walked for a few more minutes down Francis and found the Twisted Thistle and slipped inside as the ferry blared its horn behind him.

The pub was quiet. Lachlan found a small table in the back where the light and airiness from the open windows of the pub didn't stretch and took a seat, with his back to the world. He waited, quietly, for the barkeep to notice him. He knew he should wait for Euan or at least not drink too much in the meantime without him. But the smell of whiskey and regret lingered in the air around him and he craved a drink and the oblivion it promised.

"You brought the summer with you."

Her breath warm on his neck like the summer sun. Lachlan spun in his seat and then froze. Her voice wasn't so little anymore, but rather, strong and powerful. Prevailing. Womanly. She wasn't just a memory he could keep locked away, indulging in the sweet innocence of the girl he remembered her to be. She was a woman, scarred and stained, but the years had not been unkind to her. Lachlan almost found it more alluring to know that she had experienced the world like he had. He looked into her eyes and knew he had been a fool to think he could tuck her away when all he wanted to do was find her again.

Chapter Six

It had been a month. The seasons had turned, and the warmer air of spring flooded the island. The grass turned back to green and gorse began growing in patches, giving the air a sweet smell. The rain wasn't as cold, and the wind died moderately, making our walks home from school somewhat enjoyable. We had just over a month left before we were freed for the summer and none of us were any closer to making an impression with Isla Gilcrest than we were to knowing how to fly to the moon. Every boy in school, even the older boys who didn't go to our school but had heard of her from us, were in love with her, including me.

I listened to the sweetness of her voice drip from her lips while I watched her from two seats back every day in school. The days flew by now; hours ticking away like minutes, squandering the time any of us had to make our move, whatever those might be. Even Arden had been unsuccessful in his pursuit of her, which had consisted of making sure he stood next to her in the lunch line or at the water fountain when we were granted time to be outside in the garden for fresh air and sun. If anyone stood a chance of cracking her rough exterior, it would be Arden. He was the most charismatic out of all of us. When nothing materialized from what he had assured us was a foolproof method of getting her attention, he labeled her a tease and a prude and only loved her in secret.

At the end of the month, I was still the only one that had had an actual conversation with her, even if only she and I knew about it. I liked having a secret with her. It was probably just my overactive adolescent imagination, but I felt like she liked it too. Sometimes, when she'd catch me looking at her, and I could not avert my eyes in time, her lips would turn upright into the slightest of smiles. She would stare back with piercing sea-colored eyes, and it felt like we were in the hallway of the community center café again, the smell of summer and secrets hanging in the air between us.

Fridays were now our most hated day of the week, and Monday's the most coveted; that's how upside down she had turned our world. Fridays guaranteed we would not see her for two days. If we were lucky one of us might run into her at the café or see her as our parent's cars sped past one another on the road. But most weekends, she was missed, profoundly and by all. We waited like rabid dogs for Monday morning to come and raced to school on our bikes. We posted up on the school's front stairs waiting for her to materialize around the bend even though we only ever ignored her when she walked by. We made bets on who would talk to her each morning. Arden was always the favored. His cockiness got the better of him every time by stealing his tongue and only allowing him to talk to her when his back was turned.

We waited for Arden at the crux of the road that led to his house, but he never showed. If we waited any longer, we'd be made to sit in detention after school, even though we knew that Ms. McNich didn't want to be there any later on a Friday afternoon than she had to be. Unfortunately for Ms. McNich, the threat of detention was less a deterrent then was the missed opportunity to see Isla before the school bell rang.

"Maybe he's sick," Euan said eventually. We were already straddling our bikes, waiting for the final call to be made.

"He was complaining that his throat hurt yesterday," Calum added, one foot on his pedal. "And the day before, he didn't look like himself."

"Let's go," I called, already pumping the pedals on my bike. In Arden's absence, I was the leader of our group of four, then Calum and Euan were always last. It wasn't anything we'd discussed openly with each other. There was no meeting held to make these determinations. It was just something natural that happened when we'd all aged enough to make our own decisions about the world. Arden was the most confident and the loudest which put him in the front. I was the brains and remained reserved. Calum was the muscle and Euan was the reason. We rounded out each other nicely. When one was missing, it threw everything off balance, and we were scattered. Nothing good ever came from one of us missing from the group.

We flew down the road, pedaling as fast as our legs could muscle. I broke a sweat for the first time since the summer before, and the perspiration felt cool against my skin as the air raced past me. When we came around the corner of Breaclete to the gravel road leading to the school, the glow of fire caught my eye, distracting me from the care that needed to be taken in the loose rocks under my tires.

The tires bit at the gravel as I skidded across the tops of them. When a rock large enough finally caught the rubber, I was on the ground, my bike tumbling away from me before I knew what had happened. Calum and Euan had been far enough behind me and managed to stop in time before their front tires collided with me as I lay in the road, bloodied and disoriented.

I rolled to my back and was immediately blinded by the glow of sunlight from overhead. I could feel the warmth of blood rushing down my elbow and forearm. My head was spinning, and I still felt like I was tumbling. I thought I might heave but held it down when I heard a voice that most certainly did not belong to either of my friends, both of whom had yet to dismount from their bikes to make sure I was still alive.

"Are you alright?" she asked. I could feel her warmth as she crouched next to me. My eyes were sun-stained, and white spots fluttered in front of my vision only allowing me to see a mess of red hair that sprang out in every direction. The fire that had distracted me had been Isla ahead of us walking toward the school. I'd never been so glad to have been bloodied in all my life.

When the flurries in front of my eyes disappeared, and my head stopped spinning, I tried to sit up and brush the fall off like it was no big deal, despite the tremendous amount of pain I felt. My right elbow pushed against the gravel as I attempted to prop myself up and only then did I realize how hard I had landed on it. I was sure the bone might be popping through the skin, but I tried desperately to not let my face show the fear of it.

"Go get Ms. McNich or Mr. MacLean," she yelled at Calum and Euan. I looked over to my friends and saw the astonishment on their faces. Their surprise had little to do with the nasty fall I'd taken and everything to do with the fact that Isla Gilcrest was talking to them. They sped off on their bikes toward the school, both of them looking over their shoulder at Isla and I until they disappeared into the parking lot at the top of the small hill. Then, it was just the two of us.

Her touch was gentle. The skin on her hand was soft and delicate against mine as she took my arm in her hands, trying to get a better look at the damage to my elbow. The movement alone was enough to make me want to vomit, but self-preservation kept the bile back.

"Your elbow's bleeding pretty bad," she said, looking back in the direction of the school to see if help was coming. I looked with her, pleading that the road would remain empty for just a little longer.

She stood up, throwing her bag to the ground next to us, followed by her burgundy waterproof. The sun danced behind her movements and came through her hair in bits and pieces. When she lifted her arms to remove the long sleeved over shirt she was wearing, the one underneath it lifted enough that I could see the pale skin of her midsection. She was dotted with the same orange freckles that speckled her face.

"Did you want to take a picture?" she asked sternly when she caught me staring at her. Any other day, I would have looked away ashamed that I'd been so careless for my eyes. But laying on the ground underneath her, somewhat helpless, had done wonders for the sureness I had in my actions.

"I'd take a picture of you," I answered. The perturbed look on her face melted away and was replaced with the sly smile she'd given me outside the café bathroom a month ago. Until that moment, I'd been just one of the meek and cowardice faces in the sea of boys helplessly chasing after her. Confidence had to be met with confidence, which was where all other boys had failed her, except for Arden. Perhaps she could sense his show of assurance was just that, only a show to mask the inherent insecurities that laid underneath. How she hadn't seen right through my disguise, I would never understand. Maybe it was pity.

As she stooped down next to me, she wrapped her shirt around my elbow to try and stop the bleeding. She pressed firmly against my arm, and I flinched impulsively at the pain. My body shot up from the ground, and when I opened my eyes, we were face to face and a breath apart. Her eyes were deep pools the color of the shallows at Bosta Beach in summer. I got lost in them and didn't immediately hear the footsteps crunching loudly at the top of the hill.

"Sorry," she whispered, looking down at my arm.

Her breath was warm against my face. Her perfectly pink lips rested just barely parted, and I wanted nothing more than to touch them with my own.

"For what?" I whispered. There was nothing for her to be sorry about, then or ever.

I couldn't breathe. I couldn't move. I felt hot and cold at the same time, like I had a crazy fever. The pain in my arm disappeared, and it felt like I could cartwheel the rest of the way uphill to school if I wanted to. I sat as still as possible, questioning how the universe had put me in that exact location at that exact moment with Isla Gilcrest. My overanalytical brain questioned if it had been Euan or Calum or even Arden that had slipped on the rocks, would she be kissing them instead of me or was it really me she wanted to be kissing.

"For not doing that sooner," she answered, pulling away just as Mr. MacLean came upon us. Her crouched position next to me had blocked his view of us, so he'd not seen our kiss. There had been no witness, and I knew no one would believe me if I told them. But I wasn't going to tell anyone. She'd given me another secret, and I intended to keep it hidden.

**

I spent the morning at the nurse's station while Mr. MacLean picked tiny pieces of gravel out of my elbow with an old set of tweezers. I hardly felt any of it. The only thing I could feel was my lips. I didn't want to move them or talk or breathe, thinking any of the above would wash away the feeling of Isla pressed against them. He could have taken my arm clean off with a buzz saw, and I wouldn't have cared as long as the feeling of her against me remained.

"I think we should call your mother," Mr. Maclean finally said, seeing the dazed look on my face, wondering if I'd suffered a concussion.

"No!" I yelled. I had to go to class. If I didn't, I wouldn't see her again until Monday morning, and I might die between now and then. I had to see her again before she disappeared for the weekend. "I'm fine. Please don't call my mother," I assured him.

"It's a nasty gash, but I don't think it'll need stitching." He stared at me as he spoke, trying to reason away letting me return to class when he knew a parent should most likely be called.

"Can I go to class? I'm sure I'm missing a test or something this morning." I jumped up from the chair and gathered my bag from the floor, trying to not let the pain throbbing in my arm show in my expression.

He gave me a sour look, before folding his arms in a huff. "If you start to feel lightheaded, you need to come right back."

I was already galloping down the hall when Mr. MacLean yelled after me. I laughed at his insistence in returning if I felt lightheaded. I'd been dizzy since he'd scooped me up and helped me into the closet that passed as the nursing station, but it didn't have anything to do with the fall.

I received a standing ovation upon my arrival to Ms. McNish's classroom. Euan and Calum had taken it upon themselves to regale everyone with the details of the incident, skipping over the part where I almost lost my arm and jumped right to the part where Isla Gilcrest had come to my rescue. The other boys hardly believed them when they said that she'd talked to me. I could see her blush from across the room when I looked at her, our secret drifting between us.

The school day lingered in a torturous manner, putting me within arm's reach of her all day but never presenting the opportunity to talk to her. My arm throbbed and just before lunch I thought I might have to excuse myself to the bathroom and heave up my breakfast. Ms. McNish took pity on me and didn't call on me for any answers or to read any passages. I sat in the back of the classroom, with Isla two seats in front of me, daydreaming about kissing her again.

When the dismissal bell finally rang, the classroom was a flurry of movement. I didn't think I'd survive the weekend if I weren't able to at least thank her for her efforts. I frantically gathered my bag while trying to keep an eye on her at the same time. The boys in the class all circled around me in the back of the room begging me to remove the bandage on my arm to see how gruesome a cut I'd received. In the midst of the chaos, I managed to smash my elbow against a chair and fell to the floor in agony. From the floor, I could see the group of girls gathered in the front of the room, but in my discomfort, I could not focus long enough to pick her out from the crowd.

For once, I was happy to see Ms. McNich when she came to my aide and shewed the group of boys from around me. I could feel warmth under the bandage and knew that it had started to bleed again. I wondered how long it would take to come through the gauze and onto my shirt and how angry my mother would be when she saw that it would most likely be ruined.

I hurried out of the room when I realized that Ms. McNich and I were alone. I could already feel the torment of the long weekend stretching out in front of me. Desperation clung to me like stink on shit as I scurried down the empty hallway. It felt like if I didn't see her one last time, that she would instantly forget me, our moment, our kiss. I was frantic to stay in the forefront of her mind. It felt like if I slipped from her memory, I'd be lost to her again and be just another face in the crowd of the frenzied boys that filled her life.

I burst through the doors leading to the parking lot, and the negligible amount of hope I'd had of catching her was gone when I saw the lot was empty. Rain was drizzling and had sent everyone off in a hurry when usually they would have gathered to commiserate in the lot before breaking off into smaller groups of those who walked home in the same direction. I wanted to lay down on the cement stairs in the rain and let the wave of dejection I felt waft over me. I had lost her when I'd only just gotten her. Surely, over the weekend, she would forget about me and come Monday morning she wouldn't even remember my name if she'd ever known it to begin with.

"It's pretty wet out there. Where's your waterproof?" The voice came from behind, startling me into spinning around so fast that I almost lost my balance and tumbled down the stairs. When I saw that it was Isla tucked in the corner of the building, I almost wished that I had, perhaps warranting another kiss from her to reduce the pain of another injury. I must have practically squished her with the door when I'd exploded through them, anxiously trying to catch up to her. And now that I'd caught her, I couldn't find the words I'd been dreaming of saying to her all day.

"Walk me home," she said.

It wasn't a question or a request, it was an order. I had no idea where she lived in comparison to my own house. She could have lived in Ness, and I'd have walked her home a thousand times. My mother would already be furious with me about my ruined shirt, so adding to her anger by being home late was a luxury I could afford.

Isla was down the stairs and her feet crunching in the gravel before I could pull my coat from my bag. I fumbled putting it on over my elbow which was bent at a forty-five-degree angle while I chased after her, not daring to ask her to wait for me. She wasn't the kind of girl that waited for anyone.

When I finally caught up with her, we walked to the end of the road in a silence so loud, I could hear the sound of raindrops trickling on the rocks below our feet. She looked straight ahead as she walked. The hood of her coat could not contain her thick red hair, which looked like a lion's mane encircling her pale face. I could see droplets starting to form on the exposed tendrils before they sprang free with the bounce her steps produced.

When we reached the end of the no-name road that led to the school, she turned right onto Breaclete where I would have turned left to head home. At the end of Breaclete, she turned right again onto the main road heading toward Bosta. In the summer, Arden and I had made the trek to Bosta Beach on our bikes and regretted it later when we had barely enough vigor after a day of swimming to make the pedal home. I still had no idea where we were headed, but I knew enough to know it wasn't anywhere near my house.

"How's your arm?" she finally asked, still looking straight ahead as we walked.

"Ach," I answered, letting out the breath I'd been holding since the schoolhouse steps. "It's fine. It'll be fine."

We fell back into silence, listening to the rain.

"Sorry about your shirt," I said, only having just realized that I'd bled all over it. "I can buy you a new one."

"You're going to buy me a new shirt?" she laughed, finally breaking her piercing stare that had the road scared, to look at me. Her lion's mane was being soaked, and the exposed curls were beginning to fall against her skin making the color of her freckles more prominent. Her smile was faint, but it was there.

"If you want me to."

"Should I model it for you then too?"

I tried to remember the confidence I had felt when I was laying on the ground with her at my side and how she had responded to it. It was undoubtedly a mild concussion from the fall talking, but it had put a grin on her face and her lips against mine.

"Yes," I answered, doing my best to not meet her stare and only look at her out of my peripheral vision.

She laughed and then the silence found its way between us again. The rain had picked up, and my jeans were almost soaked clean through. So were hers. She'd pushed the hood back from her face, letting the rain seep into the rest of her hair. I watched slyly as she pushed the strands around her face back into the rest of the mane trailing behind her and wished that I'd thought to do it instead of her.

"What did you mean?" I blurted out before I realized what was happening.

"When?"

"Earlier, about not, you know." I couldn't get the word to pass through my lips like I was a bashful five-year-old.

"No, I don't know."

When I looked at her, her faint smile had grown into a devilish grin, her lips parting to let out a matching devilish laugh, at my expense.

"You do know what I mean." I smiled and laughed with her, starting to relax just enough to breathe.

"No." she answered, regaining her composure and forcing a bogus grimace.

I could see the game she was playing, and it made me love her more. "You're going to make me say it, aren't you?"

"Make you say what?" she spat, barely able to get the words past her lips before she began laughing again.

I took a deep breath and closed my eyes, thinking I might die of embarrassment. But at least I'd have an answer to the question that had been burning a hole in my existence since that morning.

"What did you mean, when you apologized for not kissing me sooner?"

As the words passed my lips, the sound of an engine came barreling around the corner, preceding the vehicle that was heading toward us as we walked in the road. As it moved closer to us, it slowed. I shielded my eyes from the rain as we moved to the side of the road. I could feel the tickle of panic in my chest when I finally recognized the truck and whose father it belonged to. I prayed there was no one in the cab with him.

"Raining pretty good kids," Mr. Scott yelled through the window. "Hop in, I'll give you a ride."

I left Isla standing in the muddy grass on the side of the road and walked up to the window of Mr. Scott's truck, thankful to see that he was alone. I couldn't explain why, but I didn't want Arden to see me with Isla. I knew he'd be jealous, they all would be. Maybe it was the jokes I could already hear him cracking at my expense or the betrayal I would have to look at in his eyes every day. I knew he loved her too; it just hadn't been as desperately as I had.

"I think we'll just keep walking," I heard Isla call from behind me. "I like walking in the rain."

Mr. Scott smiled with an understanding that only a man would have, wished me well and rolled up the window to carry on his way. I turned back to Isla, wanting to thank her for saving me from what was sure to be a lengthy, overexplained conversation ending with us squished in the cab of the truck, with the question I'd asked still unanswered.

"Well?"

"Well what?" she responded.

"Are you going to answer me?"

We were face to face, standing almost in the middle of the road. We'd be roadkill if someone came around the corner too fast, unable to stop short on the slick road, and yet neither of us moved.

"Since that day in the café."

"What?"

"That's how long I've been waiting."

I struggled to get past the idea that she remembered that day outside the bathrooms at the café. I'd almost thought I'd half imagined it, but she'd remember it.

"Waiting for what?" I asked, this time the tables turned, and now I wore the sly smile instead of her, waiting for her reply.

"For you to kiss me!"

I don't think she'd stopped talking before my hands were tangled in her hair, pulling her closer to me so I could kiss her like she'd ask me too. I kissed her hard, much harder than she had kissed me earlier. I cradled her neck in my hands. I could feel the tickle of her hair against my cheeks as it was blown about by the wind. The warm rain dripped between us as my lips moved gently against hers and hers against mine. I thought my hands might be stuck, tangled in the crazy fire that she wore like a crown. I didn't care if I ever got them back.

She pulled away slightly, just enough to breathe and speak. "My house is just up the way. I'd better go. My ma will be looking for me."

"Ok," I whispered, our lips still close enough to touch.

"Are you alright to get home? I didn't even ask which way your house was before we started walking." Her tough exterior had faded somewhat, showing that underneath, she genuinely cared.

"Don't worry about me," I answered. She backed up a few more steps toward her house. I looked around, trying to figure out exactly where I was and how I was going to get home. I took a few steps onto an outcropping of rock just off the road, trying to see if I could run across the craggy no man's land that ran between her side of Breaclete and mine. When I stretched onto my toes, I could just make out the peak of my roof.

"Is that your house?" I asked, pointing to the white house just up the road. It was large, much larger than mine.

She jumped up onto the rock without the need for assistance but took my hand to humor me.

"It's my grandmothers. We live with her now."

There was a hint of sadness in her voice when she answered, and I wanted to know why so I could make it go away. There were so many questions I needed the answers to. Even through the gray, I could tell the sun's position had dropped and soon it would be dark. If I had any chance of making it over no man's land I had to get moving. My questions would have to wait.

She let go of my hand and jumped down from the rock and started moving quickly toward her house.

"Isla!" I yelled after her. I thought my voice may have been muted by the rain when she didn't turn back. I watched her go for a moment before I turned toward the obstacle that stood between me and my house.

"Lachlan!" she yelled, having double backed at least half the distance she had made.

"Yeah?"

Her devilish smile was back. She was soaked to the bone. She'd unzipped her waterproof, and her shirt underneath clung to her form and slunk from one shoulder. She flicked her head, throwing a chunk of hair that had been resting heavily on her shoulder behind her. I could just make out the outline of a thin bra strap against her skin.

"Don't tell anyone?" This time it was a question and not an order, although it could have been either and I would have obeyed.

"Our secret," I yelled back before taking off over the rock, towards home and the tongue lashing I knew was waiting for me. I'd be grounded all weekend, but it didn't matter, as long as I was sent to school on Monday morning.

It was almost pitch black by the time I made it home. My arm throbbed and my clothes had significantly more wear on them after jumping several fences. My dad's car was missing from the driveway, and the windows were dark. I looked around, expecting my mother to jump out from behind something to catch me in my lie. I waited for a moment, but nothing moved, and no lights came to life in the house. Then I remembered. My mother had a standing appointment in Stornoway every second Friday of the month. They were usually late coming home, but something must have held them longer than usual, and by the grace of God I'd beaten them home.

I ran to the port on the side of the house and tore off my wet clothes except for my underwear. I opened the trash can and threw my blood-soaked shirt into the bag on top, making sure to retie it. Everything else I grabbed tight and ran inside, straight up the stairs to my room on the second floor, flicking every light switch as I went so when they pulled into the driveway there'd be no question if I had been home long enough to turn on every light. I'd be chastised for the waste, but it was minimal in comparison to what I should by right have expected. I threw my wet clothes to the bottom of my hamper and redressed. I found some old rags and rewrapped my elbow and put a bulky sweatshirt on over so it wasn't as noticeable. I grabbed some old homework from my desk and ran back downstairs to wait for my parents at the kitchen table.

I heard the sound of my father's car coming down the road and then saw the headlights as they pulled into the port. I thought my heart might pound out of my chest. I'd only made it home with minutes to spare. The car doors slammed, and I could hear my mother at the side door. Her boots squeaked as she walked down the hallway. I was pretending to read something when she looked around the corner. I didn't look up. I knew better than that.

She walked into the kitchen, dropping her purse on the counter by the sink. I watched her out of the corner of my eye, still pretending to focus on my homework. She stood by the sink her back to me for a minute and then turned to face me. I looked up quickly and then back at the papers in front of me. Her eyes were red, and she looked tired. I could feel them on me. When I looked up again, silent tears were streaming down her cheeks. She looked lost, like she didn't belong where she was.

"Ma, are you ok?" I asked, feeling the need to comfort her. "Did I do something?"

She smiled and hid her face with her hands. At first, I thought she was still crying but when she dropped her hands, I could see that she had been laughing.

"Did you do something?" she asked, all emotion having drained from her tone. "You've tracked water on the floor. And turn off some of these bloody lights." She turned and walked upstairs to her room and closed the door. Her voice was quiet as she spoke, sober, devoid of any feeling at all, good or bad.

My father came in behind her and took up in the sitting room, his face bent with distress. I couldn't tell if I didn't care about the familiar exchange because everything felt like normal or because I finally had something else to concentrate on. I quickly mopped up the water on the floor with an old rag and made a sandwich that I took to my room. I looked out the window as I ate. If I squinted hard enough, I could see faint lights across the no man's land I'd scrambled over less than an hour ago. I'd never noticed them before, but now that they belonged to Isla, they were all I could see.

Chapter Seven

It was like they were twelve years old all over again. Lachlan tried desperately to gain a piece of Isla Gilcrest's attention while she fluttered about the Twisted Thistle waiting tables and spilling drinks. She was lucky that most of the men she was serving were already too drunk to care. Lachlan watched them as they watched her with sozzled eyes. He couldn't blame them. She was as inconspicuous as a tree that might try and grow on the windswept island. The tree, like her, had everyone's attention, wanted and unwanted.

Their encounter had been brief. Lachlan found himself tongue-tied, giving Isla reason to laugh and carry on with the toils of a barkeep, only stopping briefly at his table to smile and bat her eyes. She stood with her hand on her cocked hip appearing to be only half interested in what he might be saying. He was vying for her attention all over again, and he wasn't sure he would earn it twice. He was still in disbelief that he'd won it once.

Lachlan traded his unfriendly seat in the back of the pub with his back to the world for one with a better view. The sun shone through the window in patches, and he could see the port just on the other side of the small two-lane road. Small trawlers blew their horns as they maneuvered the tight and shallow channel coming and going from the dock. But he wasn't interested in what the port or anything outside had to offer. He'd traveled nearly three hundred miles under the guise of returning home to bury his mother, but really, his return had been for her, and everything left unsaid and undone between them.

He watched her, moving in slow motion in front of him, waiting for the sun to catch her eyes in just the right way, transporting him back to the times they'd lain in grassy fields hidden from the world. Just the two of them. She caught his eye from across the pub and Lachlan saw the remnants of the smile he'd fallen in love with as a boy. He questioned how he'd made it twenty years without her and wasn't sure he'd make it another hour after finding her again.

Lachlan was red-faced by the time Euan joined him at his table. He smiled gently and took a seat on the opposite side of the table from Lachlan, out of arms reach and harm's way.

"They've got a great fish and chips here. Or skink."

Lachlan just smiled, staring at him from across the table, watching Isla out of the side of his eye and she moved in and out of his line of vision.

"Well, did you at least talk to her?"

"To who?" Lachlan asked plainly.

Euan looked around the room for Isla and then back to Lachlan. "You know, to Isla?"

"Oh, to Isla. Did I talk to Isla?"

Euan sat still, waiting for Lachlan to finish, expecting the details of their first conversation. Lachlan bent over at the waist and hovered over the table, indicating that he wanted Euan to do the same so he could share the intimate details of their conversation more privately. Euan cautiously leaned forward, looking around the room as he did. When their heads were almost touching, Lachlan grabbed Euan's collar and pulled him even closer.

"You did that on purpose, you bastard," Lachlan whispered powerfully as Euan struggled under his grasp. "A little fucking warning would have been nice. I was fucking blindsided and made an ass of myself. It was like I was twelve all over again and could barely put two fucking words together."

"She asked me to," Euan finally spat. "After she knew you were back, she asked me to drop you off here."

"What?" Lachlan's grip on Euan's collar had loosened, but he still struggled to break free of his hand.

"She asked me to bring you by," he said again. "Now let me go. I'm a man of the law now Lachlan. You can't manhandle me like you did when we were kids."

Lachlan let go of his collar, shoving him as he did. He laughed as he watched Euan correct the posture of the shirt. "A man of the law, eh?"

"Yeah, and I demand a little respect."

Lachlan leaned forward against his elbows. "You'll always be wee Euan McKenzie to me, no matter what silly uniform you wear."

"Aye, the prick's gone and got himself a complex for sure." The voice was recognizable to both men, as the third and last member of what had once been an inseparable group of four arrived at the pub. Calum sat in the chair next to Lachlan while Euan sulked like he had when they were kids, obviously hurt by Lachlan's cutting words. The men sat in momentary silence, adjusting to the idea of all three of them being together again after twenty years or maybe out of respect for their missing ringleader.

"Right then," Calum finally broke in. "What's his problem then?"

"I'm sitting right here," Euan declared. "Please don't talk about me like I'm not."

Lachlan threw Calum a look as they shared the memory of how they'd tormented the weakest link of their group as kids. "He's bent out of shape because I wrinkled his collar."

"Oh yeah," Calum said, squinting his eyes while bending over the table to get closer to Euan, who was already swatting him away. "I thought it looked a mess when I came in."

Euan stood up and pushed away from the table. "So glad to have you back Lach, just like old times."

"Oh, come on man, we're just having a bit of fun with you." Lachlan was on his feet, quickly maneuvering in front of Euan, blocking his path to the front of the pub with his arms outstretched as a peace offering.

"I wasn't. His collar's fucked," Calum said straight-faced.

Euan pushed Lachlan's outstretched arms aside as he tried to make his way past. Lachlan grabbed his friend and forced a hug against him, giving him no other choice other than to stand awkwardly next to the table until Lachlan let go of him. Lachlan tried to remember the last person he'd felt close enough toward to hug, excluding Liri, who's horizontal hugs didn't count. It was awkward and out of place for him.

The men's shenanigans had drawn the attention of other patrons in the pub. Backs that had been turned were now grimacing faces staring at Euan and Lachlan. When the gag had finally run its course, and Lachlan let go of his old friend, he could see the cop in his eyes. They were as still as an animal tracking pray, calculating its move and then his own.

"Alright," Euan finally called out in an effort to disband the onlookers. "Sorry for any disturbance."

Not a soul moved. The quiet room fell into deeper silence as Lachlan stepped out from beside Euan and met the accusatory eyes with his own. Lachlan knew the looks and the secreted words behind cupped hands. Their looks dug into him like knives, opening old wounds that had never entirely healed.

"Alright, alright, you bunch of rubberneckers, shows over. Back to your beers."

Slowly, the patrons of the Twisted Thistle averted their eyes and continued swigging on their half-drunk beers and eating their fish and chips. No one said it, but everyone found the irony in the fact that Isla had instilled more fear in the gawking onlookers than Euan had. Hushed words drifted in the air and whirled around Lachlan, around all of them. They'd all been affected by Arden's death. Some more than others.

"Ok boys, either order something or get out." Lachlan looked up at her from the table as she deliberately avoided his eyes. She chatted with his friends, reassuring Euan that he'd not been bested by a barmaid. Her smile was beguiling, and Lachlan found it hard to look away. The afternoon sun coming through the window spread like fairy dust through her thick hair. The freckles that had so prominently dotted her face as a young girl had smooth and dulled since then, but her hair was still the color of hot coals burning straight through until morning.

He was faintly aware of his name being called while he stared up at Isla, her deep green eyes finally meeting his for more than the fleeting glances she'd offered him so far. He'd fallen into her eyes, and into the memories they shared, good and bad.

"Maybe you should finally take that picture." She winked, and the mishmash of memories between them disappeared, like the end of an old film roll when the pictures run out, and only snippets of white screen flipped loudly one after another. "Just the whiskey, then?"

"Yeah, just whiskey," Lachlan answered before she disappeared into the kitchen.

"Just as smooth as ever," Euan whispered as he took a sip of his beer.

"Oh, piss off Euan. Like you could do any better."

"I have. Out of the lot of you, I'm the only one that's married."

Lachlan looked at Calum for confirmation. "Don't look at me," he said. "I haven't any interest in being tied to one lass the rest of my life."

"Yeah, because you haven't any interest, that's the reasoning," Euan spat.

"The sea's my true love anyway," Calum confessed, "and no one woman can compete with that. That's why I take a different one every night."

"It gets old," Lachlan interrupted swiftly with a soft and despondent voice, his eyes glued to the kitchen door waiting for her return.

"What's that?" Calum asked.

"It gets old, a different woman every night." He thought of Liri, and all the other women he'd slept with while feigning an interest in her just deep enough to keep her coming back. A wave of disgust for himself wafted in the air. He was glad that he'd not received any calls or texts from her since the night at the pub, but he found himself wishing she'd call just so he could apologize. "They just end up feeling empty."

"You're still in love with her?" Calum stated, a smile traipsing across his face like he knew something no one else had already figured out.

"Fuck," Lachlan muttered, shooting the warm whiskey that he'd been holding on to. "I don't know if I ever stopped being in love with her."

"It's been twenty years, brother. Surely, you've moved on. You don't really want to spend your life alone, do you? Pining after the one that got away." Euan spun the silver ring on his left hand as he asked his question as if to reassure himself of the accuracy of his own lifelong commitment.

Isla materialized from the kitchen, and it wasn't until then that Lachlan realized she'd kept their secret. Maybe out of guilt after what happened or because they'd promised it, but no one knew she'd not been the one who got away.

Lachlan didn't answer. He stared into the empty whiskey glass, wishing that more would materialize and that he had an answer to Euan's questions.

"Anyway, you did the dumbest things I've ever seen anyone do for a girl's attention. You both did." The three men fell silent, and Lachlan wondered how long it would be until they could mention his name and not feel the sting of guilt tickling in the back of their throats.

"Better you find someone who appreciates you, for how you are and doesn't make you chase after them."

Lachlan laughed because Euan was right. They had done idiotic things in the name of Isla Gilcrest, and he'd do them again. Once Lachlan had tasted the reward of the chase, there was no settling for the good girl in the schoolhouse front row.

"Christ," Calum yelled, barely able to keep his beer in his mouth as he did. "You're talking about Ross's car, aren't you? I'd completely forgotten about that."

Lachlan laughed, watching Euan across the table pursing his lips like a woman. "We all could have died."

"That was some dumb shit, caught beatings for weeks from Ross until …" Calum stopped just short of the words spilling out of his mouth. They hung heavy on his lips. Each man could see and hear the words even though they'd been caught just in time. Lachlan hoped that Ross's last memory of his brother wasn't a beating he'd laid on him for stealing his car, but he knew that it probably was.

"Why did we do it," Calum asked, trying to recover the conversation before it fell too far into the memories none of them were ready to revisit.

"He did it to show off," Euan said.

"No, no, that wasn't it. Well, that may have been part of it." Calum sat upright in his chair and jumped it a few times, knocking against the floor as he tried to get closer to the table. Leaning in, he said, "it was to get back at Ross. Remember? For asking Isla to take a drive with him."

Lachlan remembered the incident well, even if he'd tried to let it go a thousand times. He and Euan exchanged a look only they could share. An uproar at the bar over a televised match sent Calum reeling for another pint and congratulatory celebrations with men from the ferry.

"Fucking witch," Euan whispered under his breath. He never cursed, but Lachlan knew why he'd chosen to in that instance.

"Who's a witch?" The men looked up at Isla standing beside their table, bottle in hand, pouring Lachlan another whiskey. When he reached for it, it was gone and down her throat in a matter of seconds. She poured another, but it was destined for the same quick fate as the first.

"No one, it's nothing," Lachlan insisted, grabbing for the bottle.

"The woman from Hacklete? She wasn't a witch."

"How do you even know what we're talking about?" Euan asked, his face scrunched in irritation that she'd been able to eavesdrop on their conversation without them having the slightest inkling.

"Everyone knew about her or at least I thought everyone did." Isla snickered as she threw the insult at the men. Their faces were still riddled with puzzlement. "Older woman, dancing by the loch where the road splits on the way to Bosta."

Lachlan and Euan were frozen, still in disbelief that the strange woman from the Tobson footpath had been so well known seemingly to everyone but them.

"Really saggy tits," she said, holding her hands down past her waist for dramatic effect.

"How'd you know who she is?" Euan asked.

"My grandmother used to talk about her when I was young."

"What did she tell you?" Euan asked.

"She said she was a spaewife," she answered. "Like a seer."

Someone from the kitchen yelled her name with urgency. She smiled and slid the bottle into the table in front of Lachlan before rushing away. Lachlan grabbed the bottle and her hand. Her skin wasn't as soft and delicate as he remembered it being. They were rough and worn in from years of tending bar and washing dishes. As rough as they were, Lachlan had a hard time letting her hand slip from under his, feeling like he might never find it again. The confidence he never remembered her being without began to slide from her face the longer Lachlan held her hand. She wasn't the same girl. But he couldn't expect her to be, even if he did. She jumped at the shrill scream of her name and slipped away while averting Lachlan's eyes.

He poured a whiskey and then another, downing them in quick succession. Euan droned on, but he wasn't listening. His mind was a million miles away and drifting further and further away with each whiskey that slipped past his lips.

When Isla came back to retrieve the bottle, it was more than half gone. Lachlan didn't look up at her as she reached for it. When her fingers wrapped around the smooth, cool glass of the bottle, Lachlan's fingers wrapped tightly around hers again. He exploded up from the table and was pushing her backward toward the kitchen with the bottle between them before he realized the disturbance he'd left behind for Euan to explain away. It could have looked like a struggle if she wasn't walking with him willingly, their hands grasping onto each other's forearms as they danced down the back hallway.

Lachlan pushed them through the emergency exit at the back of the building and stumbled out into the parking lot. He gulped another few shots before offering the bottle to Isla, who took it and did the same, wiping her lips on the sleeve of her sweater when she was done.

"What else did your grandmother tell you?"

"I don't know, not much. My grandmother said she knew her. She said she could see things that hadn't happened yet. That's why everyone called her a spaewife."

"What kinds of things did she see?"

She hesitated.

"Is she still alive?"

"The old woman?"

"Your grandmother."

Isla didn't answer. Pain bubbled up in her eyes where a devilish stare usually rested.

"Sorry," Lachlan whispered, not needing to know more than her sad eyes already told him.

"Why do you want to know about her?" she asked, swigging on the bottle one more time before handing it back to Lachlan.

"I can't explain it." He trailed off, unable to explain himself. "Nothing. Forget it."

"What?" she asked again.

"Something she said, to Euan and I. We ran into her, literally, one day, on the footpath from Tobson back to Bosta."

"What did she say?"

The sun had all but disappeared behind the churning clouds that raced across the sky. A storm was creeping in from the west. The drive back to Bernera would be a wet one for sure. Lachlan watched as the wind pulled at her hair and he remembered how it felt tangled around his hands, soft but treacherous. He wanted to feel it against his skin again.

He took a few steps toward Isla, as her eyes jumped around, uncharacteristically unsure of herself. She had always been sure of everything she did and everything she was. She was vulnerable now, made that way by the world, just like he was.

"Can I?" He asked, only inches from her, his eyes already tangled in the strands dancing around her face. He watched as she tilted her head slightly and bit the corner of her lower lip. Lachlan reached his hand up and hesitated, his glance shifting from the burning coals to the deep green pools of her eyes. He was holding his breath, but hers, he could see was coming faster.

"I'm sorry about your mom," she whispered as Lachlan crept closer as if she was trying to sabotage the moment.

"Don't," he whispered back to her.

Her hair twisted around his fingers and he plunged them deeper and deeper into the crown of curls surrounding her face. She closed her eyes and swayed like a leaf being blown in a mild breeze. Lachlan could feel her warm breath on his lips, hurried and irregular.

"I didn't come back for her," he breathed, brushing lose tendrils behind her ear as he did.

Lachlan cupped his hands against the swell of her cheeks and tucked his fingers behind her ears, tilting her lips upwards toward his. She opened her eyes and took his breath away with one look, letting her vulnerability show through the tough exterior she tried to hold on to. Her hands found their way to his side, just above his waistline and traced the outline of his back as they moved.

***

The door behind them shifted and screeched like the sound of a banshee as it rubbed against its metal frame, sending both parties into a violent shudder in its wake. The moment was swept up in the wind and carried away. Seeing what his interruption had cost them, the busboy dropped the bag of rubbish outside the door instead of awkwardly walking past them to the dumpster and back to the door.

Isla pushed her hair away from her face and gathered what she could in her hand to keep it from tangling in the wind. "You should come see me at home," she stuttered, gathering her remaining composure as two decades of wonderment and want pulsed between them.

"I have something of yours," she admitted, brushing past him on her way to the door. "I think you might want it back."

She disappeared behind the door, letting it slam closed behind her. Lachlan stood alone in the back alley of the pub, smelling the funk of dumpster trash and impending rain, thinking about what she could possibly have of his, other than his heart, but he wasn't interested in getting that back.

***

Euan drove while Lachlan watched the evening swallow the sky. The car was silent, except for the wind whipping by them. A mist had rolled in from the west and sat over the moor, dousing it in a sleepy color. Even though summer was pushing through the air, the landscape remained unchanged for the most part. Small patches of yellow gorse poked through the red-brown color of the landscape. Black fields of heather sat on top of everything, taunting everyone with the beauty it possessed but had yet to release. Even in early summer, the majority of the island still looked dead.

Neither of the men spoke, even though Lachlan was sure that they were both thinking the same thing; neither of them was ready to verbalize it just yet. It was a memory they would have to work up to.

"She looks good, huh?"

Lachlan made sounds as air passed between his tightly clenched lips, nothing amounting to discernable words, but Euan understood them nonetheless.

"Just like you remember?"

"Almost," Lachlan replied, lying to his friend. She had far surpassed every version of her he'd conjured in his mind.

"So," Euan started, shrugging his shoulders as he drove, attempting to incite more conversation. "Are you going to see her again?"

It was the first time the thought had occurred to Lachlan, but after it entered his mind it, was all he could think of. There was going to be a point when he'd go home to Dundee, and she'd stay in Bernera or Stornoway or somewhere on the Isle of Lewis and they'd be separated by the Minch again, living in different worlds. Lewis was like an alien planet compared to Dundee. Since his arrival on Lewis, Lachlan had done nothing but wish his time away, desperate to escape back to the real world, not realizing that Isla was being wished away with it.

"What happened?" Lachlan asked, picking at the skin on his hand that had been trying to heal since the night before he left for Lewis.

"What do you mean?" Euan asked.

"What happened to her?" Lachlan fell silent, turning his gaze from his hand to the clouds twirling outside his window. "After I left. What happened to all of you?"

Euan didn't answer right away. He looked out the windshield blankly as he drove.

"It was a long time ago, Lach. Are you sure you want to go down this road? It won't change anything."

Lachlan knew he was right. Nothing would change. Arden would still be dead, and everyone on the island would still think he had murdered him. Being back on Lewis, seeing the landscape and remembering what it had been like growing up in the middle of it all had Lachlan second guessing everything he'd been made to believe about his past. The physical distance of living on the mainland had provided him with a buffer he'd needed in order to leave it all behind, as if it had never existed. Driving through the middle of it again made it real, and Lachlan wasn't sure he was ready for the truth he knew loomed in the hillsides.

"She didn't come to school for a week," Euan said, understanding Lachlan's silence was his answer. "After they'd already closed school for about a week. A lot of us didn't go back right away." His voice was unmoving, weighty. His words hung in the air between them. He realized it was just as hard for Euan to say them as it was for him to hear them, but he knew that both needed to happen.

"When she did come back, she wasn't the same. She hardly talked, just sitting at her desk staring out the window. Sometimes she'd just disappear in the middle of the day and wouldn't come back. She just started blending in with the other girls instead of standing out."

Lachlan's face shuddered in pain, and he pursed his lips enough for Euan to notice the sting his words had caused and stopped talking, letting the tenderness of the open wound dull some before continuing on.

"There was a funeral. Or a service, at least."

Lachlan closed his eyes and saw flashes as the lightning jumped across the sky. In the bits of light, he could see Arden stumbling away from him. Three quick bursts and then he was gone.

"There's a stone with his name on it too."

"Where?"

"Bosta."

Of course, it had been Bosta. How many times had they made the trip there on their bikes as kids, barely able to make it back on sore legs and in poor weather? In the summer, they braved the chilly water and swam as far as they could before turning around and heading for shore. Arden always swam the farthest.

"Your da was a mess, hardly able to leave the house for a month, I remember my da saying to my ma."

Lachlan laughed, unbelieving that the words were real. It had taken him almost three months to write and make sure he'd arrived safely at the asylum after being sent away. Lachlan had taken another four to write back, setting the tone for how their fictional relationship would continue to diminish over the next two decades.

"And my mother?"

The car was silent except for the wind licking at Euan's car as he drove. Neither of them spoke until after they'd crossed the bridge onto Bernera and only then Euan was merely confirming that he was dropping him back at his father's house, being careful not to suggest he had another option. Lachlan knew he was not the type to bring home to the Sarah Campbell's of the world, even if it was just to sleep on the sofa. He knew Euan would most likely catch an earful if he tried, so he didn't bother to ask. Nothing else was said until Euan stopped in front of Lachlan's childhood home.

"You know … It's just …" Euan's lips struggled to find the words his mind could obviously see clearly.

"Out with it."

"Just, don't be so hard on your da. He … he's done the best any man could."

"What's that supposed to mean?" Lachlan turned in his seat to face Euan, who was already averting his gaze. He could see the house just on the other side of Euan through the window, teasing him with the secrets only it and Lachlan knew. "You have no idea what …"

"And neither do you," Euan interrupted, finally turning toward Lachlan as he did. His face had changed little since their childhood. Faint red stubble peaked through the skin around his jawline, but his eyes were the same; still honest and sincere underneath whatever truth he thought he was hiding.

"Look, I'm talking out my ass." He couldn't hold Lachlan's eyes anymore and turned away, finding the storm clouds hanging ahead of them less looming. "It's just, as a dad, I know how difficult it can be, you know, to know what the right thing to do is. You never know if you're doing the right thing or mucking up their lives."

"You never said anything about kids."

"Yeah, two girls; seven and five."

Lachlan had found the idea of Euan being married, to Sarah Campbell no less, to be comical, like they were playing house and it wasn't in any way the kind of married other people were. Kids were another story altogether. Kids were real.

The car idled loudly outside Lachlan's house. His dad's car was in the drive. The house was cold and dark. The frigid sea breeze was eating the paint away, and the wind had been playing with the shingles, scooping them up by the handful and disbursing them elsewhere. He had lived there, but it wasn't his home. It felt like someone else's house he'd read about in a story, giving him an odd attachment to it built on a momentary interest, but that was it.

"Did you ever tell anyone?" Euan asked, looking down as he fiddled with his hands in his lap.

"Tell anyone what?" Lachlan was disengaged as he thought about what the old women had said to them that day along the path coming back from Tobson. He could see her lifeless eyes and the truth they held. He shuddered in his skin as he remembered her clammy hands against his arm and wished he could forget it's feel.

"Don't do that," Euan said.

"No."

"Not even the police?"

Lachlan hadn't breathed a word of it to anyone. At the time it hadn't meant anything to either of them. She was a bizarre woman, dancing naked on the moor. Even at twelve, the boys knew better than to trust in anything she had said to them. But all that had changed when Arden disappeared. Then, it meant everything, but it was too late.

"They wouldn't have believed us if we'd told them anyway," Lachlan said.

"What if I told you that I believe you, all of it."

Lachlan laughed and opened the car door, swinging one leg out onto the gravel. The cool evening breeze blew in off the water and danced around him. He'd forgotten the sweet smell it carried with it during spring and summer. He inhaled deeply, looking through all the memories it held.

"I'd say you've been reading too much into the tall tales you probably read your girls at night." He slammed the door, not bothering to look back. Rain was already falling out at sea. In about an hour it would be pounding against his father's roof, and he could lay in his old bed and drift in its pulsing lull.

Lachlan only stopped when he heard the buzz of the driver's side window but didn't turn to look at Euan.

"Arden's not the only one to go missing," Euan called, in a matter-of-fact tone.

Lachlan turned just enough to see a sliver of Euan and his car. He played nervously with the rubber weather stripping exposed by the open window.

"You just happen to be the only witness."

Euan's car sped down the road, leaving Lachlan standing in front of his childhood home for the second time that day. He walked through the unkempt grass of the front yard and slipped past where the shadow of the house would have fallen. His father stood where he always had, looking out into the stretch of sea the house sat against. As a child, Lachlan had always thought his father was looking for something, an imagined ship that would crest over the horizon one day to rescue him from the life that had swallowed him whole. He'd never understood the need for that escape as a child. He took a stance next to his father in the side yard, wet grass clinging their shoes. As an adult standing next to his aging father, he finally understood the need.

Chapter Eight

I waited for weeks, but it never came. Every time I saw Arden, my body tensed in preparation for the tongue lashing I knew was coming, followed promptly by several fists to the gut. Arden's fists were like the heads of steal hammers. Just thinking about them connecting with my midsection made me almost heave. I kept my mouth closed, my lips hiding our secret and waited for the beating that never came. But kissing Isla Gilcrest would have been worth any beating Arden could dole out, ten times over.

During the week, daydreaming of her was all I had. Having a secret, meant keeping it and I was honestly more afraid of Isla's wrath if I exposed our secreted relationship than anything Arden could do to me for sneaking around behind his back with a girl he loved almost as much as I did. I begged for the school days to drag so I could at least be near her. She'd warmed up to some of the boys in our class and even spoke to Arden, and the other's a handful of times when class work called for it, but she made well to deliberately ignore me. She'd meet my stare occasionally when no one was looking, and when she did, it felt like she could see right through me.

Friday's were the worst, knowing that I'd go the weekend pining for Monday morning when I could see her again. But this Friday was different. In a moment of desperation, I had slipped a note into her bag asking her to meet me on Saturday, and now we had plans for a picnic hidden in the rolling hillside between Bosta and Tobson when both our parents thought we were out with other friends. The warmer weather was finally sticking and meant we could be outside without question and not be expected home until dinnertime. My skin tingled at the thought of having her to myself, tucked away and hidden from the world. The day could not move fast enough.

When the bell rang, everyone filed out in a hurry. There'd be a few hours of sun and warmth left in the day, and everyone would be taking advantage of it as they dillydallied on their walks home, taking detours and the long way around when possible. I lost Isla in the shuffle, and when I usually would have felt the torturous sting of agony rip straight through me, I was relieved that the day was almost over, bring Saturday that much closer.

"What took you so long?" Arden yelled from the community center parking lot as I meandered by, too caught up in my thoughts to notice him and the others.

"What are you talking about?" I yelled. "I'm right here."

"Did you get it?" he asked.

I was clueless; lost in my own world. My obsession had turned me into a gelatinous blob who no longer knew my right from my left. Arden's frustration with me came from a place of hurt. I'd gained a relationship with Isla, but he'd unknowingly lost his best friend in the process. Even when I was there in body, my mind was a million miles away. I blamed it on family troubles, which no one who knew my family would question, but I could see the disbelief growing in his eyes nonetheless.

"God damn man, the ball, the fuckin' ball for the game! Why do you think we're all standing around with our thumbs up our asses?"

I'd forgotten that Arden had volunteered me to liberate a basketball from the fitness room after school so we could play a game before the sun went down. "I forgot," I admitted, embarrassed that I'd ruined the afternoon's activity, and guilt-ridden because all I could think was that a game would have passed the time more quickly than the lot of us standing around staring at each other's stupid faces.

"Damn!" Arden yelled as the other boys mulled around him sharing in his disappointment. "Where's your freaking head?"

"If it was so important to you, then you should have grabbed it." I didn't understand why I'd been put in charge of the ball or why Arden couldn't have just retrieved it himself. After a few minutes of our back and forth though, I could see why he was making such a big deal about the ball and the game itself.

"Look, look, look," Arden whispered, snatching at shirt sleeves to pull the group closer together. "Here they come."

I followed Arden's gaze down the road to a group of girls headed in our direction. There was no missing Isla among them. Her hair danced in the air around her as she moved. I unconsciously started twirling my fingers as if they were wrapped around the waving tendrils. Without a basketball though, we were just a group of boys standing on an otherwise empty court, staring intensely and pitifully in their direction.

The closer the group got to the court, the more we fell apart; unsure of what we should be doing since I'd dashed our opportunity to show off our marginal athletic prowess. Surely that had been Arden's plan to gain Isla's attention, and I'd foiled it. Just one more reason I'd given him to hate me.

The girls giggled behind their hands as they walked slowly by the court, glancing coyly in our direction. Except for Isla. She did not laugh but smiled confidently in our direction, returning our uninterrupted ogles of her. As she walked the sun spun through her hair, and I wanted nothing more than to grab her hand and run off. Her eyes met mine, and it felt like she knew what I was thinking. The look in her eyes whispered to stay put and wait until tomorrow.

"Ladies," Arden called, drawing their attention to him. He stepped out of the small crowd of boys to distinguish himself from the rest. "What do you have planned on this spectacular afternoon?" He asked with his hands outstretched to either side of him. He looked like what I imagined the ringmaster might. The girls giggled and waited for Isla, who was undoubtedly their fearless leader, to speak.

"Just a warm walk home," she answered politely.

The air was still and silent after she spoke. Sheep cried in the distance. The girls laughed, huddling behind Isla as she leaned comfortably against the chain link fence. She'd not left Arden with much of an opportunity, intentionally or unintentionally. We watched as he scrambled for his next move.

"Would you like some company?" he asked.

"I think we're ok," she answered, too quickly for his liking. She could see his feelings were wounded and she tried to soften the blow. "You know, just kind of a girl's afternoon. But thanks."

The rhythmic bounce of the missing ball that had foiled Arden's plan now boomed behind us, followed by the deep-throat laughter we all recognized without having to see his face.

"Of course they don't want boys walking them home," he yelled from behind us, the basketball thudding in between his words, "when they could have the men drive them home instead."

"Shut up, Ross," Arden yelled, turning to face his older brother. "Don't you have anything better to do than follow us around?"

"Free country, ain't it?" he yelled, making us flinch as he pretended to launch the ball in our direction. Everyone hated Ross Scott. If Arden was arrogant, and he was, there wasn't a word for his older brother. He'd tormented us for the year or two before he left primary when we were all stuck together with him and his disciples, day in and day out. Our coming into puberty and discovery of girls had only reignited the pleasure he took in taunting us, and I knew today would be no different. I also knew Isla wouldn't be left unscathed by whatever Ross Scott had up his sleeve.

Ross sauntered toward his brother while the rest of his gang filtered in between us, flicking hats off our heads, grabbing backpacks and throwing them to the ground, wet willies and licked palms messing up our hair. I stood and took my penance, watching the exchange between brothers I'd seen too many times to count.

Ross slapped Arden upside the head a few good times before he punched him back in the shoulder. The collective gasp from both our groups and the older boys could have been heard in Crior. Before anyone knew what was happening, Arden was in a headlock, and the rest of us were being held back against our will. Arden screamed bloody murder. I knew the feeling of Ross' headlock and wanted to help him, but the goon holding me twisted my arm to an inhuman angle, and the next scream I heard was my own.

Perhaps Ross had not seen that it was Isla we'd been talking to through the mesh fence, but when she came running around the corner and into plain sight, Ross let his brother out of the headlock but retained his tight grip around his forearm. The goons followed suit. Everyone froze in her presence like we'd been caught up to no good by our mothers.

Arden struggled against his brother, trying to save face in Isla's presence and play off the pain that he was being caused. I snagged my arm free, turned and shoved the older boy who'd had a hold of me, pushed past the rest of them, and took my place at Arden's side. I sliced through Ross' arm with my own when he wasn't looking, and he let go of Arden's arm. He winced in pain before turning his attention to me, the image of my untimely demise burning brightly in his dark eyes.

"Is that your car then?" she called, distracting everyone that could hear her. The three of us turned away from each other and toward her soft but solid voice. She stood in front of us, arms crossed against her chest, one leg kicked out to the side, rocking back and forth slightly, giving the impression that we were keeping her from something more important. The wind kicked up and tussled her hair, brushing strands across the pale skin of her face. I bit my tongue, almost in half and stared at her as she tried to save Arden and I from being beaten within an inch of our lives.

"The little red one?"

Just when I didn't think I could love her more than I did, she opened her mouth, and something cunning and crafty fell out that made me almost visibly swoon. She made sure to show her allegiance by insulting Ross's pride and joy along with his manhood while trying to help us at the same time.

"Aye, that's her," Ross responded, the insult having sailed clear over his head. We watched as he strode closer to Isla with a cocky bounce in his step. Arden and I inched together behind Ross, being careful to remain out of arms reach. His proximity to Isla made me nervous. I knew what he was capable of doing to us, but I had no idea what his intentions were toward her. I just hoped she knew well enough to keep her quick tongue quiet for as long as she could.

"How'd you like if I take you for a ride? I can get her up to about 70 on the fast road." He tilted his head and pursed his lips as he traced the outline of her form with his eyes. "And she hugs all those turns almost as tight as those jeans are hugging your hips, love."

"Knock it off Ross." The words were past my lips before I could stop them, and there were more not far behind them. "Leave her alone, she didn't do anything to you."

Ross turned slowly, laughing at what was undoubtedly the terrified look on both our faces. He could do whatever he wanted to the two of us, but Isla was off limits. Arden and I exchanged a quick glance amid Ross' blank and off-putting stare that let me know he shared the same sentiment about the girl we were both desperately in love with.

"Is this your girlfriend then Lachlan?"

"No," I yelled quickly. I should have let it fester for a second longer so as not to let on that I wanted her to be.

"Then what's it to you what I say or do with her?" Ross turned back toward Isla who still wore an expression as cold as stone. I knew she thought she could handle herself, but she didn't know Ross. Her disinterest in him would only make him push harder, just like it did his brother. "What do you think Red? Want to go for a ride?"

My skin prickled, and Arden grabbed my arm when he saw me lurch forward. Ross was standing inches away from Isla now. I could see her face sour as he expelled his cigarette-stained breath against her perfectly pale skin. He raised his left hand to the level of her hip and was about to touch her when I snapped and raced forward to grab his arm before he could. Arden was close behind me. I couldn't let her perfection be tainted by his slimy hand. I'd take the beating of a lifetime before I let that happen.

Arden jumped between Isla and Ross, pushing him backward while he flailed with me attached to his right arm. Isla backed up until I could hear her hit the fence, the metal of the chain links ringing in the air. Ross freed himself from our grips with less effort than either Arden or I would have admitted. He stood between us like a caged animal trying to escape.

"Aye, well," Ross balked, trying to save what little dignity he had left. "Your loss, you fuckin' tease."

The world spun, and it felt like I was trapped in a strong current underwater, unable to tell which way was up.

The moment my body collided with the pavement was when I finally figured out where I was in the struggle. My breath had been stolen as I laid on the ground staring up into the sky before Ross' face eclipsed the fading day's sunlight. I'd launched myself onto his back in a blind rage and held onto him like a bucking bronco for as long as I could. The churning feeling of the current was him flipping me from his back to the ground. He was kneeling down to finish the job when I caught the sweetness of her voice in the air again.

"I can't today," she yelled, grabbing Ross' attention away from me, "but maybe another day."

Ross stood up and puffed his chest out like a turkey or peacock or some other fowl trying to impress a mate with a ridiculous display. "Tomorrow." There was no inflection of a question in his voice.

I let my eyes beg and plead for me when my words couldn't. The image of her and I running through the hills and resting against the jagged rocks where I'd planned to kiss her again began to fade and was being replaced with the picture of Isla sitting in Ross' cherry red Spitfire. I'd wished he'd finished the job. At least then, I would have been in less pain.

"Four o'clock."

"Sure." She shrugged as she answered. My heart broke on the ground of the Bernera community basketball court. Isla Gilcrest had given our time away to Ross Scott like it had meant nothing to her in the first place.

Ross regrouped with his disciples, slapping hands as they congratulated him on the red-headed trophy he'd stolen away from a group of twelve-year-old boys. I questioned what he wanted with a girl so much younger than he was, but I knew what it was that he wanted because I wanted it to, or at least some version of it. I, unlike Ross, wouldn't just take it from her.

When the group of older boys was around the corner and out of sight, Isla joined Arden at my side. The group of girls meandered their way onto the court with the rest of us. Everyone stood silent and stared at one another, still too shy to talk to the opposite sex.

Isla crouched next to me. "Are you ok?" she asked.

"We've got to stop meeting like this," I laughed. With the heaviness of the mood lightened, the two homogeneous groups on the verge of becoming something other than children began to comingle. Couples formed somewhat naturally, blending everyone together. Even Euan found company with Sarah Campbell. As the pairs formed, it was noticeable that Isla was the odd girl out, stuck between Arden and myself. My guilt mixed roughly with the pain I was experiencing and churned somewhere deep inside me. As Arden helped me to my feet, I could see the light of hope twinkling in his eye, and I had to look away, unable to face him and the lie I'd put between us.

"Look," he started with almost as much cockiness as his brother. "You don't have to meet him tomorrow, I'll make sure of that."

She looked at him with the same eyes that had looked at me when I'd fallen from my bike, and I felt the bite of jealousy in my blood. I'd assumed that because I'd gotten to her first, that meant she was mine, which was just my naivete about how the world and women worked creeping through the reality of my life. She wasn't mine. We'd shared a few innocent kisses that had blinded me into thinking she was. When I saw the way she looked at Arden, I knew, she'd never belong to anyone but herself.

"That's sweet," she answered. "But it's not really a big deal. I can handle myself. I don't want to make any more trouble for the two of you."

"No trouble at all. Don't worry about it and don't be expecting to see my brother tomorrow."

"Thanks, Arden."

I watched his face blush at the sound of his name on her lips, just as I had done. He winked at her and faded into the small crowd that had formed behind us, high-fiving with Calum and receiving pats on the back from the others. Even with his back to me, I could tell that he was beaming, feeling like he'd finally broken through the steadfast façade that Isla put forward. My heart sank in my chest, and I felt like I'd lost her before I ever really had her.

"Are you ok?" she asked again.

"I'm fine." My words were curt. I stared at the grey concrete, unable to make eye contact with her. I thought if I did, I might burst into tears like a baby. "Thank you," I whispered through my bruised boyish pride at having to thank a girl for seeing me through a fight. Out of the corner of my eye, I could see her sideways smile, begging me to meet her eyes.

"You can thank me tomorrow," she breathed.

"Tomorrow? But what about ..."

"I mean if you don't want to go anymore, then ..."

"Tomorrow," I muttered, "at the end of the footpath."

"I like turkey sandwiches," she laughed as she brushed past me to rejoin the group.

I stood motionless with my back to everyone so they wouldn't see the stupid grin she'd splattered across my face. Arden's slap across my back finally broke the spell and brought me back to reality. The girls had started on their way toward Tobson, looking over their shoulders here and there before they disappeared from our view. All the boys jumped and hollered like we'd just won the game of ball we never got to play. It was the first time in all our lives we'd had the nerve to talk to girls, outside of the schoolhouse requirements which were always awkward and bumbled. But something had happened that afternoon. Maybe it was the warm air or the impending doom we all felt under the stiff arm of Ross Scott. Something had changed, even though I couldn't pinpoint what it was. We all felt more like men than boys that afternoon.

"What was all that about?" Arden asked. His face shared the same shade of green I was sure mine had when I watched Isla talking to him.

"Just saying thanks, for trying to help us."

"Oh, right, right," he said. "God damn, she's something else, isnae she?" I could hear his love for her in his voice. She'd been kind to him, and now he was running with it. I could see the wheels of his mind turning behind his glassy eyes, and I was afraid to ask what his plan to save her from his brother might be. I felt guilty knowing that she never had any intention of being home the next day at four o'clock because she had agreed to meet me. Whatever he was planning would be for nothing, but I couldn't say anything. The time for revealing the truth to Arden had come and gone. Now I was deliberately going behind his back and driving the wedge deeper and deeper between us with every lie I told him.

***

I thought it was the rain blowing in sideways against my window. After a few minutes of listening to the noise, I realized it was too inconsistent in its rhythm to be rain. I listened for a few more moments and could hear whispers outside my window coming from the garden. The sun was barely peeking above the hills in the distance when I pushed the curtains aside. Arden was standing below my window with a hand full of pebbles from the driveway and a restless look only a boy with a plan could have.

The window creaked as I pushed it open, wiping the prior night's sleep from my eyes.

"What bloody time is it?" I whispered.

"Six thirty," he answered with excitement in his voice. "I've already woken Calum and Euan."

"Why?"

"I've got a plan," Arden whispered, his words calm but calculated. "To get back at Ross for yesterday."

I was scared to ask, but I knew that I had to. "What plan?"

He didn't say anything but pulled a set of keys from his pocket and shook them in the air. He turned to look at his brother's car parked strategically so that it peeked around the corner of my house enough for me to see it from my window.

"Are you fucking crazy? What the hell are you doing?"

"What we're doing! And, yes. I am crazy. But she's worth the beating."

He was right. She was worth the beating, but by stealing Ross' car, we would incur more than a beating. We'd be lucky to come away from it with our lives.

"Are you coming or not?" Arden yelled.

"Shhhhh, you'll wake my ma and then I won't be able to go."

"You're coming then?"

I could see movement down the road, and when I strained my eyes, I could see it was Euan cresting the small hill on his bike. I knew Calum wouldn't be far behind. A hopeful smile broke out across Arden's face. He knew I'd never let Euan and Calum show me up. I quickly dressed and scribbled a note which I push-pinned to the outside of my bedroom door, telling anyone who read it that I had left early with Arden to tend to Mr. MacLeod's cattle for him while he was laid up. I knew where Mr. MacLeod kept the hay and I knew where to find the cows if they weren't meandering about the beach waiting to be fed. No one could claim that I'd lied if we quickly spread some hay in the midst of the insanity of what was Arden's plan.

When I reappeared at the window, Calum and Euan had joined Arden in the garden and were whispering loudly to each other. I shimmied out my bedroom window onto the pitched roof before dropping onto the crown of the carport. The tin of the roof bucked and yawed like an unsteady boat under my weight, it's loud thudding calls filling the silence around us. I was sure I'd woken my parents by the time I made it to the garden.

We stuck to the side of my house like glue, out of sight from my parent's bedroom window, waiting to see if either of them had taken notice of the clatter. When the house remained still, Arden tiptoed to the car, and we all followed. Euan was the last one of us to get into the small two-seat Spitfire and only after my insistence that he'd be beaten worse by us if he didn't get in than by Ross if he did. In the end, he caved and crammed in next to us. After the door slammed closed behind him, we all looked at each other like it might be the last time we would, knowing it very well could be.

"Do you even know how to drive this thing?" Euan asked, pushing his glasses up to the ridge of his nose.

"I've known how to drive since I was ten. I've driven Mr. McLeod's tractor with my dad before. This puny thing will be a piece of cake."

Arden turned the engine over, and we all stared out the windshield waiting for him to put it in gear, but he hesitated.

"What's wrong?" I asked as we twisted in our seats assuming his stillness was because we'd been spotted by someone out for an early morning walk.

"You're straddling the shifter," Arden laughed. "Unless you want me handlin' your junk for however long we're in here, I suggest you figure something else out."

"There's hardly any room in here as it is," Euan cried as I shoved over out of the way of the shifter. "This is a two-person car!"

"You could always sit in the trunk if you think that'd be more comfortable." Arden's voice was confident and crazed. He knew what we were about to do could kill us in more ways than one, but he was blinded by his promise to Isla. I sank in my seat knowing it was all a waste.

"We'll make it work," I said, sitting cross-legged on the center console with the emergency brake firmly against the crack of my ass. "We aren't going to be in here for long." Arden hadn't shared the details of his plan before the four of us piled in the stolen car. I had no idea where he was taking us. I wasn't convinced he knew either.

Arden put the car in gear and pounded his foot on the gas, spinning the tires and spitting gravel as we took off. Anyone that saw us would assume it was Ross driving, leaving him to reap whatever ridicule our reckless driving collected. Arden took advantage of that knowledge and sped down the single-track road, taking turns too tight and skidding out. I could feel Euan's hand behind me looking for something to grab ahold of as we splashed around the small car, our bodies swaying heavily against each other. I wasn't sure if Arden meant to just steal his brother's car, rendering it missing when he attempted to leave to pick up Isla, or if he was intent on wrecking it all together.

The turn for Tobson, coming from our direction, was almost blind and even though we all knew it was coming, we nearly missed it. The tires tried to grab ahold of the loose gravel in the road, but couldn't, spending us into a nauseating spin in the middle of the small intersection. When Arden regained control, we sped down the road toward Tobson at a clip far too fast for the twisting road and his abilities.

"Arden, you're going to kill us, slow down!" Euan yelled from somewhere underneath Calum and myself.

"It's fine, I've done this a thousand times."

"Arden, really, you should slow down." My voice was calm, but stern overtop the fear of dying I was trying to hide from him. The road jogged back and forth, and Arden didn't even bother to downshift, speeding through the turns with the ass end coming out from underneath us each time.

"I'm gonna barf if you don't stop," Euan mumbled.

"Come on you bunch of girls, live a little!" He finally yelled.

The road disappeared from in front of us, falling below the cresting hill. I questioned if it would be a sheep in the middle of the road or another car coming from the opposite direction that would send us careening off the road; either were good possibilities. I almost hoped it'd be another car. At least that way, we'd have a better chance of perishing in the accident rather than limping away to our mothers who would surely have all our balls in vice grips by dinner.

My stomach fell out from underneath me as the car jumped the small hill. I wanted to close my eyes but couldn't. I could feel Arden jerk the car to the right trying to avoid the dark mass that had jutted out in front of us. We nearly missed it but found a cattle fence and the soft dirt of the hillside instead. Our bodies lurched forward when the car's movement stopped abruptly. When the dust settled, and the shouting stopped, I was surprised everyone was still whole.

"What was that?" Arden yelled, pushing his door open and jumping out of the car as if we'd not just totaled it into the hillside.

"God damn sheep, just like I said!" Euan yelled, pushing Calum off his lap and scrambling for the door handle. Once he was free from, he let his stomach heave, spilling his breakfast into the turned-up dirt.

"That wasn't no sheep, it was freaking huge!" Arden was already scrambling up the steep hillside, chasing whatever had jumped in front of us.

"Arden!" I yelled, watching the smoke spit from the hood of Ross' car. "The car!"

He didn't stop. Maybe it had been his plan all along. Maybe stealing Ross' car and abandoning it somewhere on the island wasn't enough. He had to be sure he wouldn't randomly find it and still be able to pick Isla up at four o'clock. Wrecking the car into the hillside would ensure that even if he did find it, he wouldn't be able to drive it that afternoon.

I watched as Calum scrambled up the hillside a few feet behind Arden, who was already almost at the top. Euan was sitting in the dirt, leaned up against the back tire of the Spitfire and I was stuck in the middle of all of it.

"Lachlan, get up here!" Arden yelled before disappearing over the top.

I looked around at the houses in the distance that made up the village of Tobson. The closest one was several hundred feet away, and while the crash had surely been loud, I doubted that they were close enough for anyone to have heard it. The road was quiet except for the sound of the wind whistling through the valley. Sheep screamed in the distance, but there was no movement I could see. If we were going to escape persecution for the stealing and wrecking of Ross' car, we had to get out of sight.

"Euan, we've got to move. We can't stay here."

Vomit had run down his chin and onto his shirt leaving the air smelling like cereal and stomach acid. I pulled him to his feet, and he stumbled behind me to the faint path leading up to Arden and Calum at the top.

I froze, standing motionless while Euan collected himself, whining the entire time. A shiver crept down my spine and across my skin. I looked around for the eyes I could feel eating me alive but could not find them.

"Hurry up," I whispered. "Before someone sees us."

"Are we walking all the way back?" he called from behind me.

"Yes," I answered.

"God damn Arden, why'd he have to wreck the car? I hate walking."

"We were always walking back, even if he hadn't wrecked it."

He was silent for a moment and then mumbled, "freaking hell," under his breath as we continued to scramble toward the top, grabbing hold of rocks as our feet slipped in the wet grass. I looked back at Euan before disappearing over the lip, the smoke from the car still rising into the air. I wondered how long it would take before someone found it.

Arden and Calum were a good deal ahead of us when we left the village of Tobson behind, twisting and turning through the rocky outcropping that stood between us and home. It was going to be a long hike back with Euan in tow complaining the entire morning. I tried to find the good in the shit situation Arden had forced us into and reminded myself that it could have been raining. Instead, the sun was up, warming us as we walked. We finally caught Arden and Calum once they stopped close to a marker for the footpath back to Bosta. Arden was pointing at something down below them with one hand, motioning for us to hurry with the other.

I ran ahead of Euan, who was hopelessly behind. Arden, Calum and I stood on the edge of a large, smooth boulder that jutted out over the edge, looking down over the large loch that created a gully between Tobson and Crior. The sun sparkled on top of the water and made it shine like glass. The fluttering reflection was mesmerizing; so much so that I initially missed what all the commotion was about.

"Where did it come from?" Calum asked. "I've never seen one out here."

On the far bank, almost directly across from us, a patch of darkness sped through the gauntlet of boulders that sprang up out of the dirt. It was fast and sprightly as it moved; too fast for any animal that normally roamed the pastures. Its hair flew behind it as it ran, catching the sun's light just right so that it looked almost silver instead of black. When it reached the top of the hillside, it bucked and kicked, letting out a scream we could hear on our side of the water. When it calmed, we all swore it was looking in our direction, pawing at the ground.

"When was the last time you saw a bloody horse?" Arden asked. "Who would have bought a horse?"

"Is it looking at us?" I asked, watching its sudden stillness.

"I don't know, can horses even see that far?" Arden waved his hands above his head in the air, as if to signal to the beast. We watched as it pawed at the ground and reared up again, screaming into the still air before turning and disappearing over the ridge.

"What's that?" Euan asked, out of breath, when he finally reached the rest of us.

"A horse, you fuckin' dolt," Arden answered.

"That's not a freaking horse, you idiot," he spat quickly, pointing down toward the bank of the loch on our side of the gully. "It's a person, a woman."

We followed the direction Euan's finger was pointed and at the end of it, found what looked like a woman walking by the water's edge.

"What's she doing?" Calum asked, squinting his eyes like the rest of us.

"She's naked!" Arden yelled, before covering his mouth once he realized how loud he'd called out. We all flattened out on the rocks underneath us to hide from her view. When we found enough bravery to sneak to the edge and look over, she'd disappeared, just like the stallion had on the other side.

"Where'd she go?" Euan asked as we scrambled to our feet.

Arden was already back on the footpath heading down to the bank to find her. Calum took off behind him, and Euan and I were left making our way down slowly behind them. On a good day, Euan was pretty useless in the hills. The ground was soggy and deep in places from the rain the day before, making the downhill slope that much harder for him to traverse.

"We don't see her," I heard one of them cry from down below us, having reached the bank.

"She's not a ghost," Euan scoffed behind me. "She didn't just evaporate into thin air."

We rounded a small bend in the path, and I heard Euan yell out behind me just as he collided with my legs, sending us both toppling over one another in the muddy grass. As we tried to untangle ourselves from one another, Euan became panicked, smacking my shoulder with something between disgust and terror in his eyes. As I turned back toward the path, the naked woman appeared a couple feet below us.

Her eyes were empty. They instantly reminded me of my mothers. Her long, dirty hair fell over her front but was too thin to cover everything. What we had assumed, or perhaps just wished, would be a young and beautiful naked woman dancing next to the loch on a warm spring day had turned into every boy's nightmare. She was old, and her skin was wrinkled like worn out leather. Calling her ugly would have been a compliment. Her skin sagged and was covered in filth. She stank of sheep shit and made me wonder if the filth covering her wasn't one in the same. Her uncovered breasts hung low and continued to sway even though she'd stopped moving. I didn't dare look further than that. I'd not seen a naked woman before, at least not in real life, and didn't want the image of whatever she had between her legs to be the first honeypot I'd see.

I felt Euan behind me scrambling to get to his feet, sending small rocks and clumps of dirt tumbling down the path, but I didn't dare move. She looked like she was ready to snatch me if I did. I stood still, looking into her empty eyes, my own reflection staring back at me.

"Late spring, 1985," she whispered. Her voice cracked as she spoke, and her lips stuck together in places like she hadn't spoken to anyone in years.

"What?" I asked in a slight panic; my voice shaking as if I stood on tottering ground.

"Stay clear of th' water's edge. That's where th' beast lives." She spoke like she was in a trance, hypnotized by something only she could see in the distance.

"He's a shapeshifter. Th' devil's seed. Bred, not born. Singed by th' sins of th' devil himself. You saw him; didnae you?"

"Arden!" Euan yelled from behind me, terrified at what he was witnessing. "Arden get up here!"

The shrill screech of Euan's voice pulled the woman from her trance, and there was life in her eyes looking back at me.

"Stay clear of th' water, sweet laddie." She grabbed my arm with a grip that could have rivaled any full-grown man's. Her skin burned like dying coals, and I struggled against her in vain. "He's stealin' bodies and souls, killin' barons when no one's lookin'. Th' water's edge, that's where it eats 'em - alive, bones and all, leaving nothing of him or 'em behind."

"What?" I begged, frozen in her hypnotic glare.

"There's a footpath that leads to th' bank where feet can walk on water." She pointed east, toward Bosta, but otherwise didn't move. "That's where it waits for you," she whispered. "Th' water's edge - that's where he kills you."

Her eyes were the color of milky marbles. They almost glistened in the bits and pieces of sun filtering through the morning clouds. Her mouth barely opened when she spoke.

"It's not your fault," she whispered, sweetly. Her eyes began to water and filled with a sense of sadness I recognized in another woman's eyes. "But you will pay th' price."

My heart was pounding. I was panicking under her grip, unable to find oxygen in the air around me. It felt like my blood was boiling under the skin she had a grip on. Something passed between us, something unexplainable. She smiled, exposing her blackened teeth. She pulled me close enough to smell her rotten breath, and my stomach heaved when its stench hit my nose.

"What are you talking about?" I pled as I tried to pull my arm from her grip.

"Th' bedtime stories you've read are true. You've seen it, the beast as black as night and fast as wind, serpent's mane and skin that sticks. It swims in the deep and comes ashore by day as man, and by night – he's evils beast. The devil's seed," she whispered, "come to claim what's his."

I could hear Arden and Calum behind her before I could see them. They came around the corner and caught an eyeful of old woman ass as they did. Her eyes filled with sadness which welled over her lids silently. She let go of my arm and slowly backed away from me, mumbling as she went. Arden and Calum threw rocks at her as she scurried up the hillside, eventually disappearing behind the rocks we'd been standing on when we saw her dancing below.

"What'd ya think Euan? Eh? She'd do for your first time alright." Arden never missed a moment to tease Euan, and this inexplicable moment would be no different.

"Shut up, Arden. You talk like you've done it when we all know you haven't."

"Yeah, well ..." Arden struggled for a comeback, bringing out the Ross in him as he stammered. It was foolish to think he'd turn out any different than his brother.

It was painful even to think it, but I didn't see our friendship lasting if he turned out like Ross. "I've done more than you have!"

"You've done nothing, just like the rest of us." I tried to hide my smile as I thought of Isla's lips against my own. Had I been honest, I would have won the contest for who'd done more with a girl, but I kept quiet and hid the secret under the lie.

Arden flung his hand in the air, dismissing the truth of my comment as he did. In a vain attempt to focus the attention somewhere else, he yelled, "was she whispering sweet nothings to the two of you, about how she'd take you behind the rocks."

"No! She said ..."

I cut Euan off before he had a chance to repeat anything close to what the woman had said to us. I couldn't explain it, but I didn't want it repeated. There was no doubt in my mind that the woman was crazy, but something in her words felt true. I just didn't know which part. Something inside me told me to keep it a secret.

"She was rambling on about some magic crystals she found on the rocks by the water. She's crazy, she's wandering around completely naked for fuck's sake."

Arden threw a handful of rocks in our direction before he and Calum took off ahead of us again heading toward Bosta. We could just make out the yellow sand of the beach and the call of gulls flying over the rocks which had been exposed by the receding tide. Euan and I got to our feet and regrouped, before following after them.

"What was that all about?" he asked me.

"I don't know, just - just keep it between us."

The muscles under Euan's chubby face tensed. "Why?" he asked.

"I dunnae know, just ..." I didn't have an answer for him, or myself. It just seemed like the thing to be kept secret.

"She wasn't actually suggesting that …" he snorted as he laughed as the thought took shape in his mind. "Well, that – that the horse we saw was a …"

"Don't say it," I interrupted, brushing mud from my pants. Saying it out loud somehow gave it merit, even though we were both thinking the same thing. We'd all read the tales of the water horse that lured women and children to the water's edge, so it could drag them to the depths and devour them whole. We'd always just assumed it was an old wife's tale to keep non-swimming children away from lochs and streams. We'd never in our wildest dreams thought there was any truth to it.

Chapter Nine

The house was as still as the death that lived in it. Lachlan laid in the same bed he had as a child, listening to the ticking of the wall clock on the other side of the room. He remembered how it had lulled him to sleep as a child, but now, every second it recorded with its mechanical beat was another second of his life being stripped away. The realization that he'd done little with his life since the last time he'd laid there made him wince with each second that passed. The island felt untouched by time, just as he remembered it, yet everything had changed.

The smell of coffee wafting up the steep staircase finally roused him from his bed and the depression he'd fallen into. If he'd believed in heaven, which he didn't, he would have pictured her looking down at him, laughing. Instead, he thought of his mother how she was; dead, laying in the morgue in Stornoway until they brought her back for burial. He had been confident that her death would bring, at the very least, a small sense of relief in his life. Even though they hadn't spoken in almost twenty years, her memory was still a stranglehold on Lachlan's life. All the times she'd failed him as a mother bubbled when he needed to be loved the most, preventing him from moving past the emptiness her inability to love him. Her death had loosened the noose, but the scar tissue around his neck felt permanent.

He stood at the window, peeking out from behind the curtain. The sky was the same color as dirty dishwater. The clouds were beginning to leak tiny bits of early light as the sun crept over the horizon. He strained his eyes to see what had once been Isla's house. If there had been anything good to come of his return home, it had been seeing her again, even if merely seeing her was all that ever came of it. At least he had that.

The crashing sound of glass breaking came as he sat on the edge of the bed, mentally preparing for another encounter with his father. Lachlan jumped to his feet and pulled on a pair of dirty jeans before bounding down the stairs toward the sound of chaos. Shards of broken tableware dappled the floor from the bottom of the stairs through the sitting room and into the kitchen. Lachlan remembered the mismatched bright pink and yellow plates and bowls he ate from as a child and how he always thought that they were too cheery for the drab house they served.

The side door to the garden smacked against its frame as the morning's breeze blew in, kicking up papers on the kitchen table. He tiptoed through the mess covering the linoleum floor, making his way to the side door but stopped at the kitchen table when he noticed a familiar face looking out at him from underneath handfuls of paperwork and old newspaper clippings.

The woman in the picture was undoubtedly his mother, but her smile and bright eyes made her almost unrecognizable. His brain struggled to comprehend the look of happiness on his mother's face; it wasn't something he'd ever seen before.

She was thin. Her face was plump and round, framed in dark red curls. She wore makeup, most noticeably lipstick almost as dark as her hair. Her lips were parted like she'd been caught mid-laugh as the picture had been snapped. She wore a simple black dress that hugged her girlish form. Her eyes were filled with promises as deep as the sea that shared their color. The emptiness Lachlan remembered looking back at him throughout his childhood was gone. She looked alive for the first time in his life. The irony of her liveliness only after her death was not lost on

Lachlan as he thumbed through the rest of the papers on the wobbly kitchen table.

On the top of the pile was an application for her death certificate that his father had half completed. Strewn about underneath were countless other official documents and bills, most of them unpaid. Letters and notices from several different doctors' offices and the hospital in Stornoway were sewn into the pile, large dollar amounts highlighted in yellow or pink to catch the eye. For the first time since his arrival, Lachlan found himself feeling sorry for his father in the wake of his mother's death. He found it hard to think of his mother as anything other than the callous woman she'd been to him. Even so, she'd been his wife, for better or worse, for far longer than half their lives.

Underneath the legality of death were more pictures of the same woman. Lachlan flipped through handfuls, looking at his mother, studying the liveliness in her eyes which leapt off the paper more than it ever had in life. Near the bottom of the pile was a newspaper clipping with a picture of her standing in an art gallery. The headline read *the biggest thing to hit contemporary art since the color red.* His mother stood underneath the boldfaced headline with her arms crossed and a confident smugness glazed across her face. Surrounding her on the wall were dozens of paintings of all different sizes, encompassing a multitude of different subjects. The smock she wore was covered in paint smudges, and the heads of paintbrushes poked out from the pocket in the front. Lachlan stared at the stranger in the picture, questioning what had happened to her, even though in the back of his mind, he already knew.

The old and faded paper felt more like fabric in his hand as he slipped through the side door to find his father. The garden had always been his refuge from persecution, and now it had just become habit. The sun struggled to break through the blanket of clouds covering the sky. The little pieces of light that were able to break free glinted off the still surface of the water which was otherwise dark with depth. His father turned toward Lachlan with alarm when the door slammed behind him. He'd been alone so long, even his son's presence was easily forgotten.

"What is this?" Lachlan asked, handing his father the faded article. "Why have I never seen this before?"

Lachlan's father took the paper and held it in his hands. A small smile spread across his face. If Lachlan hadn't been there to see it himself, he would not have believed it. His father looked like a different person with the slightest bit of happiness dancing through him. But as quickly as it had appeared, it was gone. He crumbled the paper and dropped it to the ground, letting the wind play with it before Lachlan stomped his foot on top of it to keep it from being carried away.

"It's ancient history," he father answered.

"But it's my history," Lachlan shouted, annoyed with his father's lackluster response.

"Let it be, son," he responded with a voice that sounded a thousand miles. "It doesnae have to do with you."

"It doesnae have to do with me?" Lachlan's voice found strength in the anger he felt towards his unsympathetic father. He'd always been somewhat indifferent towards him, neither loving nor hating him. He knew too little of the man to make an accurate assumption of him. More times than not he'd just felt sorry for him.

"It has everything to do with me!" he yelled. "This is why she hated me; isn't it? She had this amazing life planned, to be somebody, to get off this bloody island; right? And then I came along and ruined everything. Is that it? Is that what happened?"

He could see his father's face trying to hide the truth. The secret life his mother had before his birth had been exposed, and the reason for the hatred Lachlan grew up seeing behind her eyes was exposed. The revulsion in her eyes finally made sense. She'd had an escape plan, but only one ticket. A husband and baby had never been a part of her plan.

His heart raced. He wanted to jump up and down. Scream loud ridiculous obscenities at his father. Shove the truth right in his face, but he knew his father's stone façade wouldn't crack. It never had. She'd worn him down to a shell of a man with little to no emotion left in his body. Lachlan needed a reaction, any reaction, to know that his father was still human.

"So, what happened? Did she blow up into this amazing artist headed for the mainland and you had to think of a way to make her stay behind because you knew you'd never make it anywhere but here?" There was a smugness in Lachlan's voice. It hung the air between the two men like the sea fog that rolled in with the morning, shadowing things until they were right under your nose.

"That's it, isnae it?" he continued. "You had this out of your league woman that you'd somehow managed to score. You knew you'd never do better than her, but she could do better than you in the city by lunchtime. Was that it? You knew if you couldn't get her to stay, you'd lose her forever?"

"Lachlan, you dinnae ken what you're talking about." His father continued his steadfast stare out into the oblivion in front of them, refusing to react to Lachlan's ploy for some type of emotional exchange.

"That's it, isnae it?" The floodgates had been lifted, and Lachlan was intent on putting all their cards on the table. His hands shook at his side and his skin pimpled with fear and anger. There was no reason to hold anything back anymore. It was all or nothing.

"You knocked her up to make her stay. That's what you did, didnae you? You knew she'd keep it if you got her pregnant because what other option would she have? There aren't abortions here. She'd be cast out by the island and left for dead. She'd have to marry you and stay, trapped on this island while her dreams faded away." His whole body was shaking. His cheeks were red, and sweat was beginning to bead just above the surface of his skin. Anger that had been festering for more than half his life was spilling out violently, and he couldn't stop if he'd wanted to.

"Lachlan, stop." There was a forcefulness affixed to his words that Lachlan never remembered hearing, but it was too little too late.

"Why should I? You obviously didnae. Did she ask you to stop? Beg you not to do it? Did she tell you to stop and you didnae listen?

"Stop!" The vigor of his voice stunned Lachlan. He couldn't remember his father ever yelling, even when as a child when it would have been warranted.

"That's it." Lachlan's voice was mocking, almost laughing at the truth between them. "You stole her dream by giving her a child she never wanted. You fucking cursed all of us. Of course, she'd never known how to love me, she never even wanted me." He paused as another revelation passed through the forefront of his mind. "She may have hated me, but she resented you. I can see it now. She always pulled away from you, never wanting you to touch her. I dinnae even have an image of the two of you hugging at any point in my entire childhood? Not even a fucking hug. Nothing! And now I know why."

His father turned his lifeless stare to the ground, rubbing his forehead. Lachlan picked him apart as he looked at him; his balding head and wrinkled skin were just concealing the parts holding a lifetime of lies and half-truths held in the deep recesses of who he was. Lachlan had never known him well enough as a child to justify hating him. He almost wished for the bliss his ignorance had afforded him then.

"How could she love you? You were insufferable to her. She didn't want anything to do with you. And why would she?" Lachlan drew in a long breath to steady himself. "What woman loves a man that rapes her."

It was an explosion. Suddenly the space between the two men disappeared. Hot air rocketed by Lachlan's face and his body was falling. The grass was wet with morning dew and clung to the skin on Lachlan's face as he lay against it, with his father's knee in his chest and hands wrapped tight around the collar of his undershirt. His eyes were wild with anger, but Lachlan could tell it was not meant for him. His father crouched on top of him, but his mind was somewhere else, remembering another instance in which he'd let his rage run free. He'd never known his father's strength and was surprised the old man had any fight left in him. They'd maybe shaken hands half a dozen times in his life, and his grip had been nothing to write home about.

The air was quiet for several minutes before his father spoke again. "I didn't rape my wife." His voice was deep, pulling from a place that had most likely never seen the light of day. "And she didn't hate you," his father offered, removing his knee from Lachlan's chest, holding out a hand to help him to his feet.

Lachlan scrambled up from the ground, swatting the wet grass from his clothes as much as he was his ego at having been bested by a man almost thirty years his senior. Both men breathed heavy, pulling in the fresh air spinning in off the water.

"Son, you have to …" His father's words were desperate and fraught with anguish. His voice shook as he spoke them, and tears welled in the corner of his eyes.

"You know what, dinnae call me that. Not anymore. You had your chance to be my father, but you just …" The two men faced each other like stranger's passing in the night, neither one wanting to do the polite thing and make eye contact with the other. Lachlan could feel the pain of unreturned love welling up in the back of his throat. He opened his mouth several times to try and speak but struggled to push the words past his lips. He turned away from his father, not wanting to show him just how much he'd been affected. He'd managed to tuck his emotions away in deep places for most of his life, but since returning home, they'd found their way out, leaving Lachlan unsure of how to handle such foreignness.

"You just let her hate me," he finally whispered, still unable to meet his father's eyes. Instead, he looked up to the sun as its warmth dripped against his skin. The morning clouds had disappeared, leaving no trace that they'd ever existed. He felt the pain of his life trickle down his cheek and hang at the edge of his chin before wiping it away.

"Maybe you hated me too," he said, before turning and walking away, past the house and down the road, without so much as a look over his shoulder as he went.

Chapter Ten

There was only darkness creeping under the curtain yet, but my eyes had already been open for over an hour. The thud of the clock on the opposite wall taunted me with each second that passed, moving slower and slower as if it meant to torture me. The day hadn't even begun yet, and already it was dragging. It felt like morning would never come.

At the first sign of light, I was at the window craning my neck to see over the boggy moor that separated me from Isla. As the dingy gray color of predawn began to give way to morning, I could see the peaks of the house and the top floor window that I knew belonged to her. I thought about her, laying in a warm bed surrounded by heavy blankets and woolen throws her grandmother had woven for her. She felt safe hidden in their folds, she'd told me. I hadn't been brave enough to ask her what she thought she needed saving from.

I dressed quickly and quietly. I grabbed the thin checkered blanket I'd been hiding under my bed and shoved it in my bag. I glanced out the window again, looking up at the pale blue of the sky, praying that it would stay as clear as it was just then. Visible rays of yellow and orange hurried across their blue background, igniting like a fire set in the sky. My gaze shifted back to the peaks of the white house in the distance, and my thoughts drifted to the meadow hidden in the hills behind Bosta.

I crept downstairs, listening to my father in the kitchen fiddling with the kettle and then the newspaper. He was already dressed in the same monochromatic drab dark blue uniform he always wore, even when there wasn't any work to be done. He turned cautiously when he heard footsteps behind him, hunching like a beaten dog, looking around for my mother.

"She's gone for milk," he said, relaxing as he turned back to the kettle.

I let out an audible sigh of relief and my body's tense posture loosened. I thought I heard my father laugh, but I couldn't be sure. I crossed the kitchen to the cupboard and grabbed a box of cereal, poured a bowl and sat down at the table. I watched my father as he stood at the counter, waiting for his coffee to finish. Except for the hiss of the kettle the room was quiet. The silence screamed between us.

When his coffee was ready, he poured a mug full, and I watched the steam waft into the air above it until he began to stir in a spoonful of fine sugar. The metal spoon clanked rhythmically against the porcelain coffee mug as he stirred. When it was perfect, he placed the spoon in the basin of the sink and took a seat with me at the table. The chair creaked under his fidgeting weight until he was comfortable and took a sip of the dark liquid.

We sat together in the stillness of the room, enjoying the peace my mother's absence afforded us. My mind started to drift towards thoughts of Isla and things boys tend to think when they think about girls. I looked at my father across from me with his arm bent at the elbow holding his coffee parallel with his chin, his eyes staring aimlessly around the kitchen. If there were ever an opportunity for a man to man discussion, this would have been it. The idea of discussing girls with my father triggered anxiety and my body tensed as I tried to finish my cereal. Our eyes met briefly before they darted off in opposite directions and I wondered if the same thought had occurred to him. Thinking that it had made the awkwardness between us thicken and stick like wet cement.

I took a few more bites of cereal, letting the rough crunch of it between my teeth fill the silence. When there wasn't anything left, I drank the little bit of liquid in the bottom of the bowl, trying to swallow my pride along with the milk.

"So," I spit out, pathetically unsure of where I was going after that. My father grunted in response, sipped his coffee, and refusing to meet my eyes, for which I was thankful. It was already awkward enough without having to look at each other.

"I was just curious ... I mean ... there's this ..." I couldn't finish a sentence or thought. I decided it wasn't worth the embarrassment and jumped up from the table in a huff of frustration and placed my empty bowl in the sink.

"What's her name?" He asked before disappearing into his coffee again.

I was hesitant to divulge the details. I didn't want him or my mother to know it was Isla Gilcrest. I'd already been inadvertently warned that I was not to associate with the little Catholic girl, I believed was how my mother put it. Frankly, I didn't see where we got off assuming we were higher or mightier than the anyone else. In my opinion, neither side had it right.

"I guess that's not important," he continued when I didn't respond. "They're all the same, I suppose."

I let out a laugh that disagreed with his assumption that Isla was like the rest. She was nothing like anything I'd ever experienced before. The other girls at school no longer existed in my eyes, their colors had dulled and faded into the background of my vision, rarely making enough noise for me to take notice of them anymore. Isla burned like the sun over the ocean in the morning, crazy and untamed.

"I see," my father whispered. I stood in his spot at the counter, looking out the window to the glasslike surface of the cove. The wind was absent from the morning, and the only ripples on the water came from two Goldeneyes diving and chasing after one another, calling back and forth as they did. I wondered if their pursuit of the fairer sex was more straightforward than ours.

We both jumped as we heard the tires of my father's car crunching over the loose gravel of the driveway. In unison, we met each other's eyes with the same disconcerting look. I had planned to be gone before she returned and not show my face in the house again until just before dinner so there would be no chance of being kept from what the day held for me. I'd squandered my time away thinking about human anatomy questions I honestly knew I didn't need the answers to. My boyish curiosity was going to be the end of any need for answers if I didn't get out of the house before my mother found an asinine reason to squander my Saturday away.

I was stuffing snacks into my backpack and frantically looking for my shoes when he asked, "do you love her?"

His question stopped me in my tracks. I'd been in love with Isla since the second I knew she existed. There was no explaining it to him in a way he would understand. I didn't even understand it. It was like she existed solely for me. I still wasn't confident she felt the same toward me, but I knew there was something different between us.

"Then tell her how you feel. Don't waste it." My father's voice was commanding like he was physically trying to push his words into my ears with force. I heard the door to the car slam shut and could already hear my mother calling out from the carport. I had seconds to get out the side door to freedom, but something held me in the kitchen with my father. Maybe it was the intensity with which he'd spoken, or perhaps it was the realization that for the first time in my life I felt connected to him. I was torn between staying and leaving.

"And protect her with your life," he whispered with a breathy voice as if he'd just run laps around the house and come in for a glass of water. We looked at each other, listening to my mother's key turn in the lock on the other side of the house. In seconds she'd be inside, but I couldn't drop my father's weighty look. There was something in his eyes that said he was speaking from experience, and for a second, I could see past the pain in his eyes to a time when they'd been filled with nothing but happiness.

The door creaked open slowly. It was like a gust of wind blew in and clouded the happiness he'd let me glimpse and then it was gone, clouded over with pain.

"Go," he whispered, jumping up from the table, making unnecessary clatter with the chair as he did to cover the sound of the side door slamming behind me. I could hear her penetrating voice through the walls of the house, slamming cabinets in the kitchen and tossing my empty cereal bowl at my father. I stood in the carport listening for half a second, wondering if I should go back and offer myself up in my father's place. I caught the wind down the small hill and pedaled away from the house. Something told me he wouldn't have wanted me to come back. He'd had his time to protect what he loved. Now it was mine.

***

They were silhouettes leaning into the morning sun, bobbing like buoys at the end of the pier. I hadn't had time in my haste to grab my pole. I was lucky to have made it out with my freedom, and that was enough. The water was still, mirroring the sky and the cliff breaks that lined the coast. Gulls scuttled above, riding the updrafts into the clear sky before diving back down to look for sustenance under the surface. Over their calls, I could hear Arden yelling at the other end of the pier. Not yelling at anyone, just yelling, like the birds above. Just because he could.

"Where's your pole?" he asked when I finally joined them, dropping my bag onto the bench in the middle of the pier before taking a seat next to Euan on the edge. We hung our feet over and kicked the pylons beneath the bridge.

"I didn't have time to grab it," I said. "I was in a rush to get out of the house before my ma found me."

"Here," Arden said, holding a half-smoked cigarette out to me. I shaded my eyes from the midmorning glare coming off the water's surface to look up at Arden above me. His arm was covered in bruises. He turned out of the sun, and I could see matching ones on the underside of his jawline. I'd never been the recipient of one of his brother's vicious uppercuts, but I'd seen him dole them out. He tried to hide the pain under his cockiness, but there was no denying how bad a beating Ross had given him.

"How much longer do you think until Ross lets it go?" I asked, plucking the cigarette from between his fingers. I took a short drag, coughed lightly, and handed it back.

"Does he know it was us?" Euan asked, twisting around toward Arden and shielding his eyes the same as me.

Arden knelt down, inhaling a long drag as he did, inflaming the cherry on the end until it was deep orange in color. "No, he doesn't fucking know it was us. And he better never find out." He exhaled the drag slowly and methodically into Euan's face. Euan never smoked with us. It gave him horrible coughing fits. I only did it because it was something to do. Calum stood in Arden's shadow smoking a cigarette of his own, following quietly in the footsteps of his fearless leader, as always.

"Leave him alone," I said as Euan coughed and spat at the smoke lingering in his face.

"That goes for you too," Arden snapped back, taking another drag. "You'll be in just as much shit as the rest of us if your ma finds out, probably more. He better keep his girlish mouth shut."

"Screw you," Euan whispered under his breath as he reeled his line in. "I don't have a girlish mouth."

"They're big pouty girl lips," Arden laughed. "They'll make your boyfriend very happy one day."

Euan scrambled like a newborn lamb to get to his feet, but it was all for show. He was no match for Arden, and he knew it. He ran at Arden, bumping chests with him like a bunch of apes in the zoo.

"No, you missed," Arden laughed, pushing Euan back a few steps. "My junk's down here." He grabbed and shook himself, laughing in Euan's face.

Euan went after Arden as best he could, but it wasn't close to a fair fight. Arden shoved him one good time, and he nearly went over the flimsy railing into the shallow murk ebbing below us.

"Come on man, that was my good pole," Euan whined as he watched it begin to sink to the bottom of the shallow cove.

"I've got a pole ..."

"Shut up!" I yelled after we'd all had our fill of the pissing contest. "Why are you being such a shit this morning? You should've just sent Ross in your place if that's how it's gonna be."

Arden's stern and taunting grimace melted away at the mention of his brother's name. Arden was what he was, and even if it was something close to being his brother, he hated being called out for it. He hated his brother, but he hated being compared to him more.

"Sorry," he mumbled under his arrogance, offering his hand in apology to Euan, who smacked it away and almost started the who thing over again.

"I got something!" Calum yelled from the other side, sending Arden and I running to investigate.

"It's just seaweed," Euan yelled, already on his belly hanging out over the edge trying to fish his pole out of the water with a net. "Or the bottom."

"No, I really got something this time. It's moving back and forth." Calum tugged at the line for a few more seconds before it snapped, sending he, Arden and I toppling over one another into a pile onto the unforgiving concrete surface of the pier. Euan stood next to us laughing to the point of tears. The sound was infectious, and soon we were all laughing at our own stupidity. Arden rolled and jumped to his feet, offering me his hand. I took it, even though I knew the peace was only as short-lived as his temper.

"What's your problem?" I asked, brushing pier dust from my pants. "It's too early to be so freaking angry."

He didn't answer right away. In his hesitation, I saw a familiar forlorn look, and I knew what was coming.

"God damn Red," he mumbled, somewhat ashamed that his sour attitude was due to a girl, or rather, the lack of a particular girl. I cringed when he called her Red. She said she didn't mind it, but I hated it. It didn't suit her. Her hair wasn't red. It was the color of a fire blazing in the middle of winter, scorching and all-consuming.

"I don't get it," he continued. "After everything I did, she still won't ..." He trailed off. "I mean, she still barely talks to me." There was heartache in his words and guilt in my throat. I swallowed hard, forcing the lump as far down as it would go, but it was still there.

"Maybe she just doesn't like your face," Euan spat from a few feet away. "Ever think about that one?"

"Shut up, Euan! What's not to like?" he asked, but I could already see the self-doubt welling in his eyes as the idea that he might not be all that he thought he was finally occurred to him.

"Did you actually ask her out or did you just dance around it?" Calum asked as he fiddled with the remains of his reel.

"I flat out asked," Arden answered, looking dejected as he flounced around the pier with his hands in his pockets and his heart on his sleeve. He hadn't said anything about asking her out. Not that we told each other everything, but we were best friends. I would have thought something as big as asking out Isla Gilcrest would have come up in conversation. The fact that it hadn't made me question what else he wasn't divulging to me, as if I had room to judge. I was the one keeping the secrets, as far as I knew.

"What did she say?" I asked, needing to know exactly how the exchange had transpired.

"What do you mean? She said no, obviously or I wouldn't be sitting here pissing my heart out to you dobbers now, would I."

"I mean, did she give you a reason why not?" I asked with a tone too confident to have gone unnoticed.

Arden stopped walking the circular path he'd worn into the pier and looked at me with accusatory eyes. Euan and Calum were busy treading hooks and casting off into the shallow water to notice the silent exchange. His eyes dug into me as we stared at each other across the benches. I tried not to look guilty, which proved harder than I would have thought. I dodged his glare, darting my eyes around so he wouldn't see the images of Isla that were looping through my mind.

He jumped onto the bench and sat, straddling the back. He pulled another cigarette from his pocket and placed it between his lips while he fished for the lighter. "Maybe she just didn't like my face," he responded. "What's it to you; you think she'll like yours better?"

"Yours is even worse than Arden's!" Euan laughed from behind us, trying unsuccessfully to solicit a high five from Calum.

"Shut up!" we both yelled, before turning back to each other.

"Maybe you should ask her out," Arden proposed, hopping down from the bench to offer me a drag on his cigarette.

"Nah," I said waving it off.

"What? Are you going to tell us you're not in love with her anymore?" he asked brashly.

I didn't answer. I couldn't. I could keep her a secret from my best friend, from the world, but I couldn't admit that I wasn't in love with her. At least so that it would be believable.

"Milksop," Arden whispered as he jumped back to the benches, laying down and placing his hat over his face as if readying for a nap. "At least I had the bullocks to ask. We'll see if her tune's changed when she comes to thank me for rescuing her from my brother."

He was right. He had had the bullocks to ask her out, regardless of what her response had been. I had never had the nerve to ask her anything, at first. I'd only managed to fall ass-backward into her world, and when I did, she hadn't pushed me out. The secret burned in my throat, but I kept it quiet, just like she'd asked.

***

Arden slept for hours on the stone bench while Euan and Calum and I trawled for nonexistent fish in the cove. The wind stayed silent for most of the morning and the sky cloudless, exposing its pristine blue color we almost never got to enjoy. We were joined at times by men from Crior and Kirkibost who'd come to escape for a few hours and enjoy the sun. They knew better than to waste their time with poles and bait and simply sat on the benches or leaned against the railings staring aimlessly out into the oblivion that surrounded our island. I watched impatiently as the seconds ticked by on my watch, waiting for my time to come.

"Let's catch the bus," Arden yelled abruptly, startling us and several other men in the vicinity. He jumped up from the bench, energized and with a plan already spinning in his mind. I looked at my watch, and with just over two hours until I was due at the bottom on the Tobson footpath, I wasn't going anywhere but there.

"To where?" Euan asked foully.

"I want to do something," Arden started, already gathering the spilled tackle box next to the benches. "It's only like what noon or something. There's plenty of time to catch the bus to Stornoway and hang out and get back before anyone knows we're gone."

"The ferry should be docked for a while before leaving on the evening sail," Calum added. "We could beg my dad for some money."

"I'm not allowed to take to the bus to Stornoway," Euan noted. "And neither are you, Arden."

"Says who?" he asked, even though we all knew the answer. Except for Calum, none of us had been granted the freedom to travel on the island bus to Stornoway on our own. That freedom only came with acceptance at the Nicolson Institute and only because there was no other way to get there from Bernera. Because Calum's father worked in Stornoway on the ferry, his mother often times sent him on the bus by himself to meet his father who would either bring him home later or send him back on the bus.

"I'm not going," Euan professed and moved with his pole further down the pier.

I looked at Arden, panicked that I'd not come up with an explanation for excusing myself from their company when the time came. There was a million reason I could give him, but I knew he'd have a million rebuttals waiting for each one. I needed something that would stick, something that would make him not come looking for me later.

"I can't go either," I finally admitted, still unsure of the reason I was going to put forth.

"Why the hell not? What the fuck else are you going to do?"

"I can't," I repeated, already feeling his resentment.

"Why not?" he asked again, stone-faced, letting me know that no answer would be acceptable.

"I've got an appointment ... with my parents in Shawbost."

"An appointment? What kind of appointment?"

"Can you just let it go. It's just an appointment. Does it really matter what it's for?"

To Arden, it did. He looked at me with incredulous eyes, combing me over like a hunting dog sniffing the air for whatever beast it had been trained to find. Something had changed between us and the trust we'd placed in each other for the whole of our short lives so far was fading like mist on the water when the sun rips through it in the afternoon. Maybe it was puberty or girls or the inevitability that I saw in Arden. The boy he had been was disappearing and being replaced with the spitting image of his older brother. It was hard to continue liking him as I had when I knew what he was becoming.

His glare was relentless, and he wasn't going to let it go. I could see in his eyes that he didn't believe me, and I couldn't blame him. It was a pathetic excuse, but it was the only one I could come up with. I cursed myself internally for not having thought of a better one ahead of time. I needed something better if I'd be escaping more often, which I hoped would be the case.

"It's a doctor's appointment, ok, happy?" I finally offered when he refused to let it go.

"What kind of doctor's appointment?" Calum asked, perpetuating the lie even further. He had a knack for being so quiet you'd forget he was there, only making his presence known at the most inopportune moment.

Arden turned back to me with eyebrows raised, waiting for the answer to Calum's question.

"It's a therapy session, ok, there, are you all happy? Can we move the fuck on now please?"

The excuse had developed into something not half bad. It was personal and plausible enough that it shouldn't have warranted more questioning. It would be reusable.

Therapy usually lasted more than one session. It could be a standing appointment. But still, Arden's stare told me he was not convinced, that he knew deep down it was all a lie.

"What?" I finally yelled with force, pushing back against his disbelief. He shook his head and pursed his lips as if to say *if you say so, but I still don't believe you.*

"What time is the bus, Calum?" Arden yelled, still questioning my loyalty with his eyes.

"Fifteen minutes," Calum yelled back, swinging his bag over his shoulder as he did. "If we hurry, we'll make it."

"You coming, Euan? Or do you have a doctor's appointment too?"

I scoffed at Arden's inability to let it go. Euan rambled on with his overly formal explanation of why he couldn't go with them. We all walked our bikes to the end of the pier in silence, listening to the gulls scream overhead, just as desperate for a catch as we were. When the gray concrete of the pier gave way to the black asphalt of the road, Arden and Calum turned and headed to the covered bus stop a few hundred feet down the road.

"See you girls later," Arden yelled, stealing one last disbelieving look over his shoulder before jumping on his bike and pedaling away.

"He's turning out just like …"

"Don't say it," I yelled back to Euan, stopping him mid-sentence before the words escaped his pouty girl lips. It was one thing to think Arden was turning into Ross, it was another to say it out loud, as if breathing the words into existence would make them real.

"See you later," I exhaled as I jumped on my bike, leaving boyhood concerns behind for ones about a girl waiting for me at Bosta Beach.

I skidded to a stop at the end of the road just before the large boulders that had been placed in the road years ago to prevent people from driving on the beach. The air whipped in off the open ocean, cooling the beach and surrounding area. The tide was as far out as it could be, exposing the rocky bed usually covered by the blue-green water. Black slippery seaweed blanketed the rocks and reflected the sun beating down from above. My eyes darted about the landscape, searching the hillside when I didn't see her waiting on the beach. The only movement I saw was sheep traversing back and forth through the narrow paths up to the top of the outcroppings and two of Mr. MacLeod's cattle meandering about the backside of the beach near the stream that trickled down from the top. I hadn't expected her to leave herself out in the open. We were keeping secrets after all, but I wasn't planning on having to search for her either. Knowing her though, I should have.

I ditched my bike behind the small shed at the cattle fence, knowing the only person who'd see it there would be Mr. MacLeod, if he saw it at all. I walked down the path, the tips of my fingers dragging against the old stone wall enclosing the war memorial cemetery that had been erected just above the beach itself. The stones, which were usually cold and wet, were warm to the touch, having been baking in the sun most of the day. I followed the sandy path past the picnic tables and made my way to the beach. I walked toward the water's edge, dodging small tidal pools and slippery rocks, trying to get a better glimpse of the hidden cove just past a piece of the island that jutted out from the rest. When I got as far as the tide clock and didn't see her, I doubled back and headed into the hills that stretched upwards toward the sky.

Sheep gamboled along the thin rocky ledges. Some gathered inside the shambled walls of an old ruined croft. When they heard me shuffling through the thick grasses, they huddled close together in one of the corners and watched quietly as I passed, swishing their jaws back and forth as they continued to chew the heather at their feet. I stopped to watch them, listening to the soft wind blowing through the valley, when I caught a glimpse of fire burning up above.

"I've got her now," I whispered to the sheep as a scrambled my way up one of the paths they'd carved into the hillside, trying to stay out of sight. I followed the switchbacks working my way up, staying hidden behind the stone protruding from the earth. At the top, I skulked between the rocks, making my way closer and closer toward the wisps of red hair fretting in the wind. I was almost on top of her, and she didn't even know it.

I pounced like a stalking cat jumping out from the shadows, ready to sink my teeth into my prey. "Got you!" I yelled as I leapt up over the formations between us, startling another of Mr. McLeod's cattle, sending both of us scrambling as we screamed. My heart was pounding out of my chest as I watched the auburn-haired beast tramp away, long tufts of reddish fur trailing behind it.

"Silly boy," she whispered as her breath tickled the skin on my neck. I yelped uncontrollably. I spun quickly on the uneven rock and lost my footing, sending the two of us tumbling off the edge in a whirlwind of appendages and tangled mane onto the grass below. When we landed, we were pressed together in ways I knew to be too advanced for our age, but neither of us tried to move right away.

Her eyes sparkled in the sun, calling, the way the ocean cries when it wants the taste of summer flesh. The wind blew through and tangled her wild hair in the long grass. She smiled up at me as I gently brushed specs of dirt from her cheeks. I could have died right there on top of her.

"Sorry," she laughed. "I didn't think I'd scare you that bad."

"You didn't scare me. This was all just part of the plan," I said trying to play off my embarrassment at having confused the cow's fur with her hair, but I wasn't sorry for what had resulted.

"Are you ok?" I asked, realizing that we'd taken quite the tumble together.

She wiggled out from underneath me, brushing off the dirt and grass we'd accumulated in our fall. "I think so," she answered, jumping to her feet. She extended her hand and helped me to my feet but forgot to let go. "Should we go then?" she asked, already leading the way.

"Are we going somewhere specific," I asked, assuming we'd just be hiking through the valley aimlessly before we stopped for the picnic lunch I'd grabbed from the co-op on my way to meet her. She didn't answer me, at least not with words. She looked back at me over her shoulder. Her face was buried in a sea of fire twirling all around us in the wind. Her smile was devilish. I swallowed the lump in my throat, mildly intimidated by the plan she obviously already had in her mind.

We walked hand in hand traversing through the landscape, leaving the marked footpath behind us as we descended from the top of the ridge to the valley floor. The foothills blocked the wind and in its absence the afternoon sun warming us almost to the point of being hot.

"There," she exclaimed, dropping my hand to point at the abandoned croft a few hundred feet in front of us. It sat on the edge of the massive loch that created the divide between Tobson and the other side of Bernera. Had I been inclined to ask what exactly it was we were looking at, it would have been in vain. She was already thirty feet ahead of me, rushing toward the croft. When I caught her, she'd stopped outside the skeleton of the building and was quickly removing her shoes.

"What are you doing?" I asked, watching with confusion.

"We're," she emphasized, "going swimming."

I laughed, assuming she was joking. The sun hadn't warmed me enough to warrant a dip in what I knew would be unsympathetically cold water.

"I didn't bring a suit," I said, as I watched her kick her shoes toward the croft and begin to unbutton her jeans.

"Me either," she said, stripping her jeans off, revealing her solid, pale legs. Next went her thin jacket and then her top, leaving her standing in the middle of the late spring air in nothing but a pair of striped panties and mismatched bra she was just beginning to fill.

She looked at the cold water and then back at me, winking devilishly before tearing off toward the water. I watched in astonishment as I realized that Isla Gilcrest was standing in front of me in nothing but her underwear, while I was standing, like a Nancy, on the shore still fully clothed.

She ran fast and kept going when she hit the water's edge. I had my shoes off and one pant leg when I stopped, struck by utter confusion at what I was seeing. She'd run well past the shallow edge and should have been at least waist deep, but the water barely licked the back of her calves. She ran harder, picking up her knees as high as they would go before she dove headfirst, disappearing under the darkness of the surface almost three-quarters of the way into the loch. Seconds later, her head bobbed up a few more feet further out. Reluctantly, I stripped to my boxers and eased my way to the edge of the water.

"You can't do it like that," she yelled, floating effortlessly on her back. "You just have to run and dive in head first." I wasn't sure if she was referring to the water or to us; it felt like it could have been either. I waved her off, giving the impression that I knew what I was doing in either instance and backed up to give myself enough room for a running start.

The cold stung my feet, and I thought I'd stepped on something spiny in the water, but I kept going. Even though I'd seen Isla only moments before defying gravity and run across the surface of the water, I braced thinking that I was close to running off the edge of the hidden shelf, but it just continued. She got closer and closer, and I ran harder and harder.

"Now!" she yelled, splashing her arms intensely.

I took two more steps and launched myself into the air, streamlining my arms above my head. The water felt like fire as I passed through it. The cold, thick liquid stole my breath, and I burst through the surface gasping, blinded by the sun's glare on the rippling water. When I could finally see again, I was alone in the water.

"Told you," she laughed from behind me. She splashed as I spun to find her, blinding me again and giving her time to swim back to the shelf.

We played like kids half our age, chasing each other, forgetting the feeling of the frigid water as we did. The sun beat down, doing its best to warm us while the sound of our laughter echoed in the valley. I raced her back to the shelf, pretending like I was letting her win when really, I had to concede that she was a much better swimmer than I was.

Her hair was much darker and clung to the skin around the small of her back as she scrambled against the muddy shelf's edge, slipping before her feet caught. I watched as she started running back toward the bank when she suddenly froze. I swam hard, face down in the water, desperate to reach the shelf and finally catch my prize after an afternoon of our cat and mouse game.

When she didn't move at hearing me splash behind her, I knew something was wrong. My playful steps became more purposeful. The afternoon of careless jest melted away in an instant, and I could not get to Isla quick enough.

"What," I whispered when I finally caught up with her, grabbing her shaking hand.

She didn't answer immediately and stared blankly at the hillside behind the croft. "There was a man, up there," she finally replied, pointing to a faint path worn into the grass.

"It's probably just Mr. MacLeod, out to check on the cattle."

"He was just standing there, watching us."

"Did it look like Mr. MacLeod?"

"No," she answered.

The hillside was still. The wind was still. We stood calf-deep in the water, looking and waiting for something to move, but nothing did. The sun shone down on us but being stationary in the cold water began to make our teeth rattle and skin pimple.

"Where does your mom think you are right now?" I asked, realizing how careless we'd been with our secret. Someone had seen us. There would be a price to pay for our recklessness.

"I don't know," she answered quietly.

"Where'd you tell her you were going when you left?"

"She didn't ask." She shivered violently as a wind blew through, rippling the water and our skin. I couldn't help but hope the everydayness of my appearance had enabled me to remain unidentifiable to the stranger watching us as we swam, labeling me as potentially any boy from the island. Isla, however, was recognizable a mile away just by the color of her hair.

"Let's go," I said, grabbing her hand as we started walking as quickly as we could through the water. The enjoyment of the afternoon was lost, replaced by an oddity riding on a new air that had blown in. I held her hand as tight as I thought she would let me, and then she squeezed it harder.

"There!" she whispered loudly. "There, there!" She pointed up to a man perched on the path, his eyes watching us in the same stalking way I'd watch Isla earlier.

His arms hung oddly at his side like they were too long or too heavy for his frame. He didn't move except to sway gently in the breeze. We didn't move either as we stared back at him. There was nothing particularly sinister looking about him, it was just a feeling. Finally, he smiled, a cock-eyed type smile. His lips were unevenly parted to one side of his face. Then he started walking, bobbling peculiarly down the path toward the croft, toward us.

She tried to stop, but my legs started moving faster, dragging her behind me. I felt an uncontrollable need to get to my backpack, to our clothes, to the only possessions we had in the world before the strange man on the path made it to level ground. It wasn't Mr. McLeod like I had hoped. The man was a stranger in a place where everyone knew each other by first name. Even from several hundred feet away, I could smell the stench of sin on him.

We made it to the bank and Isla dropped my hand, pumping her arms faster without it, perhaps having felt the same thing I had. We dove into the shadow of the old croft and lost sight of the man in the pitch of the hillside. I grabbed my bag while Isla grabbed our shoes and clothes. We stood like statues, waiting, listening for the man to come running around the front corner. When he didn't appear, the fear grew stronger. Without looking away, I reached into my bag for the blanket I'd packed and handed it back to Isla as she passes me our clothes. Once she'd wrapped herself in it, I pulled her close behind me, holding my arm around her in a protective fashion, my father's words running through my head; *protect her with your life.*

"Put your shoes on," I whispered back to her, thinking we'd take our chances and make a run for it. I could hear her rustling in the grass behind me, slipping on one shoe, and then the other.

"Here," she whispered, poking my side with my own shoes. "Where'd he go?" she asked, pressing herself against my back. I could feel shivers through the blanket. I wanted to think it was from being cold, but I could feel my own body shaking, and the cold of the water had long since faded.

"I don't know," I answered, inching forward slightly. "Can you run?"

"Faster than you," she answered, putting a smile on my face despite the irrational fear that was ravishing us. There was no explaining it, other than saying there was evil in the air. The sun disappeared. Birds stopped calling. The distant cries of sheep up above faded, like even nature was afraid of him.

"When I say so, run," I instructed. She didn't respond, but I knew she would be ready.

I inched forward again, quietly, listening to the way the wind moved through the grass. We pressed our backs against the stone wall of the croft, waiting. When I reached the corner, we stopped, and my heart almost leapt out of my chest. I didn't want to round the corner, but I knew I had to. I pressed myself firmly against the cold stone, closed my eyes, and took several deep breaths. I felt her fingers weave into mine and my heart beat began to both slow and quicken.

I let go of her hand, not wanting to drag her with me toward whatever was waiting on the other side of the croft. I opened my eyes and swung my body around the stones, making loud, ominous grunting noises as I did, but there was nothing there.

I turned back to Isla with a dumbfounded look on my face. Whoever he was, he wasn't waiting for us on the blind side of the croft as I'd expected. He'd vanished in the wind that was blowing gently through the grasses around our feet.

"Let's go," I said, but her feet were already moving, dashing through the rocks and boggy spots ten feet ahead of me. She'd tied the blanket around her otherwise exposed body like a toga, and it, along with her partially dried hair sailed in the rush of air trailing behind her. I focused on her, not wanting to look back, trying to leave the sickening feeling in the pit of my stomach behind me.

We were almost back to Bosta when she finally stopped, collapsing against a small outcropping as she panted heavily. I stopped just short of the rocks with my hands clasped tight on my knees trying to force air into my burning lungs.

"What was that?" she finally asked. "Where did he go?"

I didn't want to answer her and give truth to what had just happened. The feeling of nervous trepidation was still there, pumping heavily just under my skin. I wanted to vomit the feeling out of my stomach, but when I tried, nothing came out.

I pulled my bag from my back, realizing that we were both still only in our underwear. I started rummaging through handing Isla pieces of her outfit little by little. We dressed awkwardly in front of each other, not willing to separate and dash behind a nearby boulder to find privacy. I wanted to enjoy what should have been a momentous occasion in my life, in any young boy's life, but I was riddled with a fear too paramount to even speak, much less conjure any type of enjoyment from the moment.

Clouds began rolling in off the open water. Without the sun the air turned cool, and the sky grayed overhead. Our wet underwear bled through our clothes, casting shadows of the day in certain places. When we were both dressed, I turned back toward the loch. The absence of the sun's glare on the water made it look dull and deep. It lacked any of the flirtatious qualities it had possessed only an hour ago. I couldn't believe we'd been brave enough to swim in the same water.

We turned to go, but a swift breeze swept an unfamiliar sound through the valley and up to where we were perched. The still top of the water's surface broke viciously as the beast pawed at the edge of the shelf. Its skin was the same dark color as the water. It kicked and bucked violently, trying to throw an unseen rider, letting out a scream that boomed like thunder. I didn't know if Isla saw it or not. When I turned, she was already halfway down the last peak to Bosta, begging for the yellow sand of the beach to be underfoot, instead of the evil that we'd stumbled upon.

Chapter Eleven

Ghosts were following Lachlan, taunting him with every step he took. He'd hoped that the distance between him and his childhood would lessen the sting of reality, but the wounds were festering with each forgotten memory he'd found since returning to Lewis. He kicked at stones lying in the road as he made his way away from his father's house, trying to leave the truth of his mother's hatred and his father's lies behind him.

A horn blared, sending sheep scrambling from their perches. Lachlan moved to the side of the road. The horn blasted again. He stepped into the grass to make room for the vehicle to pass. The shriek of the horn came a third time, pulsing in Lachlan's blood as it rang through the air. He turned, the middle finger on his left hand already extended and raised in the air as he did.

"What the hell, man, get out of the bloody road," Euan yelled, trying to hold back laughter as he screamed at Lachlan from his car. "If you're not careful, you'll end up like that one over there." He pointed to a sheep carcass lying just off the road about a hundred feet up from them.

"What the hell are you doing anyway?" Lachlan asked, shielding his eyes from the sun.

"Looking for you," he answered, half hanging out of the car window.

"What'd you want?"

"What?"

Lachlan rubbed his face, already tired of the trivial niceties of the conversation. "You said you were looking for me. What'd you want?"

"Right, right," he said, hesitant to say more.

"What man, what? Spit it the fuck out already!"

Euan looked around like he expected someone to be hiding in the miles of open expanse that surrounded them. Lachlan humored his friend and spun in a circle looking for the mysterious person or persons Euan expected might be listening in on their apparent top-secret conversation.

"There's no one here Euan!" Lachlan yelled, holding his arms out at his sides to further foster his point. "There's never anyone here!" He bent down and grabbed a handful of pebbles, launching them into the still air. "It's just damn sheep and rocks, and God damn peat and the smell of shit." Lachlan was flat out yelling now, but not at Euan. Just yelling to yell, because he could and no one but Euan would hear him. "This God damn place," he gasped, searching for breath. "This damn island…"

"I know, man," Euan agreed. "I know."

Euan slid back inside the car and reached across the seat, pushing the passenger door open from the inside. Lachlan looked at the world around him; the muted landscape, the distant islands rising out of the sea covered with haze, the sun sparkling like diamonds on the still water. He wondered how something so beautiful could have been so cruel to him. The island had stolen his childhood; all their childhoods. He couldn't help but feel like it might not be done with them yet.

The men rode with the windows down for the few minutes it took to get to Euan's house in Kirkibost. The wind whistled in the air as they thought about their version of life and what Lewis had both taken and given to each of them. Euan pulled into the drive of a familiar house before cutting off the engine. Lachlan remembered it, but as one of the crofts Euan's family managed for someone much wealthier than most of them. Euan had done well for himself, and it showed in the smug grin on his face.

"Wait," Lachlan gasped as Euan opened his door and swung a leg out.

"What?"

"I need to ask you something."

"Ok."

Lachlan sat motionless for a moment, trying to gather his thoughts. He could see the questions drifting in his mind. It was the answers he was afraid of that made him hesitant to ask.

"What was it, with her and Ross?" Having to put the two of them together in a sentence was painful and dried Lachlan's throat, the thought of them together strangling him from the inside out.

Euan sighed, unsure of how to answer the loaded question. "I really think you should talk to her about it, not me."

"Just tell me," Lachlan pled.

"It just happened. One second they were and then they weren't. Don't think too much into it. It's not what you're picturing in your head."

Lachlan was sure there had been others, but the idea of her and Ross irked him in his depths. Maybe it wasn't Ross that bothered him. Maybe it was the idea that she'd love him, or anyone, the way he loved her still.

"Why?" he finally asked.

"Why what?"

"Why him?"

"I don't know," Euan answered uncomfortable answering for a woman he knew could inflict severe damage on him. "I think ..." he trailed off in thought.

"What?"

"I think they were both lonely and somehow they just found comfort in each other's loneliness."

"Why was she lonely?"

Euan rubbed his hand against the scruff poking through his cheeks, producing a scratching sound as he did. "She wasn't the same, after everything, after you were gone. I don't really know. I think we were all different, after." He paused before admitting the rest of the truth.

"Even Ross was different. I think he'd realized that he'd been a horrible older brother and decided to try and change. He's not the same person you remember. At least not completely."

Lachlan twitched uncomfortably in his seat, his hand against his chest, feeling like someone had a hold of his heart and was squeezing it tight before letting it go so he could breathe before compressing it again. It pained him, but at the same time, he found contentment in knowing that Isla had been lost without him, just as he had been lost without her.

"I want to show you something," Euan said, tearing out of the car to avoid any further conversation.

The house was quiet and smelled of lavender. Dolls and puppies and other stuffed animals dominated the front room. Backpacks and little pink waterproofs hung on the hooks next to Euan's uniform jacket. A family of four's boots from biggest to smallest sat underneath the hooks. It was a scene out of a magazine for women and soon-to-be mothers. Lachlan wanted to laugh at the absurdity of Euan playing house, but it was more than any accomplishment he'd made in his own life. The laughter would have been a cover, and Euan would have seen right through it.

They dropped their shoes in the make-shift mud room, and Lachlan followed Euan down a hallway toward the back of the house. As they walked, he could hear little voices in one of the rooms, laughing behind closed doors. They left the airiness of the house behind for the dark and dank room at the end of the hallway. The stale smell of beer wafted in the air as Euan quickly closed the door behind them. A television balanced on a small stand in the corner opposite an old and tattered corduroy sofa. It reminded Lachlan of his flat in Dundee and of the life he'd been living only days ago. He'd almost forgotten it even existed, as Lewis worked to swallow him whole.

"Nice room," he laughed.

"Yeah, it's pretty sweet. Got it all to myself. The girls aren't allowed in here, not even Sarah."

"Yeah, I can tell."

Lachlan roamed around the room as Euan moved to the desk behind the door and started shuffling through papers. On the bookshelf were pictures of Euan's life; graduation from the academy in Stornoway, a wedding picture, his girls as infants. Lachlan couldn't help but envy the life he was looking at. Euan had come out on the other side of everything and moved on and made something of himself. He wanted to ask how he'd done it; how he'd let it go like nothing had happened. It wasn't the kind of thing you could ask any more than it was the kind of thing he could have answered. He found himself jealous of Euan for the first time in his life.

"Are you happy?" Lachlan asked, holding the wedding picture in his hand.

Euan crossed the room and took the picture from Lachlan and looked at it with doting eyes.

"I can't imagine my life without any of them. It's like, before I was holding my breath, and now, I can breathe."

"How old are your girls?" Lachlan picked up a picture of Euan holding an infant while Sarah slept in the background.

"Nora's almost eight, and Annabel is five."

Lachlan looked at the smile on his friend's face in the picture, his eyes looking down on the person he'd created and brought into this world. His eyes were bloodshot and dark circles spilled out underneath them, but he looked like the happiest man on the planet as he held his daughter for the first time. He placed the picture back on the shelf wondering what his own mother's eyes had looked like when she held him for the first time.

Lachlan patted his friend on the back. "You've done well for yourself, Euan. I'm happy for you."

Euan smiled proudly, trying not to boast. "Come here, I want to show you something."

On the desk were stacks of papers and piles of notebooks. Euan pushed the piles to the edges of the flimsy table, exposing faded maps of Lewis underneath. Euan stood back once he'd cleared the table so Lachlan could take it in.

Notes had been scribbled in the margins and out over the empty blue spaces of the Minch and the Atlantic. Arrows with lines leading back out to the notes crisscrossed over the island and each other making it almost impossible to connect one to the other. Lachlan leaned against the table which began to rock under his weight. Familiar names jumped out, circled in thick marker. He followed the lines leading to corresponding notes and found Arden's name drifting like a ghost in the blue of the map.

Lachlan stepped back from the table without taking his eyes off the map. "What is all this?" he asked, trying to rub the disbelief of it from his expression.

"It's … well … it's something I've been working on, for a while." Euan gulped audibly, realizing he'd not completely thought out his explanation. He stepped toward the table placing his hands against the map. "All these," he began, sliding his hand over the smooth paper, "are missing kids, like Arden."

"Arden's not missing, Euan, he's dead." Lachlan professed, turning his back on everything Euan was trying to show him.

"Yeah, I know," he whispered, turning inward and falling back into his old habit of self-doubt. "I didn't mean … I've done a lot of research, put in a lot of time combing through records and files and statements."

"Euan, I dunnae know where you're going with this, but in case it's where I think it's going, please, just fuckin' stop."

"But, you should see this. You need to see this. There's ..."

"See what? Eh? See what? I was there, remember." Lachlan's voice grew louder the longer he talked. "There's nothing for me to see. I saw it all that night. I saw him stumble away toward the water. I saw him go under. There's nothing else to see." Lachlan's words shook with guilt and pain as he spoke, unsure of which had a tighter grip.

Euan stood with his back to Lachlan, staring down at the map. "That's not what you told the police. I've read the reports."

"I was twelve years old! My best friend was missing, and everyone thought I killed him. My brain was freakin' scrambled. It wasn't real, Euan." He wouldn't say it outright, but he was begging his friend not to force him to relive that night. He'd already done it a thousand times.

"If you look at this though, just look at it with me and you'll ..."

"No, man. No. This is insanity. Have you lost it?" Lachlan was pacing back and forth across the room, panicked at the idea of facing the lie he'd made up twenty years ago. "How can you stand here and look me in the eye and tell me you believe any of it? You're a damn cop for God's sake. It wasn't bloody real. I made it up."

Euan reached for the stack of papers flipping frantically back and forth through looking for something specific as he mumbled censored obscenities to himself quietly. Pages began falling on the floor in his haste. When he didn't stop to pick them up, Lachlan knelt to gather them and was startled when he found a familiar face staring back at him.

He was already engrossed in the article and barely heard Euan as he droned on at a high rate of speed. His voice was distant and then disappeared altogether, and he was alone in the room with the picture of a ghost. She was much younger and not so thin or pale as he remembered. Her hair was dark and longer, resting just above her shoulders. The life in her eyes and the small smile on her face made her seem made-up, like she was a doll created from someone's imagination, but there was no question as to her identity. It was Moira staring back at him.

"No, man," he heard Euan say as he reached to grab the paper from him. "The other side."

Lachlan turned quickly, dashing the paper just out of Euan's reach. When he was finally able to pull his eyes away from Moira's picture, they leapt to the headline; *search called off for local woman's attacker after months and no leads*. The life in Moira's eyes began to drain the more Lachlan read. She'd been walking home from a get-together with girlfriends on a Thursday night when she had been grabbed from the street, blindfolded and taken somewhere. The whole thing happened so fast that she never even saw the man who grabbed her and had been unable to give any type of physical description to the police. He held her for six days and tortured her, never removing her blindfold. When it was finally over, she was left in a dirty horse trailer in the middle of a field. She'd been left unbound and naked, forced to find help while being humiliated in the process. No one was ever caught or even held for longer than an hour for questioning.

"Who is she?" Euan asked, having sidled up next to Lachlan to see what had so profoundly grabbed his attention.

"Why do you have this?" Lachlan asked, ignoring the question entirely, paralyzed by Moira's beyond-the-grave stare.

Euan stood next to Lachlan, reading the article over his shoulder, furrowing his brow as he tried to make sense of where the article had come from.

"I dunnae know," he finally admitted, continuing to read. "I bet it was just something I grabbed accidentally.

See look, here." He pointed about three-quarters of the way down the page where it described that the attack had taken place just outside of Inverness. "See, it's just a mistake, this wasn't even anything from Lewis. This is what I was trying to show you," he said, placing another clipping over top of Moira's picture.

It was an unfamiliar face staring out at him. A woman, not unattractive but obviously caught in the middle of something that didn't warrant time for makeup or even the brushing of her hair it seemed. Even though Lachlan had no idea who the woman was starting out at him, her eyes looked familiar. Sad and distraught, adrift somewhere other than where they were. The picture was tagged with a headline that read *Angus Campbell found dead, Kieran Campbell missing, presumed dead.*

Lachlan skimmed the article quickly, searching for the reason Euan had insisted he read it. It wasn't unlike any other story you'd expect to follow the ominous headline. The woman in the picture was Gretchen Campbell, the wife, and mother to the two dead men. The husband had been found not far from their home, in the hills where their sheep grazed. He had been severely beaten but at the time the article was printed, the cause of death had yet to be determined. The boy, who had been in the hills with his father tending the sheep that morning, had vanished and was presumed dead due to preexisting health conditions. Whatever had overpowered the father was most certainly no match for a boy of sixteen with a limp.

"Do you know who that is?" Euan asked.

"Should I?"

"I think she's the old woman we found in the hills, as kids. I know she is."

The feeling of panic set in, grabbing hold of his lungs, squeezing them tighter until he felt dizzy. At first, she looked nothing like the women they'd seen in the hills, but the longer Lachlan studied her, the more pieces of her he found. Her eyes were just as he remembered them; wide and glossed with a pain he hadn't understood at the time. Lachlan's arm began to burn like it had when she had ahold of him and things he'd done well to forget bubbled over.

"Beware of the water's edge," he whispered almost incoherently. "That's where he waits for you."

The ghostly sensation of restraints grabbed ahold of his wrists and wouldn't let go. A mechanical buzz hummed quietly in his ear until it zapped like a bug catcher in summer but with the intensity of a lightning strike. He gasped for air as his head sunk below the surface of reality, unsure which way was up, what was real, what the truth was, what it had been all along.

"Who is she?" Euan asked, crouching to look at Moira's picture on the other side, utterly unaware of the panic attack ripping through his friend.

"She was at Inverness with me," Lachlan answered in a shallow voice, pulling himself back from the edge to a reality that felt spliced and poorly patched back together. "She killed herself while I was there."

Euan shuffled uncomfortably, clearing his throat when he couldn't think of what to say.

"She ..." Lachlan tried to think of how to put her into words for Euan but couldn't come up with the right combination to do her justice, so he let the moment pass.

A woman's voice called from down the hall, pulling both men from the trancelike episode they'd fallen into. Euan began shuffling papers around on the table, trying to gather them into a pile before throwing them into folders he'd discarded onto the floor. Lachlan watched, still shaken. The voice grew louder and was accompanied by smaller, shriller voices following behind it. Lachlan watched as Euan desperately rushed to hide the project he'd kept hidden from his wife.

"Euan!" the voice called again.

"Shit," Euan whispered, shoving the last of the papers into a brown folder and placing it back on the shelf behind him. He gave Lachlan a don't ask look before pulling an old sports magazine from the shelf and tossing it at Lachlan. As he did, several other books spilled onto the ground, one with a familiar blue cover and fanciful golden script. He remembered the book from his childhood and the scary stories used to instill good morals in children when the fear of God and lashings had failed. But the stories weren't what made him fear the book.

"Euan McKenzie, what on God's green earth did you track in on the floor and where ..." The noise coming out of Sarah Campbell's, now Sarah McKenzie's, mouth stopped the second she flung the flimsy door open and saw the stranger standing in front of her. The little girl who followed quickly behind her mother shared the same reaction and instantly gravitated toward her mother, who wrapped her arm tightly around the girl's shoulder.

"Sorry," she coughed. "I didn't realize you had anyone ... I mean, someone." Her words were short and jumpy. "Shit, Lachlan, is that you?"

"Mommy, that's a bad word," the little girl squealed.

"Go find your sister," Sarah said, pushing the girl out of the room without breaking her stare with Lachlan.

"Sarah Campbell," he said, "or I guess it's Sarah McKenzie now."

"I never thought we'd be seeing the likes of you again."

There was a tone in her voice, leaving Lachlan to wonder if she'd wished it had stayed that way. The ends of her lips turned up in a way that made her smile look mad, like she wanted you to know that it was being forced. Her eyes fluttered between the two men and to the table behind her husband, probing for clues of what the two had been doing behind the closed door.

"Lachlan's managed to become a teacher." Euan's words were as forced as his wife's smile. He could see she wanted to laugh at what she assumed was a joke but knew better than to let it out.

"Is that so," she answered, barely moving her lips as she did. "Euan, can I see you in the kitchen, please. Nora needs ... can I just see you please."

She gave Lachlan one last look and backed out of the room awkwardly, refusing to let go of him with her eyes. He looked at Euan, whose face was red with embarrassment and emasculation. He shrugged his shoulders as he pushed past to follow the keeper of his balls down the hall to the kitchen.

"I'll be right back," he whispered as he went.

"Sure."

Lachlan tossed the magazine Euan had forced into his hand onto the small sofa and watched it gently bounce. He looked back at the books that had fallen on the floor, craning his neck to read the titles without bending down and pick them up.

"Daddy said he needed to borrow them for his big work project." The little girl from before was standing in the doorframe when Lachlan looked up. She was the spitting image of her father, but with long blonde hair. The glasses she wore were too big for her face, just like Euan's had always been. She was past the age a child would be considered cute and instead was awkward and stiff, uncomfortable in her own skin.

"What big project is that?" Lachlan asked.

"It's a secret," she whispered, cupping her hand against the side of her mouth.

"A secret about fairy tales?" He asked, kicking the edge of one of the books with his foot. "You must be an expert then." The age of the girl didn't matter, Lachlan knew how to get what he needed from the opposite sex at any age.

"I guess you could say that." The girl took a few steps into the room and looked at the books on the floor. Lachlan could see her hesitation to get too close to a stranger, but she wanted the praise to continue.

"I'm Lachlan," he said, holding out his hand. "I'm a friend of your parents, from when we were about your age probably."

"I'm Nora. My birthday's in a couple months, and I'll be eight."

"Well, I hope you have a happy birthday, Nora. Maybe I could send you something. Do you need anything else to help your dad with his secret project?"

"No," she answered, skipping past him into the room to retrieve the books from the floor. Lachlan stood next to her as she began to flip through them. "I think we're all set. I've told daddy the whole story, made sure not to leave anything out. He said I'd make a great police lady when I get bigger."

"I bet you would." Lachlan cooed, watching as she flipped through the pages, pictures of all the stories he remembered reading as a child skipping in front of him. "What story was your dad most interested in."

"That's easy. The kelpie," the girl answered quickly.

"Why that one?"

The little girl hesitated, flipping the pages slowly as she looked at Lachlan out of the side of her eye.

"I won't tell anyone," he whispered, kneeling down to her level. "It'll be our secret."

"Well … I think he wants to catch one, or something."

Lachlan held back a burst of laughter, biting his tongue so as not to lose the girl's confidence.

"But kelpies aren't real. They're just stories. So how would he catch one?"

"He said someone's seen one." The girl's voice shook as she answered him. She'd found the story in the book, and her fingers traced the image of the water horse on the page. Its eyes burned like fire and steam rushed from its nose. She looked at the illustration like it might leap from the page and into the room itself.

"Who's seen one?" Lachlan asked.

She turned her eyes from the book to Lachlan. "You," she answered, before running out of the room to her mother calling her from down the hall.

Chapter Twelve

My heart raced as I ran down the hallway. The sound of my shoes smacking against the tile floor echoed through the emptiness around me. My breath came faster and faster. I felt like I'd swallowed a balloon and it was expanding in my lungs. My mouth and lips were dry as dust, but I couldn't stop. The news of room inspections was already minutes old by the time I'd overheard the whispers in the mess hall. The orderlies could have been anywhere. I didn't care if they tossed my room. There was barely anything in it for them to go through, except for the book taped to the underside of the toilet tank. I prayed I hadn't been careless when I replaced it in its hiding place the night before. The book was all I had left in the world.

The door to my room was open when I rounded the corner, and I knew I was too late. I could hear orderlies mucking through my cabinets, talking to each other about something one on of them had watched on television the night before. Patients were not allowed in rooms during inspections; too many fights and near stabbings of orderlies. I stood outside the door, panting for air until I heard the door to the bathroom creek open. I felt my stomach jump and knew I had to do something.

Their faces were plastered with shock when I barged into the room holding my stomach, doubled over in fabricated pain.

"You can't be in here," one yelled. "Wait outside."

"I'm gonna be sick," I cried, trying to look as pitiful as possible.

The orderly moved toward me with his arm outstretched to escort me back into the hallway while his partner continued with his search of my room. He pushed the bathroom door all the way open and flicked the light on. The yellow glow covered the room, and I could hear its rhythmic hum from where I stood. I was being pushed out of the room as I watched him begin to lift the top of the tank off the toilet.

I push my finger to the back of my throat and felt my stomach heave one good time. I held it back as best I could, ducking under the arm of the orderly escorting me and made for the bathroom. My hand was pressed firmly against my mouth until it dropped to my side as I passed through the bathroom doorway, vomiting my barely digested lunch all over the second orderly. He twisted at the waist with the top firmly between his hands, resembling someone preparing to take one good whack at a golf ball. Horror covered his face when he looked down at the front of his uniform which was now covered in greens and the catch of the day. I relaxed when I saw the underside of the top facing inward toward the shower, secreting the plastic wrapped book taped to its underside. I heaved two more times, partially onto his shoes, but mostly into the toilet before it stopped.

"You've got to be fuckin' kidding me," he finally yelled when I stood up to face him, vomit still running down my chin.

"I told you I was going to be sick." I held my stomach and made like I might heave again, hoping he'd want nothing more than to remove himself from the line of fire. When I covered my mouth again, he slammed the top against the back of the tank and pushed past me holding his hands in the air. I kicked the door closed with my foot and made noises like I might be dying while I shimmied the top back in its place. The book wasn't safe anymore. It was only a matter of time before they found it.

"I hear you were sick yesterday," Dr. Rutherford noted as he lit a cigarette. "Threw up all over one of the orderlies, did you?"

I looked at him as he fidgeted on the other side of the desk. I rarely spoke during our appointments. It felt pedantic. He was never going to believe me. After Moira, it felt like no one would. Dr. Rutherford watched me through his rounded glass, trying to read my silence. I knew he believed me to be the one in the room with Moira, but he'd not been able to prove it. It didn't really matter anyway. She was gone, leaving me with more questions than answers.

"Are we going to do any talking today?" the doctor asked.

"What do you want to talk about?" I asked.

"I would like to talk about your progress," he answered with a sly smile. "Or rather, your lack of progress."

He got up from his chair and strolled slowly to the window behind him looking down to the garden below. The trees in the courtyard brushed their branches against the glass. Summer was all but gone. Soon the trees would drop their remaining leaves and be nothing more than skeletal remains of what they had once been, just like those of us inside.

"It's been four months now, Lachlan," he started with his back turned toward me. "Typically, we like to see some sort of development past the coping mechanism in the first three months or so. By that time, the shock of most situations has worn off, and the sane come back to life while the rest..." His voice trailed off as he twirled the hand holding his cigarette in a circular motion near his face. "Well, we don't have to go there just yet." I could tell he wanted to though. He didn't care if anyone recovered or what the truth was. None of that seemed to matter to good old Dr. Rutherford in the long run.

He turned and smiled at me. His eyes were wide, overly expressive. The glasses he wore magnified their peculiarity, making it hard to hold his stare without feeling like you were being emotionally undressed. He sashayed from behind his desk toward me, picking up trinkets from the shelves and putting them back as he walked.

"Here's where we are then." He was standing behind me now, awkwardly close to my chair so that his manhood pressed gingerly between my shoulder blades. "I've written to your parents to let them know that I've not seen as much improvement as I would have expected."

"My parents don't care about me," I whispered, standing and moving my chair a hair forward to get out from underneath his stance. I could see the handle of his brass letter opener shoved under a pile of unopened mail at the corner of his desk. I'd heard the rumors, but I wasn't sure what his game was; if he asked for certain favors from certain patients in lieu of punishment or as payment for extra drugs. Moira had known him well enough to know his first name. There was something personal in the way she'd said his name, something unforgiving. I wondered if I would be able to grab the opener and stab him if it came to that. I wondered if I'd be looked at differently after killing a second time when everyone already thinks you did it once.

"That may be true," he responded, strutting back around to the front of his desk. "They may not care about you, but I'm still required by law to ask their permission since you are still a minor. It's just the formality of it all."

He sat back in his chair and placed his hands behind his head in a relaxed posture. His cigarette clung to his lip as he spoke. His smile made it difficult to understand him without straining to listen.

"I've given you a month to show progress before we implement more, result-oriented methods," he said.

I wanted to laugh, but for the first time in the months since my arrival, I felt fear and self-doubt creeping in. I forced a smile to show I wasn't afraid of his threat, but I knew it was only a matter of time.

I left Dr. Rutherford's office less concerned about my future than I was about that of the little blue book. I'd become obsessed with it. Moira thought its message was real enough to die for. That deserved my respect in and of itself, even if I'd not made any sense of how she'd come to know words spoken to me in secret or their significance to the truth. Sense or not, the book wasn't safe inside the walls of the asylum anymore, and I had to get it out.

***

Days fluttered by, and I had yet to devise a plan to get the book to safety. Patients were allowed to send packages, but only after they were thoroughly searched, and every letter read, looking for accusatory truths of what was really happening inside the walls of Inverness District. The warmth of summer was almost gone, but on sunny days, I spent the afternoons in the garden soaking up the last of the sun's rays. I knew the dreary days of winter were coming and so did everyone else. The loss of warmth had already sent several patients into unrecoverable spirals. Two had been sent out for specialized treatments and had not returned. I tried not to think about them as I sat in the last of the summer, watching the birds jump from branch to branch, singing to each other in the rustling of the wind.

I'd almost given up hope when I watched the royal post truck pull onto the grounds while I sat in the courtyard. It was simple and stupid at best, but there was no other way to get the book out without the orderlies seeing what it was and taking it straight to Dr. Rutherford. I watched the mail carrier open the back of the truck and gather the day's delivery before closing the hatch and walking through the courtyard to the front doors.

I watched the rest of the week. Each day it was the same truck, the same carrier at roughly the same time. The route ran like clockwork. At first, I thought I could befriend the driver and perhaps persuade him to take my package as my last will and testament. It might work. Maybe he would feel sorry for me and see it as his good deed for the day. But he could become curious and open it himself. It wouldn't serve him any purpose, but I wasn't willing to take that risk. He was always in a hurry to get in and out in as little time as possible, leaving me a short window to sneak the book into the back of the truck with the mail he'd already have collected. I only needed seconds. I watched for a few more days and then decided there was no other way.

From the mess hall, I liberated a few pieces of the brown packing paper and string the butcher used to pack meat. It made a crinkling noise in the back of my pants as I walked to my room. I laid in bed thinking about the only person in the world I could trust with the book. She was caught in the middle of everything, even if she didn't realize it. I imagined her sitting next to me like she had in the hills behind Bosta. I closed my eyes and tried to find her face, but it was blurry and hidden behind her wild hair. I reached out to touch her, but she was already gone.

When the sky was as dark as it was going to get, I skulked from my bed to the bathroom and shut the door. I took the book from its hiding place and held it in my hand, unsure of what to do with it on our last night together. Part of me wanted to get it wrapped and re-hidden before there was any chance for it to be found. But another part of me wanted to hold it in my hands for as long as possible.

The cover was soft and worn through in places, especially along the spine. I crouched down on the bathroom floor under the pulsing yellow light and traced the golden letters with my fingers. I opened the book and let the pages dance together in the air, tilting it ever so slightly in either direction to make them move. When I'd had my fun, I let the pages fall open to the place where the spine was creased from having been held open too many times.

My hands rested on the worn-out pages, tracing the handwritten words scribbled deep into the pages overtop of the print of the story. *Pay the price* repeated over and over for pages. The letters were more profound in some places than they were in others, bleeding over to other pages. I flipped to the page where the repetition stopped and where the handwritten story scribbled in the margins began.

I thought about Moira and the way her eyes looked right before I lost sight of her. I thought about how the blood from her feet continued to drip down the wall for several minutes after she was gone. I let my tears drip quietly onto the pages of the book as I looked down at the words. The things she'd scribbled in the book were secrets I thought were only mine, but somehow Moira had known them as her own.

I thought about Arden, and the look on his face before he disappeared; the way his hand sank into the flesh of the beast in front of him; the way I tried to warn him. The old woman's words of caution whirled in my mind. Had I been a better friend, I wondered in Arden would have listened to me about what the animal was or what it was there for, but that only lead me to the thought that if I'd been a better friend, we probably wouldn't have been in that valley that night, and Arden would still be alive.

I thought about Isla the most; what she'd think when she opened the book and saw handwritten words scribbled in the story. I'd never even had the chance to say goodbye to her before they'd ushered me off the island. My heart sank into the cold peeling linoleum floor underneath me, knowing that I'd lost her just when I almost had her.

I closed the book, but it didn't matter, I could still see everything; the old woman, Moira, Arden, Isla, even my parents. They were ghosts; each leaving me with a different haunting look in their eyes I felt might never go away. I tried not to close my eyes. The images were always worse in the dark.

***

"One more time, Mr. McGinley. Tell me what happened the last night you saw him." Doctor Rutherford's back was to me as he spoke. He stood in front of the large bay window behind his desk looking out to the grounds below. The trees were holding onto the last of their leaves as I held onto the last of my sanity. "What happened to your friend, Arden Scott?"

"We were fighting," I said, just as tired of telling him the story as he was of hearing it.

"Why?"

Every time he asked that question, I found a different image of Isla in my mind. Sometimes it was as simple as her smile. Other times I could see her laying in a field, her hair laying in the wet grass, her deep, penetrating eyes staring up at me. Each time though, it felt like I was losing more and more detail. She was becoming fuzzy and felt like a ghost. I knew I had to let her go, but I didn't know how. *Protect her with your life*, my father's voice echoed.

"I can't remember," I lied.

The doctor chuckled and took a drag from the new pipe he'd been sucking on for the last thirty minutes. I could tell when he looked at me that he knew I was lying, but I'd never utter Isla's name to him. I'd protect her from this and him until the end.

"You can't remember what you were fighting about?"

I raised my hand to my face, and my fingers began tracing the half-moon shaped indent above my right eye. It was still tender to the touch months later. The doctors in

Stornoway had told my parents that I was lucky to be alive but living in the aftermath made me think otherwise.

"Yes," the doctor mumbled as he sat on the edge of his desk in front of me, awkwardly adjusting himself as he did. "How'd you get that scar?" He asked, reaching his hand toward my face. At first, his fingers gently caressed my forehead and the area around the scar. I kept his stare, letting him know that I wasn't afraid of him, even though I was. When I appeared unphased by his advances, he quickly dug his thumb into my eyebrow, pushing steadily on the scar. "Was it the horse that kicked you?"

I pulled away and jumped over the back of the chair, taking the opportunity to look at the clock above the door. Our time was almost up. I prayed he would just end it and send me on my way. Even though I had plenty of time to make it to my room, grab the book and make it out to the courtyard before the mail carrier arrived, I wanted the session to be over. I had nothing else to say.

"Are you sure you don't remember?" He asked again. His tone wasn't hopeful like it usually was. It was excited, enthused. I could hear him fidgeting with papers on his desk, moving and shuffling them around.

"No," I answered with my back still to him. "Can we be done for the day?"

"I'm afraid not," he answered. "Why don't you take a seat."

There were five minutes left in our session, giving me thirty-five minutes until the mail truck pulled into the drive abutting the front courtyard. My heart beat hastened, but it was still plenty of time.

"Your month is up." He said coldly. "I won't be seeing you for a couple of months, give or take. Hopefully, once we've resumed our sessions, we'll have more to talk about." He tried to look like the discontinuation of our sessions grieved him, but it was all an act, and we both knew it.

"Frankly, I've grown tired of hearing it over and over again," he continued, shuffling through the papers on his desk again. "So we're going to give you something new to talk about."

My skin prickled, and my heart began pumping faster. Panic set in at the thought that I'd missed my opportunity to get the book out of the asylum and into someone else's safekeeping. Internally I was screaming at myself for waiting so long to get rid of it, but it had become a type of security. Having it close by gave me hope that I was not insane and that I'd not killed my best friend. Sending it away felt like cutting out a piece of myself and throwing it away, not knowing what would become of it.

I tried to hide my anxiety under arrogance. "You said you needed permission," I responded, unsure of what my parents would have said to one another when they'd received his letter. Despite our differences, they were still my parents. I had to rest on that fact because I had little else in the way of hope.

"Yes," the doctor answered, returning to the papers. It was a calculated ploy to drag out what he already knew. "I did say that, didn't I."

Over the sound of rustling paperwork, I could hear the seconds ticking by on the clock behind me. My leg began to bounce in place, and I could feel my underarms start to sweat. I knew I still had time, but it felt like Rutherford knew my plan, and he was taking his time to ruin it.

"Ah, here it is!" He stood up from his chair and hurried around to the front of his desk where he sat and opened the small envelope. He unfolded the piece of paper and read it to himself, moving his lips, mocking me as he did.

I jumped from the chair and snatched the piece of paper from his hand. I turned my back to him as I did and glanced quickly at the clock. I still had time. I could feel

him behind me, lurking. I hadn't even looked at the letter
when he put his hands on my shoulders, rubbing them like I
was a woman. I didn't know what the letter said, but it
didn't really matter. Rutherford had said everything with
his cockiness. I glanced up at the clock and made a
decision. I knew I was already headed for the first floor;
what difference did it make how I got there?

When I could feel his warm breath on my neck, I
bolted from his office, wishing I could leave behind every
piece of skin he'd ever touched. The orderly was nearly
asleep in a chair outside the office and nearly fell over with
the commotion of the door slamming against the wall and
Rutherford yelling after me. I ran as fast as I could to the
end of the hallway, crunching the paper in my hand as I
pumped my arms. I made it to the stairwell and turned back
to flick the doctor off before bounding down the stairs.

I was in my room in seconds, moving the top to the
tank and ripping the book from the underside. Once it was
in my hands, I froze, knowing I now had too much time. I
couldn't stay in my room, but I needed to stay hidden until
I saw the mail truck. I tucked the book addressed to Isla
Gilcrest on the Isle of Lewis inside my waistband and stuck
my head into the empty hallway.

I floated through the stairwells and drifted in and
out of rooms on the east side of the building, checking the
windows facing the courtyard in every new room I entered.
Without realizing it, I found myself in the library for the
first time since Moira's death. It had been closed and
locked for several weeks after the incident, and when it
reopened, I had little interest in going back. The window
that the chair had flown through had yet to be replaced, and
instead, large pieces of plywood filled the space where the
glass should have been. I crossed the room toward the
would-be window and crouched by the wall underneath.
Someone had run a cloth against the paint and smeared her
dark blood around in circles, leaving behind a faint shadow

of her existence. Shards of glass still sat precariously in the sill. I placed my hand against the sill where her feet had last touched the earth. I wanted to thank her, but I wasn't sure what I was thanking her for.

I lost track of the orderlies as I thought about Moira. An uneasy silence hung in the air around me until I realized I was no longer alone in the room. Two orderlies stood side by side almost touching elbows just inside the doorway. Their eyes were fixated on me; predators stalking their prey. I got up from the ground, unsure of my next move. I felt for the book tucked into my waistband, desperate for a way out.

"Come on kid, let's just do this the nice way, ok. We don't want to hurt you. We're just doing our job." The second orderly chimed in with other similar sentiments. Their act was almost genuine enough that I thought about bargaining with them; if they took the book and promised to mail it for me, I wouldn't put up a fight. My eyes darted around the room, and my breathing hastened as the feeling of being trapped sunk in.

Something scratched against the plywood outside the missing window. I thought I was hallucinating, but one of the orderlies scrunched his face at the sound of the peculiar noise. It stopped for a moment and then started again, louder and more erratic than before. I chuckled at the thought of someone or something trying to get in when all I wanted to do was get out.

The orderlies inched toward me slowly. Every step they took, I took one in the opposite direction, like we were the wrong end of magnets being pushed against each other. After a few steps, I was just past the end of the plywood and craned my neck to see through the next window. Outside, the wind blew through the leafless tree, and I watched as the branches rubbed against the outside of the building like shriveled fingers.

"Were either of you here when Moira jumped through the window?" I asked, unsure if they had been. They all looked the same to me in their white nursing uniforms. Neither of the men flinched or gave an answer.

"She threw a chair through this window," I continued, moving toward the plywood, tapping it with my hand to test its sturdiness. The corner whistled as the wind picked up again, exposing a weakness otherwise missed.

My retelling of Moira's story had stopped the orderly's advancement, at least for the time being. I took a few steps back so I could see out the window again, looking down to the courtyard below. "She landed right there," I said, pointing down to the cobblestoned entranceway leading to the front steps. The last thing they needed was another dead patient.

"Did they tell you what she yelled?" I asked, turning my attention from the window back to the orderlies. "Just before she jumped. Did they tell you?"

"Come on kid," one of them started, relying on the minimal training he'd received before becoming responsible for human life. "You don't want to do this kid. Look, we'll tell Dr. Rutherford that you cooperated and gave no trouble. He'll be lenient. We'll make sure of it."

I knew they meant well, but there was nothing they could do. I'd be punished just the same, with or without their help. I turned back to look out the window. I felt for the book again, making sure it was tucked snuggly into my waistband. I watched as the tree danced with the wind, remembering the warm summer days I sat in the courtyard daydreaming of home. I never thought it would be possible to miss the desolation of Lewis, but I did. There was peace in its familiarity and seclusion. I could still smell the burning peat lingering in the air and hear the rustle of the long grass moving in the wind.

I'd give anything to be on the footpath to Tobson. I closed my eyes trying to see the beach or the sun's sparkle on the water, but all I could see was her. I was at peace knowing she would be the last thing my mind saw before I jumped.

"Mr. McGinley," the doctor called, turning into the room. We locked eyes for a moment, waiting to see what the other had up his sleeve; thankfully the sleeves of patient garbs weren't as restrictive as the three-piece suits he wore.

The room filled with the white gas from the fire extinguisher I pulled from the wall just as Dr. Rutherford entered the room. The plume filled the space between us and gave me enough time to act. I bashed the bottom of the fire extinguisher against the plywood with a jolt of resistance ringing through my arms. The cloud was weakening behind me, and I could hear them yelling. I threw the extinguisher against the plywood again sending a terrible cracking noise into the air. I struck the flimsy wood again and again until a section large enough gave way. I tossed the extinguisher and pulled the plywood back, sending it splintering onto the floor. The cloud of white gas was all but gone, but so was I.

Horrified at the prospect of another suicide within months of the last and in the exact same manner, would not escape the notice of someone above Rutherford, and he knew it. His face softened, and he called the orderlies off, giving me space to breathe.

"Lachlan, we can talk this through," he said calmly. "We can give it some more time if you think it will help."

"If I think it will help?" I laughed back at him. I looked over my shoulder, out into the open space behind me as I teeter on the edge of the sill. The wind was rolling through in spurts, kicking up wildly before dying down again. The branches that had been scratching on the plywood now stretched out for me like a hand calling me home. I suddenly realized that I was still grasping the letter Dr. Rutherford had handed me in his office. I steadied myself against the empty frame and began unfolding the thin paper. "Since when am I in charge?" I asked as I did.

"Lachlan, just come down, and we will figure this out," he promised with a hint of desperation creeping into his voice.

I looked down at the scribbled letter. My mother's hand was most noticeable, fanciful beyond its need. *Dr. Rutherford*, she began. *He was a bad seed from the beginning, cursed to become what I always feared he would. Do what you think will help him, but I cannot claim him as my own. He's the devil's son now.*

I looked up at Dr. Rutherford, who had also read the letter. For a vile man, his eyes hung low with sympathy for me at that moment. We shared the understanding that it was one thing to be crazy, but it was quite another to be disowned by the woman who'd given birth to you. Even though I knew his kindness was fleeting and would only last as long as I stood on death's door, I appreciated the sentiment.

I turned slightly, facing out toward the courtyard. The letter fell from my hand, taking with it any hope I had been holding onto that my mother may have loved me. I let my attachment to her, good and bad, fall with it. I didn't want my mother's hatred of me to be the last thing I thought of if I didn't make it.

I looked out toward the horizon while Rutherford's voice boomed behind me, but his words were lost in the emptiness of the situation. Instead, I focused on the trees and the cool breeze blowing through them. The sun was hidden behind the moving clouds, but I could still see red glowing bright; she was a flame keeping me at bay while calling me home simultaneously.

The rush of air around me was exhilarating. The feeling of flying was freeing until it turned into intense falling and it felt like my stomach was in my throat. The branches of the trees were rough and tangled together. I broke through them violently, grasping for one strong enough to hold my weight. The sound was like firecrackers spouting off in every direction, one louder than the next. I kept my mind focused on the color red as I fell, needing something to guide me safely to the ground.

There hadn't been enough time to alert other orderlies before I jumped. Rutherford's astonishment bought me time. When the tree dropped me to the ground, he and the orderlies were hanging out the window, waiting to see if I'd make it down alive. When I rolled to look up at them, the smile on my face sent the two orderlies dashing down the hall, while Rutherford stood at the window and lit a cigarette, shaking his head as he did.

I rolled onto my stomach, knowing I had only minutes before the orderlies would be on me. I could see the red mail truck as I laid on the lawn. My skin was stinging and split open in places. I felt for the book, praying for the strength to keep going. I collected everything I had left to get to my feet and made for the truck, hoping I still had enough time.

My feet skidded to a stop in the gravel of the driveway. I hugged the side of the mail truck, slinking against its smooth exterior, making my way to the back hatch. The crisp feel of the metal against my skin brought relief, if only temporarily. I slid my fingers around the silver handle and took a deep breath, yanking it upward.

The thudding in my chest stopped almost immediately when the door would not give. Every other day I watched the carrier open and reopened the hatch without reaching for a key to unlock it. I assumed in his haste to make deliveries he'd not bothered to lock it. It must have been self-locking, I thought, as I moved to one of the other doors and yanked on the handle. When the door didn't open, panic raced through my body.

Without knowing what I was doing, I sprinted toward the large double doors leading toward reception. I gained speed the closer I got. I could hear shouting echoing down the hallway and through open windows. I had seconds before they had me.

I couldn't stop my legs from moving as the front door swung open. When I saw the neon yellow fabric of the carrier's jacket instead of the bleach white nursing uniform, I picked up speed. My legs burned, and my lungs screamed for air. The collision was crude and took the carrier by surprise. By the time he looked up from the mail he was sorting in his hand, we were already tumbling down the front steps.

There was no pain, and everything moved in slow motion as we twisted and tangled together. The bag spilled as we fell, sending a sea of white envelopes spilling out over the stone walkway. When it ended, we were both laying on top of the contents of his bag, stunned, but otherwise intact.

"Ach, I'm so sorry lad," he carrier professed. "Are you alright?"

He looked at me as he spoke, but his hands were already picking up the spilled parcels and slipping them back into his bag which lay on the ground between us.

"Aye," I said enthusiastically. "Aye, I'm fine. Let me help you, it's the least I can do."

I started grabbing handfuls of letters, shoving them into the bag. I could hear pounding footsteps from down the hall echoing toward us. I reached behind me for the book tucked in my waistband, but there was nothing there. The orderlies burst through the door and grabbed me off the ground. The carrier vouched that it had been an accident and that I was attempting to help him with the mess. None of it matter. Somewhere in the shuffle, I'd lost the book. I tried to retrace my steps as I bucked in the orderly's arms but couldn't remember being without it. I'd been caught, and now I was headed for the first floor, and the book was lost in the world again, like I knew I would be.

The carrier walked slowly back to his truck taking with him any hope that I'd had. I wasn't even sure what I was supposed to be hopeful of, but it was hope nonetheless. I struggled in the orderly's arms as the carrier's neon yellow jacket disappeared behind the back hatch. I kicked and screamed until I ended up face down on the steps watching my only chance for redemption drift away.

With my arms restrained behind me and a knee between my shoulders, I laid calmly against the cool stones, no doubt waiting for Dr. Rutherford to present himself. As I watched in disbelief, the stout carrier began to shut the back hatch to his truck when he stopped abruptly, looking at something at his feet. He bent down, steadying himself on the truck as he did, and picked up a small brown parcel from the ground.

Chapter Thirteen

He'd never been inside her house as a kid. He'd only ever seen it from the outside and from a distance. He thought about the countless nights he'd stood at his window, craning his neck to see the peaks of its roof over the moor, waiting for the light in her room to go out. He would lay in bed afterward, thinking about what her house looked like, causing him to feel awkward about being in it so many years later. It wasn't at all how he'd pictured it.

He sat in the dim room, waiting. He wanted to open the curtain that hung heavy against the large window on the backside of the house but assumed that would be rude to do in someone else's house. He fidgeted on the sofa, trying to find a comfortable position, and when he couldn't, he stood up, still waiting. He paced nervously about the room, pretending to look at the knickknacks on the shelves and tables, wondering if he'd been forgotten.

"Sorry," Isla called, bounding down the stairs. She was holding a gray towel in her hand, ringing out her wet hair. She swayed into the room and took a seat in an old chair opposite Lachlan. "I was in the shower."

Lachlan smiled, trying not to stare. She was dressed in a thin pair of cotton shorts and a white low-cut t-shirt that had slid halfway down her shoulder. Lachlan couldn't help but note the absence of a bra strap. She'd still been wet when she dressed, and certain spots of her shirt clung to her damp skin underneath, reminding him of swimming in the lake and how their clothes stuck to their wet skin after they'd fled. He stared, studying the changes in her body since then.

"You know, this is the first time I've ever been in your house," he said, looking around. "It's very, holy?" He turned to look at the multitude of paintings of Christ in varies stages of his life. He'd counted them while he waited and had come up with sixteen separate representations of Jesus in the sitting room. "Do all Catholics decorate like this?" he asked.

"Just the hardcore ones," she laughed. "I wasn't here too long after my grandmother died, and I guess my ma just never got around to updating it. Not that she'd do it much differently." They glanced around the room together, looking at all the eyes staring back at them. Lachlan shivered in his skin, off-put by the feeling of being watched.

"Sorry," he responded in a pathetic attempt to offer condolences for the death of her grandmother. He'd met her once or twice, at the café or curbside store before Isla had moved to the island. She'd always smiled at Lachlan, before returning his mother's scowl.

"Ach, it was a long time ago," Isla said, drifting somewhere in her nearest memories of her grandmother for a second before the moment faded. "You're lucky you caught me, I'm on my way out, back to Stornoway for a day or two."

"Back to the Twisted Thistle, I presume?" he asked with a hint of mockery on his tongue.

"Aye," she answered shamelessly. "You got something against barmaids then?"

"No, not at all," he professed. "I'm very fond of anyone peddling copious amounts of alcohol."

"How 'bout a whiskey then?" she asked, crossing the room and opening a small cabinet to retrieve a bottle and a couple of glasses. In the absence of any natural light in the room, the liquid appeared dull and cloudy. Lachlan watched as she downed a shot before pouring both glasses again, carrying them in one hand and the bottle in the other.

"The other day," Lachlan started as he reached for one of the glasses. She teased him, pulling it just out of his reach. Even though her face had changed, matured, she had the same cunning smile at times. He grabbed for the glass again, and again she moved it just out of his reach, further behind her. Lachlan leaned forward, scooting to the edge of the sofa. He brushed against her hip with his arm, and his face was inches from her midsection. She smelled like fresh picked heather and childhood memories. He stood up from the sofa, almost pressing against Isla, finally grabbing ahold of the glass. He downed the whiskey and held it out for another pour. "You said you had something of mine," he whispered as her eyes dissected his.

The playfulness of her manner melted away. She poured another drink and threw it back, without offering Lachlan another. She set the bottle on the coffee table, meeting Lachlan's gaze with a painful look, almost apologizing for something that hadn't happened yet.

She slid past him, deliberately brushing against him as she moved. Her hair was mostly dried, except for the tips of the longer strands. They were still dark and heavy with the weight of water. The curls bounced freely as she moved, tickling the small of her back. Dark freckles dappled her pale arms and matched the ones on her face and legs. He remembered the cluster on her midsection, to the right of her belly button, and how he'd once touched them with the tips of three fingers.

"Are you coming?" she asked from the bottom stair.

Lachlan's heart began to thump hard enough he was sure she'd hear it if he got to close. He felt like a daft kid again, like he didn't know what he was doing. He was flustered and felt hot under his shirt and wanted to rip it off. His years of experience with the faceless women of his past was gone. He felt like a teenager on the verge of finally becoming a man. She stood on the bottom stair, waiting for him, in the only light the house seemed to let in. She was burning, just like he was.

The room was simple, except for the intricate web of blankets dressing her bed. It was a mound of warmth and softness like cotton candy melting on a warm summer day. A small white dresser sat against the wall opposite the bed, along with a wardrobe and a small bookshelf with a collection of little odds and ends. The curtains were drawn back on one side letting in the day. Lachlan couldn't help but wonder if she had been able to see his house as well as he'd been able to see hers.

"Well," she laughed. "This is it. Is it all that you thought it would be?"

"And more," Lachlan whispered. "May I?" he asked, pointing to the mass of blankets on the bed. She motioned he was free to do as he wished.

He removed his boots before launching himself onto her bed, twirling and twisting in the blankets and throws until they swaddled him like a baby. She stood at the dresser with her arms folded across her chest and one leg crossed in front of the other, watching with disapproving, almost motherly eyes.

"I like blankets, what can I say?" she laughed when he finally came up for air.

"I remember," Lachlan answered. "They made you feel safe."

"Very good, Mr. McGinley," she answered, surprised at his retention for trivial childhood information. "What else do you remember?"

"Everything," he answered quickly, the entirety of their brief relationship together flashing before his eyes. It seemed like it stretched out forever, but in reality, it had only been a matter of months. He sat up in the bed, digging himself out of his cocoon to look at her. He realized for the first time that they were at best strangers with shared memories. She looked back at him with eyes that said there was still a measure of what they had been to each other, whatever it had been.

He flopped back on her bed wondering why he'd never thought to surround himself with warm blankets. His bed at home in Dundee was dressed in a thin blanket and thinner sheet. There was no warmth in them. He was always cold at night, until he woke up in a sweaty panic, throwing the blankets to the floor as he gasped for air.

He began to feel strangled by the blankets, their soft exteriors suffocating him as they wrapped around him. He slunk to the floor with his knees pressed against his chest. She stood in front of him, the paleness of her legs shining in his eyes. She knelt down, sitting in the space just in front of his legs, with the little blue book resting brashly on her lap.

Lachlan stared at the book without moving, like he had done night after night in the asylum. He thought of Moira and the stain her blood had left on the wall in the library. He could see the old woman from the loch and feel her grip on his arm, burning like hot ash against his skin. Images of Arden at the water's edge accompanied the sound of his scream. He could feel Dr. Rutherford's breath against his neck and the way his skin prickled when he said he knew that he was lying. The images all danced together in his mind until all be could see was Isla, unsure of which one held his truth.

"You never wrote," he said glumly, trying to focus on her eyes and stay in reality.

She looked back at him for a moment, but then dropped her gaze to the book.

"I did," she said quietly as she opened the book. Inside the cover were small pieces of paper folded together in odd shapes and sizes. Some looked as if they'd been torn in half and put back together. The tape running down the middle of them gleamed in the sun breaking through the second story window.

Lachlan reached for the top letter, unfolding it. *It was real,* it read, printed in fanciful twelve-year-old girl script. *From the beginning to the end, it was real.*

"You asked me to tell you the truth," she whispered. "I tried, but …"

"It's ok," Lachlan responded, dropped his legs pulling her closer, taking her face in his hands to comfort her. "It's ok."

She smiled half-heartedly at him, knowing it was a lie meant to lessen her guilt. "When I knew you were out, and you didn't come back for it … I figured …"

Lachlan rubbed her cheek with his thumb, looking into the penetrating eyes that had haunted him for so long. They had been hardened by the world and Lachlan couldn't help but feel somewhat to blame. He'd put her in the middle of it all and then disappeared without so much as a goodbye, leaving her behind to pick up the pieces as best she could. He wanted to take her pain away, even if he didn't have the room to keep it for her.

"You kept it, all this time," he whispered, now inches from her face. His hand glided against the smooth skin of her neck and into the crown of fire surrounding her. She sat still, her breath coming quicker. She had not looked up from the book and was tracing the golden inlay lettering with her fingertips. Lachlan brushed loose tendrils away from her face, tucking them behind her ear like he'd done once before.

"It was hope," she breathed, finally lifting her eyes to meet his. The light from the window caught her tears and made her eyes look more like the ocean than ever before.

"Hope that you'd come back."

The electricity only found in decades of lost love pulsed in the air between them and tears spilled over and onto her cheeks. Her upper lip trembled. She sighed quietly. Waiting. Wanting. He couldn't be sure if the pounding he heard was his heart or hers. Lachlan leaned in, squeezing the energy between them as the scream of the house phone rang through the air. They both jumped at the sound, panting and winded by the missed opportunity.

Isla sprang to answer the phone on the dresser. She spoke quickly, but Lachlan wasn't listening. He tried to wipe the look of desperation from his face as he clamored to his feet and slipped his feet back into his shoes.

"Euan's looking for you," she said with her back to him.

"What for?" he asked.

"He wanted to know if I'd given the book back to you yet?" She turned to look at him, truth and fear fighting for room in her expression.

"How does he know about the book?"

"I told him." She covered the shame of having betrayed him with somber honesty. "He needed to see it?"

"Why?"

"Because," she said forcefully. "Because you weren't here."

She'd had no reason to believe he'd ever return so he knew he had no right to think she'd keep the book to herself. He couldn't blame her any more than he could blame her for hoping he'd come back.

"He showed me his files, and the maps, and everything."

"You dunnae believe him, do you?" he laughed.

She paused, picking her words carefully in her head. She crossed the room quickly, knelt to retrieve the book from the floor, shoving it into Lachlan's chest with force and purpose.

"I believed you."

***

His head was already spinning as the motion sickness grabbed ahold of his stomach. He couldn't help but open the book and thumb through it as she sped along the 858 toward Stornoway. He dragged his fingers across the pages, sensing the indentations that the tip of her pen had left behind as she'd pressed with force to make them. He wanted the words to mean something, anything, but as he read them, they became more and more distant and devoid of any meaning. The significance they once held had faded with time, leaving them as the nonsensical ramblings of a crazy person. He laughed at himself for ever having believed them.

"You've read all this?" he asked, holding the book flippantly in her direction.

"Yes," she replied, almost yelling over the roar of the wind coming in through the open windows.

"And?"

"And what?"

"And what? He laughed, shaking his head. "What exactly is it that you believe about it?"

She didn't answer. Her eyes stayed on the road, hidden behind dark sunglasses and her wild hair as they sped toward Stornoway.

Lachlan continued to skim through pages, reading bits and pieces, but never quite finishing a sentence; *hurried feet, open windows, brunette or blonde*. None of it made any sense. They were just strings of words put together after a date, which was the only thing that felt concrete. The letters at the end of each entry written out in all caps rounded out the crazy ramblings. The wind swept over the pages, flipping them rapidly until Lachlan slammed the book closed trying to forget the words.

The air was warm, and she drove fast with one hand on the wheel and the other tapping her fingers to the music's beat on the door frame. He tried to think of anything other than what she'd looked like as she ran over the top of the water, her feet pounding against the hidden shelf underneath the water's surface, tucked away from the world. The faint sound of the old woman's voice drifted in the air; *you'll pay the price*. He let belief flood his mind for a split second before it faded to dust and the wind that shook the car stole it away. Then, all he could hear was Dr. Rutherford's voice, and his own, which he didn't recognize at first. He couldn't believe anymore, even if he wanted to.

Lachlan looked up as the car lurched forward, slowing as they entered the village of Achmore, the halfway point between Bernera and Stornoway. They passed through the sleepy village slowly, watching the rundown houses pass by. Years of accumulation filled the yards; broken down vehicles and other machinery strewn about, old bathtubs, tattered fences that could no longer keep sheep. Lachlan knew to the outsider driving through, it would look like poverty. He could see it with foreign eyes. But it was just life on Lewis. The old may have been discarded to the lawn or pastures, but it was never forgotten. The relics of crofts that served their ancestors hundreds of years prior still stood on their land; cast-off and derelict but never gone.

"Why are we stopping?" Lachlan asked, trying to rub the sick feeling from his cheeks.

"Gas," she yelled, jumping out of the car. She leaned into with the window flashing a playful smile. "Unless you want to walk the rest of the way," she laughed.

Lachlan opened his door and stepped out, hoping the fresh air would relieve the nauseated feeling in his stomach. The sun was almost directly overhead, warming the fresh air around him as it mixed with the smell of petrol wafting off the pump. He took a few steps into the rough grass, noticing the smallest purple blooms beginning to peek through the dead vegetation overtop of it. Soon the air would smell like lavender; like summer.

"Want anything?" Isla yelled from across the hood, pointing behind her to the small convenience store. He glanced down through the window at the blue book sitting on his seat staring up at him. He wanted to understand. He wanted his life back. He wanted the truth. He crossed in front of the car, following Isla into the small roadside store, having to settle for a bag of crisps and a can of soda instead, instead of what he really wanted.

The store was still, except for voices he could hear chatting at the register. Lachlan reached for the door of the drink cooler hoping the carbonation would help settle what the reading while moving had done to his stomach. He felt what he thought were playful taunts from Isla as she poked him in the side. He turned, laughing, and preparing for his revenge, but stopped when he saw the frightful look plastered on her face.

"Fuck," he murmured to himself, looking at the frail woman standing in front of them. She seemed shorter than he remembered, and the bags under her eyes made it look like she hadn't slept since he'd gone missing. Lachlan wondered if she had.

She stood motionless in front of them, shifting her gaze between Isla and Lachlan. Her face was expressionless, except for the tiny quiver in her chin. Lachlan begged that she not begin to bawl and cause a scene in the drink aisle of the gas station grocery. He didn't think she was that kind of woman, but he imagined a child's death has a way of stealing away the person you were before.

She blinked away the beginnings of tears in her eyes and forced a smile onto her sullen face. She moved slowly towards them, her eyes fixed on Lachlan. The thought of crossing paths with Mrs. Scott had never occurred to him until she was standing in front of him, desperately searching his eyes for answers to questions that had been burning in her gut for twenty years. Lachlan only wished he had them for her.

"I was sorry to hear about your mother," she said, looking up at him.

Lachlan just stared back, tongue-tied. There were no words, and even if there were, he wasn't sure he could get them past the lump in his throat that was making it hard to breathe.

"It's been too long," she whispered, grabbing his hand lightly and patting it, the way a grandmother would. "It's good that you've come home." She smiled and dropped his hand.

"And you, missy," she squeaked, with ten times more energy than she had only seconds prior. "It's been way too long for you too."

"I know Mrs. Scott, it's just ..."

"Oh, don't be sorry, dear, just come by and see me once in a while. Bring me some cakes or something, and I'll make tea."

The frail and fragile woman stroked the side of Isla's face and fidgeted with the tips of her wild hair. Isla's eyes were sad and apologetic as she looked down at what remained of Arden's mother.

"You're the closest thing I ever had to a daughter," she cooed. "Such a shame you lost ..."

The bell for the front door broke through the moment and startled the three of them. The customer pushed past them in a hurry and disappeared behind one of the displays.

"Well," Mrs. Scott finally offered. "I should be going."

She smiled at both Isla and Lachlan, letting her eyes linger on him a little longer before she meekly walked past them toward the door. Lachlan felt something burning in his chest as he watched her go; a firestorm trying to escape. He tried repeatedly to bury it under quick swings of the soda in his hand, but the tingle of the bubbles only inflamed it. He was sure it would burn his throat on the way out, but he couldn't keep it buried inside. Not any longer.

"Mrs. Scott!" he yelled as she stood in the open door letting the wind rush in, wild and warm with the beginnings of summer. He could feel both their eyes on him as he fumbled for the right words, if they even existed.

"I didn't ..." He swallowed hard, trying to lessen the burn of the words in his throat. "I didn't kill Arden."

It was like the world froze the second the words left his mouth. Nothing moved, not even the wind. Mrs. Scott's face was filled with confusion at first, and Lachlan began to fear that she'd misheard him, thinking that he was admitting to heinous acts. When her face sweetened, the world started to move again.

She breathed deep, looking at Lachlan with empathetic eyes. They were the mother's eyes he'd never seen looking back at him as a child. He found the irony of it comical; a mother without a child and a child without a mother. He wanted to laugh but didn't.

"I never thought you did child," she exhaled, "but something did."

Chapter Fourteen

We shuffled in a single file line down the hall in silence, lunch sacks in hand. We could hear the cries of sweet freedom from the kids on the other side of the doors as we got closer. The lunchroom was our time. Sometimes the assigned teacher would sneak out for a smoke break or use the bathroom, and we'd be left alone for a few minutes of true independence. None of us could wait until next year when we would be across the island from what felt like nursery school and from our parent's. We could taste manhood on the tips of our tongues, but six weeks felt like a lifetime away.

"I'm gonna do it," Arden said plainly as we all sat and emptied the lunches our mothers still packed for us. "On the trip, I'm gonna do it."

"Do what?" Euan asked snidely.

"Ross said all the girls get loose on the trip and that she's just protecting her good girl image. Ross says on the trip, if I make a move, she'll ..." Arden's voice trailed off into the uncharted territory of what boys did alone with girls, which we all claimed to be experts in but knew nearly nothing about. We all knew what men did, but not boys. We were in an awkward phase where we knew too much for our own good and couldn't expect much from the opposite sex. But we all knew the rumors about the St. Kilda trip.

"She'll what?" Euan asked, still chewing.

Arden leaned in toward the center of the table, looking around for listening ears and teacher's eyes as he did. "Ross said, when his class went, he made it to third base with Meredith Murry and that one of his friends," he poked his head up from the huddle the four of us had formed over the table top before continuing. "He said one of his friends actually got to put it in a few times before the girl stopped him because she was worried she'd get pregnant."

None of us moved as the reality of sex, however brief, hung in the hot air between us. Arden's eyes twinkled like shallow pools reflecting the sun. He'd become obsessed with the idea of sex, no doubt, at the influence of older brother who'd given him the idea that the St. Kilda trip was his best chance at getting it. I slouched back into my seat, watching Arden as his eyes darted quickly away toward the girl's table, toward Isla.

"You should all be making plans too, so, you know, you're not caught off guard if the opportunity presents itself." Arden tore into his sandwich, glancing obviously around the lunchroom.

"You're delusional," Euan said, spitting half-chewed pieces of crisps across the table as he did, "if you think any of those girls are going to let us have sex with them. They don't even talk to us! What makes you think they'll let us, you know."

Arden kicked at Euan under the table. "Not you, tubby. No girl wants another girl's lips on them. I wasn't talking to you. I meant the rest of us."

"They're not girly lips," Euan yelled, kicking back at Arden under the table but missing and smacking his shin into one of the supports. The noise quieted the room and drew the attention of the girls. They stopped eating and looked at us with eyes that made us feel like we were a different species; a pack of rabid dogs with fleas and ticks and covered in our own shit. They turned back to their conversation, disregarding us like the foul animals we were.

"I'm gonna do it," he said again. "You'll see. She'll come around on the trip."

I laughed and tried to play it off like I had choked on a part of my lunch, but it was poorly executed. I committed myself to it and played it out like I might have almost died, but he knew. They all knew.

"You got something you want to add to the conversation McGinley?"

"No," I coughed, still committed to my ruse, but in typical fashion, Arden wouldn't let it go.

"You think you can get her?" His words were weighted. There was no playfulness in his voice if there had been before.

I laughed again, cursing myself as the sound rushed past my lips. "I'm not laughing at you, man. It's just ..." I didn't know how to finish the sentence. I was laughing at him and the distorted version of reality he lived in. Isla'd never have sex with him. I didn't expect her to have sex with me, and she liked me, at least enough to tolerate me.

"Just what?"

"Nothing. Never mind. Just forget it."

"Do you think I can't get her?" he asked.

"We know you can't," Euan interjected before slurping down a gulp of soda. "You already asked her, and she said no."

That wouldn't stop him. She was a trophy that he intended to win, a conquest he planned to overcome. She'd become nothing more than a prize to him.

"Ask her," Arden said calmly.

I ignored him, concentrating on my lunch and the shrill voices ringing throughout the room.

"If you think you're better than me, if you think you can get her before I can, go ask her. Right now." His body was stiff and unmoving as he spoke.

"I'm not asking her," I answered, ignoring him while his eyes burned a hole in my forehead.

"At least I have the balls to talk to her instead of just being secretly in love with her."

"I'm not secretly in love with her," I said calmly because it was the truth. She knew at least to some extent that I was in love with her. That much wasn't a secret.

They erupted into laughter and table slapping, drawing the attention of the tables around us. Arden was almost in tears by the time he caught his breath enough to respond.

"Prove it," he howled, wiping the tears from the corners of his eyes while Calum and Euan held their aching sides. "If you're not in love with her anymore, prove it."

"How the hell do you want me to prove that?"

"Go ask her out. If you don't love her anymore, it won't matter when she rejects you."

"Are you so sure she'll reject me?" I asked, almost too quickly. Everyone's eyes were on me as the possibility spun in Arden's mind. He'd proposed the experiment, confident that she'd never take me over him. His ego was preventing him from seeing truths outside the one he wanted to see.

Euan mumbled something through the food in his mouth as Arden and I stared across the table at one another, at somewhat of a stalemate while I held all the cards. I watched as he squirmed in his self-doubt and smiled.

"You know what, I think that's a great idea. I'll go ask her out, and we'll just see what happens."

Euan and Calum stopped chewing as their eyes darted back and forth between Arden and I, waiting.

"Why don't you do it now?" Calum interjected.

"Why not?" I said, gathering the mess left over from my lunch to throw it away on my way to talk to Isla. My eyes never left Arden's and his never wavered from mine. The tension between us began to hiss and burn like a perfectly arranged fire. Arden would never back down or admit his fear that he'd pushed me into the arms of the girl he desperately wanted to win over. The only way to put it to rest would be for me to be rejected, in front of everyone, by the girl I secretly loved. I only hoped she'd play along.

The bell rang out overhead, echoing through the small lunchroom. Groups began gathering trash from their tables and slowly exiting the room to head back to class for the rest of the afternoon.

"Saved by the bell," Arden smiled, finally able to breathe again. I just grinned back.

We gathered our things and pushed through the large double doors leading out to the hallway behind the group of girls from our class. To them, we didn't even exist. We were flies on the wall. If only they knew how much they meant to all of us.

"Hold this," I said quickly, shoving my lunch sack into Euan's arms before taking off ahead of the group to catch up to the girls. I looked back to see Euan and Calum's jaws drop to the floor while Arden's face twisted with the pain of adolescent insecurity. I wanted to feel sorry for the torture I was putting my friend through knowing full well that he'd have his victory in the end when Isla publically rejected me, but I didn't. He deserved it.

As soon as I was side-by-side with the group, they went silent, grabbing quick, confused glances in my direction. I smiled gently at them with the confidence she'd given me. I no longer feared them like the boys behind me did. I understood them now, or at least her.

"Isla, can I talk to you for a second?" I asked loudly. All eyes spun toward Isla who had yet to look in my direction.

"Sure," she answered, giving her clique the cue to hurry on without her.

Her stride slowed as we walked alone the rest of the way toward the classroom. Euan, Calum, and Arden hurried past us, forgetting to avert their eyes as they did. She stopped at the water fountain a few doors down from our room, and I watched as everyone except Arden slipped through the door. I turned my back to him as I leaned casually on the wall next to her as she drank from the fountain.

"Will you go out with me?" I whispered down to her trying not to laugh.

She stood up, clean, fresh water dripping from her bottom lip. I wanted to smear it away for her and had to stop myself from doing so.

"What?" she asked.

"I need you to pretend like I'm asking you out, and then reject me, so I can get Arden off my back about being ..." The words *love* hung on the tip of my tongue, wanting to escape. I blushed with embarrassment at having almost said the word, even though I suspected she already knew its truth.

"About being what?" she asked, pretending to play dumb. She leaned against the wall in front of me with her arms overlapping across her chest. I watched her eyes look past me to Arden who was still standing in the doorway, no doubt. Her eyes drifted back to me, and I wanted to tell her the truth, that I was in love with her, but I knew this wasn't the time or the place.

"About having a secret with you," I finally answered. "He's obsessed with you and thinks I am too. I need you to act like I'm asking you out, so you can reject me, and show him that I don't care."

She tilted her head slightly to the left so Arden could see her smile past the back of my head. "Is he watching us?" I asked, confident that he was.

"He looks like a little kid who's lost his puppy," she answered pouting her bottom lip.

I was happy he was suffering, and I was sure it showed on my face. Isla laughed at my enjoyment, which only made my smile intensify. I'd have given my left arm to see the look on his face as she giggled girlishly, playing her part well, just like I'd hoped she would.

"Are you still walking me home today?" she asked even though she already knew the answer.

"Of course." It was all I had been thinking about since the last time.

"We better get going then," she said, "or he might start to suspect that I've said yes to your proposition and think that you are in fact in love with me."

"I never said ..." but I didn't finish. I could lie to Arden, but I couldn't lie to her. I didn't want to.

She touched the side of the arm gently with a consoling look of pity in her eyes. She brushed past me and winked at me as she did. I turned, following her with my eyes as she walked past Arden and disappeared into our classroom. I walked toward him, reveling as he tried to comprehend what he'd just seen. It wasn't until I saw the disbelief on his face that I began to feel anything close to guilt. He was supposed to be my best friend, and yet, it didn't feel that way. We were becoming rivals, and it wasn't just because of Isla. She may have been the catalyst, but she wasn't the reason.

"Are you happy?" I asked, a hundred times cockier than a kid who'd just been shot down by the most beautiful girl in school rightfully should have been. "I asked, she said no, can we move on?"

"What'd you say to her?" he asked, still unconvinced.

"I asked if I could sit with her at lunch tomorrow."

"And what'd she say?"

"She said she had other plans," I laughed.

Arden's expression was full of confusion for how'd I'd overcome the witchy spell she'd cast over all the boys in our class. Perhaps because he wanted to get out from under it as well. Even the ones who knew they'd never talk to her once in their lives were still in love with her. She'd given them no other choice; she'd given me no other choice.

The confusion grew as Arden's eyes darted past me. I turned to see my father walking towards us slowly, his hands in his pockets and his works boot squishing loudly against the tile floor. He glanced awkwardly at the doors of the rooms he passed, trying to avoid our baffled glares. I couldn't think of a day when my father had picked me up from school, much less come inside in the middle of the day. Arden tried to slip into the classroom, catching my father's attention with his movement. He motioned for him to stay where he was. Whatever it was, it was for both of us.

"What are you doing here?" I asked crassly. "School's not out for another couple hours."

Arden looked at me like I had three heads. What did I care if we had time left on the clock? To him, anything was better than sitting in class. But seeing my dad where he didn't belong made me question what was so wrong that he'd come in the first place. My second thought was whether or not it was going to affect my ability to walk Isla home like we'd planned. It was Friday, he should have been driving my mother to Stornoway, giving me the whole afternoon to walk Isla home as slowly as I could.

The look on my father's face said that there would be no walking tall girls home that afternoon. I watched him as he stood, swaying from one foot to the other, uncomfortable even in his own skin. For half a second, I wondered if it was my mother, but the thought vanished before I allowed myself to feel the reaction or lack of response to any news involving her.

"Mr. McLeod was up checking on his pastures this afternoon and found one of the cattle …" he stopped short of the details, looking Arden and I over as he tried to determine what boys our age were capable of handling.

"Found what?" Arden asked, signifying to my father that we were old enough to hear what he had to say.

"It was, well, it was decapitated. Just no other way to put it. A clean decapitation."

Arden and I exchanged horrified but captivated glances with each other. "What could do that to a cow?" They weren't the smartest of beasts, but they were big, and they understood fight or flight the same as any animal. It was not an animal easily beheaded.

"Can we see it?" Arden asked, excitedly.

"Your father's up there now with Hamish. Sent me to fetch the both of you, since you'd been feeding them and whatnot, while he was laid up. Wanted to ask you if you had seen anything peculiar or out of place."

"Not that I can remember," I answered quickly, half turning to step into the classroom. Ms. McNish had already started her lesson and glared at us out of the side of her eye.

"All the same, you should probably come with me, help us take a look around and see if we find anything. Hamish will probably want to talk to the both of you."

"Yes!" Arden half yelled.

"Can I help you with something?" Ms. McNish asked my father, poking her head into the hallway and interrupting Arden's celebration.

"Sorry, ma'am," my father offered. "I'm here for the boys. We've got a bit of a situation, and I've been sent to fetch them for some assistance."

She looked my father up and down, not buying his made-up sounding story. She looked at Arden and I as if to say what help could we possibly have to offer.

"You've got to sign them out in the front office," she said, pointing down the hallway. "To the left. They'll give you a pass. Then you can come back and collect them."

"Yes, ma'am."

My father turned without another word to us. Ms. McNish stood expectantly in the doorway, waiting for us to take our seats until my father came back for us. All eyes were on us and whispers passed behind hands as we took our seats. Ms. McNish attempted to continue with her lesson, even though it was obvious no one was paying attention. The wrinkling sound of folding notebook paper was all anyone could hear in the back of the room. All I could hear was the scratching of my pencil as it flew across a scrap piece of paper as I scribbled a note to Isla, letting her know that I couldn't walk her home, to stay out of the pastures behind Bosta and to beg her to meet me Saturday instead.

My father returned and knocked gently on the door just as I finished. Arden was already walking toward the front of the room and missed me dropping the note on Isla's desk as I passed by. I slid it carefully into the crux between her arm and the notebook she was drawing in. She sat up and used her hair as cover so she could read it in secret.

Just as I reached the door, I smacked myself on the forehead, playing dumb for the second time that day. "Forgot my bag. Sorry, Ms. McNish."

She glared at me from the front of the room and even when my back was to her, I could feel her eyes digging into me. I dilly-dallied on the way back to my desk, waiting for Isla to look up and give me some type of acknowledgment that she'd meet me tomorrow. If not, I'd go all weekend without seeing her, the pain of which was already starting to take hold of me. I didn't realize it, but I had been holding my breath and only started breathing again when she finally looked up at me at the last second before I passed her desk. She bit her bottom lip slightly and winked discretely before returning to her drawings. I grabbed my bag and was in the hallway with Arden and my father in seconds, not wanting to linger and ruin the moment.

***

It wasn't what I was expecting. I didn't know exactly what to expect, but when my father said we were going to see a severed cow head, my imagination ran with it, leaving the truth of the matter much less shocking than I had anticipated.

The grass was smeared with blood, which looked more black than red. Flies were already eating the exposed flesh, buzzing incessantly around our ankles as Arden, myself, my father, Arden's father and Mr. McLeod all stood in a circle around the head, which was a good five or six feet from the rest of the body.

"You boys seen anything strange while you're slogging around back in the hillside?" Mr. McLeod asked. He was angry, but not with us. He loved his cows. They were more like pets than livestock to him. They didn't serve any purpose other than to give his life some small sense of purpose. The dead one was the youngest of the seven that he had. She'd just had her first calf, and now it was an orphan. We could hear its worried calls from the pen at the end of the road next to the cemetery.

"Nothing," Arden answered, squatting down to get a closer look at the inside of the beast's neck.

The adult's eyes were on me, not having answered when Arden did. I was unsure of what to say. I had seen something strange the week prior, but I didn't see how that had anything to do with a dead cow. I looked down at the head, it's eyes still half open and its large tongue hanging out of its mouth, licking at the grass like it had done all its life.

"I haven't seen anything," I finally answered. The immediacy of my guilt was surprising as it began to ravage my insides. Somehow, I knew the incident Isla and I had experienced the week before had something to do with the dead cow. I thought maybe I'd tell my dad the truth later when it was just the two of us, but not with Arden there. He was already suspicious of me, and it would only add fuel to his raging fire. I kept my mouth shut and hated myself for lying instead.

"Wait," Arden yelled, standing up to rejoin us. "We saw that horse, what was it, a couple weeks ago now?"

The men exchanged odd glances with one another. "What horse?" Mr. Scott asked.

"It was a black horse, just running up on the ridge like it had a firecracker up its arse," he laughed, but the description was not that far off.

"What's a horse got to do with anything," Mr. McLeod lamented, "a horse ain't doin' this to my poor girl."

But a stranger wandering in the hills could have. We stood still, staring down at Mr. McLeod's poor girl and listening to its baby cry for it. I wondered if cows made good mothers. From the sounds of the orphaned calf, I would have had to say yes.

"There's nothing can be done about this one," my dad finally offered, "but we should collect the rest of them, keep 'em in the pen 'til we get some kind of answers on this."

Mr. McLeod looked as if he might cry as he shook his head in agreement. He sniffled and turned to look toward the beach. The tide was out, and the black seaweed covering the exposed rocks sparkled under the remaining sun.

"I'll check the other side of the cove," he yelled, with his back towards us so we couldn't see the tears in his eyes. But it didn't matter. We could hear them in his voice. "They like to go in there sometimes." He walked toward the beach without turning back.

Arden, I, and our fathers took off in the other direction, up over the ridges until we were looking down on a familiar scene. The water danced with the wind and reflected the light, just like it had in the first part of the day when I'd been there with Isla. The sereneness made it easier for my mind to reject the memory of the wickedness we'd found later on.

From the top, we could see almost clear to Tobson. Woven into the herds of sheep grazing on the hillsides, we could see several of the cows meandering around, heads down, eating the grass as they walked. We counted four that we could see, not including a new calf glued to its mother's side; three on the right side of the gully and one on the left. We split up, and Arden and I jogged down the shallow path to the left to retrieve the mother and her calf and bring them back to pen where they'd stay until our parents could make sense of what had happened.

"What do you think did that?" I asked Arden when we reached the bottom of the path and started walking at a less hurried pace.

"No idea," he answered, "but it had to be bigger than that cow. And stronger. Those things are powerful." He continued to ramble on, but I stopped listening. I thought about the man on the path and how he'd hobbled down toward us. From where we had been standing I couldn't tell if it was just the ground that had given him trouble, causing him to bobble, or if there was something wrong with his legs. Even at the time, I wanted to believe it was the second because it gave us the advantage to get away. If something was ailing about the man, then he couldn't have been capable of enough strength and force to chop the cows head clean off. That's what I wanted to believe, but I couldn't be sure.

"So," I heard him say as he punched me in the arm.

"What?" I asked in a daze.

"What the shit man, haven't you been listening to me?"

"Sorry, I was thinking about something. What'd you say?"

"I said Ross and some of the guys are going to Stornoway tomorrow, and I begged him to take us with him, and finally he said yes as long as we sat in the back of one of the cars and don't talk. We're also not allowed to hang out with them while we're there, but who cares, right? It's just a ride. Do you want my dad to tell your dad when we get back so it's all settled?"

"What time?"

"They're leaving when they get up, which isn't usually until like eleven. Depends on how much drinking they do tonight," Arden laughed, but the jealousy was thick on his tongue.

"I can't go," I said quietly. Even if I had been able to go, I would have lied and said I couldn't. I didn't want to go anywhere with Ross.

"Why the hell not?"

"I've got that appointment."

"What time?" he asked, skeptical of my excuse.

"One."

He wanted to be angry with me but couldn't. He knew better than anyone that my family needed therapy, however real or imagined I had made it out to be.

"Whatever, man," was all he replied, powerless to really say anything else in the face of my very believable lie.

We'd gotten close enough to the cow and her calf that they'd taken notice and stopped pulling at the dry grass beneath them. We could barely see the mother's eyes under the auburn fur that hung in front of them. Her horns we could see clear as day though.

"They aren't just going to follow us back," I said, looking around for something better than grass to entice them back to the beach. We looked across the water to our father's who'd already roped two of the three cattle at the top of the ridge. "Are you wearing a belt?"

"Ach, no. What the hell are we going to use?"

"Look around. Maybe there's a feed bucket nearby. That should get her moving."

We split up and scavenged the grass for something to lure the mother and her baby back toward the beach. Arden bounded up the incline ahead of me. Within seconds he was shouting and holding something above his head he'd pulled from a patch of long, tangled grass.

"This should work!" he yelled back to me.

"What is it?"

"It's rope," he yelled, bouncing back down toward me. "It's got something on it," he said, opening and closing his hands which were covered in a black, sticky substance. "It should be ok to rope her with, you think?"

"I guess," I answered, looking at the black smudges left behind on his hands. "I don't think we have another option."

Arden roped the mother, and after some encouragement, she began moving. Her baby followed loudly behind her. We could see our father's ahead of us, about to disappear over the ridge back down to the beach with their three cows in tow. We meandered, dragging our feet in the long grass as the mother and baby traipsed behind us.

"How do you think I should ask her?" he finally said, breaking the uncomfortable silence that had been following us.

"Ask her what?"

"The St. Kilda trip. I want to ask her if we can, you know, do something, on the trip."

I couldn't look at him. I was afraid he'd see the truth in my eyes or, at the very least, my revulsion. "I don't think it's the kind of thing you ask. I think it just happens.," I finally offered, unsure of what else to say. But it was the truth. A preplanned hook up on the St. Kilda trip was not something you asked for.

"How'd you do it?" he asked.

"Do what?"

"Get over her?"

"I don't know, I just did."

"It's probably for the best," he said as we started to ascend out of the valley. The calf fell behind, and we moved slowly to allow it the chance to catch up.

"What's that supposed to mean?" I asked after digesting his comment.

"Just, you know ..." he answered, tapering off at the end.

"No, I don't know. That's why I'm asking."

"Just that you aren't all tied up in knots over her anymore." We crested the top of the ridge and could see the beach down below. Our fathers had rejoined with Mr. McLeod. I counted five cows in the pen, not including calves. Ours would make six, and the dead one they were huddled around made seven.

"It probably wouldn't have worked out anyway," he teased.

"Why the hell not!" I yelled, stopping our progress completely.

"I don't know," he laughed, handing me the rope while he rubbed the flaky black substance on his palms in the wet grass. "She doesn't seem like a good fit for you. You're more in the background. You're quiet and don't like to be the center of attention."

"And she does?" I asked.

"Whether she likes it or not, she is," he gushed. "She needs someone that can stand in the middle of it all, next to her."

"And I suppose you think you're that someone?"

He didn't answer. He didn't have to. I could hear his father yelling for us from down below, and when we looked, we could see them waving their hands at us to hurry up. We still had a couple of hours of light left in the sky, but I could see the shadowy clouds looming over the water. The murky sheet of rain connecting the clouds and the open ocean would be overtop of us within an hour.

I watched Arden trot down the hill, away from me. I stayed behind, letting him go. I wanted to scream at the top of my lungs so that everyone within a mile, easily, maybe even two, would know that I knew what her lips felt like pressed gently against mine, what she looked like in her underwear, what her hair felt like tickling against my skin. But I couldn't. Not because of him, but because of her. I turned and tugged on the lead connected to the stubborn cow behind me. When she was close enough, I whispered all of it to her instead, brushing the fur out of her eyes so she could see me clearly; so she could see my truth.

Chapter Fifteen

Lachlan sat with his head up against the window watching the world fly by. The sky had turned from blue to gray with a green tint lining the thick clumps of storm clouds following behind them. He closed his eyes, and all he could see was Mrs. Scott's face. Lachlan was ashamed to admit that he'd never given much thought to all the others affected by Arden's death, even his own mother. He replayed her words in his mind, wishing he'd had an answer to give her.

The small, barely paved road cutting through the peat fields between Achmore and the coastline gave way to signs of life as it dumped them out in Marybank and then quickly into the heart of Stornoway. Busses and cars moved quickly down the streets, pedestrians clogged the sidewalks, and young people on bikes raced through the openings in the traffic. Isla turned and headed towards the Castle College in the hills above the bay.

The car jerked to a stop in the library parking lot. Isla slipped out, stretching her legs and grabbing her waterproof from the backseat before slamming the door shut. Lachlan looked around, unfamiliar with the buildings in front of them.

"What was it?" he called to Isla as she hurried toward the front door.

"What was what?" she called back.

"Between you and Ross?"

His words stopped her in her tracks, but she did not turn to face him.

"Nothing," she answered simply.

"It had to be something," he responded. "Mrs. Scott pretty much called you her daughter back there."

"It was nothing," she yelled, turning toward Lachlan slightly but avoiding his eyes. She ran her hand across her stomach slowly and shivered slightly. Lachlan was happy to see that the mention of Ross' name made her as physically sick as it had him. Even though he knew there was more to it than nothing, her physical revulsion of him was enough for the moment.

"What are we doing here?" he yelled.

"Looking for Euan," she called back, turning slightly toward Lachlan with a heavy hand resting against her midsection like she might be sick.

The library was quiet and smelled like vanilla. The front desk was empty. Rows of bookshelves spilled out in front of them. Lachlan could hear the click-clack of someone typing away on a keyboard nearby. He followed behind Isla who was already leading the way to the back of the building.

"He's in here," she whispered over her shoulder as they approached the back wall where banks of doors and small rooms extended in either direction. Euan wasn't surprised to see them as they walked through the door and barely looked up from the maps and papers spread clear across the large table. The computer screen in the opposite corner flickered and pulsed, begging to be used.

"Right," he finally said in what felt like an official capacity, calling their meeting to order. "Did you bring it?"

Lachlan looked at him across the table, unsure of what it was he was supposed to have brought with them. Isla wrestled with something in her jacket and retrieved the small blue book from her pocket. She placed it on the table and pushed it toward Euan.

As if they weren't in the same room, Euan picked up the book and started leafing through it, mumbling to himself as he did. Isla had moved to the corner of the room and was tapping away at the computer while the monitor flickered. Lachlan felt invisible as he stood in the middle of the room, in the middle of something he couldn't believe.

"Is someone going to tell me what's going on?" he finally asked. "What exactly are we doing here."

Isla looked to Euan, who, in turn, finally stood up from the table and recognized Lachlan as being in the room.

"This," he started, motioning to the mounds of paperwork on the table between them. "This is the closest thing we have to the truth."

Lachlan glanced over everything on the table, trying not to laugh as he did. At best, the materials were random and far-reaching as far as any type of believable truth.

"What exactly is this?" Lachlan asked.

Euan started shuffling through papers and black and white photographs as he spoke. "I told you," he started, "Arden isn't the only one to go missing. Look."

He sent several pieces of paper sailing across the table toward Lachlan. Old newspaper articles about babies stolen straight from their cribs at night, a young girl out for a swim thought to have possibly drowned, boys gone missing in the hills while tending their family cattle and sheep.

"Euan, this doesn't mean anything. These," he said, looking down at the papers again, "the girl probably did drown and …"

Lachlan believed that the girl in the article had most likely drowned, and perhaps the boys missing from their family's field had befallen some other type of foul play, but babies missing in the morning was something else entirely.

"Look at these," Euan said, sending more paperwork across the table.

More articles about children gone missing, the faces of their loved ones left behind calling out for them. Behind the clippings were black and white photos, obviously official police pictures from suspected crime scenes. The drowned girl's clothes left behind on the beach, a backpack from a missing kid on his route home from school, another's jacket left splayed across shrubbery in the hills. But that was it.

"Is this a joke," Lachlan laughed, tossing the papers back toward Euan. "What exactly do you think is going on Euan?"

"It's not about what I think," he said, finally stopping and looking at Lachlan.

"It is," Lachlan laughed again. "This is all in your head."

"No," Euan said with force, returning to the piles of paperwork. "Here, look at this."

Euan sped around the table forcing another handful of pictures into Lachlan's hands.

"See," he said, pointing to an unraveled piece of rope in one picture, before grabbing the stack back and flipping through them at a high rate of speed.

"And here, look at this."

His finger jumped and stabbed the picture of hoof prints in Lachlan's hand.

"They were found in almost every case of someone who'd gone missing."

"So what!" Lachlan yelled back. "Almost all of these cases are in the middle of nowhere, where the only thing out there is cattle or sheep, or god only knows what other animals muckin' about. I bet you walk out in the hills right now anywhere on the island and you'll find the same exact thing; rope and fuckin hoof prints. It doesn't mean anything!"

"It means everything!" Euan yelled, smashing his hand onto the table, sending papers jumping into the air. Lachlan held his scowl for several moments, trying to make sense of his friend's momentary insanity, but there was no sense in it.

"Euan, please," Lachlan insisted. "This has to stop. I made it up, all of it, and I spent years locked away in the loony bin because of this ridiculous lie. If you keep screamin' 'bout hoof prints and fairy creatures, you'll be lucky if the same thing doesnae happen to you."

Euan froze as if the idea had never occurred to him. The sound of the keyboard had stopped, and Isla sat in the corner shifting her gaze between the two of them, stuck in the middle.

"They found them by the loch after Arden disappeared," Euan breathed, tossing yet another article across the table.

Instead of indulging him further by reading it, Lachlan rubbed his hands across his face. The several days of stubble scratched loudly against his hands, but no amount of rubbing could get rid of his disbelief.

"I'm sorry," he said, turning to leave. "I can't do this, not again."

Lachlan watched as the last bits of hope Euan had resurrected since his return to Lewis fade into dust. He had to wonder if Euan had been harboring his theories since it had happened. He'd hidden it from his wife, the department, but not his eldest daughter. Lachlan felt some comfort in the fact that he wasn't the only one lost in the mess left behind by Arden's death, but he couldn't drown in it any longer.

"This was a mistake," he whispered as he turned to leave.

The metal doorknob was underhand when Euan spoke again.

"They found them when Gretchen Campbell's husband and boy went missing too."

The paper slid across the table, biting at all the other's as it moved. It sounded heavy, weighted with something Lachlan had been looking for but never found.

Out of the corner of his eye, Lachlan watched Euan slide the photos across the table before he turned back to the book in his hand. He listened to the swish of pages moving in Euan's fingers, trying not to turn and look at the table. He never would have admitted it out loud, but he was afraid to.

In the distance, a mechanical hum started pulsing, and the scar on his forehead throbbed lightly. The bottom of his eye twitched rapidly as he tried to rub it away. He tried desperately not to think about it, but it was almost impossible with Euan spoon feeding him memories and ideas, wild fantasies about his version of the truth. His skin was hot, and he needed a drink by the time anyone spoke again.

"And there's this," Euan said, holding a clipping in his hand over top of the book. Lachlan turned slightly but could not open his eyes all the way. The pounding in his head made it almost impossible. "You ran out the other day, and I didn't get a chance to show you."

Euan held the clipping in one hand and the book in the other. Lachlan walked back toward the table, rubbing the scar above his eye as he did. He reached for the clipping with one hand and steadied himself on the table with the other.

The headline read *Lewis woman and self-proclaimed "seer" committed after affirming her husband and son were killed by a monster from the deep.*

Her eyes were distant, looking out at something only she could see. They looked just like Lachlan remembered when he'd seen them as a boy. The pounding in his head continued the deeper into the past he fell. His stomach turned and had he had anything in his gut, it might have ended up on the table between them. Lachlan scanned the article as best he could with only one eye able to open enough to read until he found what he'd been looking for.

"She was at Inverness," Lachlan mumbled, resting against the table.

They'd never been Moira's words. She'd only been the messenger. The words themselves still made little if any sense, but it made more sense that Moira was merely repeating them. They'd been the Spaewife's words, her predictions, her words of warning.

There was static in the room, a thickness to the air that made breathing difficult. Lachlan wanted to run out of the room, out of the library, away from Lewis, away from everything. He stumbled back from the table and crashed into the bank of floor to ceiling windows behind him, remembering the penalty he'd paid for a truth he couldn't have possibly understood at the time; the electrodes, the restraints, the buzzing, the humming, the flashes of light, the intensity of the electricity arching through his body. The terror he felt that first night resurfaced and his blood began to curdle in his veins.

"They must have been friends," Euan offered.

"It still doesnae mean anything," Lachlan laughed, raising his head to look at Euan.

"You don't know what they mean?" Euan asked.

"They dunnae mean anything, it's just madness."

"They have to mean something," Euan professed, desperation clinging to his words, and Lachlan wondered if his distress for it all to mean something came from a want to find out what happened to Arden, or if it had more to do with the mountain of paperwork sitting in front of them.

"Give me the book," Lachlan finally shouted.

Euan slid the book across the table as a preemptive smile broke out across his face. Lachlan scooped the book up and began flipping through it rapidly, the pages swishing in the air as they moved.

"The dates," Lachlan started, slamming the book against the desk and sliding it on top of the map Euan had splayed out in front of them. "The dates, don't match up, not one of them. Look! Some of them are decades apart from the reports."

Euan rubbed the smile from his face. Lachlan wasn't telling him anything he hadn't already seen for himself. Lachlan couldn't understand what it was his friend was holding on to if the one concrete element left behind by the Spaewife didn't match any of the cases he'd dug up.

"It's just nonsense," Lachlan whispered, as they both leaned over the table looking at the truth of it in front of them. "Whatever you think this is, Euan, it's not. Trust me."

"But, I thought … we thought," Euan's voice broke as he spoke, gesturing toward Isla sitting quietly in the corner. "I thought, some of these, looked like locations. Places, maybe."

Silence took over. Lachlan and Euan started across the table at each other, both searching for what they needed from the other.

"You have to let it go," Lachlan flipped the book closed without another look and pushed back from the table. "We all do."

"No," Euan said forcefully, unable to let any of it go. "No, this is something. This means something, it has to."

"Why? Why does it have to mean something? Who is this helping? Is this bringing anyone back? Have you found anyone? Is this bringing Arden back!" Lachlan's voice was unfaltering, steadfast in his position. "It doesn't mean anything, and even if it did …"

Lachlan stopped short of finishing his sentence, not wanting to breathe hope back into the hopeless. Despite knowing the truth of who's words were scribbled in the book, Lachlan knew the words were still meaningless, at least to them. Maybe they'd meant something to Gretchen Campbell at one point in her life. Maybe writing them down had given her some type of relief from the gut-wrenching pain she suffered having lost a husband and son in one fell swoop. Whatever their purpose, they weren't the key to bring Arden back. Arden was dead, and they all needed to accept that he was and figure out how to move on without him.

"Why don't we just ask her?"

Isla's voice startled both men who reeled in her direction at her sudden insertion into the conversation. Her eyes were glued to the flickering screen in front of her.

"Because she's dead," Lachlan answered, facing away from everyone in the room. "I watched Moira jump out a window at Inverness."

"Not, Moira, Gretchen Campbell," she said, pointing to something on the screen that neither man could see. "The Spaewife."

Chapter Sixteen

Everything was foggy, like someone had opened the all the windows on a crisp morning after a night of rain and let the mist roll in from off moor. It reminded me of home, of the hills behind the beach and the way the valley disappeared in the fog when you looked down at it from the top. As kids, we'd run from the ridge and stop just before the haze began to cover the ground. We'd tiptoe like ballerinas just above the clouds until someone had dared to fall below the surface and disappear into whatever lay beneath it. Even though we'd been in the valley a thousand times and knew the landscape well enough to traverse it in the dead of night, we still held our breath until we came out on the other side. The middle, where you lived for a moment in the damp grayness surrounding you before you came out underneath the cloud mimicked the haze I found myself in after visits to the first floor. I didn't know how much time I'd lost, but it felt significant.

I knew I was alive in the sense that I was still breathing, and that blood was still moving through my veins, but I felt little else other than air go in and out or the beat of my own heart. A thin film of confusion clouded the halls as I was escorted from the treatment area back to my room. The fog softened the sharp fluorescent lights, giving the rough edges of the asylum a more palpable feeling. The end of the hallway was always barely visible as I walked, and it felt like in a million years I'd never reach the end. My room was dim and didn't feel like mine anymore. Even the bathroom, which was usually nauseatingly bright, felt murky. I was alive, but lifeless at the same time.

Days ran together, and I was sure I was losing significant chunks of time. Things were being lost, taken from me and hidden away where they knew I'd never find them, but I didn't care. They'd made sure of that with medication and conditioning and the assurance that it was all part of the process. Had I been able to feel anything other than nothing, I might have laughed at the assertion that losing my memory and possibly my mind was part of the process.

***

There was a man's voice in the distance. It sounded like he was underwater. Or maybe I was underwater, and he was yelling from the surface. They must have been meant for someone else, not me.

"Lachlan," I could finally make out from under the surface. The man's voice felt close. I could feel the heat from his throat in my ear. I could taste stale tobacco wafting in the air around me, strangling me as much as the water it felt like my head could not get above. I struggled, but it only made it worse. Eventually, I knew I'd have to give up if I ever wanted to breathe again.

"Lachlan," Dr. Rutherford boomed. I turned my head towards the sound of his voice, but the restraint run against my forehead stopped me from moving. I couldn't see him, but I knew he was there. I could feel the pleasure he took from seeing me restrained wafting in the air between us.

"Can you hear me?" he asked.

"I can."

"Very good," he cooed. The metal legs of the chair he'd been sitting in screamed as he pushed back and came into my limited sightline. He hovered over me, pipe and all. "We're going to try something new today. How does that sound?"

He asked the question as if I had a choice. I pulled my arms against the restraints and then did the same with my legs. Something close to pain shot through my leg and I could feel something warm take over my foot as blood began to leak from the rawness of my skin. I'd been there before but couldn't remember it.

"Normally, during these procedures, the patient is put to sleep, a twilight state, to let the mind and body relax."

I felt my body tense, realizing that there was no way to know for sure how many times I'd been in that room with him hovering over top of me; how many times I'd been put under; how many times my unconscious body had been left alone with Benjamin, as Moira had called him. I wanted to cry out, scream, let the tears I could feel behind my eyes paint my cheeks, but I didn't have the means to do so.

"I'm going to keep you awake and ask you some questions, to try and ..." he paused to stare off into the distance as he searched for the right word, but I knew it was all just for dramatic effect.

"We'll say isolate the memory we're looking for."

He was a black and white cartoon character in the shadow of the fluorescent light backlighting him. I could see little else. There were other people in the room, moving about, flipping switches and calling out numbers I didn't understand. There was pressure against my arm, and then it felt like it was on fire.

"Ready?" he asked, but not to me.

Something hummed behind me, pulsing like it was being brought to life. The rhythmic movement of it was lulling, and maybe that was the point. Rutherford moved out of my field of vision, and I was left with nothing to look at but the lights above me.

"We'll start with something easy," Rutherford began. He sounded distant again and had I not been able to feel his breath against my skin I would have thought he stepped out of the room. The warming sensation that had started in my arm had moved, migrated through my body and was making its way down my legs when he spoke again.

"What were you and Arden fighting over, that night, in the valley?"

I could feel the excitement in his voice. It dripped from his lips like a dog slurping water in summer, the excess continuing to drip from his mouth even minutes later.

"What were you fighting over?" he asked again.

I could hear a man's voice, but it wasn't Rutherford. It was filled with a familiar sadness. Sorrow clung to the words as they drifted in and out of my ears. *Protect her with your life*, they echoed, and even in my drug-riddled state, I understood what my father had meant.

I closed my eyes and blinked away tears and sunspots burnt into vision by the blinding lights shining down on me. When I opened them again, all I could see was the glowing crown of red she wore as if we were back in the hills, laying lazily in the long grass as I looked up at the clouds behind her and she looked down at me.

"What was the fight about?" Rutherford asked, the heat of his breath feeling like the downdraft of warm summer heat.

Protect her, my father whispered again.

"I don't remember."

The light disappeared, along with the image of Isla and any memory of her. Arden vanished, quickly followed by the whole of Lewis. There was nothing but darkness, like it was the only thing that had ever existed as far as I was concerned; until all I could feel was the pain. Pinpricks and shallow needle stabs against my skin, over and over again. They weren't particularly deep, but they burned like wildfire and made me beg for the darkness.

I sat in front of his desk, looking out the large bay window at the tree branches being pounded by the wind.

The rain smacking into the glass sounded like tiny pebbles instead of liquid. In between the almost metallic pelting sound, I could hear the tick and the tock of the wall clock behind me, timing me until I made some type of verbal response.

I turned slightly in the uncomfortable chair, towards the sound of Dr. Rutherford's voice behind me. "Yes, Dr. Rutherford?" I answered.

"There we are," he answered with the same wry smile I remembered from before. "It's been awhile."

I had no memory, no way to judge how much time I'd lost; how much time they'd stolen from me.

"How long?" I asked. The words did not sound like my own despite the feeling of my lips and tongue moving in sequence with the words.

He smiled behind his pipe as he moved aimlessly around the office. "It took longer than we anticipated," he breathed laboriously, as if the treatment of patients interfered with his other duties. "You were resistant, at first."

"How long?" I asked again calmly.

"You were insistent that your tall tale was the truth, convinced that the water horse was the only truth." He fidgeted with the tobacco spilling out of his pipe and relit it as he spoke. "In the end, I think we helped you to see, there's always more than one truth."

"How long?"

"Three months," he finally answered, "give or take."

I had no recollection of it. There may not have been much to remember, I thought, as I searched my memory for something, anything that had happened in the last three months, but there was nothing but pain covered in darkness.

"How are you feeling?" he asked, taking a seat on the edge of his desk.

I thought about his question, trying to find the answer. I looked at my hands and arms, picking them up, turning them over and then back. I pushed the sleeves of my shirt back from my wrist and looked at the tender pink skin just below the bone of my wrists. The irritation from the restraints was beginning to heal. I did the same to the cuffs of my pants, pulling them up to look at the healing skin around my ankles. They were worse off than my arms. Red and black puffy scabs had formed. I picked at them at night until they bled which was why they hadn't healed as fast. I ran my fingers against my skull and the prickly pieces of hair that they'd let me retain. I'd never thought much about what my hair meant to me until they were taking it away. The tooth I'd cracked during the first treatment still throbbed, preventing me from eating solid food. My clothes hung loosely against my skin, which hung slack against my bones. I wanted to tell him that I felt worse than I was sure I looked, that I felt violated, that I felt dead underneath it all. But I felt nothing. I was a shell with nothing underneath. There was only the emptiness where I use to be.

"Ok, I guess," I finally answered, unsure of how to put the truth into words, not that it would have mattered.

"Great," the doctor answered happily, "I think we're going to make some great progress together now that we're on the same page."

He clapped his hands together and jumped up from his seat on the edge of the desk. He spun around and raced to his desk chair, scooted in quickly and gave me a look like I was welcome to proceed. His eyes were large, magnified behind his rounded glasses. His mustache looked like it needed a trim and he had something from his last meal hanging on at one of the edges. I wanted to laugh but felt like I'd forgotten how.

"I'm not sure where you want me to begin," I uttered after we'd stared at each other for an awkward amount of time.

"Let's start with Arden," he squealed like a child who'd been told he was going to the fair. "Or start at the beginning or the middle. Wherever you'd like to begin, that's where I want you to begin." He wore a crazed grin, stretching from ear to ear. The whites of his perfect teeth glistened in the light from the desk lamp. He looked like a madman waiting for his fix, and I was it.

I sat for a moment, thinking about where to start. The story was so convoluted, even the beginning wasn't really the beginning, but I knew Dr. Rutherford didn't want the trivial idiocrasies of my life before what had been the main event thus far. I watched the wind dancing with the trees outside and listened to the rain, remembering how it had felt against my skin that night. I remembered the evening fog rolling in from the beach, blanketing the valley as it moved quickly over land. I'd been alone when the first sound of thunder cracked, but I'd felt eyes on me since I left the sandy path at the crux of the beach and the hillside.

"Someone's watching me," I said as my skin prickled. "I can't see anyone, but I know there's someone there."

"Is it Arden? Is he there yet?" his words were quick, pushing through the spittle accumulating around his rabid mouth.

"I don't see him."

"Who is it then? Who's looking at you?"

I could feel the cold stone of the croft trailing underneath my fingers as I paced back and forth, waiting. The wind pushed across the valley floor in spirts, brushing against my skin. On it, I can hear an unfamiliar voice carrying a message. The words are faint, but they're there, telling me what's about to happen. They keep repeating, over and over again, like a song left on repeat.

"Relax Lachlan, you're in a safe place. Tell me who's watching you."

I can see Arden in snippets like a film roll that's about to run out. There are short bursts of light that hurt my eyes, and I want to look away, but I can't. He's yelling at me, but I can't hear him, only the unfamiliar voice, narrating the scene in my head. Arden points at me as he screams, panic and terror written all over his face, which don't match the narrator's words. *It's all your fault*, the voice says calmly.

"He's in the water," I whimper. But something isn't right. Something's missing.

"What's he doing in the water, Lachlan? Is he with the person who was watching you?" The doctor was almost on top of his desk he was so far out of his seat, salivating, hanging on my every word.

"He's … he's … he's yelling at me, reaching out toward me." Something's still missing, but I can't hold on to it.

"Tell me what you see Lachlan!" the doctor instructed, his elbows pressed firmly against his desk and his ass no longer touching his seat.

Something moved the darkness. It was the same color as the black surrounding us, which was why I hadn't seen it before. Arden's eyes widened, and his screams stopped. He's moving away from me, still yelling, but his words are not his own. *Why'd you do this to me Lachlan,* the voice says for him.

"It's …"

"Hold onto it Lachlan!" he yelled, slamming his fists angrily against the desk.

Something started burning inside me. My skin turned hot, and beads of sweat began to take shape in my forehead. I shook in my chair. I could taste rust in my mouth and feel sweat in the corners of my eyes. A low buzz hummed in my ear and there was an immense pressure inside my head. I tried to scream but couldn't find my voice. My lap felt warm, and I knew that I'd pissed myself, but I couldn't do anything about it. I couldn't open my eyes much less move the rest of my body.

The image of Arden began to fade like the ghost I knew he is. Lightning flashed in the sky, three times, quickly, and then there's nothing but the darkness. Thunder crashed and rumbled, almost like it was happening inside my head, just above my right eye. Then, all I could feel was the cold mud against my cheek. Everything froze, and I could hear Arden as if he were still standing next to me.

Watch out, I see him mouth. Then there's nothing.

Chapter Seventeen

"I cannae believe you never even fuckin' thought to check if she was still alive!" Lachlan screamed, smashing his hands against the dash of Isla's car as she sped clear across the island toward Gallen Head; toward the Spaewife; toward the truth.

"What kind of cop are you? Isnae that police work 101 for fuck's sake!"

"She shouldnae be alive," Euan yelled from the back seat. "How was I supposed to know that in that she should also flippin' live forever. She's got to be as old as dirt by now. She looked like she might die right in front of us when we saw her as kids."

"What kind of inspector are you?" Lachlan yelled in anger, but his anger wasn't meant for Euan. Lachlan didn't know who it was intended for. Maybe himself, the old woman, the island itself. Euan had only accidentally stumbled into something he couldn't explain. It wasn't his fault.

Isla sped down the 858 with the windows partially down trying to outrun the sun. They had only hours to make it before the sun went down and they were lost in the darkness of the isolated village of Gallen Head, just north of Uig. Lachlan had been there once as a boy. He remembered it even then being a place he would not want to visit after dark.

Euan wrestled with his stacks of paper in the back seat, losing the battle against the wind whipping through the car. Lachlan thumbed through the pages of the Spaewife's book like it was the first time he'd read it. The words still hid secrets Lachlan didn't know the answers to, but as the barren landscape that made up the middle of

Lewis gave way to the mountainous peaks of the eastwardly coast, he felt that he might have a chance at finding what he'd lost.

***

By the time they arrived in Uig, the sky was streaked with reds and oranges as the sun was preparing to set on the other side of the island. Euan read more of the reports in the backseat of Isla's car as she drove. Lachlan stared out the window at the rocky cove hidden between two towering bluffs on either side. As they sped up the hillside toward the village of Gallan Head, just outside Uig, Lachlan watched the waves lapping at the stone shoreline and the sun disappearing from the sky.

The village itself felt deserted. There was no movement in any direction. The majority of the homes that had been fashioned out of old Conex box type structures were dark. Junk and debris littered the small yards, giving the appearance that all its inhabitants had just picked up and left while in the middle of everyday tasks.

The Gallan Head Hotel, a rectangular shaped, red-sided building, was the first building that showed any evidence of life with a small front light illuminating a faded sign bearing its name. The car crept past slowly, the tires crunching loudly on the loose gravel and absolute silence surrounding them.

"It's that one," Isla said, pointing ahead of them to a small building that had once been painted purple. The sun had stolen its vibrance long ago and was now a dingy relic of what it had once been.

"Are you sure?" Euan asked, hopeful that no human could live in such squalor.

Isla stopped in front of the small croft, holding up a picture she'd printed from the library to show that it was a match to the one in front of them. "Pretty sure," she answered, opening the door and stepping out.

Euan knocked on the door, despite it only being attached at the top hinge. It looked like rats, or some other vermin had eaten the bottom half of it. The walls looked like they were leaning to one side, having been pushed by the relentless wind that skipped across what felt like the edge of the world. It was most certainly the edge of Lewis.

"There's no one here," Euan yelled back to Isla and Lachlan, still standing by the car. "I don't think there's anyone here, anywhere."

They all stood and looked around, feeling like the only three people in the world. The last bits of the sun were holding on to the edges of the sky. Soon it would be pitch black, and the stars and the moon would be their only source of light.

"Listen," Lachlan said quietly, "do you hear that?"

No one spoke for a moment. But then it came, a low, murmured hum being carried on the wind spinning around them.

"Look around," Lachlan yelled as he stepped over a small dilapidated fence in front of the old woman's house, moving in the direction the wind was pulling from. The closer to the back of the house he moved, the louder her voice sang, calling him to find her.

On what had once been the back porch of the rundown croft was the old woman, sitting in the fresh summer wind, watching the day disappear from view. Lachlan recognized her immediately. She didn't look that different from when they'd encountered one another the first time. He was frozen, watching her rock back and forth in the wind.

"Th' one that got away." Her voice was frail, and the words mumbled. Lachlan stared at her from across the small courtyard, listening, waiting to be invited into her world again.

The old woman went silent and stood up from her rickety chair, shuffling her feet as she walked towards

Lachlan. There was almost no light left in the sky, and the stars were beginning to make themselves visible. In the background, he could hear Isla and Euan calling for him, but he ignored their calls.

She stood on the other side of a short stone wall that had at one point divided the neighboring yards. In the waning light, Lachlan could see the clouds covering her eyes. He needed to know what lingered on the other side of them.

He reached into his back pocket, pulling out the little blue book that had belonged to her. Lachlan held it in his hands, unsure of what her reaction to seeing it again would be.

"I think this is yours," he whispered, holding the book out to the woman.

The clouds in her eyes began to fade as she reached for the book. Lachlan had shoved papers and articles in between the pages, making it awkward and bulky for her frail hands. The book spilled on the stones below her feet, loose pages and pictures being kicked up in the wind.

"Lachlan!" Isla yelled from behind him. He turned expecting to see her around the corner of the house.

"Lachlan!" she yelled again, sounding more distant than before.

He stepped back to look for any sign on Isla or Euan when a penetrating sting took over his arm. He wanted to jump back, out of the way of the pain, but couldn't. The woman had ahold of his arm again, her fingers burning against his skin, just like before.

"Th' one that got away, Spring, 1985," she whispered in a throaty voice, tightening her grip on Lachlan's arm, just like she had when he was a boy. "I warned you, didn't I, laddie" she hissed.

"You said that to me before," Lachlan breathed hurriedly. "What does it mean?"

Light from a torch bobbed between them, and Lachlan could see through her eyes when it caught them just right. They were tired, begging for something she couldn't put into words.

"It was there, waiting at th' water's edge for you, wasnae it, wee Lachlan?" Her lips pursed, and a bony hand reached for his cheek like a grandmother would have done, had he ever known one.

"Not so wee anymore, I see."

"How do you know what happened to me?" he asked, unbelieving that the skeleton with skin in front of him knew what century it was, much less who he was. "How do you know who I am?"

"I've known you since befor' ye was born," she hissed, "since before your mother even knew you." Her grip on Lachlan's arm tightened; unkempt and dirty nails beginning to dig into his skin. "I see th' things o' th' devil's seed, passing in mah mind."

"What is the book? What does it mean, the dates? What is spring 1985? What does that have to do with what happened to me?"

She pulled Lachlan in closer, and he let her, despite every atom in his body screaming to the contrary. Her breath came faster, and her eyes glazed over.

"You've been livin' on borrowed time, sweet laddie, these last twenty years. He's waiting for you – to claim th' one that got away. It's your turn to pay the price."

She let go of Lachlan's arm, and he stumbled backward, tripping over discarded fragments of past lives behind him. The clatter drew Isla and Euan's attention, sending them running in the dark, narrow path between the dilapidated homes. She was hard to see, but they both jumped at the site of her, hunched over gathering the book from the ground around her feet.

"Don't forget your book," she exhaled holding the book out to Lachlan as Euan helped him to his feet. They looked at the women with wide eyes, uneased by her strange smile. The weight of the book made her arm shake, and Lachlan grabbed it back from her before it found the ground again.

"Let's go," he whispered, backing away from the woman.

"What?" Euan questions. "Wait, but I thought ..."

"Read them again," she laughed loudly as she turned to make her way back to the chair hidden in the corner. "It'll all make sense. Follow the path to th' loch where you walked on water – where you saw him first. He'll be waiting." She fell roughly into the old chair, mumbling distant words as she did. "It's your turn to pay the price, wee Lachlan."

"What the hell was that?" Euan asked as they all piled into Isla's car and hurried down the hill as if running from a crazed murderer instead of a harmless old woman. Lachlan rubbed his arm where she'd grabbed him, expecting there to be a burn mark, but it wasn't even chaffed from her chapped skin.

"What'd she say?" Euan asked, hunched over the front seat looking back at Lachlan.

"Walk on water," Lachlan repeated. "Saw him first."

"What the hell does that mean? Is that it? Is that all she said?"

"Just, shut up for a second," Lachlan yelled back at him, frustrated and cramped in the backseat, stifled by piles and piles of paperwork. Let me think, was what he meant to say, but it came out as "I need a drink."

At the bottom of the hill, Isla pulled to the side of the road, leaving her headlights burning to give them light in the darkness. She pulled a bottle of whiskey from behind her seat, offering it to Lachlan first. The liquid burned as it went down, but he welcomed it. He passed the bottle to

Euan, who in return handing him the hoard of papers he'd grabbed from the car.

"She warned me to stay away from the water, that something was waiting for me where feet walk on water."

"Warned you.?" Isla asked, stealing the bottle back from Euan. "When"

"The day we crashed Ross' car."

Isla's eyes grew to the size of twin moons, unwavering in a cloudless sky. She tried to speak, but disbelief had stolen her voice clean from her throat. All she could do was stare back at Lachlan, the memory of that day reflecting in her glassy eyes.

"We found her in the hills on the way back from Tobson." Lachlan took a deep breath, trying to organize the flood of thoughts and truths he needed to let out. "It was like she'd seen it, in her mind, before it happened. Like she knew it was coming."

Lachlan's words came faster and faster. "There's no other explanation for it. It happened exactly like she said it would, except, instead of me, it was …" His voice trailed off as the memory washed over him.

***

Isla moved toward Lachlan, leaning against the hood of the car. She stood in the space between his stance, whiskey bottle to her lips. "Drink," she said, handing him the bottle, "and then tell him."

Lachlan gulped the fiery liquid down without issue, wishing it would wash away the craziness he was on the verge of believing. There was no way it could be possible.

"Tell him what we saw that day."

The air was still. Fog rolled slowly in front of the headlights like ghosts' swimming around them. Below, waves crashed into the jagged edge of the cliffs. They'd never spoken a word about anything that happened that day. Lachlan had tried to salvage the bits and pieces worth saving, but the feeling of something wicked had always tainted them.

"You saw it?" he asked standing upright, leaving Euan's hard work sitting loosely on the hood of the car. "You never said anything. I wasn't sure, I mean. I never knew for sure."

There was barely room for the stillness of the wind to move between them. Lachlan looked down at Isla, her pale skin reflecting in the headlights. Her eyes were bloodshot, like she hadn't slept well in days, maybe longer. She moved, but her eyes never wavered. Her fingers traced his, winding in between them and the neck of the whiskey bottle until she grabbed ahold of it and took another drink.

"I saw it," she choked out, wiping whiskey from her lips. Lachlan wished he'd thought to do it for her instead.

"What the shit is going on?" Euan finally yelled. "Or did you forget I was even here?"

"Aye, we know you're there," Lachlan yelled, holding Isla's eyes as he spoke, reliving the memory with her. "There's a loch, behind Bosta – there's a shelf that leads out from the shore, and you can run damn near to the middle before it drops off."

"Walk on water," Euan whispered, pacing back and forth beside the two of them.

"Walk on water," Lachlan repeated, invigorated and terrified by his own words. "We went swimming on a Saturday, and there was a man, in the hills, above the croft that's there at the edge."

He gulped another shot and felt the crown of Isla's head push against his chest and her hands resting on his hips.

"He was on the path, and then he just ..."

Lachlan paused, still somewhat unable to comprehend what had happened.

"He just what?" Euan begged. "What?"

"He disappeared, just vanished when he got to the bottom of the trail."

"What?"

Lachlan ran his fingers through Isla's hair, pulling her head from his chest. He met her gaze again, trying to find the right words in her eyes.

"I can't explain it, it was more than just him being there and then vanishing. The second I saw him, I felt ..."

"Evil." Isla voice wavered as she finished Lachlan's thought. "It felt like evil running through the valley."

Euan stood still, a dumbfounded look across his face and his arms stretched out to his side. "Ok, so what then?"

Lachlan swept Isla's hair behind her ear and smiled. "We tore out of the valley and when we got to the top, after we dressed and before we ran back down the other side – a black horse was racing across the shelf, away from us."

The wind kicked and wrapped both Lachlan and Isla in a whirlwind of red hair and papers lifting from the hood of the car. Euan dove frantically on the hood, trying to catch as much as he could before the wind took them all.

"Grab them!" he yelled desperately, watching however many years of hard work and secrets fly away into the night.

The three of them dashed around like birds scattering from a tree into the sky, stopping and pawing at the papers as they fluttered in the darkness. Had it not been devastatingly gruesome to watch in terms of the time and effort Euan had taken to compile all the papers that danced around them, it would have been almost beautiful. The wind eventually died and what was left of Euan's work drifted to the ground, and they chased pathetically after it.

Euan moaned in the background while Lachlan moved away from him and Isla chasing after what he felt he could grab. Maps and newspaper clippings swished around his feet as he walked. He grabbed what he could before turning back towards the car, trying to organize the remnants in his hands.

The gravel of the unpaved roads crunched as he walked, tilting the papers into the beam from the headlights to see what he'd managed to save. He pulled the picture from the pile, slowly, as if moving it too quickly would cause it to disappear. First, it had only been her eyes he had seen, but as he inched it out from behind the page on top, she was completely exposed. A familiar set of indignant eyes staring back at him.

He read the headline; *Local woman attacked.* Lachlan skimmed the article trying to make sense of why her picture had been printed next to such a headline. Keywords began to stand out from the blur of black and white that sped past his eyes as he read. *Young woman, severely injured but will recover, ligature marks, blindfolded, transported to a secondary location, torn undergarments, evidence of rape, victim declined full examination.*

The world began to spin around him. The air was thin and unbreathable. Lachlan felt like for the first time in his life he could see, despite being in the middle of the darkened coast.

"What is this," he asked soberly, holding the paper out in front of him.

Euan and Isla had regrouped by the car, trying to account for what each of them had found and what was still missing. Euan whined like he had always done as a child. The incessant high-pitched sound moving past his lips made Lachlan's skin curl.

"Shut the fuck up, Euan!" he screamed as he stumbled back toward the car, unable to take his eyes off the picture in his hand. The other papers he'd managed to catch had been lost again, drifting in the sea breeze behind him.

"Just shut up! What is this? Why do you have this?"

"What?"

Euan grabbed for the clipping, but Lachlan was already pushing him away.

"Why do you have this?" he yelled again, the fingers of both hands already wrapped around the folds of Euan's collar. "Answer the fuckin' question, why do you have it?"

"I don't even know what it is, let go of me." Euan struggled against Lachlan, but he was no match, and they both knew it. Lachlan pulled his old friend in close, so they were eye to eye. His chest heaved, and spittle flew from his tightly clenched lips as he tried to breathe.

Lachlan let go and shoved Euan backward, sending him teetering against the front of Isla's car.

"What the fuck!" he yelled once he had his balance, and Lachlan dove at him again, crushing the clipping in his hand as he did.

"Stop it," Isla yelled, putting herself between the two men.

Dust kicked up from the gravel wafted in the air, clouding over the yellow of the headlights. His chest tightened, and his skin was hot. Beads of sweat dripped into the corners of his eyes and stung like the sea when he'd swum at Bosta or Seilebost. His vision tunneled, and Lachlan could feel his knees begin to buckle. Euan's face remained clueless until Lachlan waved the clipping in the air.

"This!" he yelled again. "Why do you have this."

"What is it?" Isla asked, still standing in the space between them.

"It's about my mother," Lachlan replied, shaking the words as with his trembling lips. "It says - she was raped."

Lachlan turned away from them and looked at the article again, rereading the date to make sure he'd seen it right. His laughter was frantic, fraught with disgust and disbelief.

"April," he gasped as his knees buckled beneath him. "1985."

Chapter Eighteen

"I can't stay long," she said softly as we ran, hand in hand, off the main road to the middle of the field not far from her house. I thought we'd lie in the afternoon sun looking at the clouds as they passed by, the wind transforming them into pictures of funny things. Her bad news should have been abysmal, but I was there with her at that moment for however brief; that was all that mattered.

"Why?" I asked, finally slowing once we were out of view of the road, hidden behind a small outcropping of rocks that jutted up out of nowhere. Our parents had forbidden us from the pastures behind Bosta once word of Mr. McLeod's decapitated cow had spread, not that it mattered to Isla and I. I wasn't sure we'd ever go back there after the last time.

"I have to watch my little sister," she answered without the slightest sound of discomfort in her voice.

"How long can you stay?"

"Not long," she answered, taunting me with her smile. She wanted me to think that it didn't matter to her, but I knew that it did.

"Then we better get to it," I laughed, pulling a blanket from my bag and letting it sail in the mild breeze before laying it on the dry grass.

"That's mighty presumptuous of you, Mr. McGinley," she said straight-faced with her arms crossed over her chest. Her smile had melted away and in its place was a look of absolute disgust for me and my insidious suggestion.

"No, it's not ... I didn't mean ..." What the hell had I just done? I'd swallowed my tongue, and the more I tried to recant my proposition the more tongue-tied I became. I bent down to gather the blanket and regroup when a wild roar of laughter rang out into the emptiness surrounding us. She was red in the face and near tears when I was finally able to look at her. She grabbed the two furthest corners of the blanket and straightened them out before falling on top of it, still laughing and holding her sides in hysterical pain.

"You should have seen your face," she was finally able to get out through the laughter. "You turned ghost white."

Embarrassment paralyzed my legs, and I couldn't move as I watched her roll around on the black and white checked blanket. The situation just proved that I was in over my head with her.

"Well," she called up to me. She laid on her side, with one hand resting gently on her hip and her hair fanned out around her. "Are you coming down or not?"

My skin was hot, and the sound dizziness makes echoed between my ears. It was like a floor fan stuck in some weird, annoying rhythm. I had no idea what I was doing with Isla Gilcrest. I'd gotten her alone in the middle of nowhere laying on a blanket underneath me, and realized I was utterly and completely incapable of handling her, just like Arden had said. I wanted to rip her clothes off just to spite him but didn't even know where to begin.

She took pity on me but only after toying with me long enough to make it worth her while, like a cat with its catch. The cat keeps the catch alive long enough to let it think it has a chance just before it dispatches the poor thing. I was the poor thing, and I made it easy for her toy with me. She reached out her hand and smiled a sweet smile I knew well enough to know that she didn't show to many people.

"I didn't mean it like that," I whispered, dropping to my knees pathetically.

"I know what you meant," she whispered, shifting from her side to her knees, putting us face to face. "You're a good boy." She put both her hands in mine, looking down at them as she did.

"You're not like the rest of them," she said, and I was forced to wonder which Scott brother she was referring to.

Her lips tasted like berries and sweet biscuits as they pressed gently against mine. The wind tossed her hair like the grass swaying around us, tickling me in the space between our faces. I let go of her hands only to cup them around her cheeks and pull her closer, kissing her harder as I did. There was nothing else like it. Not just the kiss, but the connection I felt to her. I was aware that I knew little about the world, but I knew love, and it had scarlet hair, soft pink lips, eyes as deep as the ocean and a smile that could bring me to my knees - and had.

"Lay with me," she whispered while our lips still touched, "and look at the clouds." She pulled away and smiled modestly.

We laid in the sun, shielding our eyes to look at the clouds as they passed us by. She snuggled on my shoulder as her hair twirled around us as wild as the wind. It was warm enough that she wore short sleeves and I tickled the skin on her arms with the tips of my fingers, making her squirm and shy away.

"Watch out for Arden," I whispered abruptly.

"What? Why?" she asked, still giggling as I pulled at the tiny peach-colored hairs on her arm.

"He's obsessed with you."

"What? Shut-up, he is not."

I didn't respond and just watched her as she lay against my chest.

"He thinks he's going to ... well, he wants to ..."

"Out with it!" she yelled jumping up to her knees.

"He thinks he's going to get somewhere with you on the trip - the St. Kilda trip."

"I see," she smiled, spinning her hair into a messy braid to keep the wind from carrying it away. "The infamous St. Kilda trip, where girls lose their morals and their panties on the boat ride over."

"No, I didn't say that's what I thought, I just …"

She was laughing again, at me, but I knew I made it too easy.

"Why are you here?" I asked. My brain was on shuffle, and random thoughts were escaping at a rapid pace.

"I don't know," she answered. "I like being with you. I can be myself around you."

"Why are we keeping this a secret?" I blurted out.

She puckered her lips in an attempt to not laugh at the humility leaking from mine. "It's more fun that way," she answered with an over exaggerated wink.

I knew that wasn't the truth, and so did she. I didn't think she had an answer for it, any more than I did. Keeping it a secret made it ours and no one else's, and that's all that seemed to matter when we were together.

"What is this, exactly?" I wanted to take the words back the second I heard them. My heart began to race, unsure if I wanted or even needed to know the answer. The wind kicked up and blew the lazy braid she'd spun clean out of her hair. It flew in every direction, just like fire in the wind.

"I think they call it love," she whispered confidently, unashamed of her forwardness when most other girls would have blushed and run away.

I could barely see her face through the flames that burned around her, but she was there, and I was there with her. "I think you're right," I said, before grabbing her and kissing her so hard that it hurt somewhere deep inside both of us.

"Find me first," she whispered in between kisses and our breath.

"What do you mean?"

"On the trip, find me first, so I don't have to pretend with some other boy."

"I'll find you first," I panted, clamoring for as much of her as I could get in that moment, "and always."

She left me in the empty field, but I watched from atop the outcropping until she skipped up the stairs of her house and waved me off. We didn't talk about it, but we both knew the implications of what we'd seen and kept secret. I tried not to think about it, and just watched to make sure the door closed behind her before I fell back to the blanket, pretending I'd seen nothing at all.

I stayed for a while looking up at the sky and imagining her lying next to me. I wandered to Bosta even though I knew I wasn't supposed to. I didn't go into the hillside, but stayed at the beach and walked barefoot, letting the warm sand squish between my toes. As the tide came back in, it brought with it the smell of a storm. The tide bell clanged loudly with each ebb that rolled, and I made my way home unhurriedly.

***

The house was quiet, but the lights were on, and my father's car was in the drive, so I knew they had to be home. I crept into the kitchen and caught my father off guard as he stood at the sink washing the kettle. When he heard me behind him, he turned brutishly, the look of dread ringing loudly in his eyes. He didn't even have enough time to warn me.

"Oh, Lachlan, you're back," my mother hissed from behind me. "I didn't hear you come in. Where have you been?"

Her simulated jollity gave her away. Something had happened. She knew something. I just didn't know what. I backtracked through all the lies I'd told recently, but they were all too muddied together to understand which one had been found out.

"Just out, riding bikes and stuff."

"That's nice," she said, trying to make her face smile, but instead it came off as toleration. "With who?"

"Just kids from school." I tried to as vague as possible, leaving myself outs all over the place in case I needed to back my way out of whatever lie I'd been caught in.

"Who, specifically," she demanded. My back was against the counter. My father stood next to me at the sink. He'd turned the water off and was looking out the window, listening vapidly to my mother.

"Was Euan there?" she asked. "Or how about Calum? Maybe Alister or Ian or the little Stewart kid. I can't remember his first name. Were they with you?"

I didn't answer. I just stood in front of her with my hands pressed against the counter behind my back, waiting for what I knew was coming.

"I know Arden wasn't there," she whispered, trying to meet my eyes as they darted away from hers. "He came lookin' for ya 'round lunchtime. Said he hadn't seen you all day."

My fear of my mother ended where my hatred for Arden began. He hadn't believed my lie about the appointment. He'd gone to my house knowing that I wouldn't be home and that my mother would be expecting the two of us to be together. He'd done it on purpose.

"Where were you?" she asked again, doubling the number of syllables in each word as she drew them out.

My anger made me brave, and I pushed past her, bumping her shoulder as I did. "What do you care. I was just out. Why does it matter who I was or wasn't with?"

First, I felt her hand wrap tightly around my arm, pulling and spinning me back towards her. Then I felt the tips of her fingers and their sting against my cheek before I could even comprehend that she'd slapped me.

"It matters because I'm your mother and the last thing I need is you out making trouble just like ..." she caught her tongue and stared at me with hate-filled eyes. "Tell me right now," she yelled as her face shook. "Where were you and who were you with? And don't lie to me! I've called every other mother on this godforsaken island and asked them where their boys were, so don't lie to me!"

I figured I was already in trouble. What difference did the truth make? She was like Arden; she'd beat the dead horse until she got what she wanted. I decided swift punishment was better than dragging it out.

"I was with a girl, ok, that's it," I yelled back, rubbing my cheek.

My answer had shocked her as if the thought of her son being interested in a girl had never occurred to her.

"What girl?" she let slide through her teeth.

I didn't answer and instead, looked back to my father who was bracing himself against the counter, with his head hung low and eyes closed waiting for it to be over.

"What were you doing with her?"

My eyes darted to my bag and back to her as if to tell her that's where she'd find the answer. She stared at me for a moment longer before tearing off to grab my bag from the bottom of the stairs, ripping it open and dumping it onto the kitchen floor. The blanket spilled out onto the floor, followed by Isla's jacket she'd left behind and the rope I'd used to lead Mr. McLeod's cow with the day before. I wanted to laugh when I saw that my mother's assumption was the same as Isla's when she saw the blanket, only I knew my mother's supposition wouldn't end with playful banter.

"What is this?" she whispered, picking up the pieces of rope and holding them out like it might be a dead snake instead. Her face was horrified as she looked at me. In that moment she stopped being my mother and became someone else. The anger in her face faded and turned to fear. She began mumbling and dropped the rope back onto the blanket. "What are you doing? What are you doing?"

she repeated over and over. "I knew it, I knew this would happen," she whispered to my father behind me.

"It's just a piece of rope from ..." my father started.

"Shut up!" she yelled, now pacing back and forth in front of us. "I told you, I knew ..." but her words turned to mumbles, and I couldn't understand her. I just stared at her, unable to understand the reaction she was having.

"Go to your room," she finally yelled. "You're grounded, for ... until I say otherwise. Go to your room. I don't want to see you. Go to your room."

Her voice shook, and she twiddled her fingers in front of her mouth like a child. Tears clung to the bottom of her eyes which looked back at me with shame and remorse.

"What?" I yelled, "but I didn't do anything. That's not fair!"

"Fair!" she yelled, almost hysterical, shaking her head back and forth like she was trying to shake something from her mind. "Fair!" she yelled again lunging at me. My father stepped between us without saying anything. It was the first time he'd intervened in an argument, ever.

"Fair, you want to know about fair?" she screamed, trying to push past my father. He never raised a hand to her but moved with her like they were dancing.

"Get upstairs," my father shouted back to me through my mother's incoherent screams. "Just go."

She stopped screaming and stood still, panting for breath like a dog gone rabid. "You're not to see whoever she is, ever again, or any girl. You're too ... it's in your blood, and I'll not have it be true."

"What?" I yelled, uncertain of what her crazed statement was supposed to mean.

"You're not allowed out of this house anymore unless it's to go to school. I'll lock you in your room if I have to!"

"But I didn't do anything!"

"Yeah," she laughed, "but you might. I'll not have some little girl be …"

"Lachlan, just go upstairs," my father begged, "please."

I moved out of my father's shadow and watched her fight off his attempts to calm her. Her words were incoherent, and every attempt my father made to console her with his touch were met with thrashing arms and banshee screeches.

"I wish you weren't my mother," I yelled as I bounded up the stairs to my room. "I hate you!"

I could hear them struggling against each other from the top of the stairs. Before I slammed my door, my mother yelled back "most days I wish I wasn't your mother either!"

***

I was at the crux of the road where Arden and I always met before school. I was there a whole fifteen minutes before I saw him gliding down the hill toward me. I stood next to my bike, desperately trying to control my anger as it pulsed with each beat my heart made. When he was close enough, I shoved my bike directly into his path, sending him flying and into the wet gravel on the other side. I was on top of him before he knew what was happening.

"Why'd you do it?" I yelled in his face, grabbing the collar of his shirt to pull him as close to me as I could. "Why?"

He didn't struggle. He laid underneath me like a silent rag doll until he started to laugh. "I knew you were lying about something," he said. "You suck at lying."

"You're not my keeper Arden, I don't have to tell you everything I'm doing." I pushed him to the ground and stood up.

"You're right, you don't have to," he yelled as he jumped to his feet, brushing the grime off his back as he did. "We're supposed to be best friends. But lately, it's like you can't be bothered with me, or with any of us. I knew you were lying about the fuckin' appointment and I want to know why."

"So, you came to my house looking for me when I told you I wouldn't be there, you fuckin' asshole! I'm grounded for like the rest of my life thanks to you."

"Why were you lying, then? What were you doing that you had to lie to me? Just tell me that you don't want to fucking hang out, I'm a big boy, I'm not gonna cry about it."

"Fuck you, Arden, you always cry about it. You'll bug me about it until I finally give up and do whatever dumb shit it is you want to do."

"That's not true. You can do whatever you want, see if I care."

"If you didn't care," I yelled, "then what the shit are we fighting about?"

"Because you lied about it, and I knew you were lying about it. What the hell do you have going on in your life that's so much more entertaining than what we've always done?"

"I was with Isla, ok! I was with Isla." I was breathless by the end of the sentence. It didn't matter anymore, I was never going to be allowed out of the house to see her again anyway, thanks to him.

"Shut up," Arden laughed, picking up his bike. "Now that's a lie."

"Is it?" I asked. "Are you so sure about that?"

We stood like statues across the road from each other, and I watched gleefully as Arden wrestled with the possibility of Isla and me being true.

"You wouldn't know what to do with that girl even if you did manage to get her attention somehow." He grabbed his bike and walked toward the main road without looking back at me.

"I've seen her in her underwear!" I yelled at him, making him stop dead in his tracks. "The day we crashed

Ross' car, when you thought she'd just be sitting at home waiting for your bother, she was with me. She was never going to be there. We went swimming in the loch behind Bosta in our underwear that afternoon. That's why I blew you off."

He didn't turn to look at me until I stopped. He let his bike go, and it tumbled in the gravel. He walked toward me, laughing in disbelief. His fist was fast, like his brother's, but it didn't hurt as bad as I was expecting. After a few more hits he knelt on top of me while the gravel pushed jaggedly against my back.

"We aren't friends anymore," he whispered in my face.

I thought his words would sting more, but they were hollow. We hadn't been friends in months. This was just the formality of it all.

Chapter Nineteen

The world was on its side, tinted the golden-brown color of bottom shelf whiskey. The coolness of the sticky tabletop did little to chill Lachlan's burning skin. A half-smoked cigarette rested in the corner of his mouth. He could hear the whispers twirling around him, shouts from burly locals to the barkeeps for more whiskey, glasses clinking together in celebration of nothing more than collective drinking. He tried holding onto the words he knew were significant, the ones he'd heard the old woman say before, but they were slipping away with each drink that slid down his throat. He threw back another swig from the bottle of Grouse on the table, stealing looks around the Twisted Thistle as he did. The pub was alive, but Lachlan felt dead inside.

"Should we do something? Call someone?" she whispered to Euan across the table.

"Who would we call?" he responded, shrugging his shoulders.

Lachlan's mind drifted as he downed another shot, spilling half of it on its way to his mouth, eager to find the oblivion he never fully appreciated before. The warm liquid washed over, but it couldn't wash away the truth. Not anymore.

"No," he spat sloppily between drinks, "let's call him. Then we can ask him if it's true. That'll be a fun conversation."

Lachlan slurred his words and drool oozed onto the tabletop, as he'd not bothered to lift his head to talk. The pub erupted in a riotous clamor. Men and women yelled and cheered and clinked glasses and pounded on the bar top. Lachlan shot up from the table, applauding sarcastically with them, throwing his hands into the air as he did.

"Maybe we should go," Isla suggested when the brief distraction lifted.

"Where're you gonna take me?" he slurred. "Back to my house?" He smiled drunkenly across the table at Isla. He'd drunk so much the golden liquid was just peeking over the bottoms his eyes, sloshing back and forth as he swayed in his chair.

He leaned over the table toward Isla, reaching clumsily for any part of her he could find. "Maybe we go back to your place, and I push you up against the wall a few good times. 'Bout time I got it in with you."

"Lachlan," Euan barked, but his words were lost in the ringing between Lachlan's ears after the palm of Isla's hand struck the side of his face.

She grabbed for the bottle as she jumped from her seat, but his reflexes when it came to booze were quick. Lachlan's hand covered hers, squeezing it against the glass neck of the bottle he was determined to finish on his own.

They stood across the table from each other, in a drunk's version of hand in hand. They struggled over the bottle, but really it was a struggle against the people they'd become versus the memories of who they'd once been. The girl he'd known before was disappearing the longer he looked at her. He had caught glimpses of her, but a squandered past they'd never get back had all but buried her.

The struggle became violent as they pulled against each other. Euan pushed back from the table and tried to intervene but decided to let them have their scuffle. They had twenty years' worth of time to work out between them.

The warm liquid began to spill, causing their grip on each other to loosen. Desperation took over; he couldn't lose her again. Lachlan let go of her hand, and the release of pressure caused the bottle to slip through her fingers.

The table that had been in between them was spinning through the air before either of them knew what was happening. The bottle fell in slow motion as he grabbed for Isla, pulling her to him with the impact of a high-speed collision.

The kiss was powerful. She resisted at first, but Lachlan could pinpoint the second her hesitation gave way to want. The world fell away, and they were the only two people left on earth. Her lips were warm and pushed back against his. His hands tangled in her hair, and hers tangled together in his. Everything burned. He could smell heather on her skin, mixed with whiskey and hope.

"Where have you been?" she panted when she came up for air.

Lachlan looked at her and looking back was the vivacious girl he'd fallen in love with. The ache of what life had dealt them was dissolving, leaving them as they had been before; untouched by what was yet to come. Lachlan let his mind drift to realities where Arden had never died; where he'd never been sent away; where he and Isla had been allowed to love each other out in the open; where he was still who he'd thought he was. The what-if images were devastatingly beautiful and heartbreaking all at the same time. They'd never get their missing time back, but maybe hope was not lost for them. The look in her eyes made him think there were still possibilities left to come.

"I'll thank you to be takin' your hands off my wife."

The voice was deep, deliberate. Lachlan stood motionless, torn between the fear of breaking the connection he felt to Isla at that moment and the need know who had dared to make such a claim. Isla whispered a slew of curse words into the folds of Lachlan's shirt before she pushed away from him.

"What do you want Ross?" she asked with resentment stiff on her tongue.

"I'd like it if I didn't walk into our pub and see some strange man's hands fondling my wife, we'll start there."

He spoke with a smile that stretched ear to ear so that his words sounded overextended. Lachlan felt like he'd been caught in the middle of a bad visual effect; the one where the camera zooms in but pans out all at the same time inducing a dizzying feeling in the viewer. The walls of the pub behind Isla began to melt, stripping away a world that had only just begun to exist.

Lachlan looked at Isla standing a foot away from him, but she flickered in what felt like the distance. He opened his mouth to speak, but nothing came out except the need to vomit.

"This ain't your fuckin' pub, Ross," she spat, bending down with Euan to pick the table up from the floor.

"What are you all looking at?" she yelled at the crowd of lookie-loos. "Rounds for everyone, on the house."

"It's our bar sweetheart," Ross corrected her, "remember, what's yours is mine and what's mine is mine," he laughed, almost cackled the last few words out of his mouth.

He twirled a toothpick in the corner of his mouth with his tongue as he turned to either side and high fived with the entourage he still traveled with. He was still the same seventeen-year-old boy, only now, he was draped in the skin of a man who'd not been treated well by life. Lachlan almost felt sorry for him, but the feeling faded almost as quickly as it had materialized.

Lachlan felt a million miles away as he watched Ross move closer to Isla and push up against her. His movements were deliberate and cocky. Lachlan moved his jaw back and forth, recalling his last encounter with Ross and the pain he'd left him in. But it was too late. Lachlan had already recoiled his right arm as he spun Ross around with his left. The connection sounded like wood splintering and rang through the boisterous pub like no other sound had ever existed.

The two men erupted in a hail fire of blows before Euan intervened and pulled them apart. Ross' face was covered in blood. From what looked like a broken nose and Lachlan stood by, hands cocked, ready for more.

The sting Lachlan felt break out across his cheek was unexpected. Gasps from the crowd of onlookers accompanied her hand as it flew through the air, coming to rest against Lachlan's face in the most puzzling delivery of a thank you he'd ever received.

"What the fuck was that for?" he yelled, energized by the tingling in his skin.

"I didn't ask for your help," she yelled back at him, shaking the sting from her hand. "I can take care of myself. I've done just fine without you for twenty years."

Her pain spread like thick, slow-moving molasses on top of her words. It clung to each letter and stuck in Lachlan's ears as he digested them. The words *without you* played on repeat. They stung more than anything she'd ever said to him.

"Is it true?" Lachlan asked, choking on his own words.

She didn't answer, at least not with words. Her reply slid down her throat in the form of whiskey she gulped straight from the bottle. When he found her eyes again, a different person was staring back. She wasn't Isla Gilcrest anymore. She was Mrs. Scott.

Maybe she'd suffered a blow to the head, rendering her temporarily incapable of making rational decisions. Lachlan wouldn't put it past Ross to take advantage of a helpless girl in that situation. Anything would have made more sense than her simple want of him; his greasy hair, his pockmarked skin, and slim-man build.

Ross' laughter broke the stillness of the room. Lachlan could feel the dozens of droopy, work tired, inebriated eyes watching him, waiting for what was to happen next. He and Isla stood at arm's length, allowing just enough space for the last secret between them to breathe in the whiskey-soaked air.

"You didn't know, did you?" Ross finally managed to get out as he wiped contrived tears from his eyes.

"Ross," Euan spoke up, without having anything more to add to the conversation except for eyes that begged him to have mercy on Lachlan.

"That's right," Ross whispered. His breath was as rancid as his teeth. Lachlan felt sorry for the toothpick lodged in the corner of his mouth. "She's my wife."

He leaned in enough for Lachlan to feel the heat from his breath on his neck. "But I could be persuaded to share her with yah, for the right price, of course."

The floor was sticky and smelled like dirty water left behind in a mop bucket at the end of the night, but it was cold against Lachlan's skin. He clashed with Ross, throwing fists that were aimed at something he couldn't see. Their arms flailed in the air as they rolled on the floor, more like lovers than enemies. The only thing Lachlan could see was Ross, the look of victory spreading like wildfire on his pitted, sour face.

Euan and a few other men from the bar intervened and pulled the two apart before any serious harm could befall them, but the damage had been done. Lachlan gasped for breath, spinning around to look for Isla. He needed to see the truth of it in her eyes, hear it on her tongue, so he could believe it and let her go entirely.

When he found her, he begged with his eyes for it not to be true, but hers said that she could lie to him any longer.

"What the fuck," Lachlan whispered. He felt like he might be hallucinating, having drunk enough that there was more whiskey in his blood than blood, causing oxygen deprivation to his brain and inducing an uncontrollable nightmare that he couldn't wake up from.

"Say it," he demanded.

She stumbled, moving closer to him as she opened and closed her mouth in quick succession as she searched for the right words, but Lachlan knew they didn't exist.

"It's a long …"

"Is it true??" Lachlan yelled, grabbing her by the shoulders and shaking her, harder than he intended.

Her hand flew again, but Lachlan grabbed it midair and squeezed her wrist. His hand shook uncontrollably, and his skin burned against her touch. He had an uncontrollable urge to kiss her. He tilted her head up toward him like he might but stopped with only inches between them.

"Yes or no?" he asked, the words barely sliding past his clenched lips.

She stared back at him, tears slipping down her soft skin, her eyes already apologizing for what she was about to say. "Yes," she whispered, without attempting to offer any further explanation.

He let go of her like she was infected with the plague, holding his hands out in the air like surgeons did before gloving up. The heavy smell of cheap whiskey wafted in the air and nauseated him more than he already was.

"God damn," he finally laughed, no longer bothering to keep it together. "And I thought I was the crazy one this whole time."

Uneasy chuckles sprang from the crowd of spectators gathered around them.

"Come on man, let me take you home," Euan whispered, taking up next for him.

"Home?" he laughed. "Where? To my dad, who turns out isn't even my father. The home where I lived with a woman who hated me because I was the living reminder that someone had raped her? That home? Is that where you want to take me? Well let's go, I don't think I can get there fast enough."

He tilted the bottle back but found it empty. It dropped to the floor with a resounding emptiness that rang through both the room and Lachlan.

"Come on, I'm just trying to help."

"You're trying to help me?" Lachlan laughed in an overexaggerated manor, bending over at the waist as if he'd developed a stitch from the hilarity of his comment.

"How exactly is it that you're trying to help me? Are you helping me by convincing me that a make-believe monster murdered our friend; by taking me on a wild goose chase through our past; by taking me to an old woman's house you think has the answers to the whereabouts of all the missing Lewis children!"

The whispers began and didn't stop until there was a gentle roar in the room.

"That's right," Lachlan confirmed to the crowd, "your darling Inspector McKenzie believes he's cracked the case of decade-old missing and murdered children all over Lewis. And the prime suspect ..." His speech was cut short as Euan grabbed ahold of him, pulling him in close.

"What the fuck are you doing? An hour ago, you believed everything just as much as I do. I saw it in your eyes. You're just drunk and upset. Let me take you somewhere to sleep it off."

An hour ago, the world was a completely different place he thought. An hour ago, he was still madly in love with a woman he barely knew but craved with every ounce of his being. An hour ago, his mother hadn't been a rape victim, and his father was still his father, both of them inexplicably incapable of loving him, but even that was better than the reality.

"I have a better idea," Lachlan mumbled as he fished in his pocket for his wallet. From it, he pulled what barely amounted to more than twenty pounds.

"Ross," he yelled over the dismantling crowd, grabbing everyone's attention again. "Is this enough to borrow her for an hour?"

Drops of whiskey splattered on Lachlan's face as a bottle went whizzing by his head, landing a few feet from him in a mess of shattered glass.

"The next one won't miss," she articulated. "Get the hell out of my pub."

"Whatever you say, Mrs. Scott." The words were painful on his lips. He watched as she internalized them. He wondered if the regret on her face was because he'd found out her secret or that it existed at all. He couldn't be sure. He wasn't even sure he cared.

Lachlan turned his back on Isla, painfully leaving her behind. With the altercation seemingly over, the remaining onlookers broke up, returning to their half-drunk pints. Ross stood between Lachlan and the door, wearing a smile broader than the Devil's pulpit, but just as secretive. He tried to ignore him, wanting nothing more in life than to be anywhere other than on the Isle of Lewis. He prayed he'd make the last ferry to the mainland.

"I'd of let you have her for half," he whispered.

"Fuck you, Ross!" he shouted, still feeling the need to defend her out of principle. His skin prickled as he looked at Ross up close and thinking of him between Isla's legs. The whiskey in his gut churned violently, and Lachlan had to catch himself before he vomited all over Ross.

"You've not changed a bit since we were kids, have you? You were a shit person then, always tormenting us, picking on us. You were a shit older brother. Arden hated you. We all hated you."

Ross' smile faded at the mention of his younger brother. His thin lips curled around his soured teeth, and the whistle of swift-moving air in his nostrils made him sound like a bull ready to charge.

"Take it back," Ross whispered angrily.

"Fuck you. It's the truth." They were standing chest to chest, breathing in each other's anger.

"Arden hated you just like the rest of us did."

"That's not true, I was a good older brother; gave him booze and cigarettes, showed him how to talk to girls, how to sneak out of the house. I taught him how to be a man." His voice began to shake at the end, but Lachlan couldn't have helped himself if it wanted to. It was too late. He needed to get everything out, leave it all on the island and head back to the mainland, never again looking over his shoulder.

"He hated you so much Ross, he crashed your car and almost killed all of us, just to keep you away from Isla."

Ross didn't respond.

"Arden loved her, in his own way, and almost killed himself, me, Euan and Calum, to keep you away from her, because he knew ..." Lachlan's voice broke off in the painful realization that he had treated Arden no better than Ross. "He knew you didn't love her. He was just protecting her from you. We both were."

Lachlan turned slightly toward Isla. "Don't stand here and act all innocent, like you had no idea. You knew exactly what you were doing, with him, with me, even with Ross. Girls like you always know what they're doing, calculating each smile, each bat of your eyes, each soft glance at the exact right time." The feeling of her seduction burned like a kerosene fire on the underside of his skin, and despite everything, he'd give the world to feel it one more time.

"You were a tease, and you know it. You pitted every single boy you looked at against each other, including Arden and me."

He looked at her, watching tears stain her pale skin. The girl he'd loved didn't exist anymore. She was a ghost, like everything else.

"He died that night, because I betrayed his friendship, for you!" Lachlan was whimpering by the end, watching the horrifying scene from that night replay behind his eyes.

"Don't put this on her," Euan yelled, "it's not her fault."

It was, and it wasn't. She was just as much to blame as he was.

"I killed my best friend," Lachlan whispered into the palms of his sweaty hands. "Because of you. He wasn't supposed to be there that day, you were."

The whispers grew louder as the crowd of onlookers digested his confession. Accusatory eyes peered out at him from the crowd. Smiles developed at his admission of what most of them had assumed to already be the truth.

"You didn't kill Arden, man, you're just drunk," Euan whispered to him, drawing more attention with their hushed words.

"Didn't I?" he posed. He wasn't sure anymore. His head began to spin. Faster and faster. Nothing made sense anymore. The frayed threads that had been holding his life together had ripped as far as they could without letting go completely.

"He just admitted to killing the Scott boy! Aren't you going to arrest him," yelled a faceless voice from the crowd, followed by cheers and other indistinguishable demands.

"Lachlan, I'm not going to be able to help you if you keep talking. Just keep your mouth shut and let me help you."

His knees buckled but caught himself on a table before hitting the floor. He wanted to run but he wasn't sure his legs would carry him, so he stumbled toward the door instead. He heard Isla call his name in a broken cry. He turned, but all he could do was smile at her sullenly, as he watched their love slip away a second time.

From just outside the door Lachlan could hear Ross yelling at Euan and his friend's faithless attempt at defending him. He let their voices and memories slip away as he stumbled away from the pub, only stopping when a flash of metallic red glinted in the street light stopped him in his tracks.

It stared back at him with a familiar, crooked smile. Lachlan rubbed the astonishment of seeing it again from his eyes, moving closer to confirm that it was one in the same. The right headlight had never sat correctly after they'd slammed into the rock face of the Tobson hillside. Even in the darkness of the alley, Lachlan could see it was still cockeyed.

The pub erupted into madness behind him. Loud, angry voices called out over the sound of crashing glass. He could pick out bits and pieces of Euan's and Ross' voices clamoring to outshout the rest of the crowd.

Pieces of plastic headlight recoiled in the air before falling and splintering even more against the cobblestone. The sound of weak wood against the metal hood sounded surprisingly like thunder, booming down and through the empty alleyway. Lachlan wanted to smash the windshield but knew the picket he'd found wouldn't survive the hit. Instead, he struck the side-view mirror, hurling it further into the dark alley with panting effort.

Sweat began to bead on his arms and neck, and he found it hard to pull a good breath through his uncontrollable laughter. At the end of it, the red Spitfire looked much like it did the first time they'd wrecked it, maybe worse. A misty rain began to fill the air, cooling his skin. The wooden picket clattered against the cobblestone street after crumbling in Lachlan's hand. He stood back to look at his handiwork, remembering how scared he'd felt when they'd crashed it in Tobson. Now, he just felt hollow.

"I doubt Ross'll find this as funny."

Her voice cut through the beginnings of the passing rain like glass rubbing softy against the skin of his neck. He turned his face toward the falling rain, letting it wash over him, hoping it would take away the sting of having to say goodbye to her a second time.

"Make sure to tell your husband I did it," Lachlan finally laughed, turning to look at Isla through the rain.

The rain became thicker and soaked her through to the bone in a matter of seconds. She looked back at Lachlan with lips scrunched like she caught the smell of something sour in the air. "It's not what you think," she yelled. "Ross and I."

"It doesn't matter what I think, just that it is." He wiped the rainwater through his hair, slicking it back and away from his face. "Of all the men on this bloody island, you had to marry him. I'd of forgiven you for marrying anyone else, given my blessing even, but not him."

"Forgiven me?" she smirked. "What exactly do I need to be forgiven for?"

He looked at her, thousands of memories and thoughts and words racing through his mind; each of them interconnected because she existed in all of them. He wanted to forgive her for marrying Ross, but that wasn't really what he needed to forgive her for.

"How about for not showing up," he yelled, with more pain and hurt than he expected. His words turned up at the end of the sentence as a tingling lump developed in the back of his throat.

She stared back at him with penetrating eyes. "Let's go somewhere so we can talk."

"I can't Isla," he yelled over the roar of mother nature, but it came out sounding unkind.

"You can't, or you won't?" she asked.

"It's too much. This place is …" He didn't know how to finish his thought without sounding witchy. He wanted to say that the island had it out for him, for all of them, but he knew it would sound too crazy, even for him. "You're married to Ross for fuck's sake! What's left to talk about?"

"There's everything left." Her words were sharp, forceful, like they'd always been, but they didn't fall below the surface. They were empty promises he couldn't hold onto any longer.

"This was a mistake," he yelled.

They stood in the dark alley, only feet apart, but a million miles away from each other.

"Was choosing me a mistake?" she asked, shielding her face from the rain with her hand.

It was the last truth lingering between them. Her gray shirt clung to her form and her dark, heavy hair fell over her shoulders and trailed down over her breathless chest. He could see the slightest hint of her bra strap peeking out from under her the thin collar of her shirt, reminding him of the first day he'd walked her home from school. He could have shrugged it off as coincidence. Any two people could realistically be caught in a rain shower together more than once over the course of twenty years. It rained more often than it didn't, especially on Lewis. But Lachlan knew it was more than that. It felt like the world telling him it was time to let her go – for good.

The ferry horn blared brashly from the harbor several streets away. "I can't stay," Lachlan finally said when it quieted.

"That's not what I asked you."

There was no right answer. He couldn't answer her without betraying Arden one last time. He couldn't remain faithful to him without hurting Isla. It felt like he would always be caught between them.

"I guess that's for you then," she yelled, motioning to the ferry making its final approach to dock.

"I'm sorry, Isla," he yelled to her as she turned back toward her disheveled pub. "For everything that went wrong between us."

She paused and turned just enough for him to see the soft skin of her cheek. "I'm not," she said, "because it was us."

***

The rain was comforting as Lachlan stood on the massive dock, waiting for the ferry to unload before reloading and heading back to the mainland. The rain was warm against his soaked skin. He stood like a statue leaning against the cement wall, still trying to process the fact that he had been a completely different person standing on the same dock only days before. He felt numb and whatever was left of his rational thought process knew he was in shock. He wanted to breathe but needed to get off the island first, away from whatever was infecting him. It had been like a fast-moving cancer pulsing through his body, and if he didn't get away from it, he felt like it would quickly consume the rest of him.

A steady hand on Lachlan's shoulder pulled him back to reality, and he was surprised to see Calum standing next to him, seemingly out of nowhere.

"Shit, Calum, you scared me," he breathed, wiping the rain from his face.

Calum's eyes peered out from underneath his yellow waterproof. "What're you doing standing out here in the rain?" he asked, looking back to the several guests waiting in the well-appointed waiting area inside the terminal behind them.

"I'm going home, back to Dundee," he shouted over the sound of the working pier.

"I gathered that," Calum said, "being that you're at the ferry terminal and all. You smell just as sloshed as the first time I found you here."

"This was a mistake."

"To get hammered before taking the ferry? After last time, I would have to agree with you."

Lachlan had to smile at his friends dry, sarcastic humor. It hadn't changed in all the years since he'd seen him last. He'd forgotten how refreshing it could be. Even as his world was crumbling beneath him, Calum could make him want to laugh.

"No, you prick," Lachlan laughed, shoving Calum playfully on the shoulder. "Just, coming back here, you know. I don't know what I thought or expected would happen, I just ... I don't know."

"What happened?" he asked sincerely.

"I spent almost half my childhood locked away with people trying to convince me of a different truth than I thought I knew, and then I come here, and Euan tries to convince me that the lie is actually the truth. I don't know which way is up anymore."

Despite the heavy rain and strong winds, Lachlan watched the gulls hanging in the air as he spoke. When their wings tired, they wrapped their feet around the wire banisters, heads down, determined to weather the storm.

"I found out my mother was raped and that my father probably isn't my father." He'd expected the words to sting, like the zap of an electric fence touching his skin, but there was nothing. He knew the pain was there, just under the surface, waiting to be exposed. He'd exchanged the pain of thinking his mother hated him for the knowledge that she did, but for reasons out of her control. In the end, his existence had still pained her beyond what she was capable of. He wanted to blame his lot on the idea that his father was an unknown man that had attacked his mother in the middle of the night, bound her, raped her, and left her naked in the street, but he'd lost himself way before he knew that truth.

"And Isla's married to Ross fuckin' Scott," he laughed with exaggeration, almost howling up at the moon hanging heavy over the Minch.

Out of all of them, the last one stung the most, because if there had been anything worth coming back to, it would have been her. Lachlan wanted to go back to the perfect image he had of her in his mind; the one who's sea green eyes he had searched for in the darkness when he needed them most; the one who brought him out of boyhood into manhood, the one who'd never given him any other option other than to love her.

"Aye, that's a lot of shite," Calum agreed. "She was in a bad way for a long time. Mrs. Scott too. Such a fluke thing too, to get pregnant only after one time together, and as drunk as they were. I don't even know if she knew who she was going home with that night."

"What?" Lachlan asked, the feeling of vertigo both pulling and pushing against him simultaneously.

"Aye, Mr. Scott promised her mother that Ross would make it right. A couple days after they were married she lost the baby, and he's been holdin' it over her head ever since."

Lachlan watched as men in lime green jumpsuits began waving traffic onto the ferry, lane by lane. The gulls still clung to the railings in front of them, waiting patiently.

"Probably for the best, you know. Ross would have made a shite father." He lost Calum's voice in the ferry horn. The gulls who looked like they were sleeping jumped from their perches and floated in the rough air above the dock, looking for food with piercing eyes like they thought they were hawks instead.

"What?" Lachlan yelled back.

Calum waited for the noise to fade, looking out to the Minch as it disappeared under a thin fog. The darkness swirled until it just looked like emptiness. The rain broke, and Calum tore the hood from his waterproof back like it had been smothering him. Lachlan stepped toward the railings, looking back at the lights of Stornoway burning behind him. The gulls hadn't waited in vain. Someone from the kitchen strolled by with a cart full of sweet smelling treats, some of which managed to spill out onto the dock. The birds squawked and squabbled with each other, each fighting for their fair share.

"Maybe it's good, you know, to know the truth," Calum offered. "You can't fix it if you're still living in the lie."

Lachlan watched, captivated by the gulls tearing apart pieces of pastry and potato scones with their yellow beaks. The scraps were gone in a matter of seconds, and when every last bit was spoken for, they leapt back to the railing where they perched waiting contently for the next feeding.

"Fix what?" Lachlan asked.

"You know," Calum said, shooing the birds from their perches only for them to return seconds later like nothing had happened. "All of it."

Chapter Twenty

"Remember," Ms. McNish yelled from the front of the room. "Permission slips for the St. Kilda trip are due next week. If you plan on going, please have them to me no later than Wednesday."

The widely anticipated St. Kilda trip was less than a month away, and the mere utterance of its name sent the room into a tailspin as the girls whispered secrets behind their hands to each other and the boys craned their necks to try and hear them. I didn't bother to lift my head from the desk and continued to stare blankly out the window, despising every second of sunshine pouring through. I knew there was no chance I'd be allowed to go on the St. Kilda trip. Not now, thanks to Arden.

I had barely spoken to anyone, including Isla in the weeks since my falling out with Arden and my homestead incarceration. My mother couldn't stomach my sight and barely spoke to me unless it was imperative to my survival, and even then, it felt purely out of legal duty instead of motherly love. My father had scarcely spoken to me before, and nothing about that had changed that. The division had been drawn between myself and Euan and Arden and Calum, each of us taking our assigned sidekick to a different lunch table or the opposite corner of the field when we were let out for gym or recess. Arden had yet to divulge the reason for our rift, unable to admit the truth even to himself. I watched joyfully as it festered under his skin.

I'd begged Ms. McNish to move my seat away from Arden after it happened, and she was only too excited to separate us. I was moved to the other side of the room, to the third row from the front and just behind Isla. Arden stood by and watched as our falling out pushed Isla and I closer together, at least terms of our seats. His only saving grace was he knew I'd never be allowed out of my house to see her, and it showed in his crooked smile.

I could hear her voice over the clatter circling around us. It was the only thing that could pull me from my deep depression, if even just momentarily. It was like silk wafting in the air around me, wrapping me loosely in its lightweight refuge. She turned in her chair slightly, just enough to give the impression to anyone watching that we might be talking, but not enough to draw Ms. McNish's daggered stare.

"Your mom's not gonna let you go, is she?" she asked quietly.

I lifted my head from the desk and propped my chin against my hands folded underneath. "No."

Her face was sullen, and her eyes darted back and forth like she was reading something I couldn't see. "Can you ask your dad?" she posed, to which I just scoffed. He'd probably have dinner thrown at him for me even thinking to ask him over my mother, even if he didn't respond.

I laid my head back down on the cool surface of the desk, and Isla turned back around. There was nothing more we could say to each other. My incarceration was indefinite, meaning the next time I would be able to see her outside of school was too. I wanted to cry and probably would have if she'd not been sitting right in front of me. It felt like I might die.

"What if you forged the slip?" she whispered quietly from her seat, without shielding her deception. "And just went anyway. You're already in trouble. What's a little more?"

She was trouble. Her deviousness made me love her even more even though I tried not to. It was uncontrollable, like everything else with her.

"I'd never see the light of day again," I mumbled into the void between my face and the desk so that it echoed louder than I expected. She'd be worth it. I knew it, and what was worse, was that she knew I knew it.

The rest of the day slipped away from me. Ms. McNish droned on at the front of the class and Isla didn't speak to me for the few remaining hours we had left. Euan threw balled up pieces of paper at me from his seat a few spaces back and one row over, but it wasn't worth the trouble of moving to see what he wanted. The next time I moved was at the sound of the final bell and at the sound of mine and Arden's names on Ms. McNish's tongue.

The room cleared quickly, leaving us alone. We could hear whispers in the hallway and see eyeballs trying to steal glances through the crack in the doorframe, but there was nothing much to see. Arden and I remained in our seats utterly indifferent to the other as Ms. McNish fidgeted at the front of the class.

"Boys," she said finally. "I can't help but take notice to what's going on between you, and I have to admit, at first I was delighted with the reprieve your falling out gave me, but now ..." she looked back and forth between us with dour eyes. Even she, who had more reasons than most to revel in our falling out, even she couldn't dismiss it as trivial. "I'm sure whatever has happened between you, it can't be worth your friendship."

Arden scoffed before she'd even finished her thought. The sound stung under my skin while the question hung heavy in the air between us. I began to question myself and everything that had happened between Arden and I. I had never intended to hurt him, but as that thought entered my mind, I realized that I'd never actually taken his feelings into account because more often than not, he didn't appear to have any. He operated like a robot, and even though I knew he loved Isla in his own way, I never expected such a visceral reaction from him.

"Nothing?" Ms. McNich posed, holding out her hands to both of us, waiting for some type of response. I knew Arden would never be the first to speak. If I didn't say something first, we might never speak again. I wrestled with the idea and wasn't sure I cared either way.

"Alright then, that's it," she huffed. "You can go."

Arden darted out of the room ahead of me, as if to claim his position in the right and solidify mine in the wrong. I let him go, feeling like I needed to give him something. I'd already won the girl. I could let him think he was right.

I followed him into the hallway, unable to stop spiteful thoughts of him and our crumbling friendship from creeping into my thought process. I wanted to think I was better than him and his crass exterior but underneath, I knew what I'd done was wrong. I wondered if he would have done the same thing to me if it had been reversed. The thought made me laugh and reassured me that I was not the monster he'd made me feel I might be.

The parking lot was empty except for a few teachers gathered around their cars in the corner, trying to hide their cigarettes from us. Arden was ten paces ahead of me, walking next to his bike as if he were taunting me to catch up to him and attempt to resolve our issue. I could smell the smugness wafting behind him. It stank like spoiled eggs. I crossed to the other side of the road, and sped up, walking parallel with him, mocking his taunt.

Just as the feeling of triumph and righteousness flooded my blood, they were replaced with guilt and repentance and the acknowledgment that I, perhaps, was in the wrong despite everything to the contrary. The betrayal stung in my chest, and I felt needle pricks in the back of my throat when I tried to swallow. I looked over at Arden, and when there was no acknowledgment on his part, the culpability began to fade back into innocence. She'd chosen me, after all, out of everyone. I couldn't help that.

A car came speeding around the bend just ahead of us in a flash of red. We both laughed when we saw that the front bumper still smashed in, one headlight still hanging loosely by the internal wires that were now exposed. Whatever we'd done to damage Ross' car hadn't been permanent, but it was enough to take pleasure in. I only saw her when he slowed to show off his prize.

I could almost hear the sinister laugh I was sure was spilling from his mouth as they passed. She didn't look up as they passed. I wasn't entirely sure she'd even seen me. Just as quickly as they'd rounded the bend, they were gone, back towards school and the community center, creating a void in the thick air between Arden and I.

We looked at each other, and when I saw his face, I knew I hadn't imagined seeing Isla in his brother's car. He looked just as dumbfounded as I was sure I did, and all we could do was laugh.

"Did you just see that?" I yelled across the road.

"What a fucking tease!" he shouted back, laughing under his breath.

"Did that really just happen?" I asked again, still in shock.

"I think so."

When the words ran out, we were left on opposite sides of the road, staring at each other uncomfortably. I tried to hide the agony I felt at having seemingly lost the love of my life to Ross Scott, and Arden averted his eyes to let me wallow in it. It was like a horrible accident, the kind you can't look away from. I kept replaying it in my mind over and over again, and every time the smugness on Ross' face grew, and her feelings for me faded further from the surface until they disappeared entirely. Of all the boys on the island, even the limited options we presented the girls of Lewis with, why, out of all of them, did it have to be him? He was vile. The feeling of betrayal churned in the pit of my stomach, sinking down into my feet and it was only then that I realized how Arden must have felt. I'd never felt so low in my entire life.

"Sorry," he muttered so quietly it was almost silent.

"Me too."

We'd both acknowledged our wrongdoing and silently agreed that we'd never let a girl come between us again. And that was it.

***

Ms. McNish had a sideways smirk when I took back my seat next to Arden the following day, no doubt thinking that her intrusion had somehow impacted our lives enough for us to reconcile. I smiled back, letting her have her imagined victory. Euan and Calum sat behind us like they always had. They didn't ask, and we didn't offer any explanation for the sudden rekindling. Everything went back to normal, as it had before Isla Gilcrest arrived on our desolate island, except now we knew she existed. She wasn't a secret anymore, and there was no going back to the way things had been, but we had to try.

I ignored her as best I could, but she wasn't the kind of girl you could just disregard. She knew it, and I knew it. When I was desperate for reasons to hate her, I thought of her sitting in Ross' car, and all the immoral things I was sure had passed between them. My stomach turned when images of them together came to mind, but it made me despise her as much as anyone could who was still in love with her.

"I have something for you," she whispered as the cold water from the fountain outside our classroom slid down my throat. The sound of her voice made me jump, and my throat closed briefly, causing a fleeting instant of breathless panic.

I didn't answer. I watched my reflection glint in the basin of the fountain, wishing I had the willpower to walk away from her, but I knew that that amount of strength didn't exist.

"What is it?" I asked. The coldness in my voice was surprising, even to me. My resentment had been building the longer we went without talking. It needed an outlet, but I didn't want it to be her.

"Can you walk me home today?" she asked.

"Are you sure you don't already have a ride?"

She mocked my pain with her smile and her deep eyes never wavered from mine. She didn't belong in Bernera, or on Lewis, yet here she was, standing in front of me. I tried to hate her, but she wouldn't let me.

"Is that what this is about?"

I was screaming inside. I was sure there was steam spewing from the top of my head while wildly inappropriate obscenities flew through the air.

"It's not a big deal," she said mockingly as she flipped strands of her hair away from her face.

"Not a big deal," I whispered harshly. The crowd in the hall was beginning to thin. Soon we'd be alone. I grabbed her arm roughly and pulled her into the alcove of the empty music room a few doors from where we'd been standing. I loosened my grip and let myself enjoy the feel of her warm skin under my fingers. I melted, like summer butter left out too long.

"Ross Scott?" I asked, secreted in the crux of the empty room. Out of the corner of my eye, I could see the metal music stands glinting in the sun floating in through the window. The churning clouds cast shadows that danced on the walls, giving the stationary objects in the room movement, making it feel like we had an audience watching as a poured my heart out.

"Of all people, why did it have to be him?" I tried to keep my voice at a whisper, but it was difficult. My love for her still burned as deep as my hatred for Ross, and they both manifested in the ripple of my voice when I spoke.

"Him?" she asked. She scrunched her nose and forehead in confusion.

"You know, to ... just ... why him? You could have anyone. Why him?"

Her confusion bloomed into a pity-filled grin. She dropped her arms to her side and moved toward me. "You're such a silly boy," she whispered.

I felt like a deer in headlights, unable to move or look away from her. My skin prickled like a cold draft had wafted through despite the sweat I could feel pooling in my armpits. I had no idea what was on the other side of the headlights. I just hoped it hit me hard enough, so I didn't have to limp away.

"My mom had to go into work early and asked Mrs. Scott if she could bring me and my sisters to her at the hotel. She couldn't but said that she'd get Ross to do it."

Her smile was crooked and cocky like she knew the whole time that I was being tormented by the idea of her and Ross.

"That's it?" I asked.

"But..."

"Why didn't you say something then?"

"You never asked."

My heart was pounding, and it felt like I was gulping for air that was right in front of my face. I'd never thought to ask her what it was about, her joyride with Ross, and assumed the worst of it. Her lips turn upward, teasing me and my stupidity. I had almost thrown her away, and for nothing, the realization of which left me even more breathless than I already was.

"Your parents are in Stornoway until late; right?" she asked without the inflection of a question. They were just words floating in the empty space between us. I fought against it, even though we both knew, in the end, I couldn't say no to her. I tried to remember how her betrayal had felt, desperate to find the sting of it in my gut so I could find the will to walk away from her and keep my silent promises to Arden to stay clear of her, but the sting had disappeared in an instant. My body had already replaced it with the sweet memory of her hair tickling my skin.

I let her walk back to the classroom ahead of me. We were already late, and our simultaneous entrance back into the classroom would be too obvious for some to ignore. I counted in my head slowly, waiting for enough time to pass before I followed behind her. I tried to put her out of my mind and focus on Arden and what I was going to tell him, but she was all I could see.

I walked back into class a few minutes later, interrupting Ms. McNish and drawing unwanted attention to myself. I walked to my seat, and it felt like everyone already knew I was hiding another secret; the same secret.

"Where were you?" Arden whispered out of the side of his mouth as he pretended to read.

"Bathroom," I whispered back, not wanting to lie to him but at the same time knowing that telling him I was walking Isla home that afternoon wasn't a conversation we could have out the side of our mouths.

Rain began to tap lightly against the windows. Ms. McNish's hand smacked a small piece of white chalk against the board at the front of the room. I looked up at the wall clock hanging precariously above the door, watching and listening to the mechanical arms move at a snail's pace. I felt light headed and laid my head down on my desk, but that only amplified the sound of guilt and betrayal colliding like they'd always belonged together for me.

The final bell screamed, and everyone jumped to their feet in a hurry. The rain had stopped, giving us a few hours of daylight before dusk took over.

"Hey," I called to Arden over the uproar of clattering seats and idle chatter. "I've got to talk to you."

"Lachlan, I need to see you, please," Ms. McNish called.

"Busted," Arden laughed, throwing his bag over his shoulder.

"Not so fast, Mr. Scott. I believe Mr. Maclean is expecting you in detention."

"You were serious about that?" Arden whined.

"Mr. Maclean doesn't respond well to tardiness," she answered, pointing to the door.

"Fuck," he whispered, sluffing his bag off his shoulder and dragging it on the ground behind him laboriously.

"Mr. Scott, do you want me to start a detention list for Monday as well?"

"No, ma'am." He moved slowly toward the front of the room, pushing past and through small groups that were still congregating. My guilt eased as he disappeared. I rationalized it in my mind that I'd tried to tell him, but unforeseen circumstances had gotten in the way. He'd be stuck in detention and therefore not even be aware that I wasn't walking home with him. It felt like it was meant to be.

"Mr. McGinley?" Ms. McNish called in the background, but my attention was elsewhere; watching Isla in the doorway.

It was subtle and was I not always watching her when she was in view, I might have missed the quick wink and glance down at her hand. We made it look accidental. It almost felt like it could have been. We said our apologizes for bumping into each other as she slipped the note into my hand while walking briskly past me to retrieve something from her desk.

"I don't have your permission slip for the St. Kilda trip," Ms. McNish pointed out. "You are coming with us; aren't you?"

Despite our rekindled friendship, I knew I'd be sitting at home watching from my window as the boat carrying my classmates to St. Kilda sped out of site. Isla slipped through the classroom door and into the hallway as if on cue with my thoughts. She would slip away to St.

Kilda with the rest of our class, including Arden, for a night of debauchery I'd only know second hand. I knew Arden well enough to know that he'd not give up on Isla as easily as he may have wanted me to believe. I began to wonder if he'd been one step ahead of me the whole time.

"I don't think so," I said, shaking my head in disbelief that I would miss one of the most coveted events in all our lives.

"Are you sure?" Ms. McNish asked again, "you've really earned it."

An image of my mother hurling a dinner plate across the room because I'd let wet laundry sit overnight in the washer came to mind. It smelled of mildew the next morning when she'd opened the machine and found it. I'd spent the better part of two weeks in my room for that. I didn't even know how I would begin a conversation with her to ask her for permission to leave the house much less the island altogether after lying to her about so many different things. Ms. McNish's insistence that I be allowed to go only made it worse. Even the teachers were excited to go.

"I don't think so," I said reluctantly.

It was strange to see such care on her face. It wasn't something we saw often. We knew we drove her crazy. It was our job as kids. But we knew, deep down, she cared about our wellbeing. It made me wish my mother was capable of such emotion.

I turned away from Ms. McNish unable to take her pity any longer. I balled my fist in anger, and the corners of Isla's note poked into my palm, reminding me that I was holding it at all. While Ms. McNish busied herself at her desk, I unfolded the paper and held it in my hand.

Meet me at Bosta, it read. *I want to go swimming again.*

The air was warm enough for a dip in a sun-drenched loch, but my skin chilled at the thought. I didn't understand why she'd want to go back, but who was I to argue with a girl who wanted to strip down to her underwear in front of me? I tucked the note into my back pocket before making my way to the door and the temporary freedom ahead of me.

I crashed into Arden as I walked out of the room with my head hung low in defeat. My palms instantly turned clammy as the opportunity to tell the truth presented itself. I opened my mouth to admit the truth, but nothing came out, other than the reassurance that I was a coward.

"Mr. Scott, back so soon?"

Arden and I passed in the doorway, exchanging glances and a shoulder bump but little else. I wanted to be a good friend, but I wanted Isla more. I knew if I told him the truth, I'd be chastised anyway, so not telling him seemed to be the best decision for everyone involved. If I'd been able to do it without looking certifiable, I would have punched myself in the face for being the owner of such a stupid thought process. But it was what it was; I couldn't stop having feelings for Isla, and even if I were capable of such a feat, I wouldn't want to.

"Cleaning duty," I heard him say to Ms. McNish as I walked down the hall.

"Great, you can start with that trash in front of my desk."

Chapter Twenty-One

Menacing clouds hung low in the distance, threatening to rain down on them with maddening furry. They gathered speed the longer Lachlan watched them move, twirling like bathwater down the drain. The sun behind them broke through in thin patches that painted the water below with a luminous shimmer. They danced together, the sunlight and the sea, moving as one before disappearing altogether. When the daylight was gone, hidden in the thick, fast moving clouds, the water was dark and deep, hiding things in the shadows and folds of the waves rolling on the surface. In the middle of it all, Lachlan's eyes were glued to the silhouette of the man he'd called his father his whole life, and between them, the truth they had yet to realize.

Lachlan watched as Calum's car petered down the road and out of site. His hand drifted down to his pocket, to the piece of paper with his mother's picture that was burning against his thigh. He didn't have the right words as he stepped from the gravel into the soggy grass of the yard. His feet felt like they'd been cast in cement, almost impossible to move with any type of purpose or ease. His anger built with each step, bringing them closer together and yet further apart.

Lachlan didn't know if the truth would have made any difference, but it felt like it might have. At least there would have been a reason, an understanding of why his mother was the way she was, instead of just thinking that she hated him without cause. Hate with purpose felt like it would have stung less. He looked at his father as he felt for the clipping in his pocket, angered by the secret and the truth they'd both robbed him. It may not have made any difference, but at least he'd have had a chance. Instead, he'd been kept in the dark, hidden behind the lie that now consumed his entire existence.

His father was dressed in the same navy jumpsuit he always wore. He hunched over at the shoulders, which he hadn't used to do. He'd thinned, instead of gaining weight like most older men seemed to do. His hair was white, and his skin was thin. He'd aged what felt like overnight. Despite Lachlan's indifference to him, seeing him as an old man made him seem more human than he ever had before. The robotic tendencies he'd displayed had faded with his youth, leaving behind even more of a stranger than he'd been before.

They didn't look at each other when Lachlan finally reached the water's edge. Instead, they stared out into the gray abyss that stared back at them with just as much infinite wonderment. Gulls glided in the warm updrafts over the water as the clouds continued to turn, thinning as they did, letting in more and more sunlight. Dark specs on the horizon came into view as the hulls of the fishing ships crashed against the churning sea, trying to outrun the storm chasing them in from open water.

"Coming back from St. Kilda, no doubt," his father said, nodding out to the small ships, the ache for the open sea thick on his every word.

They stood in silence watching the ships putter past on their way to the small port. Gulls followed behind them, waiting for their share of the haul. The wake rippled against the thin bank in front of them, bathing the rocks until they shone and sparkled in the little bits of light sifting through the clouds. The ships were gone, down the inlet, in a matter of minutes but the smile on his father's face remained.

The anger that had been stirring inside Lachlan since the night before began to wane as he watched the frail man in front of him, his life having been swept away, caught up in something no one could have prepared for. Lachlan had misplaced his anger in him. He'd done nothing but blame and punish himself for what happened. The sadness in his eyes finally made sense. He only wished there was something he could do to ease it, but he knew the depths of that type of pain and knew there was nothing to be done about it except to live with it.

Protect her with your life, he had whispered before letting Lachlan sneak out the side door and away from his mother's persecution. They'd sat at the table that morning, eating breakfast off his mother's lifeless china, talking, man to man about the one thing all men could relate to; women. It was the most genuine conversation Lachlan and his father had ever had and the best advice anyone had ever given him, but he'd squandered it. He loved Isla still, even after everything that had passed between them. If he was honest, he loved his father, somewhere deep down under the pain they'd been dealt. He may have even loved his mother, somewhere underneath it all.

"You still up for the trip then son," his dad growled, "out to the rock?"

Everything melted away. The truth didn't matter, not like Lachlan had thought it did. Calum had been right. The purpose of the truth hadn't been purely for self-discovery, it had been to move past it, fix it, start new. The reality, which he thought would bury him, had actually set him free.

"I'd like that dad," he answered, wanting to hug him but settling for patting him on the shoulder.

The wrinkled clipping tucked away in Lachlan's pocket stopped burning as hot as it had been. He wondered if they'd ever talk about what happened but for the moment the conversation posed little importance. Looking at the man that may or may not be his biological father, he never felt more at home.

"I'm sorry I didn't come home sooner," Lachlan offered. He watched as his father's stone-like surface softened around the edges.

"You're here now," his father answered, turning to look at his son. Lachlan felt like it was the first time they'd ever truly seen each other in their thirty-some years as father and son.

***

The phone rang and rang, over and over, it's high pitched howl echoing in Lachlan's ear as he mumbled Euan's name under obscenities into the receiver. But there was no one home to answer the other end. Lachlan tried two more times before giving up and leaving a message he hoped Sarah wouldn't erase before Euan had the chance to hear it. He didn't know what he would have said if he'd answered but knew he needed to say something. Euan had stumbled into something, and even if Lachlan didn't believe his theory, he deserved his help to puzzle the truth out of the mess he'd found. Lachlan owed him that much.

"Da, I need to borrow the car," he yelled out to his father, still standing in the garden. "I need to ..."

His father turned and smiled. The clouds they'd been watching earlier had dissolved, and blue sky stretched from the water's edge as far as they could see. "Just tell her the truth," he shouted back, waving his son off. "Tell her how you feel."

Lachlan sped down the twisting road, heading south just to make the hard, right turn at Crior to head back north toward Bosta. The big house came into view, the sun reflecting off the white siding in a blinding shimmer. He could just make out the window of Isla's bedroom on the backside of the house before it disappeared as the tires crunched in the rough gravel of the driveway.

He was on the porch without a clue of what he was doing, already knocking purposefully on the door when he realized it. He tried putting faith in knowing what to say when he saw her, but as the door began to creak open and his throat closed shut with panic. It was obvious he should have devised more of a plan. When the woman answering the door did not resemble Isla in any way, he let out a lightened gasp, knowing he at least had a few more seconds to think.

"She's not here," her sister spat without Lachlan having to ask. The look of disapproval painted on her sour face let Lachlan know he'd not be let off the hook as easily as he may have hoped.

"She's in the hills ..." Her words trailed off in the rush of wind whipping past Lachlan's face. He didn't need the sister to tell him where she was. He already knew.

The tires of his father's old Corsa bounced and jumped as Lachlan sped the rest of the way to Bosta Beach. He wasn't sure the old car could handle it, but he couldn't fight the urge to find her quickly. He had to hold onto the feeling of wanting her, needing her, the person she was and not the girl he'd still expected her to be. He skidded to a stop at the end of the road as Bosta spilled out in front of him.

The tarnished tide bell sounded with each ebb of the water. The fine, white sand of the beach was disappearing, each wave eating away at it. Soon, the ocean would fill the entire cove, hiding the pathways leading into the hills. Lachlan skirted the encroaching tidal pools and cut along the small sandy ridge just outside the wall of the cemetery before crossing the footbridge at the bottom of the hills. From there, it was up and over the ridge. He passed small flocks of sheep as he ran up the grassy incline. They moved as one organism the closer he got to them, sounding off one by one in high pitched screams. The carcass of one of its own lay still, half eaten, next to the remains of an old croft, just as eaten by time as the animal was by death.

At the top of the ridge, Lachlan stopped, catching his breath not from the physical exertion but in the forgotten beauty the glen held in secret. The hills stretched out for miles, only interrupted by the dark rippling surface of the lochs that ran between them, snaking through the landscape like they had for thousands of years. The sun beat down, sparkling on the water's surface in places where the clouds did not block it, shifting patches of luminous color like a spotlight above them. In the middle of it all, a fire burned, brighter and more vivid than the first time he remembered seeing it.

He wanted to yell for her, but stopped himself and instead, squatted down against a rock, out of the wind to watch her swim. Her body was microscopic compared to the massive loch spreading out on every side of her. He may have missed her had it not been for the contrast of her pale skin and rich hair against the shadowy surface of the water. He could see bits of her naked skin as she fluttered about in the water, unencumbered by life, by him, by her past.

She swam a few quick strokes and disappeared under the water, leaving ringlets vibrating on the surface in her wake. Lachlan counted quietly to himself, waiting for her to resurface. At thirty seconds, he stood up and shielded his eyes from the sun, thinking he'd missed her, but he still couldn't see her. A minute passed and still nothing. Lachlan was moving down the hill towards the water's edge and the abandoned croft, still counting and looking for the fiery crown of hair to surface, but the water had gone still except for the movement made by the wind. He stripped to his underwear, dropping his clothes next to hers and the stone wall, but there was still nothing.

The water was colder than he remembered the last time he'd been swimming in it. It wasn't bone-chilling, but it wasn't pleasant. His bare skin prickled as he ran through it, causing small eruptions with each pounding step he took. His pace slowed the further out on the shelf he moved, not knowing where it would end, and the true depths of the loch began.

He stopped and slid his feet forward inches at a time until his toes curled over what felt like the edge. His unsure movements sent wrinkles swirling out over the surface. He was panicked, unsure of where to start his search for her body or if he'd even be able to see under the dark surface. His heart began to pound painfully in his chest forcing him to take deep breathes that felt empty of air in his burning lungs.

"Took you long enough," she laughed while splashing water in Lachlan's direction. "It's a good thing I wasnae in any real danger, I'd be dead by now."

Her hair was dark, made even darker matted against her fair skin. Even though her mouth remained hidden, he knew the devilish grin the surface line hid from him. Lachlan let out an exacerbated huff, before falling over into the chilled water, welcoming the relief it brought to his burning skin. He should have guessed that she'd been able to pick him out of the hillside when he thought he was well hidden.

She kept her distance, acting aloof once Lachlan surfaced. They were halfway across the loch by the time she stopped long enough that he might be able to get a word in. But when the opportunity presented itself, he was tongue-tied and awkward, like he was a teenage boy on the verge of manhood all over again.

"This is the part where you apologize to me," she said sternly, treading water in front of him.

"I know," he laughed, embarrassed by his inability to form a complete sentence. "I am sorry, for everything, it's just ..."

They floated in the water, moving their arms back and forth, sending small waves out into the space between them until they crashed together, casting the ripples back in the opposite direction. Lachlan watched the ripples as they moved, letting the anxieties of the last few days wash over him before letting them go.

"There's nothing else," he finally admitted. "I'm just sorry."

"Yes," she agreed, sending a splash in his direction again. "You did turn out quite sorry if you thought you'd come back here and things wouldnae have changed."

"I wanted it to be the same," he said. "I wanted you to be the same. The way I remembered you."

She didn't answer right away. She couldn't. There was pain in his voice, and she knew not to mock it. Maybe she'd wanted it too, to be the same person she had been before he left, but life had happened in the twenty years they'd been apart. Lachlan knew he couldn't fault her for that. He'd done things he wasn't proud of, things he'd never admit to even if she asked.

"I held onto the memory ... the image of you. When I needed to escape, all I could see was the fire around you." He smiled at her, both their bodies bobbing idly in the water. Clouds moved overhead, casting shadows on the water shaped like large beasts swimming below the surface. But Lachlan knew it was just the two of them. It always had been.

"None of what happened was your fault," he said calmly, staring at Isla, remembering the look in Arden's eyes when he'd shown instead of Isla. "You know that; right?" The question was just as much for her as it was for him.

"I saw you," she admitted after a quiet moment. "That afternoon. I was here but when I came over the ridge the two of you were already fighting."

"What?" Lachlan asked, confused.

"I was here, but when I saw the two of you ... it was something, inhumane. You looked like you wanted to kill each other."

Lachlan splashed water on his face, trying to wash the images away. Arden may well have wanted to kill him, but that's not how things turned out.

"I ran," Isla continued. "I ran back to the road, halfway back to Bernera before I found Mr. McLeod on his way back up to check on the cattle in the storm. Maybe if I had stayed, maybe …"

"God, no," Lachlan uttered, "is that what you've thought this whole time?"

Their stillness had him chilled. The wind swept down into the valley in bursts, brushing over the water in slight undulations. The ripples deepened as he swam toward her. The question of why she'd been late to begin with burned in Lachlan's mind, and he wondered if too much time had passed to ask the question.

"There's nothing you could have done."

"I could have left you alone. I knew what I was doing with you, I knew I was teasing you. From the first time I saw you, I knew, but I just …" she breathed, tiring. He could feel her invisible strokes growing wider and deeper as she searched for something tangible to hold on to.

Lachlan smiled trying not to laugh. "You could have tried, but I dunnae think it would have worked." He was close enough he could have reached out to her, but he wasn't sure she would let him. "You didnae know. It was my choice, and I made it." He moved closer, so their arms began to tangle as they paddled to stay afloat. "And I'd make it again."

The admission shocked even him. It had always felt like either/or until that moment. He couldn't have Isla without Arden being dead or the other way around. One couldn't exist unless the other didn't. But he'd had it wrong the whole time.

"Tell me what really happened that night," she said, neither asking or telling. "And then let's leave it in the past, where it belongs."

Lachlan reached up to brush strands of hair from her face, letting his hand follow the curve of her cheek down to her neck and then her shoulder, realizing that there was nothing between them but the water.

He traced the outline of her arm and then his fingers found their way to her bare hip. He found courage he'd forgotten he had when it came to Isla Gilcrest. She wasn't like the other women he'd conquered in his life. She wasn't a trophy, or a means to an end, a drunken night ending in a clumsy morning. She was real. He took her firmly in his hand, as something soft, and unfamiliar rubbed against him, sending a paralyzing jolt through his chilled body.

Over the sounds of his own shouts and frantic splashing, he could hear hysterical laughter. She had her head bent back resting gently on the water, and her body heaved as she attempted to laugh while keeping gulps of water from slipping into her throat.

"What the hell was that?" Lachlan yelled, spinning in circles in the water, looking for the mysterious creature that had brushed against his arm.

Isla composed herself as much as she could and swam toward him softly with only her eyes above the water. She stopped inches away from him and began treading water again, looking around her as she did.

"Such a silly boy," she whispered as she fanned her weightless hair out around her, letting it glide like seaweed floating freely in the water. She moved closer and the tips of her hair tickled against Lachlan's skin. He'd dreamed of that feeling, but he'd never had it quite right.

The white clouds overhead had curdled and turned a thick gray color and hung heavy with rain. The absence of the sun above cooled the air as it swept over the loch, but despite the physical discomfort around him, Lachlan had nowhere else in the world he would have rather been at that moment.

"So, what happens now?" Isla asked with wide eyes.

"I guess we pick up where we left off." Lachlan's cheeks hurt from the size and intensity of his smile.

"And where was that?" she asked.

"It was here," he answered, both physically and symbolically. He moved quickly, wrapping his arm around her midsection, pulling her against himself. Their kicks and paddles became tangled as their bodies fought to keep their heads above water even though they were already drowning in each other.

Her lips shook against his, along with the rest of her body. Lachlan wanted to believe it was from his touch, but he could feel his own body shivering. The kiss was tender, almost shy. For all intents and purposes, it could have been considered their first kiss which justified their hesitation. They weren't the same people they'd been before.

Lachlan pushed against the water with her in his arms, moving them closer to the shelf. Their lips barely parted as they moved simultaneously, their kicks and treads no longer fighting against the others. He watched her eyes, darting back and forth. She felt like nothing and everything in his arms all at once.

The cold mud of the shelf squished in Lachlan's hand when he finally reached solid ground. But they stayed, holding on to the edge for support while letting the rest of their bodies hang weightlessly in the deep. Individual raindrops began to dot the water's surface. They were oddly warm against his skin as the rest of his body fought the feeling of the cold water surrounding him. He looked up toward the sky, letting the rain pepper his skin, thankful for every second of life he'd been granted knowing that he'd squandered his life. He wasn't sure he deserved it, but life had put them together a second time, and he'd not miss the opportunity to be hers again.

The second kiss was impassioned, frenzied. The shy, coyness from before had melted away with the subtle rain pattering around them. With only the raw, submerged earth around them, Lachlan lifted her against it, setting her so she sat with her legs hanging over, buried in the cold water from the waist down. Her dark hair hung in front of her, covering the slight swell of her chest. He kissed her hard, and she kissed back, enfolding her hands around his cheeks, pulling him closer as she did.

The chill of the water disappeared. The rain almost sizzled on his flushed skin as it fell. They couldn't get close enough, no matter how hard they tried. Lachlan's lips moved from hers to her cheeks and then her ear, and then her neck where he let his teeth graze her skin gently. He could feel the quickness of her breath under her skin in the rise and fall of her chest. Her hands tangled in his hair as he kissed her gently between her breasts.

Thunder screamed out above, frightening them enough to pause in their place. Lachlan rested his head against Isla's chest, listening to the pounding of her heart just below the surface. He could feel her start to slip away but didn't want to move. He let her go, and when he looked up again, he found her empty hand extended, waiting to take his.

They ran like they had as kids, kicking and splashing clutches of water at each other. Their laughter rang through the valley, outlasting the roar coming from the sky. Everything moved in slow motion. Individual beads of water hung stagnant in the air. Her smile never faltered. The deep pools of open ocean water where her eyes should have been called him home, but all he could do was look at her, realizing it was the first time he was really seeing her since he'd been back. The images he'd kept of her in his mind, his memories, the scarred woman he'd thought she was, disappeared, leaving behind the woman who'd grown out of the girl he'd loved so many years ago.

She stopped at the door to the ramshackle croft that sat almost at the water's edge. It should have been a painting, the way her fair skin contrasted with the deep stone color and her burgundy hair fell almost to her navel. Lachlan was still ankle deep in the loch committing the moment to memory when the sky screamed out again, sending not so distant memories flooding into his blood. Isla reached her hand out to him, almost as if she knew, and he let her smile wash the memories of that place away, replacing it with entirely new ones. Ones that were unquestionably true.

Chapter Twenty-Two

The hands on my watch felt frozen. Each time I looked down to confirm that it had been another hour that had passed, in reality, it had been barely minutes. I had time, but not infinite amounts of it. I had to allow for travel time over the craggy rocks and fields between her house and mine, making sure I'd left time to slip inside and power up all the house lights to give the impression I'd been home for hours. My mother would scream at me for having all the lights on, demanding I get a job to pay for the increase in the bill due to my carelessness. The threat was idle. If it weren't the lights, it would be mud on the floor, the door not closed properly, eating too much of her food, looking at her in the wrong way, merely existing. She'd always find something to justify her miserable existence.

I looked again at my watch, lying to myself when I said I would give her five more minutes before leaving. I'd wait forever for her. I couldn't think of anything outside of two broken legs that could keep me from her. It was magnetic, whatever it was between us.

The sun disappeared behind slow moving clouds. Their crisp white color meant they weren't yet filled with rain, but it was only a matter of time. From the top of the ridge, I looked off into the distance, out over the ocean, and could see the storm steeping on the horizon, and still, she hadn't shown.

I paced across the ridge, looking down at the path I'd taken to get there, waiting impatiently. The tide was coming in, burying the silvery sand with each slow-moving wave that rolled in. Soon, the briny rocks covered in urchins and slippery seaweed would disappear along with the beach, and it would be like they never existed at all.

They would be lurking shadows below the surface, waiting for the tide to change, clamoring for the sun's warmth over the sea's cold current.

The path remained empty. The long grass on either side swayed and sang in the wind, mocking me with every blade that rustled. Any elation I had felt before arriving at Bosta to meet her was beginning to wane with the realization that she might not show. I looked at my watch again. Her five minutes was up, twenty minutes ago. Five more minutes, I promised myself, knowing it was just another lie.

The rock was stiff and chilled, even through the fabric of my clothes. I turned away from the empty path and looked down to the bottom of the valley and the loch below. The clouds hid the sun, and in its absence, the water's surface was murky and uninviting. I tried to imagine how the valley had looked when Isla and I had gone swimming, but it felt like a different place entirely. The shadows of the clouds above moved quickly over the landscape, painting the stillness of hillside with ghostly movement; the only movement.

There was a rustling in the long grass. I sat up confused and disoriented by the missing light from the afternoon sky. My eyes were heavy with the sudden sleep that had found me. The wind ripped over the ledge, pulling intensely at my clothes as if trying to wake me up before the thing rustling in the grass pounced, or maybe it was just the wind tattling on itself.

I looked at my watch. It had only been half an hour since the last time I remembered looking at it, and in that time the storm resting on the horizon had been pushed inland by the wind and was directly overhead. Grey clouds spun overhead, pregnant with rain, and I could feel the wetness looming in the air. Still, she hadn't come.

I crouched on the south side of the outcropping and ducked out of the wind. Any hope that I had been harboring foolishly was gone, swept away by the winds biting at the landscape. It would be a race against the elements to make it home before the rain, but that wasn't enough to energize me to move. I sat against the rock, pathetically unable and unwilling to move, stuck inside my inability to understand why Isla hadn't shown.

I stared down to the valley floor aimlessly. The wind pushed small ripples and white caps over the water's surface. The grasses bent over, pulsing with the flux of the winds intensity. The only thing that didn't move was the remains of the stone croft. Through the beginnings of tears, I saw something move against the steadfast croft. Something human.

My feet tore through the bending grass, and I was halfway down the path when I lost sight of her. I questioned how she'd missed me sleeping the afternoon away on the ridge but banished the thought almost immediately. It didn't matter. The closer to the bottom I bounded, the more forgiving the wind became, allowing me to move faster toward what was waiting for me.

The ground was soggy, like it had already rained. My boots squished and sank in the sodden dirt creating the sound of suction every time I pushed off for another step. Once on the valley floor, I picked up speed. My heart raced, pounding so loud I was sure she would hear it when I finally found her, and laugh. I'd forgive her for it, and being late, and anything else she did in life.

"Isla!" I yelled, bursting through the mouth of the croft, thinking she'd taken refuge from the elements inside its unshakable walls. But it was as empty as the path had been.

Thunder crashed, and even though it was still in the distance, the ground shook. I stood in the doorway looking out to the loch as rain began to dot the surface of the water, sending ringlets out in each direction until they collided with others moving in the opposite direction.

"Isla?" I yelled again. My skin prickled but not because of the cool kisses from the rain. A familiar feeling grew in my chest. I stood, motionless, hoping that my lack of movement would help me blend in and disguise me from whatever was watching. But I had it wrong. My lack of movement made me stand out against the whirling hillside.

I let myself think, hope, that it was Isla playing a game with me. She might be hiding behind one of the rocks just up the path, waiting until my fear peaked before jumping out to reveal herself. The eyes felt familiar, but they weren't hers watching me.

Chapter Twenty-Three

The world had shifted. Decades worth of want and wonderment had come to an end. She would no longer be the girl that got away. It felt like a dream; one Lachlan had had a thousand times before; one that fell tragically short of reality.

Lachlan lay in the dark, unable and unwilling to move, as he committed every detail of the encounter to memory; the smell of her sweet stained skin; the rush of hurried breath on his neck; the movement of her body under his. He could still taste her on his lips; the sweetness of heather and gorse melded together into what he believed her to be – the embodiment of summer.

The thunder roared incessantly across the sky. The remnants of a poorly stacked fire burned in the corner, giving off barely enough light for Lachlan to see his hand in front of his face. In the darkness, he slid his hand along the blanket in search of Isla, but she was a ghost, the sweet smells of summer the only part of her she left behind.

Lighting flashed, rushing through the bits of the croft it could reach, and then there was nothing but the darkness again. The emptiness grew the longer he laid in the dark, and he searched his memory for when Isla had left, but it was like fighting through a drunken haze even though they'd not had a drop since the night before. He'd made sure of that. He wanted to remember every detail of his apology to Isla, whereas before, he'd drunk to make sure he forgot the night.

Thunder cracked around him, stirring distant memories better left forgotten. Images of Isla melted, giving way to other things entirely. The storm felt just as it had before. The change in air pressure was palpable. The world felt lighter, freer. The rain came and went in sheets, pouring for a few minutes then relenting. He could feel the chill of the wet mud against his cheek as he remembered sinking deeper and deeper, unable to move. The rain pelted from above, making it hard to see, but not impossible. In the bursts of light, he could see a figure.

Lachlan knew it was his imagination playing tricks on him, but he decided to let it, one last time before he let it go. What had happened between him and Arden would always be there, something just below the surface, but he knew he had to move on. There might never be an explanation for what happened to Arden, or the other missing children Euan had brought to light, but that didn't mean that Lachlan wasn't allowed to live. He realized his life had been a punishment pushed upon himself for having survived when Arden hadn't, the same way his father's life had been a punishment for not protecting the woman he loved. They had both been shells of men, living parallel lives on paths that had never crossed until the truth brought them together. He knew it was time to let Arden go, and he could not have thought of a more fitting place than where it had begun.

He dressed quickly in the darkness, before turning his attention back to the scant fire in the corner. Crawling on the ground, he found bits and pieces of what could be used as fuel to build it back to something functional. In moments, the inside of the croft was cast in an orange glow, as the fire roared confidently in the corner.

Lachlan took stock of the space around him with his newfound sight. There wasn't much to look at except the rubble that had befallen the croft and the makeshift bed he'd made for Isla and him to lay on. Seeing the beige color sheet lying against the earthen ground, the impressions of their bodies still outlined in the simple cloth, gave truth what had happened between them in the dark.

The existence of their evening together, laying there, staring back at him, left Lachlan in stitches, laughing at the unbelievable sequence of events that had led him back to her. Days ago, Isla Gilcrest had been but a figment of his imagination, a ghost he clung to, unable to let her go completely. But it wasn't just her, it was everything. The island had been holding him hostage from hundreds of miles away, and he'd let it. His night with Isla had freed him from the trapped feeling. With her, he felt like he could finally find a future that didn't revolve around what had happened or who he had been in the past. With her, he could be someone new; someone different.

Thunder rumbled as a second wave of storms moved overhead. The ground and the walls vibrated, shaking loose from its hiding place Isla's backpack that had been sitting precariously in the doorway of the croft. Lachlan grabbed the bag, but it was already soaked clean through. As he stood in the doorway, he stared out into the darkness, picturing the hillside and the loch he knew was there but couldn't see, hoping that Isla wasn't caught in the midst of the mounting storm. He couldn't make sense of where she'd gone or why, but in the back of his mind, it felt like something she would do.

He unzipped the backpack and turned it upside down in haste, spilling its contents onto the ground below. Clothes and a few bags of crisps and a half-drunk bottle of water piled together at Lachlan's feet. Giving the bag one last shake, he watched, paralyzed, as a small blue book with gold lettering fell to the ground, coming to rest face up, as if to stare him down, one last time.

Lachlan stood motionless staring back at the book. He tapped it with the toes on his right foot, like it might be a dead animal he wasn't quite sure was dead. He was able to draw a deep breath when it didn't leap from the pile and attack him. Lachlan knew its bite was subtler than that.

He stooped down and picked it up, flipping through the pages with a speed too fast to possibly read any of its words. But it wasn't words he was looking for. Halfway through, the handwritten scribbles began to fill the margins with their nonsensical ramblings. He looked at them but didn't read them, he didn't have to, he knew them all by heart.

Outside, the storm screeched unnatural sounds as the wind whipped through the valley. Rain pelted against what remained of the roof above Lachlan, but small streams of water were beginning to find their way in, leaking down the stone walls. Quick gusts pushed in through the open doorway, stirring up the fire and throwing embers spinning in the air.

He couldn't help but think of Moira as he looked down at the book, and the blood-stained wall under her feet as she stood with a giddy smile where the window should have been. It felt like a betrayal, not believing in the things written in it. She had believed the words had been worth her life. Lachlan stood above the fire with the book in his outstretched arm, questioning what would be worth his life.

The world went silent as if to listen in on Lachlan as he whispered goodbye to the book. The wind and the rain stopped. The only sound left was the trickle of water making its way inside and the crackling hiss of what was left of the fire. Lachlan opened his hand, and the book landed open-faced in the fire with a deafening thud.

Embers crackled with excitement, as the fire began devouring the thick, blue cover. Lachlan wanted to look away but couldn't take his eyes off the glowing orange line that was working its way slowly down from the top corner. He'd assumed there would be a sense of release at letting it go and watching it burn, but all he could do was trace the handwritten words with his eyes. He knew the scribbled words by heart. He didn't even need the book. He could have recited them in his sleep. Lachlan watched as the burn line flowed like liquid on the page, illuminating something new; something that hadn't been there before.

The heat singed his cheeks as he crouched closer to the fire, trying to read words he'd never seen before. He scoured the page frantically, his eyes trying to outrun the graceful embers closing in. How had he never noticed the page or read the words in front of him before? He'd picked the book apart, at night on the cold bathroom floor, scouring it for the truth Moira had purported it to hold. But he'd never seen the words before; he never would have been able to miss the date.

April, 1985. Spring sprung early this year, making April late, hot and the air pregnant with midges already. She's a redhead this time with lips that match. Pretty, wide smile you'd not soon forget. Layered thick and splattered all the colors of the rainbow as she leaves the studio she rents on from a man named Kenneth Street. Where feet can walk on water, hidden from the light, he finds them both, but only one paid the price that night. The one that got away – he'll be back, we're sure. The girl draws him near whenever he is far. LEWSTOR

When he finally finished, the book was half gone. His hand was in the fire as he listened to the way it licked at the tattered pages. Perhaps it was shock that kept him from feeling the pain he rightfully should have endured as the cinders clung to his skin. He swatted at the flames, trying feverishly to save what was left of the book and the words he'd never seen before.

Lachlan dropped to his knees and doused the book with the dirt and sand that made up the floor of the derelict croft. The gritty sand stung the skin on his hand at first but eventually cooled the burn he was finally able to feel. He stiffened, staring down at the corners of the book poking out from the dust covering it, hoping he'd not been too late.

Most of the cover was gone. The innards of the book remained, in various stages of decay. What endured of the page marked April 1985 was badly charred, but the words were there, staring Lachlan in the face. They were words he'd never seen before in a book he'd read a thousand times; words he'd heard before; words he'd seen before in other places.

He could hear the old woman, calling him by the name she'd given him; late spring, 1985, the date of his mother's attack, the date of her rape, the date he was likely conceived. The dates weren't recording the disappearances of children. It was the mothers she was keeping track of. But why?

It took everything he had to turn the pages, as if the April 1985 entry might disappear if he took his eyes off of it. Every page, every entry was new. The dates spanned several years in either direction of 1985. Lachlan flipped gingerly through the remains until it became clear as day that he wasn't reading the same book he'd spent night after night agonizing over as an adolescent in Inverness District. The book in front of him was a different book entirely, with different dates, different vague descriptions of places that could have conceivably been around any corner of Scotland. Except they weren't. They were catalogues of attacks, things the Spaewife had seen. She'd written them down and marked them with coded letters at the end of each entry; his mother's being LEWSTOR for Lewis, Stornoway.

Lachlan began wondering how many books there were. How many attacks had the Spaewife seen? How many other children had she warned of the creature in the deep waiting for them at the edge? How many more would there have to be before it stopped? Lachlan got to his feet, questioning if Euan had been right all along; if he had somehow had it right all along. Was what Lachlan thought to be his own made up story, actually the truth?

His concentration broke with a familiar sound riding on the breeze; one he'd not heard in twenty years.

He'd heard the cry roll through the valley once before. It sounded like thunder, in animal form.

Lachlan stood at the mouth of the croft, straining to see through the shadows whirling around him, but there was nothing but the darkness. He squinted and listened for the sound again, but the air was still. His body relaxed when it didn't come again. It had been his mind and the valley playing tricks on him again. He leaned against the stone wall, for one last look; final confirmation that he hadn't heard what he thought he had.

A low rumble stirred above, growing stronger the longer it rang out. Lachlan focused on where he knew the loch to be, waiting for the flash.

Two bursts in quick succession lit the valley floor. Her pale skin against the darkness surrounding made her look like a ghost floating just above the surface of the water. The beast shared the color of night, making it almost impossible to see, same as before. It reared up, kicking at the water, but she didn't move.

Lachlan tried to yell for her, but the sight of what he'd taken as imaginary had stolen his speech.

Chapter Twenty-Four

I'd make a run for it, back to the parking lot and grab my bike from behind the feed station for Mr. McLeod's cattle. I'd made the run hundreds, if not thousands of times before. I was confident I could make it in the waning light.

Steam rose from the top of the loch in the shapes of ghosts and fluttered above the water before the wind carried them away. I stood in the doorway of the croft as I scanned the hillside for the eyes I could still feel on me, but the only thing that moved was the grass in the wind. I watched, looking for a break in the rhythm, but there was nothing. I hoped I could outrun it; whatever it was.

I'd ride to Isla's house to make sure she was home safe, before cursing her for standing me up, followed by a pleading apology for one in the same. I'd leave my bike by the back of her house, where she said her mother would never look, before tearing off across the empty expanse between our houses. I'd pray there was nothing to light my way home except the lightning jumping from the clouds above me. Any light out in front of me meant I was too late.

I stood motionless in the doorway, waiting for something to tell me it was time to go. The rain was thick. It would be like trying to run underwater, but I had little in the way of choices. Flashes skipped across the sky in quick succession, briefly illuminating my path. The hillside remained empty. It was time to go.

In seconds, my jeans and shoes were soaked. My waterproof did the best it could, but I could feel individual drops creeping in through the collar and running down my back and chest, sending chills through my body as they moved.

I was only feet from the croft when I heard a voice calling over the downpour. It was faint but unmistakable. He was behind me and had been, most likely standing under the overhang of the croft's roof waiting for me to make my move. We'd only been feet if not inches apart. I realized how dumb I'd been to think I could outrun him out of the valley. He'd have caught me in seconds.

I froze, refusing to face him as if keeping him to my back meant he wasn't really standing behind me, but he was. I knew in the back of my mind that I'd have to face him sooner or later. I just always assumed it would be later.

"Where do you think you're going?" Arden yelled, through the sheet of rain between us.

I searched for the explanation, the rationalization that I'd gone over a dozen times in my head. There was no excuse. There was no explanation; other than I'd broken our pact to not let Isla come between us again. I began to turn towards him, listening to the sound of the mud squishing around my feet as I tried to pull them free. The only thing I had in my corner with me was the knowledge that he'd have done the same to me if the roles had been reversed. He could deny it all he wanted. We both knew it was a lie.

The rain was so thick I could only make out his outline. All detail was washed away. We stood motionless, staring at each other, the people we'd become. We weren't the same boys we'd been even the year before. Something had changed, and we both knew there was no going back to how things had been. We felt like enemies before anything was even said.

"How'd you know where I was?" I yelled back.

"You told me."

"What?" I yelled. "I can barely hear you." I took a few steps back toward the croft, and the sheet of rain let up as if trying to listen in on our conversation. I looked around like someone had flipped a switch, but Arden's glare didn't waver.

"What do you mean I told you? What the hell are you talking about."

With minimal movement, Arden reached into his back pocket and retrieved a wad of wet paper. He didn't have to open it for me to know what it was. I reached into my back pocket, and when my hand didn't find the note Isla had given to me, I knew it was because it was in his hand.

"Not a great day for a swim," he said, throwing the wadded-up piece of paper in my direction.

"I guess not."

I wanted to apologize, but only because it was the right thing to do, not because I wanted to or because I felt like I was in the wrong. It wouldn't have mattered anyway. Arden would see it for what it was.

"Where's Isla?" I asked, assuming that Arden was responsible for her absence.

The smile on Arden's face spread until it looked painful. The corners of his mouth almost reached his eyes, which beamed like shiny coins we'd collected and polished as children. He looked like pure evil.

"She needed a ride, rather unexpectedly," he spit through his upturned lips. "There's only so many people we know with a car and nothing better to do than rescue a young girl in need."

There were a million names I wanted to call him and a million more things I wanted to say to him. He had no spine or conscience putting Isla in the car with his brother. Maybe they'd worked out a deal where Ross would save a piece of her for him. Lachlan knew he'd never speak to him again after they finished what they had to say to one another at the bottom of the valley, but he'd never forgive Arden if something happened to Isla.

"I should beat your ass," Arden admitted.

"Why, so you can be just like him, following behind like his little puppy. Is that what you want?"

"No, because you deserve it," he yelled.

He wasn't wrong, but neither was I, and we both knew it. We stood, face to face, at a crossroads in our lives. There was an invisible line drawn in the mud between us; a line that once we crossed there was no going back. I looked at him and the clown-sized smile he still had on his face and took the first step over the line.

"She picked me," I said. "That's all this is about. You're angry because she picked me instead of you. Your feelings got hurt, and you don't know how to fucking deal."

He was on top of me in less than a second in a barrage of clenched fists. They hurt more than I remembered. Ross must have been working him over often, schooling him on how to follow in his footsteps.

"She doesn't know what she's missing!" he yelled as we rolled in the wet sludge, coating our skin and clothes in dark mud.

"And what's that," I grunted, pushing him off me before trying to get back to my feet. The mud was like quicksand, sucking me in deeper the more I struggled against it.

"What exactly is it that you think she's missing?" I asked. "Your incredible good looks? Your conversation? Or maybe it's your witty charm that she can't do without. The charm that makes the rest of us cringe because it's so over the top forceful. How else would you convince a girl to go with you? It would be borderline kidnapping if you ever got a girl to go with you because she'd feel like she had no other choice. You'd probably just take what you wanted from her anyway."

Arden stopped struggling. His eyes widened as if taunting me to say what I really wanted to say. He looked back at me, waiting for me to finish it.

"You're turning into Ross. That's what this is about. Not Isla, not even me." The truth burned like fire in my throat. "And we all hate Ross. Even you, at one point. And now ... now it's like you can't wait to be him."

He must have been secretly wiggling himself free while I spoke. He sprang free of the mud's grasp, jumping to his feet in one movement. He immediately began to sink again, teetering from one foot then the other trying to escape it.

The rain had begun to fall harder, and any light the sun had left in the sky had faded. I wormed my way free of the ground and made for the cover of the croft, when a forceful gush of wind rounded the corner of the structure and pushed past me in a devilish blur.

It split the rain like its skin was on fire. Its fiendish cries tore through the valley. In the fading light, all either of us could see was the red of its eyes and the other's incredulous expression. We both looked in the direction it had gone but lost sight of it in the steam hanging just above the ground. Thunder cracked an ungodly crash, and the ground shook. I watched as the water gathered in the puddles closest to me as they echoed and rippled the sky's rage.

When I looked up, Arden was gone, already tearing out towards the water's edge. I lost him in the mist, and as I did, the moment froze. I looked at the mist dancing with the wind, the ripples in the standing water and the darkness that was coming. Her scratchy voice bubbled up inside me until her haunting words finally found meaning in my world. *Stay clear of th' water's edge ... that's where he waits for you ... that's where he kills you.*

The world moved again, but faster than normal. I couldn't see Arden or the beast, but I knew where they were. The mud gurgled and sucked at my feet as I ran toward the water's edge, hoping I wasn't too late. Lightning jumped in the sky, and I could see Arden standing ankle deep on the hidden shelf, arm outstretched toward the beast who, in the mist, looked like he could walk on water, just like she had said.

Chapter Twenty-Five

The chill of the water stung against Lachlan's skin as it seeped through his shoes and the cuffs of his jeans. The sky had quieted and gave him no light to see. He was blindly easing out onto the shelf. The spaewife's words sped through his mind; *that's where he waits for you.*

"Isla!" he screamed through a whisper. They weren't alone. Lachlan could feel eyes on him, the same eyes that had watched him and Isla once before.

Lachlan continued inching forward, dragging his feet in the mud as he moved, swinging them out to the sides, surveying the water as he moved. He could hear the beast somewhere in front of my him and feel the vibrations of his hooves rippling across the surface, but he had no sense of Isla in the darkness.

His steps became slighter the further from the bank he moved. He remembered the feeling of fear he'd experienced inching toward the edge of the shelf the last time he'd been there with Isla. It had been a fear laced with tender adolescent exhilaration. He'd give anything to experience that sense of freeing anticipation again. It was like being tied to the earth and set free of its gravity at the same time. The perfect moment going over a steep rise in the road when his stomach both soared and fell to earth. He'd been both tied inexplicably to her, but somehow set free at the same time. His father's words echoed inside him; *protect her with your life.*

A low rumble rolled above him, and he pled for light, but it didn't come.

"Isla!" he called again, louder this time. "Isla, answer me!"

He continued edging forward. He stooped down so his hands dragged in the water, sifting through the seaweed and long grasses growing under the surface. He imagined it would feel rough against his skin, and not slip through his fingers as easily as the things that were meant to be there. It would feel out of place. Woven. Frayed. Lachlan stood motionless in the dark, waiting for something to move, to give him a clue of where it was, but the world was still.

"Isla!" he yelled, splashing and kicking at the water. "Answer me!"

The animal shrieked, sounding as terrified to be there as he was. Lachlan could feel its movements in the way the water moved. He moved too fast and tripped over his own arm dangling in the water and somersaulted until he was on his hands and knees.

"God damn it, Isla, answer me!" he yelled, thrashing viciously against the helpless water. He sat back on his heels and wiped the murk from his face. The idea that he was too late began to bubble up, and he screamed unrecognizable noises into the darkness around him before smashing his fists into the water again. At first, he thought it was just the water moving against him, but the more it pulled, the more familiar it felt.

The pull was gentle, not the violent struggle he remembered from twenty years ago. He fished in the mud, his fingers searching through the seaweed for something that didn't belong. He swayed back and forth on his hands and knees until the rough fibers of what felt like a rope slid into his fingers.

At first, he just held it limp in his hand. It could have been anything; a line cast off from a dingy or trawler lost in the loch having taken a wrong turn somewhere near its mouth. It could have drifted from miles away and just tangled in the reeds, unable to break free for further aimless exploration of the depths. Or it could have been a tether that the stories said was made of serpents. He tugged against the rope, waiting for the other end to respond in kind.

Lachlan jumped to his feet and followed the rope like a trail of breadcrumbs left for him to find. When the slack went limp he pulled again, and the beast pulled back, crying in the darkness as it did.

The sky had begun to clear, and the dense clouds obstructing the moon had thinned enough to let its white light filter through. Silver patches danced on the waters dark surface, shifting as the wind swept through the remaining clouds. As if on purpose, the wind stopped suddenly, casting a focus of moonlight against her pale skin and the thin bleached summer dress she wore. The gleam was almost blinding.

"Isla!" Lachlan yelled.

She turned, surprise covering her face as if she hadn't heard him yelling for her in the dark.

"It real," she half yelled, gulping air as much as belief. She turned back to look at the beast still trying to take it all in. "You were right. All this time, you were right."

Lachlan wanted to call her a fool, discount her statements, but it was hard to do with the beast standing in front of him. Everything he thought he knew about the world, about what had happened to him and Arden, had been wrong. The stories they were sure had been cautionary tales for misbehaving children had been real. He gulped for breath and understanding and wondered if perhaps he hadn't fallen asleep and might be dreaming, tucked in the safety of the stone croft. As much as he wanted to believe it was a dream, he knew he wasn't sleeping.

"It's not ..." he yelled, unable to finish his thought out load. It was hard to do as his eyes watched the beast sway in the shin deep water, waiting for him just like he'd been told it would be.

As if in protest of Lachlan's unsaid thoughts, the beast reared up onto its hind legs and screamed into the night. Isla recoiled, throwing her hands around her ears to shield them from the sound. Lachlan stood, frozen, still trying to convince himself that it wasn't real. It couldn't be.

When the beast settled, it moved toward Isla, slowly but deliberately. Its head hung low and heavy, nudging the water with its broad nose. The eyes were not the same as he remembered them. They no longer burned with fire. They were dark and lifeless, tawny in color with little definition between the colored part of the eye and the pupil. When the light caught them just right, they glowed slightly, but not the way he remembered.

Lachlan crept forward as the beast moved toward Isla. When the creature threw its head back, Lachlan could see the makeshift bridle tied roughly against its muzzle. There were groves, and deep-set indentations in its skin like it never had relief from the chafing of the rough rope. There was a sadness in the eyes where Lachlan had expected to find something evil, drawing him in deeper. He watched as the beast rubbed its muzzle against the inside of its leg, desperate to be free of the friction. For a second, Lachlan found pity for the animal despite everything that had happened.

He watched idly as Isla's pale hand reached out to touch the beast. It bowed its head to her, welcoming the touch. It was calm and still, almost peaceful in its pursuit of her. In the moonlight, they looked angelic, like an illustration in a book Lachlan had read before.

The pity Lachlan had fallen victim to vanished violently. It was a ruse. The books they'd all read as children talked of the water horses in lochs, mesmerizing their victims into thinking they were nothing more than ordinary horses to draw them in. The devil wouldn't catch its prey without concealing its horns; guises had to be fashioned to catch the unsuspecting.

Everything in Lachlan's body screamed that he'd gone mad. His skin tingled like it had during his shock therapy sessions with Dr. Rutherford when he mentioned the existence of the creatures from the deep. What would the good doctor have to say about the beast standing in front of him? Lachlan wanted to laugh, he could feel it in his gut, but he was paralyzed by the truth standing right in front of him. He had been right all along.

The images of Arden he'd banished from his memory began flooding his mind. He could almost see him standing between himself and Isla, a true embodiment of the ghost he'd been for the last twenty years. Lachlan watched calmly, remembering the glint of the moonlight against Arden's skin as his arm reached out for the beast and the excitement in the beast's scream when it knew it had him. His face had gone ghost white as panic took hold of his body. Lachlan could see his face as if he were standing in front of him a second time. He opened his mouth to scream, but his voice was already fading. *Watch out*, Lachlan thought he heard as the memory weakened, giving way to the reality in front of him.

"Don't touch it," he screamed, lurching forward and grabbing her hand from the air, but not before the tips of her fingers grazed wisps of hair still within her reach. Angered by Lachlan's intrusion, the beast reared and bucked violently, throwing water that sparkled in the moonlight as it flew through the air.

"Lachlan, look," she whispered, thrusting her hand in his field of view.

Black streaks trailed down Isla's fingers into the palm of her hand. Lachlan grabbed her around the wrist pulling her to his side. It looked like wet paint staining her pale skin, but it was sticky to the touch like jelly or honey.

"It feels like glue," he mumbled, taking one last look at it before grabbing a handful of seagrass and thrashing it abrasively against her skin in an attempt to rid her of whatever the substance was. When the discoloration was gone, his hand lingered in hers, and he reveled in the feel of her skin against his. The excitement that had always existed between them hadn't waned like he'd feared it might. If anything, it had intensified, knowing the truth of what lay on the other side of wanting her.

The world fell away for a moment, and the reality of their circumstances became distant half-truths. The light of the moon scattered through the gauzy clouds, catching the paleness of her skin just right. The fabric of her white shift-like dress clung to her skin like a child to its mother. The roundness of her breast showed through the thin fabric as she took in a deep breath, excited by being eyed before reality came crashing down on them.

Blinded by his concern for the black substance streaking Isla's hand, Lachlan had dropped the gristly rope back into the seaweed drifting around their legs, forgetting it ever existed, until it sprang from the water with a life of its own. Then sudden tension sent the beast into a panic. Lachlan pulled Isla close to him, turning away from the creature to face the darkness of the bank behind them.

"Can you swim?" he asked without taking his eyes from the bank. "To the other side?"

"What? Have you gone mad?" Her voice was taut and wobbly. "You want me to go into the water with that thing?"

"Whatever it is, it's me it wants, not you," Lachlan whispered, turning his attention back to the beast. The rope had gone slack again, and Lachlan stooped to find it again.

"What the devil do you mean?"

"She called me the one that got away."

The skin on Lachlan's arm began to tingle as he remembered the spaewife's touch. He couldn't dismiss the coincidence as being a fluke. The truth of it stood ten feet away from them. The old woman had seen his reality twenty years ago, and he'd been outrunning it ever since. He knew he couldn't run from it anymore.

"I can't explain it," he whispered. He couldn't even explain it to himself, much less someone else. It had never made any sense, but sense seemed to have little to do with reality, he thought, as he watched the beast in front of him scratch at its bridle as if begging to be set free. Lachlan snickered, understanding all too well the need to be set free.

"I need you to trust that I'd not put you in harm's way; that I'd do anything to protect you."

Isla looked back at the beast pacing behind them, taunting them, waiting for them. Lachlan could see the fear in her eyes. He felt the same fear in his bones, but it wasn't because of the beast or even the truth it represented. It was the fear of losing what they'd just found in each other. But there was also understanding, and Isla didn't try to convince him to swim to safety with her.

"When I say so, run as fast as you can to the edge of the shelf and swim to the other side. Don't look back, no matter what you hear or think you see."

He could feel the deep breaths moving in and out of her chest as she listened to him. The grip of her fingers against his arms clenched tighter and tighter with each word he spoke, but she never said a word.

"Get to the other side and make for the cattle path, over the ridge. Stay to the right, and you'll skirt the cemetery without having to go all the way down to the beachside. Get to McLeod's and call Euan."

Isla tilted her head up slightly, enough for them to look at each other one more time. Her eyes reminded Lachlan of the young girl he'd fallen in love with outside the bathroom of the community hall. They were filled with an assurance he'd been chasing after for two decades. The girl in the hallway had stolen his heart and never given it back. The woman in front of him still held it, and he knew then that he never wanted it back.

"Do you remember the first time we swam here together?" she asked quietly as the image of childlike frivolity danced behind her eyes.

"I do," Lachlan answered.

"I bet you never thought then that it would take twenty years to finally catch me."

Lachlan laughed, clutching her chin in his hand. "You were worth the wait," he whispered into her lips before kissing them with twenty years' worth of want.

Isla spun her arms around Lachlan's neck and kissed him back, nearly pushing him off his feet. His hands tangled in the wet hair. She felt tiny yet powerful in his grip. They stumbled in the water, until Lachlan's hands trailed down her backside and to the insides of her thighs, gripping her chilled skin and pulling her pale legs around his midsection. Lachlan could feel the rope slithering in the water around his ankles. He held Isla close, their lips never parting, as he looped his leg in the line, sealing the connection between himself and the beast and possibly his fate.

Lachlan tugged at Isla's hair, pulling her lips from his. He breathed deep, trying to find the strength to let her go again.

"When I put you down," he panted in between her hurried advances. "When I put you down, run to the edge and don't look back," he breathed. "Don't come back. I'll find you."

"Promise," she begged. "Promise you'll find me again."

So much of their lives had been built on broken promises. He didn't want the last thing between them to be another one.

"I promise that it's only ever been you. It will always be you."

Isla's pink lips turned up into the half-cocked smile she wore the first time they met, and he could see the understanding in her eyes. Only truths going forward, he thought to himself, scanning his peripheral vision and the darkness on the bank.

Their kiss was as feverish and desperate as their first. The question of whether or not it would be their last hung heavy in the thickening air around them. Rain began to sprinkle down on them, and the moon's light was fading. The clouds shifted, and the glitter the moon cast down in the middle of the loch as if to guide Isla to the other side. Lachlan felt her grip loosen as she slid back to her feet, standing in the water in front of him.

She backed away from Lachlan slowly, still holding onto his hand, trying not to draw the attention of the beast who stood further out on the shelf, still waiting. Lachlan winced as the tips of her fingers slid through his. He took one last look, expecting her to turn and make for the edge, but she stopped, her arm still outstretched as a familiar look of panic spread across her face.

"Watch out!" she yelled, pointing to something behind him.

Lachlan turned, only to see the moon catch the flash of something silver flying in the air before a familiar sickening feeling of metal on flesh caught him off guard for a second time.

Chapter Twenty-Six

The clouds held onto the tiniest bit of gray light, giving me only a few feet of vision. I wanted to yell out to him, but when I opened my mouth, my throat felt like old sandpaper left in the sun and the words scratched on the way out so that by the time they reached the air they had no noise. I only knew I'd reached the water when I felt it's burning chill seeping into my shoes and up the legs of my pants.

"Arden!" I screeched, hardly able to form his name.

I edged my way further out on the shelf to where I'd last seen them. Heavy fog crept in over the ridge stealing what little I could see in the waning light. The animal splashed violently in the water and screamed as it did. I grabbed my ears, shielding them from the blood-curdling sound.

I could see outlines moving in the dark. It pranced in the shallow water, just like Isla and I had done once before. I could only be thankful that she'd been detained even if it was by Ross. I put her out of my mind, afraid that even thinking of her would somehow expose her to the evil dancing in front of me.

Its skin was as black as the night that was closing in on us, making it appear almost invisible, but I knew it was there. I skulked forward begrudgingly as something wrapped around my leg, sending me crashing into the water behind Arden, frightening both him and the beast. Arden turned to me, and all I could see of him were the whites of his eyes. The creature beat against the water with its feet. It was still there, watching us, but waiting for me.

"You aren't taking this from me too!" Arden yelled, crouched in a football tackle stance, the fingers on his hands jumping in and out as if preparing to hit me. His eyes held the same stubbornness I'd grown up with. He never knew when to give up and call it a draw. He would fight until the death, just to prove that he was right and everyone else was wrong. I'd bested him twice when it came to Isla. It would be something he'd never forgive me for, or himself. In his eyes, I was the lesser, the inferior, his understudy. I'd had no right to step into the spotlight and play the lead. He needed something to put him back on top.

"Arden, you have to listen," I shouted. "The old woman ... she said this would happen!"

The frothy rain that was barely enough to wet my skin began to surge, and large stinging droplets crashed into the surface of the loch with violent force. I tried to move toward him, hands in the air to offer my surrender, but something strung in the water held me in my place.

"You just want it for yourself," he spat, shielding his face from the rain.

"Want what for myself? Listen to yourself, you idiot, I don't care about the horse. It isn't even a horse. The old woman said it would be here, on the bank where feet can walk on water." I pointed down to his feet. He looked down as if he hadn't even noticed he'd been submerged up to his calves despite being a good ten feet from the shore. He turned and looked at the beast as it paraded back and forth in front of us even further out on the shelf, the water barely up to its knee joint.

"She said ..." I couldn't say it even though it was standing right in front of me. The word stuck in my throat.

"The stories were true. That thing is a ..." My throat tightened and stung like I'd swallowed a thistle. The bristly bloom sat in the back of my throat, daring me to say the word.

"That thing is a fuckin' water horse!" I finally yelled into the rain, but my words felt like they were being carried away on the wind. They should have been. They were ridiculous. I couldn't believe they'd come from my mouth. Arden didn't move, and I couldn't tell if he'd heard me or not.

"She warned me," I yelled again, "when we crashed Ross' car! The naked woman in the hills, just there." I pointed up to where I assumed the path was, but in the darkness, it was invisible, just like everything else around us.

It wasn't until he started laughing that I knew he'd heard me. The idea was just as ridiculous to him as it had sounded in my head. The laughter was infectious, and soon we were both laughing like fools.

"Why should I believe anything you say? You're a fuckin' liar."

The laughter stopped immediately, and his face turned to stone. He tried to hide the sting of pain under his anger, but even in the shadow of the night, I could see it in his eyes. I didn't have an answer for him. There wasn't a reason for him to believe me then or ever again. I wasn't sure I cared if he believed anything I said for the rest of our lives, or ever spoke to me after that night. We were going our separate ways, and we both knew it. But I needed him to believe what I was telling him about the old woman's warning. At least then he'd have the option of choosing to listen to me again or not.

"I know ... I ... it's ...." The words were stuck like honey when the bottle is almost empty. It's there, you can see it, but getting it to come out is virtually impossible.

"Please, just listen to me, this one last time and then you don't ever have to listen to me again." It was all I could get out. Not I'm sorry, or I've been a horrible friend. I couldn't admit that to Arden, even if it were true; even if I thought it might save his life. I wasn't sorry that she'd picked me. I'd never be sorry for that.

Arden turned away, trying again to hide his pain. His arms hung at his side, lose, like they weren't attached to the rest of his body. He looked down at the water, and I watched the rain drip from the peak of his head into the loch, adding to the ripples and movement on the water's surface.

"Ya know," he started. His voice was broken, deflated. It didn't sound like him. "I'd of done the same thing if she'd picked me."

I guffawed at his admission, awestruck that he'd even made it. It felt like the most truthful thing he'd ever said in his life. I looked at him, and he wasn't the Arden trying unsuccessfully to escape the shadow of his malicious older brother. He looked like the kid who'd walked on Seilebost Beach with me summers ago, looking for shells and running to show them to his mother trailing behind us when he found them. Under the rough exterior he felt the need to put forward, the kind and gentle person he had once been was still there. I felt hope for our continued friendship for the first time in the months since the arrival of Isla Gilcrest and the invisible wedge she'd unknowingly driven between us.

The sky screamed, sending the beast we'd both forgotten about rearing its forelegs high into the air. We froze and watched in disbelief. Lightning flashed rapidly in the sky, each successive flash stealing the darkness from the night and exposing what I had missed.

Something moved between my legs, hidden in the murky water. I watched the ringlets that formed on the surface as it slithered around me, moving in unison with the beast. It felt like the old woman was standing behind me, shouting the words she'd barely been able to whisper before; *serpents' mane and skin that sticks.*

"Arden!" I yelled, frozen with fear, unable to move.

The sky quieted, and the darkness stole back my sight. I couldn't see the beast, but I could hear it, feel the vibrations as its hooves pounded against the shelf. The slithering between my legs stopped and went taught around my ankle as the sound of the beast moved further and further away. I could feel the grip take hold of me and then I was spinning violently in the air.

I swallowed mouthfuls of water as I twisted and then spat it back out again when I found myself above water. It felt like hours, but I knew it couldn't have been more than a few seconds. When it stopped, I gasped, unable to pull in a good breath. I didn't know how far I'd been dragged or where Arden was. I scrambled to my feet screaming for him in the darkness.

I wanted to shout to Arden, tell him not to touch its skin or mane, but I could barely breathe. He didn't know not to touch it, that it was real, that it would drag us both into the depths and eat us alive. I stumbled, half walking half crawling in the shallow water, but it was too late. When I finally found him, he was already reaching his hand out toward the beast.

"Don't touch it!" I choked out, still relieving my lung of the water they held. I doubled over and fell back to my knees trying to breathe and couldn't see if he'd heard me or not. When I looked up again, Arden was stood motionless, ghost white, pointing in my direction.

"Watch out," he yelled.

There was a flash, but not like the others. It didn't light up the whole sky. It was like it was meant just for me. A sickening sting followed. My head just above my eye was on fire, and I vomited into the mud before rolling to my side, paralyzed by the pain.

I laid still waiting for death to take me. I could feel the shallowness of my own breath as it moved in and out of my chest along with mouthfuls of dirty water. I couldn't get my body to choke it back out. It knew there was no reason. I'd be dead soon, and it wouldn't matter.

I could feel the animal's movements as the tether of serpents pulled against my legs. Ghostly screams rang through the valley, and I could no longer tell which ones belonged to the beast and which ones belonged to Arden. I mumbled his name, thinking I was screaming, but there was little strength left in my body. I closed my eyes and prayed it would be over quickly.

In my last moments, I thought of Isla. I wanted the last thing I saw before I left this world to be her gentle smile; the one where only one side of her mouth turned up, and her eyes turned downward. Her hair burned like an auburn crown, the ends of which tickled the skin on my arms as it whirled around us. I imagined pulling at the tiny white flowers buried deep in the tendrils. She pressed her hand against mine, and mine against her cheek and she nuzzled it gently. *I'll find you again*, she whispered, before her image began to fade.

The tugging against my legs stopped. I could feel the warmth of blood dripping from above my eye, down the rut my nose made on my face. I could feel it pooling in the corner of my eye, tinting the little I could see in a halo of red.

A scream rushed over my skin like wildfire. It was on top of me and a million miles away all at the same time. I tried to focus, but the harder I concentrated the more of my own life leaked from my body. I didn't feel the convulsions, just the remaining contents of my stomach trailing out of my mouth into the cool mud. I was thankful for its chill against the burning of my skin.

Light filled the sky, hanging on top of us as if to let us see the ending clearly. I watched, blurry eyed, as best I could, but my dwindling brain power couldn't comprehend what my one good eye was seeing. Arden's hands were tangled in its mane, and as the beat bucked, it lifted him off his feet only to whip him into the water like he didn't have bones. I didn't want to watch, but I couldn't look away. I begged for it to be over. And then it was.

The light left the sky for a moment, and everything was quiet. The waves of moving water had stopped, and the sounds of their screams had been carried away. Another flash burst into the sky, and they were gone. The shelf was empty. There was nothing left of either of them except the void where they'd been a second before. I wanted to scream his name. I should have cried. But all I could do was beg for forgiveness and wait for my own death. But it wouldn't come.

I don't know how long I laid in the mud. The darkness had no time. There was movement around me in the rain that trickled against the water's surface and the clouds that capered in front of the moon. I knew I was hallucinating when I heard shouting again, but I prayed that somehow, it was Arden, survived what I knew should have killed him. I felt tugging against my legs as the rope began to tangle around me again. I found some semblance of strength and screamed out.

"Calm yourself, boy, it's Hamish."

His voice was distant even though I could feel his hands working to untangle my legs of the rope woven around them.

"Where's Arden?" he asked directly.

Even in my state, I knew how ridiculous it would sound to him, but I didn't know what else to say. It was the truth, after all. I'd seen it with my own eyes.

"It grabbed him," I coughed, as Mr. McLeod sat me up and rapped me against the back, sending all the water I'd sucked in spewing into the air. I gulped, trying to find the words, when really, all I wanted him to do was scoop me up and get me out of the valley.

"What did?" he asked, directing his torch into the darkness surrounding us.

Up on the ridge, I could see more lights, bobbing their way down the path. I turned to look back out over the shelf at the nothingness that filled the space where I'd last seen Arden. Their haste was pointless. They were too late.

"The water horse," I gasped before the world went black again.

Chapter Twenty-Seven

There was screaming, but the words were unintelligible. Lachlan thrashed against the water. He was disoriented. His vision was blurred. Pressure from above drove him down on his back with considerable force pushing his body below the surface and into the muddy bank. His lungs burned as he fought to get to the surface he knew to be only inches above him. As suddenly as the pressure had found him, it released, and when he found air again, all he could hear were the screams he didn't immediately recognize as his own.

"Get to the other side," he heard himself yell, gurgling mouthfuls of water in between words as he struggled to get to his feet.

Isla didn't wait for any further confirmation that Lachlan was alright. In an instant, she reached the end of the ledge. Lachlan watched as she slowed but didn't stop to look back before launching herself off the shelf and into the deepness the loch held. He lost sight of her until she reached the other side and scrambled through the thick grass to solid ground. The white of her shift glowed against the darkness but became fainter the further out of the valley she moved. She was nothing more than a ghost on the ridge, and then she was gone, but Lachlan knew he wasn't alone.

The moon played peekaboo with the clouds, flicking bits and pieces of light onto the water's surface. A low rumble stretched out across the sky, and Lachlan let himself fall into memories of the night Arden had been carried down to the deep, hoping he'd see the thing he missed that night; the thing that was still out there in the darkness.

A long continuous rumble rolled through the clouds, booming louder in some places than in others. Warm air moving in from the beach on the other side of the ridgeline dropped into the valley, and a sallow mist began to form over the water. Lachlan kept the horse in sight and the line wrapped around his leg.

A soft rain began to fall, and Lachlan let it drip over him as scanned what he knew to be the hillside in front of him. He inched himself backward, closer to the edge of the shelf. His hand rested tenderly against his midsection and what he assumed were several broken ribs. The bones panged with each step he took and when he couldn't bear it any longer, he stopped and dropped to his knees, fighting through the pain to keep a lookout for whatever it was he couldn't see in the darkness.

There was a subtle tug against the frayed rope. When the horse did not react to the tension, the pull came again. The horse stood motionless. Lachlan began to feel the urgency through the fibers wrapped around his leg. He turned toward the beast and offered the palm of his hand. The creature moved with reluctance in its step but want in its eyes. A want to be set free.

Lightning flew in quick succession, startling both Lachlan and creature. The bursts gave only seconds of truth as the rope continued to tighten around Lachlan's leg, but seconds was all he needed. The flashes illuminated a disheveled looking man standing on the bank, the other end of the rope resting limply in his hand. Even though Lachlan knew there was someone out there, the shock of seeing that someone in the flesh sent a deep panic shuddering into his bones. Thunder screamed out above them, and the beast bucked, frightened by the sound. In the next flash, the man had become a ghost, and the bank was empty.

"I know what it is you're doing!" Lachlan yelled in the direction of the bank.

There was movement in the tall grass. Lachlan could hear him as he paced back and forth. He listened to the sound of his steps; awkward and lopsided, heavy on one side, quick and fast moving on the other.

"Aye, you're a cunnin' little bastard," the man yelled, springing vigorously from the darkness. "Have bin ever since ah let ye slide thro' mah fingers th' first time. Ah should hae kent you'd be trouble based on how much yer dear mither struggled."

His words came out in a hiss, slowed down and deliberate as if to make sure Lachlan had time to digest each syllable if not every letter. Lachlan was on his feet, ignoring the sharp pain rushing through his body, scanning the darkness, but the bank was quiet. The grass swayed evenly in the wind instead of crunching cock-eyed like it had under his feet. A dull roll of thunder labored in the clouds. Lachlan could feel the quick, haphazard jumps of the creatures agitated movements in the teether between them. Any tension he'd felt pulling against him from the bank had disappeared. The line had been left limp to ebb in the ripples, and the voice was lost again in the dark.

There was silence except for the ghosts of the victims screaming between Lachlan and the bank. Arden's shouts were only outweighed by those of his mother, who had gone to her grave with a secret even she didn't fully understand. Images of his mother floated in the mist around him, and Lachlan's heart broke when the entirety of them left him feeling ashamed of almost everything he'd ever said to her. But he knew it wasn't his fault. He'd had no way to know, and had he known, what could he have done? Lachlan had been the devil's seed in his mother's eyes, and now, the devil stood in front of him.

"I'll nae mak' that mistake again."

The whisper was inches from Lachlan's ear. He spun swiftly as the chill ran up his spine, but he could only see pieces of the man in the sudden flashes of light before the night stole back the sky.

"Why don't you come out and fight me like a man!" Lachlan yelled, almost instantly regretting his words. He was far from frail, but the stranger had already bested him once, and Lachlan knew he couldn't take another hit to the midsection without irrevocable damage. "Or do you only fight women? Maybe you're soft," Lachlan continued, "can't imagine that fighting helpless women takes much strength or skill."

"Ach," the sound came from directly in front of Lachlan, close enough to startle both him and the beast that had grown dismissive of the scene around him and was grazing on the slimy weeds swaying in the current around its legs. Lachlan squinted but could distinguish an outline moving away from him through the darkness.

"You'd be surprised." He was further away from Lachlan, closer to the bank. "Most o' 'em put up a good fight, like your friend who thought she cuid fly."

Lachlan held his breath as the image of Moira just before she threw herself out of the second story window of Inverness Asylum materialized in Lachlan's mind. Even more prominent in his memory was way her blood had continued to drip down the wall after she was gone. He could barely remember the look in her eyes, but the heavy trail of blood inching down the pale library wall had never faded.

"She paid the price," the stranger hissed, "belly was barren as th' glen midwinter."

The words were familiar. They would have been lost on anyone else, but Lachlan knew better than to let them go. He scanned his memory violently, trying to find where the words had been written. He damned himself for having burned the book; it could have proved useful after all. He scoured through every handwritten line that had been etched in the book, checking and triple checking for the words hidden away somewhere in the myriad of nonsensical ramblings, but it wasn't there. They hadn't been written but spoken.

Lachlan could hear shadows of Euan's voice as he read and recounted the gory details involving a murdered husband and a missing son whose body had never been found. The limp hadn't slowed him down like most had expected. He'd hid in plain sight for close to forty years or longer, nearly invisible to the world, because everyone thought he was already dead. Lachlan almost laughed when he realized it would take more sway to convince the people of Lewis that the Spaewife's son had survived into manhood than it had taken for them to believe he was a killer at the age of twelve. The irony of the moment was cut short when a flash of something steely flew in the air, missing Lachlan's face by inches.

"I know who you are!" Lachlan yelled into the darkness, crouched in a fighting stance, thrashing about in the water in a feeble attempt to defend himself. "Your mother warned me you'd be here. She told me I'd pay the price." Lachlan struggled for breath, fearing that the broken ribs moving freely in his abdomen could have punctured a lung. It felt like he was slowly drowning, but without being face down in the water. "I guess I'm just a little late."

His ominous cackle filled the valley, echoing between the hills surrounding them, making it sound like he was everywhere. The beast cowered at the sound but did not run.

"I remember you, from the hillside when we were kids, swimming in the loch. That was you!" Lachlan swallowed roughly, trying to find strength he didn't have. "And the night you killed Arden."

The man yelled from the darkness, his voice surging as he paced back and forth. "A've ne'er murdered a soul in mah life. Ah cannae be held responsible fur whit that creature does. That thing's a creature from th' deep, ye ken," he hissed. "A water horse th' stories mah maw cried it."

***

He started laughing again, and his movements became more erratic. The stagger in his step made him hard to follow in the darkness. His quick, illogical movements agitated the horse who almost began mimicking the movement, sashaying back and forth, kicking up water as it moved. Lachlan began to wonder if the crazed man was so far gone that he actually believed the creature in front of him was what the bedtime stories had made it out to be. Lachlan had believed it.

"Cannae believe th' auld boot is still alive wi' all she's been put throu'. Likelie I should hae killed her too, but what's a son suppose tae do? We dinnae git tae pick our maws now, dae we laddie." The movement stopped, and the air was still "Or our das fur tha' matter," he whispered. Lachlan could almost feel the swish of breath on his neck as he spoke, but he could not see him.

It was quick. Even though Lachlan had been wading in the loch, the chill of the water pilfered what little breath he had pulled into his lungs before crashing through the water's surface. The shelf wasn't more than a foot deep, but he struggled to find the top. Something heavy pressed down against his chest; a rock or boulder having fallen at the right time from the ridge above. He reached frantically for the object, and when he found it to be soft and pliable, he knew it wasn't a rock. He held the field boot in his hands as it pushed down against his chest. Lachlan stopped struggling, trying desperately to retain the lungful of air he had left. The sky flashed white again, and in it, Lachlan could see Kieran Campbell's distorted face hovering above him, laughing and screaming words that were lost in the little bit of depth between them.

His skin was pale and baggy, like his bones couldn't hold it in place. Large abscesses covered the skin on his cheeks, overtop of the scars left behind by the sores before. His teeth stuck out over his lip and his hair hung down over his eyes. Even through the murky water and deepening darkness of the night, Lachlan could see through everything and into the eyes staring down at him. They were the same eyes always looking back in the mirror, deep set so that the socket cast an uninviting shadow on them, but light blue/grey in color. Lachlan screamed and thrashed under the weight of the familiar stranger's foot, finally understanding why his mother had never been able to look him in the eye for more than a few seconds and never without being brought to tears; for her, the attack had never ended, it was always staring back at her.

Lachlan gasped as Kieran pulled him to the surface, only to wrap the rope around his throat twice before submerging him again. Kieran stood above him, inches from the surface yelling through the water at Lachlan. The words were muffled, but not all of them were lost. His foot remained on Lachlan's midsection, as he used the rope to pull just enough of him to the surface to make sure he heard his words.

"Ah remember yer mither," he spoke, "Licked th' paint from her fingers 'til they wur raw."

"You're a monster," Lachlan spat, gurgled through the strain of the lead cinched tight against his throat.

"Aye," Kieran whispered pushing even closer to Lachlan, so his lips drifted across his cheek as he spoke. "A monster I am, bred by th' hand of the' de'il 'imself."

The film of lunacy covering his eyes cracked, exposing a sadness that loomed underneath it all. It was the quiet desperation for a parent's love that Lachlan was all too familiar with. His thoughts were fuzzy and almost incoherent. They skipped around to random events throughout his life; the day he'd learned to ride his bike, the first time he'd been intimate with a woman, the smell of his father's coffee on cold Lewis mornings, the way his mother sang in the carport while folding laundry when she thought no one was listening. It was the only time he remembered her being anything close to happy.

"Is that what this is about?" Lachlan coughed, "your father not loving you, beating you and a mother that didn't love you enough to defend you!"

Lachlan was below the surface again, struggling against the man standing on his chest. He wove his hands into the folds of the rope, wrenching at them urgently, but there was no release in the pressure. He felt his limbs go limp as the last few air bubbles floated to the surface and popped. In his final moments, Lachlan could only think of Isla; the sweet smell of her pale skin, the soft touch of her lips, the flutter of her body underneath his own. He could almost feel the tickle of her hair against his arm as he felt himself slip away. Her red crown burned brighter than anything else in his memory. He was happy it would be his last.

The rope tightened. He felt the water rush around him, and he traded the pressure against on his chest for an uneven one around his neck. It jerked and shuddered, then loosened, then tightened more than before. The rope cinched forcefully around his fingers still tangled in the fibers. Everything had gone dark, even though he could feel the sting of water rushing over his open eyes. Then, everything was still. The whistle of rushing water stopped, and the rope went slack. Above him, something darker than darkness moved.

Behind him, Kieran shouted in a mixture of Gaelic and broken English. Lachlan scrambled through the water, his elbows digging into the mud as he frantically clamored to put distance between himself and Kieran. When he reached the edge of the shelf, he looked out and could barely make out the other side of the loch. Lachlan knew he'd never make it on his own.

He turned, trying to get to his knees. He grabbed the base of his neck and could feel the rawness the rope had left behind. Warm blood dripped down his neck, smelling of copper. When the wind whipped through, it stung his open flesh.

Kieran stood, twenty feet in front of Lachlan, shouting and cursing at the beast between them. Lachlan watched as he postured in the water, hands waving out to his side, calling out chants and spells, speaking with the devil's tongue to the beast he thought had been summoned from the depths of hell itself.

"Ye'r th' only one who got awa'," he called out from the darkness, in between other indistinguishable mumbles.

"My parents didn't love … couldn't love me," Lachlan yelled, "because of you and what you did to my mother. Every time she looked at me, all she could see was you!"

Lachlan listened to the sound of splashing and the garbled ramblings of a madman. The wind swept through in bursts, shifting the clouds and rustling the grasses at the water's edge. His head pounded, and his vision came and went in waves as his brain recovered from the lack of oxygen.

"I get it," Lachlan wheezed, feeling the most honest he'd ever felt in his life, perhaps because he felt like it might be his last opportunity to be so. The pain was excruciating. His lungs felt little relief in the breaths he tried to draw in. He knew his lung had to be punctured. He could feel the air leaking out of it. The only warmth he felt was from the blood pooling around his neck, soaking the collar of his shirt a deep crimson color.

"I get it, how it felt to … to know you weren't loved, to see it in their eyes."

Lachlan thought of the last time he'd seen his mother, as he was being carted away by the nurses to

Inverness, not knowing that he'd never see her again. Even through the thick window glass and the falling rain, Lachlan could see her eyes as clear as day. What he'd always thought was hatred looked more like regret in the light of the truth; regret that she'd not been a better wife or a better mother. There had always been something more behind her eyes, something Lachlan never could have understood; the idea that loving him meant that somehow, on some level, she overlooked what had brought him into this world, condoned it, accepted it, maybe even wanted it. She couldn't have one without the other.

He understood the feeling of one without the other. He'd never been able to have both Isla's love and Arden's friendship, and when he'd tried to have both, Arden had paid the price. At least that was the line Lachlan had fed his guilt for twenty years. But even that was true. The world hadn't punished Lachlan with Arden's death any more than it had punished his mother with his own existence. They'd all been connected through the delusions of a madman, who, in his own right, had suffered cruelties no child should have to endure.

Lachlan edged toward Kieran slowly, unable to move any faster than a muddled shuffle. From behind, he looked like any other man. Without being able to see the madness that leaked from his eyes, Lachlan almost felt sorry for him. Almost.

"I felt the pain of being unloved my entire life, but I'm not out there rapin' women, and killin' babies now am I. You get over it, find a way to deal. You make the best of the shit situation."

Kieran half turned toward Lachlan, arms still outstretched, clasping the lead.

"Th' best o' it? What's th' best of being beaten daily or th' best o ' huvin empty whiskey boatles hurled at yer heid? What's th' best of havin' tae listen to mah maw bein' beaten almost as much as yersel'? Th' best was putting him whaur he belonged."

Even without facing him, Lachlan could see Kieran make the sign of the cross vigorously against his chest and then look to the sky, as if in anticipation of something from above raining down on him for his evil, if not justified, deed.

"Mither said t'was her fault fur temping th' de'il 'm' then denying him her flesh, sae that he had tae take it by force. T'was her fault, but that I had tae pay th' price."

His voice was almost sorrowful, almost human.

"T'was her fault," he yelled, turning toward Lachlan and exposing the malicious grin that had slipped back onto his sour face. "So she gave mah evil a name 'n' a story, 'n' folk believed her, at least fur a time."

He laughed as if he'd told a joke, and stood expectantly waiting for Lachlan to join in.

"They barely even keeked fur th' bodies, most of th' time. Would have bin easy enough tae fin' though." His smile grew, and his eyes widened, reflecting the glow of the moon above them. "They put a marker overtop th' ones that keek doon on Bosta 'm' didnae even know it."

A pang of guilt forced its way into Lachlan's chest for having failed to make the trek to Arden's memorial stone. When nothing of him was recovered, they'd placed a marker on the peak of the farthest-reaching ridge above Bosta, looking out over the ocean. They'd stood there as kids, craning their necks to see who could see the furthest, dreaming about what the future held. It had been a fitting place to place it, even more so, if Kieran had really buried him there.

"It's not too late for you Kieran," Lachlan said, trying to appeal to the little bit of human left inside him.

His smile gave him away, and Lachlan knew it was too late. "You're th' devil's seed, same as me. It's in your blood," he mumbled, "'n' one day ye will be."

"Will be what?" Lachlan begged. His right leg gave out and brought him to his knee in a crash of pain. The feeling was familiar, a wanting for it to be over. He only hoped it would be quick.

"A killer juist lik' me."

A flash burst through the sky, and Lachlan watched as the Kieran swung the steely pipe through the air above his head. Lachlan willed himself to move, but his body was frozen, reeling from his injuries. He could do nothing in that instant but study the madman's face, his mouth opened wide enough for the loudest outcry, but the sound was missing.

A scream rang through the valley, louder than any thunder but it wasn't human. It looked like a shadow moving in the darkness behind Kieran; hidden in the night. Its hooves pounded in the shallow water, making the ground shudder and the water quiver in its wake. There was no stopping it. Even Kieran appeared to have known what was coming, thrusting every last bit of power he had into his last effort to rid the world of his devilish seed. His face contorted in a mixture of love and hate even Lachlan could not fully understand. He wanted to close his eyes or look away, but he couldn't.

Only when the horse was on top of him did Lachlan hear Kieran's screams, but they were silenced by the weight of the water on top of him. With his last bit of willpower, Lachlan stumbled to his feet and reached out for the beast as it sped past. He held his breath, ignoring the pain as he swung himself onto the animals back, trying to focus on the dry, coarse hair between his fingers and the rhythm of the animal's steps beneath him. He knew it was a risk, riding a horse when he feared his lung might already be punctured, but he wasn't about to turn down the safety its speed and strength possessed.

He felt the animal's steps shorten as they reached the edge of the shelf. He wanted to let go but realized he couldn't after it had launched them off the edge and into the deepest part of the loch. They crashed into the water with violent force, jarring Lachlan's already marred body. He clung to the animals back, appreciating the power moving below him. All four legs pumped in unison as they glided to the other bank, their speed no match for anything Kieran, or any man, could have conjured.

Their exit from the water was forceful and ill-timed. The horse slipped in the mud jarring Lachlan against its back. He held on as best he could, but he had little fight left in him. When the creature finally found its footing, it made for Bosta, recognizing the path in the dead of night. At the top of the ridge, Lachlan could see headlights speeding down the twisting road to the beach. He tried to breath knowing Isla had made it out safely and help was only a few quick twists away, but he knew it was far from over.

He turned to face the valley one last time. It was nothing but darkness. His heartbeat slowed, and he reassured himself silently that he'd made it out alive a second time. He patted the horse on its chest with his free hand and struggled to untangle his other from its mane. The darkness lifted momentarily, and Lachlan he could see a dark figure standing at the edge of the shelf looking up at him. He held his breath waiting for the next flash. When the darkness lifted again, the shelf was empty.

He slid awkwardly from the horse's back and into the long grass, taking with him a handful of its mane which stuck to the palm of his hand and twisted around his fingers. He rolled several feet from the beast, coming to rest on his back. He listened to the beat of its hooves as it galloped back into the valley, back into the depths.

The clouds had cleared, and stars were visible overhead. He'd forgotten how stunningly beautiful the night sky was on the island. There was nothing there to stop it from being so. He faded in and out, waiting for whoever found him first, laying half dead in the grass. He stared up at the sky as he waited, trying to remember the last time he'd seen a night as beautiful.

The grass rustled in the stillness of the night. Lachlan closed his eyes, listening as it moved. All he could see was Isla Gilcrest; her wry, sideways smile and wide eyes the color of the storm hidden beneath the crown of fire that encircled her. All he could hear were the stable steps of field boots swishing in the grass. Then it was only him, and the darkness.

Epilogue

Lachlan sat in the deck of the morning Calmac ferry, studying the sleepy town he was leaving behind. Colorful shopfronts lined the harbor streets. Shopkeepers fluttered about the ghostly streets, unlocking doors, sweeping steps, sipping strong coffee while greeting the passersby with warm smiles and comments about the weather. Smaller boats dotted the harbor behind the ferry, red-topped buoys bobbed in the ripples forced by the engines roaring back to life after a night of quiet slumber.

Summer had slipped away, and the air had cooled significantly. The collar of Lachlan's sweatshirt rubbed against the healing scar around his neck, still somewhat tender to the touch a month later. Just another memento of his time on Lewis.

The sun was up in the distance, its rays stretching out over the mass of land between it and the cove that hid the port. Lachlan stood, half hanging over the railing with one foot resting on the lowest rung. He watched the men in lime green jumpsuits and hard hat waving the line of vehicles into the undercarriage of the ferry, lining them up one after the other. Gulls screamed in the distance, hovering over smaller fishing boats preparing for their own departure. Lachlan looked out over the Minch, the only thing standing between him and home, questioning if he knew what he was doing.

"Are you sad to see it go?"

Her voice was soft like velvet licking at his ears. He turned toward her voice and watched as the rising sun behind her set fire to her hair. She was a shadow, bigger than either of them, eclipsing everything that had come between them.

"No, he answered, "not sad."

"What then?" She took his hand and settled against the railing, nuzzling into the collar of the oversized sweater hanging off her thin frame.

"It's freeing," he whispered, tucking a few wild strands of fire back into the collar of her coat.

Isla smiled, knowing not to push it any more than that.

"Have you heard from Euan, then?"

"Aye, yesterday, when I phoned to tell him we were leaving."

The ferry horn blared above them, sending a jarring jolt through both their bodies. A soothing woman's voice over the loudspeaker followed. Her language, which had once been all Lachlan knew in this world, was foreign now, a novelty. He smiled, appreciating that it had survived when the rest of the sleepy island had slid into modernity as best it could.

A group of children no more than ten or eleven scrambled through the heavy door and onto the deck. They spoke loudly, unable at their young age to understand that other people existed in the world. The small group shuffled toward the bow, hanging over the railing and yelling lewd comments to passengers below. The obvious ring leader stood on the second rung and pretended to piss on the others. The thicker one mumbled things their parents would say. The tall one laughed at his friend, cheering him on. The last one stood like a statue, a look of disdainful acceptance hanging heavy in his eyes as he watched his group of friends. The look was familiar to Lachlan. He missed the times when he'd been fortunate enough to give it.

"Well, then?" She asked, elbowing Lachlan tenderly between the ribs. He winced in pain at her touch and tried poorly to cover it up.

"Shit, I'm so sorry, I forgot …"

Lachlan began to laugh at her alarm. Realizing the joke, Isla sneered and elbowed him harder in the same spot.

"Alright, alright," Lachlan laughed, backing away from her slightly. "No need to reinjure me while I've just mended."

"We'll see about that," she mumbled, turning to lean against the railing.

Lachlan rubbed the stinging sensation from his ribs and fell in line behind her, wrapping himself around her as they looked out on the harbor they were slowly leaving behind.

"Well, what did he say, then?"

Lachlan rested his chin against her shoulder, barely able to see through her hair as the sea air scrambled through it.

"Four, so far," he whispered, dropping his gaze to the cold, steel floor of the ferry.

Isla wiggled in his grasp attempting to turn and face him, but Lachlan stood like stone, knowing what she wanted to ask but not wanting to face her when she did. The fresh, new wounds below the surface still stung.

"He doesn't think they've found him yet, the remains are from younger children," he said somberly, "but Euan's confident that he's there, that they're all there."

"How many others are out there?"

Four books worth, Euan had said. Fifty or so women and almost as many children in the span of thirty years. Euan had wires out to almost every agency in the country, alerting them to the web of terror he'd fallen into and the signs of what to look for in any unsolved cases they had lingering. He'd said it would take years to puzzle everything out, find all the woman and account for all the missing. He'd been assigned to head up a special unit tasked with the job of finding every victim, living and dead, and giving them the peace some had lived decades without. He'd wasted no time and made his first notification to Mrs.

Scott, who cried twenty years' worth of tears on Euan's shoulder.

"And what of him? What of Kieran?" she asked, when Lachlan didn't respond.

"She stopped talking after they moved her to the hospital, but they think he'll try and visit her at some point like he did when she was at Inverness. They've got constables playing dress up as nurses standing guard over the floor she's been assigned to." Lachlan tried not to laugh, it wasn't something to laugh about, but the levity was a welcome relief, even if he wouldn't admit it.

"Euan said it's quite a scene; big burly men dressed in their little white nursing outfits not knowing the first thing about how to look or act like a nurse.

"What will happen to her?"

Lachlan readjusted his chin against her shoulder, taking in a deep breath as if trying to digest the totality of her question and its ramifications.

"I dunno," he finally answered, because it was the truth. "She's guilty of something, maybe not as much as him, but she fed the lie to Kieran and hid the truth in her coded messages."

Lachlan closed his eyes and listened to the whisper of the Spaewife's voice echoing in his ears. He knew in time the sound would dissipate until one day it might finally be carried away by a soft breeze. But until then, not even the blare of the ferry horn could drown out her words. He opened his eyes and took one last look as the ship picked up speed, leaving behind the hills of the small seaside town.

"Why do you think he did it?" Isla asked simply. "I mean, really?"

Lachlan didn't want to admit why he thought Kieran had done it. Admitting the true nature of what Kieran was, drew an undeniable connection between father and son, flowing in the blood they shared. It was simple;

primitive even. Evil existed in many forms. For Kieran, it had existed in the form of his father. For Lachlan, in the shape of a horse. But it was all the same thing in the end; wickedness preying on the weak.

"You know, I've always loved the look of Ullapool, but I've never once been here long enough to enjoy it. Always coming or going, never staying."

"Aye, me too," she said, wiggling under his grasp as she turned to press her back against the rails, putting them face to face. "Are you sure this is what you want? To leave it all behind and come back to Lewis, to Bernera?"

Lachlan stared into her stormy eyes, unsure that he'd ever been certain of anything else in his life. The ferry left the shape of the mainland behind, pulling out into open water. In three hours, they'd be across the Minch, pulling into port in Stornoway before making the hour-long drive on barely paved back roads back to Bernera. Lachlan could see the white bridge connecting Bernera to the mainland of Lewis; a soft, fine mist settling in from the open sea, running into the hillside that sprang out of the ocean at the foot of the bridge. In the middle of it all, the fire of the sun would burn like hazy hellfire, just as Isla Gilcrest had burned at the center of Lachlan's world since he laid eyes on her.

"There's just one problem I haven't puzzled out yet," he confessed.

Isla took his face in her hand, staring back at him without waver. "We can figure anything out together."

Their lips were close enough to touch but didn't. "I'm in love with another man's wife," he said bluntly. "I'm not sure what to do about that."

"Can you keep a secret?" she whispered in the space between their shuddering lips.

About Jessica Simpkiss

Jessica Simpkiss was a student of Art History at George Mason University and now lives in Virginia Beach with her husband and young daughter. Other than writing, she enjoys traveling, camping and antiquing. She is a published poet and short-story author. The Spaewife's Secret is her debut novel.

Social Media

Website: www.jessicamsimpkiss.com

Instagram: https://www.instagram.com/jesssimpkiss/

Facebook: https://www.facebook.com/jessica.simpkiss

Amazon Author Page:
https://www.amazon.com/author/jessicasimpkiss

Acknowledgements

Many people have helped in my journey to write this book, but first and foremost is my mother, who read, reread, and then read chapter after chapter again until I felt confident enough to send it out into the publishing world. Thank you to my father, for always being level-headed and looking at the business and legal side of things when my creative brain forgets to. And to all my friends and family whose continued support and encouragement kept me writing, I cannot thank you enough.

I am fortunate to have a husband who was not only willing to travel with me to the remote Isle of Lewis knowing absolutely nothing about it other than it was a part of Scotland, but he also managed to navigate the tiny one-track, windy roads in a smart car for our entire trip and brought us both back alive. There were lots of bumps along the way, but it was a trip of a lifetime and those memories inspired me to keep writing until the end, and then some.

I also have to thank the lovely people we met during our adventure in Scotland. Form the young man on the street offering pleasantries about the weather to the woman in the jewelry store who trusted us to take our purchase and come back with cash after her credit card machine went down, you are a truly uniquely kind people. Thank you for sharing your beautifully fascinating country with us.

Most of all, I would like to thank my daughter, Sophie, whose wild and crazy imagination reminds me every day that anything is possible. Stay wild, and you will accomplish great things in this life.

46891597R00205

Made in the USA
Middletown, DE
02 June 2019